Konjo

By Samuel Sulfur

For Leia,
My Magnificent Muse.

"I am not a god... I'm just bigger than you."

(Talthielle)

Konjo was the color of stone. A dim, lavender glow glistened in his swollen eyes as he sat, hunched and sagging over a brass goblet of *roua.* His heart was empty, his mind full, and his bones dry. He could taste the sour, cinnamon draught, but he could not swallow. His lips burned. Bruises and welts from merciless beatings at the hands of petulant strangers covered his face and torso. He had not fought back tonight, and would not again tomorrow, or the next day. He would suffer their emboldened prejudice in silence. He had not even clenched his fists this time. *Murderer*, they had shouted. *Monster.* As they swung their clubs into his ribs and spine. Spurred bootheels and spit and laughter. He had only closed his eyes and wrapped his arms around his head and curled himself, helplessly, into a pathetic ball. He had no bones they could break, and no will to fight. He had longed for death they could not grant. To be snuffed out, extinguished, enveloped in that blissful black of infinite nothing. To suffer no longer.

Brinka sat beside him in equally impermeable silence, shimmering in her ethereal shade. Only a ghost now, mute and barren. If he could bring himself to look at her, he would only see her immortal sadness and pity. The hateful strangers in the tavern could see only an empty chair. Their contempt for his kind would leave always an empty seat beside him, and there would she always be, speechless and glowing her faint, haunting glimmer. A *kinja*, a ghost. A quiet manifestation of his interminable guilt and shame and loneliness. If he ran, she would float along beside. If he slept, he would dream of her. If he threw himself from the highest peaks of the great Dab, she would fall with him. If he buried himself alive, she would lay next to him. If he swam to the bottom of the Injha and tied his throat and wrists to the tangled roots of the sinana, she would float there forever.

If he reached out to touch her soft cheek, to stroke her hair, to wrap his arms around her fragile frame once more, he would find only empty space. If he begged for her forgiveness, if he fell to his knees and screamed and wailed and pleaded, she would only gaze upon his suffering and lament. She would not comfort him. If he permitted himself to sleep, he would watch her die, over and over and over again. He would dream of nothing else. His sorrow was a raging flood that would never find the sea. Konjo was the color of stone, and would never be starlight again.

The barkeep wore his impatience and suspicion in a frigid scowl. A Kenjah who sat idling and sour and sober over a single goblet of *roua* for over an hour amounted to three empty stools that might be better filled by respectable patrons otherwise. But a sober, speechless Kenjah, covered in dark bruises and bloodless welts, was a contemptible spectacle to behold, even in a wretched den of reprobates like the Titan. *The nerve of this mountain trash, showing his dull-eyed shoulder boulder in these parts.* The barkeep was just making up his mind to finally throw the intolerable creature out, once and for all, and was just about to open his mouth to give this vermin a thrashing of his own, when another old and ragged wraith in dirty rags wandered alongside and plopped himself down on a stool next to the morose looking creature, tossing a pine coin on the bar and calling out for a draught of his own in an amiable and irreverent way. The barkeep squinted at the new waif for a long moment, curious at what new kind of filth the Titan must be attracting in these uncertain times that wouldn't even balk at the hideous, stone faced mass beside him. Briefly, and with no lack of cynicism, the barkeep considered just burning the whole damned place to the ground, but the pine coin would do for now, he begrudgingly supposed. The barkeep turned to search for a dirty goblet.

Konjo, for his part, took no notice of the wild-eyed tramp, or tried not to, but out of the corner of his swollen eye, he couldn't help but see Brinka's shade seem to brighten just a little, almost imperceptibly, as the dirty old vagrant climbed onto the stool opposing. The barkeep set a fresh goblet of *roua* down and muttered something unintelligible and tonally disparaging, but the old man flicked another pine coin in the air and snatched up his drink and downed the whole thing, slamming the brass down on the bar before the coin even landed. He gave the barkeep a sharp and provocative eye and demanded another, winking as he did so. As the befuddled barkeep turned back to the tramp and reached for the second pine coin, the old man produced a third and slammed it down even harder, which made the barkeep flinch.

"And how about another round for my friend here?" The old tramp gave Konjo a rough slap on the back and stood, glaring at the barkeep as if daring him to say something else. This was more than the barkeep could take, and with venom in his voice, he began to oblige.

"Now look here, I don't know if you're a beggar or a thief, but we don't take-"

"I said How About Another Round For My Friend Here!" The stranger seemed to stand a little taller, now with both palms flat on the bar and quite a bit of piss in his own voice to match. He drilled a hole in the barkeep's eyes, leaning in over the bar, over his own elbows, grinning a toothy and menacing grin. The restless din in the tavern dimmed a little as the stranger raised his voice at the bartender, and other patrons looked up from their own draughts and conversations to observe. Something aggressive in the old stranger's voice seemed to shock and chasten the barkeep, and in the pause that followed, his callous resolve shrank.

Konjo, having been slapped on the back by an old confrontational tramp in the middle of his own distracted solemnity, was now sharply aware of his surroundings and the odd spectacle evolving beside him. He looked up and around, first at the toothy belligerent to his left, who had roused him from his despondent isolation, then at the bewildered barkeep, then at the empty stool to his right where his beloved Brinka seemed to be watching the peculiar scene unfold with some enthusiasm. She was, in fact, glowing a little more brightly than usual, which was a new phenomenon that Konjo could neither process, nor deny. He turned his eyes back to the craggy barkeep, and then back to the stranger. If Konjo was confused and intrigued, the barkeep was downright mortified. The latter seemed to shrink and relent, and turned away from both of them, clearly baffled, and then complied without another word.

At this, the stranger slid back down onto his own stool and returned to Konjo as if they had been interrupted amidst a deeply involved conversation.

"Why so glum, chum?" The stranger reached out again and slapped Konjo on the shoulder in a decidedly fraternal way. The old man was easily half of Konjo's size, and seemed bony and frail and brittle, but his friendly open palm almost knocked Konjo off of his own stool. Konjo was now even more puzzled than the barkeep, and equally speechless.

"I said why so blue, Lou?" The stranger picked up his draught and kindly thanked the barkeep as if they had grown up together. He sipped it slowly this time, peering out over the brass goblet at Konjo with glassy blue and twinkling eyes, wiping the foam off of his bushy lips with a baggy woolen sleeve. "Hey, you in there big guy? Never met a deaf Kenjah before! Snap out of it old man! Say, what's with you anyway?" The old man took another sip and set his drink down on the bar.

Konjo hadn't spoken in days. He hadn't cried out or protested during any of the back alley beatings. He had only set his pine coin down earlier and pointed at the big beaker of *roua* when the antisocial barkeep had finally condescended to notice. The last thing he wanted in the world was to be drawn out by some bizarre old bum. Konjo sighed a deep and disinterested sigh and glanced back at Brinka once more, intending to just sink back into his own thoughts and ignore the old man thereafter, but when he looked at Brinka, ostensibly just an empty barstool to everyone else around, he noticed something truly inexplicable. Brinka was smiling. Almost laughing! The sight of it hit Konjo much harder than the strange old man had. In the inescapable depths of his own sadness, she had only ever looked sad to him. He had not seen her expression change for as long as she had haunted him. He had not seen her smile since she was alive. But Brinka was unmistakably amused, and Konjo could not believe what he was seeing. While the sour, sober Kenjah stared at an empty barstool, the old man leaned in and whispered something that only Konjo could hear. Something impossible.

"You think you lost her forever, don't you?"

Konjo whirled around and stood up from his seat, staggering a little, though he hadn't swallowed a drop of that *roua* all night long. Brinka was now shining as brightly as the morning sun, and the old man was sipping casually from his brass goblet with near preternatural indifference.

"Lost...Lost *who?*" Konjo stammered, searching for words he shouldn't have to find. "Who...Who are you anyway?" Konjo hadn't heard the sound of his own voice in days, and was almost surprised by it. He looked at Brinka, who was now gazing in a friendly way at the old man, who was, in turn, watching Konjo try to orient his grasp on reality. "What are you talking about, old man?" Konjo was forcing a shout's worth of breath into a measured whisper. "What do you want with me?"

At this, the old man sat back on his stool and sipped his drink, chuckling mischievously to himself as if he had extracted all of Konjo's secrets at once. "Now, now Konjo, don't cause a scene. Don't be alarmed big guy, I come in peace! I happen to know something about what happened to you and your lovely lady friend there, and I think I might be able to help you both. But first, I need you to help me with something, if you can be persuaded. Have a seat and a fresh sip or two, and hear me out? What have you got to lose, old Konjo, old pal?"

Konjo felt his desire for this old man's abrupt and epithet laden dismissal aching in his bones. Brinka's patient indulgence with road-men and their mythical wares had been pathological. Her voiceless incandescence seemed to lean in with frantic interest, begging Konjo bide his tongue and bend his ear. She would give audience to any sobbing tale or

sermon or scheme. Konjo would have given anything he had
or must acquire to increase by a single moment the wonderful
and warm life he had known when she lived and walked and
spoke and listened and laughed and cried beside him. What
he could not bear was the obvious and deliberate exploitation
of the hopeless love of the bereaved, represented at hand by
the inevitably and egregiously scheming proposal, presently
awaiting, absurdly, his own consent. As if this preposterous
crook needed Konjo himself to sanction the picking of his
own pockets in advance. The old man was himself leaning in,
like a gambler having called his mark, refusing to say another
word until his call was checked. And there Konjo sat, the
color of ash seeping into his sinue as Brinka and this stranger
conspired against his better judgment to enlist him in some
new and calamitous folly.

 Konjo took the old man by the throat and threw him
over the bar, smashing the surly barkeep and a row of glasses,
spilling, to Konjo's own private shame, he later mused, only
the large decanter of *roua*. The patrons of this sordid
establishment at once obtained collective inertia, and silence
flooded the tavern, nearly palpable enough to drown even the
stale smell of ferment and sweat. Konjo was towering now,
the color of the rising sun, and stunned even by his own rash
implosion. Brinka's gentle light now nearly eclipsed by the
starstuff seeming to glow in the valleys between Konjo's
muscle and bone, he tried to scream before he could notice
her, and failed. Her face was a dripping wash of submissive
disappointment. She would not meet his eye, and his heart
broke again as the starstuff retreated and Konjo sank into an
ocean blue shrug. He gazed around at the disapproving eyes
and heard the hostile whispers commence. He had proven
their prejudice once again, and was ashamed.

Konjo produced his own dwindled parcel of pine coins and dumped them, one and all, clanking and clattering on the bar as the keep and the tramp worked to untangle themselves from the floor and the broken glass and the wasted draught, both chastened and mute; Konjo took no joy from the fear in their resolutely quiet eyes. But he would spend no more shame on them here. He lifted his virtually untouched goblet and drained it in a breath, slamming it beside the next, which had been proffered by the stranger only breaths ago, and this he left untouched. His eyes did fall upon it before he turned to go, and took some secret and vulgar solace in having thrown the man high enough to miss the last unwasted vessel of any worth to be found in this travesty of a town. And, turning then, away went Konjo, the color of stone again, his invisible revenant in tow, casting her one last mournful eye back at the curious stranger who had only offered to help.

Moments of paralysis and shock would restrain the patrons, Konjo knew from experience, before their anger and indignation conscripted the mob that would pursue him, and set them into motion. As the heavy doors swung closed behind him, in the unpatroned darkness beyond which greeted him, Konjo pissed in the well in peace, and then departed north towards the fields and mountains beyond. The decision now was triune. If he ran, they would never catch him. If he walked, even briskly, they would overtake him by dawn. Konjo's tired and noisy mind rang in staccato fragments and meaningless phrases. The stress of the last few days had peaked, and he felt himself breaking, as so many other treasured things had now been broken by him, their irretrievable pieces scattered as densely as his footsteps, and following a parallel path. The third option, the one which had once and long been his reflexive first, for most of his life until Brinka had come into it, that third option began to sing above the syncopated alarm bells and painful admonitions. That third option was rounding the turn on its rivals and spiriting swiftly into the lead. Konjo stopped.

Konjo, now the color of moonlight in a storm, stood as still as statues. Fists clenched. Throat aching and muscles and skin burning with the villainy of their uncompensated assaults and cruelties. He had not fought back. Not out of pity or contempt or mercy or cynicism. He had not fought back because there was no other justice to be found in these tireless lands. No penance. Konjo had surrendered so that his flesh could experience what consumed his mind and heart. Brinka knew what would come next. She knew when she shimmered around in front of him and he would not lift his eyes to meet her. When a Kenjah becomes unreachable... Brinka shouted and screamed and pumped her fists and waved her palms in front of him, to no effect. She would have pounded on his chest if her form would have done anything but plunge right through it. She would have dug her heels into the black marsh and clenched his wrists, trying to pull him forward. Walk. Run. Anything! But please Konjo. Please don't stop here. *Please Konjo!*

The shouts and torchlight began to arrive on the wind and dark from the distance. Konjo heard only the spinning overture to a forgotten symphony. Konjo was the color of the moon at sea. The Kenjah, historically speaking, had always made for magnificent mercenaries, for so many obvious reasons, chief among these their novel lethality in dispassionate, detached combat. But Kenjah made for terrible soldiers, so far as armies were concerned, if only for the strategic weakness implied by the impossibility of concealing any number of pissed off Kenjah at night, spoiling in their hearts to avenge any deplorable sin against what little any Kenjah valued enough to fight for in ranks. A squadron of angry Kenjah could be spotted from the peaks of the Dab anywhere between the opposing coasts, and thus, easily eluded for great lengths of time, if not forever. If the Kenjah pursued you long enough to find you, you had likely earned whatever followed.

Konjo turned to his six, and counted thirty, still far out, but closing. Maybe half of them armed. Dismal odds, perhaps, but Konjo would die knowing at least one thing for certain: he *had* pissed in that well. Konjo flashed their torchlight back at them, first in slow, pulsing alternations, then, as his pulse quickened and his eyes began to glow, the flashes grew brighter and faster and more intense, until he was sure that every last one of them could see his anger and resolve. Some of them, to their credit, did manage the decency of skipping awkwardly into a half step upon realizing that where they had expected perhaps a halfhearted chase before the warm spirits and the cold air brought the fray to its senses, before the preceding insult and the manageable mess obtained their proper proportions, now, there was a Kenjah standing still and burning brightly upon the high ground. Facing them down with lightning in his eyes. And the bulk of the foolish drunken horde became, as foolish drunken hordes often do, emboldened.

Brinka peered out over the pitch at the fierce throng, begging, sobbing, weeping, flailing for Konjo to turn and flee, just this one last time. He would not hear, and he would not see her visage amidst the flaring of his own anger. Konjo, it seemed, had become unreachable. She floated over his shoulders, unseen by all. Brinka had not the form for tears, or the wind to carry her shrieks and sobs, but her eternal heart could nonetheless experience fear and pain and anger, suffering for him, as he had suffered for her since her tragic end. She knew he blamed himself, but could not persuade him otherwise. He could see, when he wished, the sadness in her laden eyes, but could not see forgiveness. He could not see that she had chosen to be at his side, that she held him blameless, that her sadness was only for his broken soul and fading countenance. Her fury now, quite opaque and requiring no words, was so obviously for his stubborn and fatalistic refusal to let go just one more meaningless slight and shake from his boots the dust of one last petulant town, so obvious that he would not need the sound of her voice or the syllables it carried if he would just bring himself to see her at all.

No, Konjo. Not this way. Not like this, Konjo, please! There are too many of them, and more than half of them blameless themselves for anything but stupidity and simple minds. Konjo, please don't do this. We are so close to the hill country. Just a little further and they will lose heart and turn around go to their beds and sleep it off. Just turn and go, and we will be in the forest above the streams by morning. We can be free Konjo. So close. Konjo!

The gargling mob reached its stone's throw threshold and drew into some shambling version of inebriated columns, the worst of them to the fore, those slightly more skeptical and prone to reason shifting in their semi-conscious way toward the rear of the little provincial platoon. A proverbial standoff, shouts and curses from the brass section lobbed in provocative tones across the divide. Konjo, for his part, quiet as the stars, but burning twice as bright, waiting breathlessly, with something like joy in his swollen eyes, for contact. There were too many of them, and slurring, for anything intelligible to be discerned from their volleys; their intent was clear, but noticeably wavering. However many the mob, and however few the Kenjah, few in the world are hearty (or foolish) enough to want the privilege of first sally. They slowed to a crawl, inching forward with some indication of caution that belied better judgement, but inching forward behind the most foolish and rash nonetheless.

Brinka, feeling she could not endure another moment, finally shouted, to no one, to everyone, to anyone, to everything and nothing, at the top of her immaterial lungs: *Please! Someone please stop this! Help me! Please save him! Please save them all!"*

Konjo, the color of starlight, watching the screeching rabble now amble close enough to begin to spread out into a half moon around his position, threatening to lurch from all sides as soon as the most foolish among them finally broke ranks and charged, felt the pulse in his ears drum like thunder and the light in his eyes shine like lava. And just as one leery but grudging slog to one side lifted a stone to fling it at Konjo's face, a flash of light raked across the pitch of night and blinded one and all, accompanied by some avalanche of piercing sound that sent Konjo's senses reeling, and then everything vanished from sight altogether. The mob, the hills, the moon, all gone. Into a void of infinite nothing, to the place where dreams go at dawn's first rays. Konjo fell, stunned and frozen in the blackness, confused and moribund. Everything gone into nothing. *And Brinka.* Konjo clenched his eyes.

"BRINKA!"

Konjo, the color of stone, opened his eyes to see a goblet of untouched *roua* clenched between his palms. Brinka, to his right, watching him carefully, as if concerned. Konjo blinked and shook his head, dazed. He released the deathgrip on his drink and stared first at his hands, turning them over and over again before looking up and around at the disinterested patrons of the Titan, presumably preoccupied and undisturbed, the salty barkeep keeping a nervous eye on some disinterested spot on the floor while twirling a glass around a dry towel in a not-quite-absent kind of way. Slowly, staggeringly, Konjo turned his lavender eyes to the old tramp, sitting there with a muck-eating grin on his face, but now, wearing a very stern and serious expression behind it as Konjo met his triumphant and penetrating stare. Unblinking, the old man read a barrage of frenzied questions in Konjo's speechless terror, but answered them all with a single question of his own. Something Konjo was sure he had heard before, but couldn't quite place.

"What have you got to lose, *old Konjo, old pal?*"

***

Konjo found the old man's eyes and held them. He contemplated digging them out with his fingers. As his own senses found their stable center, Konjo remembered to breathe. Without lowering his attention from those glassy, twinkling orbs, he brought his *roua* to his lips and pulled hard. The cinnamon stung his lips and warmed his gullet. Instinctively, he thought of food for the first time in longer than he was sure he could remember. Konjo faded into the color of the forest at dusk. Intrigued, but also still quite annoyed. Control over one's own destiny was the lifeblood of a Kenjah's identity. He knew of clocksmiths, and he was sure he had met at least one in his travels, but he was slow to believe the tales of strangers and sinners alike. Wizards and sorcerers and other sorts of pilferers of the pine coin, Konjo readily dismissed at hand. He had seen many odd and inexplicable things, of course. As if cued, he observed Brinka's shade drawing in from his periphery. He pressed his eyes closed and tried to retain his sanity long enough to think. But the old man's blues found him and pulled him back into the game. Time had passed, but how long?

Konjo knew he had imagined nothing. The clocksmith had him. He was somewhat familiar with the rules, from *roua* swilling campfire revelries with old friends and fellow travellers of yore, but now he cursed himself for having been *too* skeptical to soak up the more easily dismissable bits of those stories. There was a set number of rounds, which varied according to both the prowess of clocksmith in play (there were five? *six?* in the whole history of the world? but how many were still alive?), and according to the clocksmith's intentions. Konjo was sure the set number of rounds would not be revealed to him, because that obviously defeated the purpose. But the clocksmith could flash him back to this moment from any other in his life that would follow, until he died. This served three purposes. Konjo could remember two of them. If he failed or was harmed or injured, the clocksmith could grant him additional tries, according to his own abilities and limitations. That was one. If he refused to comply, or otherwise aroused the ire of a disgruntled clocksmith, he could be made to live out his entire life, or large swaths of it, and be yanked back to start in an instant. This was the second, and why he couldn't remember the third.

He vividly remembered taking this part of a story seriously, or at least permitting himself to be moved by it. He remembered where he was and when, and who was telling the story, or at least this version of it (stories of clocksmiths were like fairy tales: they were essentially ubiquitous, but varied intensely from mountain to forest to plain to island to swamp.) Clearly, Konjo now acknowledged, at least some of them must have been true. He remembered the sauced old *swelu*, half hysterical and yet half weeping, recalling around a pitched firelight-- which itself had sent the shadows of brambles dancing for leagues in any distance, years and years ago, when Konjo's colors were fewer --a tallish sounding tale he (the old sauced *swelu*) had heard aboard ship during his own mercenary days, when Konjo's colors must have been even fewer still. The old *swelu's* mate had spoken of a clocksmith who had seized the days of a Viermah once, when that Viermah's days behind were still yet outnumbered by those ahead. Viermah, being stubborn and unruly creatures themselves, tend to feel as strongly about their freedom as do the Kenjah, although for different reasons entirely, as it goes with the Viermah. The old *swelu's* mate had alleged that the clocksmith, upon having been dismissed abruptly and with many fine epithets, went on to permit the defiant Viermah to go free, unmolested. Days, weeks, seasons, years passed. The Viermah had forgotten the old clocksmith entirely, had fallen in love, laid down his swords in exchange for plowshares, and retired comfortably in some distant villa near the Rising Coast. He watched his adored bride grow round with child as the shadows lengthened and the air turned cold. But she grew ill, as it sometimes fares with those tragic Viermah brides. Her condition worsened as the snows fell, and the fateful day came when she stumbled in the garden and hemorrhaged. In his winged arms, the Viermah flew her over the hills and valleys to the town nearby in desperate search of the local clinician, who himself took the young and perishing Viermah bride into his care while her husband shook and rattled outside, pacing the maddening steps as any mortal would, crying and praying and begging and pleading and pulling out his down as he listened to the wailing cries and whimpering moans of his beloved in her pains. Waiting for news of his bride, or of their son to be.

Finally, her cries grew still, and after an eternity, the clinician emerged, his expression hushed and grim,* and told the fading Viermah that his bride, his beloved betrothed, had not survived. The Viermah, being of pulse and skin, as any of us would, fell weeping to his knees and cried out. But then the clinician laid a hand on the suffering soul's shoulders and spoke a shade less softly. *Would you like to meet your son?* The Viermah, bless his poor soul, his heart had frozen and burst and frozen and burst with each beat of its drum. He looked up through his tears at that clinician and pulled himself to his feet. He was a father now, and he was on his own, and that little viermah in the other room was waiting for the only family he had in the whole world to look after him. Maybe he would look like his mother, and his father might be able to look into her perfect eyes once more. At the thought, the world rushed back in and the Viermah's senses returned. *Of course! Of course I want to meet my son!* And just like that, in the blink of an eye, before he could say another word or take a single step, the clocksmith whisked him right on back to the beginning. That was the old *swelu's* tale that he had heard from his mate when his own days were fewer. A good story is a good story, whether it happened or not, and that had been one of the rare occasions where, as the party had fallen still and contemplative, a younger Kenjah had leaned in and spoken up to ask, *what happened then?*

Well, then? THEN, my young Konjo, the Viermah, comprehending the clocksmith's game, beat him the only way one can beat a clocksmith.

This was the thing that stuck in Konjo's memory. It was gruesome, vile, and unthinkable. The Kenjah and the Viermah may both value their freedom, but they certainly value it...*differently.*

Konjo, winged or otherwise, was not simply content to throw himself from a nearby cliff, over and over and over again, until his rounds were used up. Trust ceases to be a virtue when time itself is used as an authoritarian system of control. No creature which could, let alone would enslave another to such an absolute extent (and the Kenjah had known the whips and chains of bondage, bitterly), no such creature can be considered in the language of trust. But, as Konjo pondered and the old tramp waited and the oblivious shade glittered, Konjo was nagged by the simple observation that, technically, the old tramp had just saved the lives of most of this people in this room, and spared many more unsalvable wounds to Konjo's soul, if not his actual life. Regardless of the mutability of the outcomes, morally speaking, Konjo was already the one on the backfoot.

As this thought finally pieced itself together in his mind, he knew his mind had made itself up. This time he was not going to spill that decanter of *roua*. He was still going to empty his parcel of pine coins, and he was definitely going to piss in that well. As for the safety and wellbeing of the whelps and scruff in the Titan this evening, well, those outcomes, as always, remained up to them.

The clocksmith, having offered his ante, quietly awaited as Konjo deliberated. It did not matter how much time had passed. The clocksmith had all the time in the world. That was the point. It mattered, Konjo supposed, in the sense that the longer Konjo sat there, stone faced and stupid and staring deeply into this old man's striking eyes, the more likely it became that the other patrons, themselves one and all never fully unaware of the Kenjah, no matter how hard they pretended, might begin to speculate in their own vulgar ways. Damn them all, of course, but circumstances now seemed to preclude the need for drawing attention, be it the right kind or the wrong. Konjo conceded that this had been the nature of his first round, in grand fashion, drawing attention to himself. One less round remained, and from this moment forward, what he did or said or did not say or do, mattered. That was the nature of the bargain. That, with the prospect of redeeming the life of his own beloved Brinka.

"You have my attention, and you may have much more than that, I begin to see and will try to accept. But as you have spoken, so shall you set your feet and fists. I will listen, and I will consent to help, whatever to and whither you may incline. But as you have me, you will now assent that I have you as well, and just the same. When this arrangement concludes, I swear on the color of stars, old man, the fates of yourself and my beloved shall be entwined. If she be shade and you be false, then shade too shall you be . You will fill no more of a cloak than she, and to this and nothing more must you agree." Konjo was the color of blood in battle, and stood and offered his hand.

The old clocksmith, of course, understood the Kenjah's colors and comprehended the Kenjah's meaning. He raised himself up to meet Konjo's eye and grasp the length of his outstretched arm, both hands, with sleeves retracted, skin to skin. "Konjo, my boy, I would have it no other way. We are agreed." A proper contract thus enjoined, and many explanations demanding, Konjo released the old tramp's hand and began to form the first of many inquiries in a row, as the process might naturally be expected to proceed, but before the words could reach his own tongue, as soon as the clocksmith's hand was free, both of the old man's hands shot to Konjo's brow and the world around him went momentarily dark, but just as it happened, it unhappened just the same, and the old man's hands went, neutral, to his hips, just a few woolen sleeves beneath an even more pronounced twinkle in those old blues than before.

Konjo, prepared to protest and not a little embarrassed by the futility of his own reflexes, tried to compose himself in that instant, if for no other reason than to refuse to be made to overplay his hand once more, but there was something in the way the light around him changed (by now dear reader, you must surely see, Kenjah are sensitive to these things), and he spun around in a moment's panic to find his Brinka's beautiful, haunting shade dissipated. A million waves slammed against the shores of his mind and heart at once, from all directions, and he was overwhelmed. Too many questions crashed into each other in the lane between his mind and mouth for any of them to manifest. Konjo was shaken and alarmed and confused. *Brinka was gone!*

Konjo whirled around to the old clocksmith once again, prepared to do much more than protest, but once again, before his hands could raise themselves or his lips could purse, the old clocksmith put a gentle arm on Konjo's shoulder and gently cocked his head towards the Titan's doors, where what Konjo now witnessed, following the nod as one cannot help but doing, even when a good brawl is brewing (and sometimes especially), what Konjo witnessed at the trail end of the old man's glance broke him, broke him as nothing else, conceivable or otherwise, ever could. Konjo swam in color and nearly collapsed, but for the gentle grip of the old man's hand. Impossible. Impossible. Impossi...

"Konjo." Her perfect voice. Her fragile frame. Her knowing eyes. She was the color of life.

"Brinka?"

Who has ever seen a Kenjah fall to the ground and weep? Taller tales have been told, one might say, taller still in a place like the Titan. Less believable even than such a tale, others would someday say, is the notion that any Kenjah could do so in front of the patrons of a place like this. Curiously, the patrons of the Titan tonight would come to find, as their paths diverged and their stories shared and their days reduced, that this latter detail provoked even more reliable skepticism than the former. *But it did happen,* they would say. And yes, this night, this round, they did live to say it.

As for whether or not Konjo pissed in that well, just the same...

So it goes.

***

Konjo and Brinka embraced deeply, forgetting the clocksmith and the Titan and everything in it, speechless as their own drums beat against one another in perfect time. Konjo and Brinka were the color of clouds. By turns, they pulled themselves apart in joyful, tongue-tied appraisal, and fell back into each other, squeezing ever tighter. The old clocksmith, himself now persuaded that moments had become relevant once more, observed with a mustered patience for a moment or two longer before pressing the issue to proceed. As he cleared his throat and took a step towards them, they both turned to him with nearly the same unspoken question in their confused eyes. Neither Konjo or Brinka could seem to find the appropriate formulation of the simple inquiry: why is the other *alive?* Such a question, however obviously pressing, is indeed much more difficult to construct in context. Something several orders of magnitude more dissonant than *why isn't my food cold?* For these moments when the tongue cannot connect to the mind, the eyes of otherwise dumbfounded mortals have learned to *implore.* And with imploring eyes, brimming also with gratitude and confusion and shuttered disbelief, Konjo and Brinka shifted slowly to the palettes of the pine and of the sinnana.

"I am Talthielle. I tire of questions easily, and I can tell both of you will burst at the seams if your questions go unanswered. For these things, there is time, I assure you, but the time is not now. You want to know why I would simply lay your winnings on the table instead of leading you around in wicked games and dangling such things over your heads like carrots before you have even heard what I want you to do, let alone had time to consider it and agree. You want to know a thousand other things you haven't even had time to consider yet. Let me tell you this much. I am not some figment of a fairy tale or fish story. I may have as much of your time now, at my disposal, as you have to spare, but my own time is neither endless nor expendable. The reason why, Konjo, I have given you your beloved Brinka back, is not to earn your trust or to ease your suffering so that you will be more useful to me. Brinka, I have brought you back, in my way, because I need the both of you, and my needs are pressing."

"Both of us?" one of them finally managed to choke out. "My dear sir, if we are both to live, then it is exactly as you said before. You *cannot* have it any other way. With your remittance now paid in advance, it is we who are now in your debt. No tricks. No false words. And we will not press you, for so long as we can manage it, for the how of what you have done, though of course we wonder at this unbelievable blessing." When Kenjah speak as one, it is a soft and harmonious sound that pleases the ear. "What was broken has been made whole again. Our questions are accordingly now twice as many, of course. But for you, dear impossible friend, Taltheille, we have only one to utter.

"How can Konjo and Brinka be of service?"

(Dab)

Konjo and Brinka were the color of midnight. Taltheille was sleepless, watching his new friends sleep and dream. The stars shone above as only stars can shine. The waxing moon climbed through the sinana branches, one by one, until it was high in the sky. Beneath it, this night, the pinnacle of Dab reached up from shadows as if trying to escape the tangible world to greet its lonely, distant consort. Taltheille, the clocksmith, the servant of the seasons, lay sprawled in his rags looking so much the common tramp. On clear nights, the cold, crisp air seemed to magnify the majesty of the stars above. He loved the clouds and the rain and the furious storms, but on nights such as these, he never missed them. A clocksmith knew many things that were hidden, but even Talthielle enjoyed the common privilege of wondering at the distant points of light, some brighter than others, some seeming so much farther away. The sky reminded him of his own limitations.

Starlight humbled him in ways the world could not.

Talthielle had sailed each of the coasts, as far out as ships could venture. He had laid a thousand eyes on the crest of the Dab, the highest point in Omnia. He had walked or ridden or rested himself on every stretch of habitable ground between, but cold air on a clear night was the only thing that ever seemed to draw the stars any nearer, no matter where he found himself. Omnia was home to Talthielle, just as to Konjo and Brinka and their beleaguered, nearly extinct Kenjah brethren. Talthielle had chosen the Kenjah because they are a lonely race. Scattered, pejorated, hunted, neglected. Perhaps Konjo had been the loneliest of them all. They are also honest creatures, by nature, if not by choice. To comprehend the Kenjah's colors is to know what a Kenjah thinks, and how a Kenjah feels. Though Talthielle had also chosen the Kenjah because they contain starlight, he mourned the simple and tragic irony that the only way to see that beautiful light is to hurt or anger a Kenjah. But all of their colors were beautiful. Beauty, alas, Talthielle reflected, is its own curse. In a more abominable age than this, the Kenjah had once been hunted for their skins. The same was true of the Viermah, for their golden wings, and of the Kalamaii, in the deep, for perhaps the most gruesome and unforgivably barbarous spoil of all, their eyes. The ancient Dab had seen many a savage age go by.

Talthielle was Epozia, a word forgotten by all but the clocksmiths themselves. The Epozia set themselves about dispelling the brutality and disorder by which early Omnia had been so markedly defined, when the stars themselves were still young in the sky. It was said of Omnia that if one put the great waters to one shoulder and followed the sea in that direction, it would take a lifetime of walking to return to the place where one began. Talthielle had tried it once, and hadn't walked for an entire season before being drawn into some local circumstance and distracted. Civilizing a land this big, with so many different kinds of creatures, required many

many lifetimes and a lot of work. The Epozia had once been many, as had the Kenjah and the Viermah and the Kalama. But as the great seas wither the stones, so had time diminished many of the magnificent lores of old. Of the Epozia, though persistent rumors and perennial superstitions seemed to proliferate with the seasons, only Talthielle remained. He longed for the days when he still had the energy to long for his kin.

Talthielle watched Konjo and Brinka beneath the stars. Talthielle was himself sleepless. A clocksmith does not dream. To be a clocksmith is to stand at the center of a still sea and watch the waves ripple away from one's feet in all directions at once. Presently, as Konjo and Brinka rested, wrapped and draped and tangled in a pile beneath the boughs of an evergreen, Talthielle was experimenting with their morning departure. The rays of the rising sun would illuminate the pinnacle of Dab a few moments after a distant crow's call, and would require approximately one hour to bathe the full face of the mountain in daylight. If Talthielle roused them before the crow's call, and insisted they eat on the road, they would miss a band of inebriants on their way home from the Titan by about ten minutes. If the Kenjah traveled at speed, they would not be overtaken and exposure would be minimized. They would make north until midday, when they would enjoin the leeward coast of the Injha River, following its leisurely meander without incident until dusk, when Konjo would spot the evening's meal galloping away from a small clearing and break off in pursuit. Brinka would sight berries along the trail throughout the day, and the three of them would have a pauper's feast right there on the banks of the river.

If Talthielle permitted them to hunt, cook, eat, and rest, Brinka would insist on camping for the night and would have no part of explaining her rather obvious motives. It went without saying that Konjo would have little interest in opposing his own beloved in such matters, and Talthielle would be obliged to play the heavy or lose several hours of travel. In all scenarios which followed, if they did not camp, the Kenjah would be surly and callow for their deprivations, which would have cascading influences upon the events of the following day. But if they stopped for the night, they ran an exceedingly close risk of being stumbled upon and discovered in the middle of the night by local trappers. Their fire must not burn after the last light of the setting sun, and they must not speak at all after the fingernail moon cleared the western ridge of the Dab. Even still, the odds of an encounter with the trappers were better than fifty-fifty, in favor of the trappers. And the trio would not make the piers of the Rising Coast at Injha by nightfall the following eve. The last schooner will have departed, and Talthielle will have to waste weeks entertaining and protecting Kenjah in boring and hostile territory before another ship capable of reaching the Kalama Temple will pass through. From there, dear reader, surely you can see how complicated things can get!

On the other hand, if the Kenjah sleep until the full face of the Dab is illuminated, the patrons of the Titan will have long left the road toward their own respective huts and cottages, and Konjo will miss his galloping game. The Kenjah will graze on Brinka's pickings throughout the day, but by midnight, the Kenjah will be starving and drained and despondent. Talthielle will have to drive them like beasts of burden for hours to gain enough ground to elude the trappers. And the next day their spirits will be severely attenuated. They will be impatient, and their questions will take on a decidedly petulant tone. By midday they will be squabbly and sour, and worst of all, slow and apathetic.

Talthielle thus worked the variations, trying this way and that to determine the proper timing. He knew, and sympathized, with the Kenjah's unspoken urge to run away and consummate their reunion in peace, in the mode of their own kind. This was not a reflection of their absence of commitment to their given word; of course they would honor their oaths to the clocksmith willingly. It was a truly happy arrangement in which no parties involved had any desire to expend any more rounds than were entirely necessary or unavoidable. They would not force Talthielle to reset the day in a punitive fashion. Circumstances being what they were, the Kenjah simply had... *competing impulses.*

Perfectly understandable.

Talthielle was sure that if he could get both Kenjah safely and inconspicuously aboard the *Marvu,* and out to sea, on schedule, the two lovebirds would make good use of a delightful and (thankfully, or at least, hopefully) uneventful voyage. But the next thirty eight hours were both critical and potentially perilous. They needed supplies and arms, as well, for the journey, and there were three possible merchants to choose from along the way, and none of them were great choices. The first of these was a simpleton who despised outsiders and overcharged them whenever he could get away with it. The second of these was a charming little witch, quite a ways off of the path, who dealt reasonably enough with her patrons, but who was indeed utterly insane and unpredictable. The third had something very precious to the clocksmith, hidden somewhere in the interior of his shop, and was, perhaps, an amicable enough fellow, except for the minor inconvenience of having sworn a blood oath against the life of Talthielle himself.

The traveling trio could lean on the imbecile, just gently enough, perhaps, to obtain a suitable cache of rations for the road east. The witch would have weapons, of course, a fine selection in fact, but many of them would be enchanted or cursed, according to none but the whims of her own chaotic mind; and even if she were disposed to reveal which was which, which she was not at all disposed to do under any circumstances, Talthielle often suspected of her that in most cases, she had indeed forgotten herself. Such dubious bargains made for interesting, if occasionally devastating surprises on the road, and were often only discovered at last under the least advantageous circumstances imaginable.

    The third, in Talthielle's estimate, was easily the most problematic, but also likely the most critical stop between this darklit glade and the sea. Three stops, less than two days. Much legging through well-traversed paths and trails, under the cover, as it were, of broad daylight, with two very conspicuous conscripts. Brinka possessed, what Talthielle knew of Brinka that Brinka did not herself know, the ability to shift her palette to obtain patterns which might render her very nearly invisible. Talthielle's luck, he mused. The smaller one could be concealed with robes or rags to satisfactory effect. The big one stood out like a sore thumb, a giant solid against any backdrop. Would that their conditions were reversed, Talthielle mused. Konjo would not permit Brinka to endure any kind of risk alone under any circumstances, and over such things, there would be little point in arguing. Talthielle could not see or discern much of anything useful beyond a conscript's interaction with most other sentient beings. Sometimes one could postulate some educated guesses, but other people's freely made choices were akin to distant stones near the opposing shores of a clocksmith's sea, where the observable waves emanating from his own decisions finally broke and scattered like the reflections in shattered glass.

Talthielle watched his quarry attentively as they slept. He would rouse them early, feed them mint bread from his own pouch, and drive them onto the road as the crow called morning.

***

Konjo and Brinka were the color of seabed, and drowning. The tangled roots of the sinana grappled their ankles and wrists as they thrashed and panicked. Strange and curious creatures of the vast deep darted around them, observing their doomed struggle and offering no aid. Konjo held Brinka's hand for dear life as he slashed and tore at the sinana around her feet. The branches moved as if compelled by some mysterious authority, swaying and dodging and reaching further around Brinka's legs with every desperate swipe. Konjo's blade left only feeble scratches in the dense throng of tendril and tine. Each could see the fear welling in the other's glowing eyes, but all else beyond was a merciless abyss of blindness. Each could hear through flooded ears the distant and sonorous wailing of some beastly leviathan form; each echoing cry seeming to grow less distant and more urgent. As Konjo flailed helplessly against the web of briar and thorn, he could see Brinka's breath beginning to fail. His beloved was choking and pulling at her throat; her pleading eyes clawed deeper scars in Konjo's heart than the constricting sinana were tearing in Brinka's legs. With each slash of Konjo's blade, the branches only constricted. The light in Brinka's eyes was beginning to dim as Konjo's own breath failed him. As his own throat closed around itself, Konjo became aware of the futility of his efforts. He let his blade fall into the roots below and knew that it was lost forever. With both hands he clutched his beloved to his chest, feeling his own tears and hers pushing against the salty tide. As he placed his lips upon hers one last time, the sonorous voice in the distance grew deafening and engulfed them both.

***

Talthielle kicked at Konjo's feet and whispered loudly, "Kenjah, awaken! The day is upon us and we have many leagues to cross. Awaken you stubborn brute! The last few stumbling patrons of the Titan will be straggling by this place within the hour. We must fly!"

Konjo, after a moment's prodding, bolted upright with a shout that cleared the birds from the branches above. Brinka, stirring, rolled lazily over and moaned in protest. Konjo stared briefly and dumb at Talthielle as the dim memories of their evening trickled into his mind, but then his eyes found Brinka and sharpened. Clarity and purpose and no small hint of gratitude flooded his eyes as he grasped which images had been dreams and which had been real. Talthielle briefly glimpsed something like fear and trepidation in the Kenjah's expression, and wondered. Konjo remembered the wretched clutch of the sinana and the panicked gurgling of his beloved's last light. "She is still dying! Drowning!" Konjo rolled over and gripped his Brinka's shoulders, gently but firmly, and called her from her sleep.

Talthielle, sure that there was no danger approaching from any direction, still sensed the urgent sincerity in Konjo's cries, and in the moment's confusion, only held his own breath and spoke nothing.

At last, Brinka came to. Talthielle saw in her own countenance all the same emotions which beset her beloved, but when she saw Konjo's worried face, and consciousness eclipsed whatever horrible nightmare had held them captive, both of them softened and breathed and collapsed in each other's arms, uttering heartfelt graces from between each other's lips, wrapping arms and legs around each other tight enough to break a man in two. As Talthielle studied his conscripts with a muted sense of alarm and a studied sense of patience, they all heard a roll of deep thunder somewhere off to the west. Neither Epozia or Kenjah could predict the weather in Omnia, any more than either could guess the number of the stars above, but the sound was as intense as that of a mallet on a steel drum, and portended fitful storms approaching fast. The rain would slow them down, and Talthielle knew he had no time to meditate on the new circumstances. Whatever dreams they had shared had clearly deprived them of rest and shaken their nerves, but these tales and their significance would have to wait until the road was beneath their feet.

"My friends, to your feet! Quickly! We must hurry from this place if we are to remain unseen. Speak your morning oaths with haste, and break bread with me as we go." Talthielle knelt beside the shaken Kenjah and proffered them his morsels of mint bread. The Kenjah eyed these unsatisfying crumbs with mournful skepticism, but accepted them without complaint, nibbling them as they clamored to their feet. Konjo and Brinka muttered their mutual thanks politely and fell into each other's arms again as life returned to their ashen skin. Konjo and Brinka were the color of roses as they turned to the clocksmith.

"We are ready."

Talthielle regarded his conscripts with a sense of resolve. In the distance, the crow called morning. He had left them to their own devices, respectful of the gravity of their reunion, and for the practical reason that he would not have gotten a word between them until shared dreams dispelled the drear of their estrangement. Konjo and Brinka had suffered, and who could say which of them had suffered more? They had deserved the night, and Talthielle had even considered expending a round or two for their indulgence. If Nanok still had the clocksmith's stones, and the three of them reached the *Marvu* on time, he might remain inclined to grant them a few extra days at sea. For now, Talthielle's own time was pressed, and the Kenjah would have many questions about the nature of their journey. Most of these had not yet even been formed.

"My friends, let us away! We will journey east toward the basin of the Dab where the Injha's tributaries feed into the Verdant. There, we will try to obtain provisions from a merchant named Jorgan, who is a very sour fellow and surly. We will follow one of these tributaries into the marshlands where we will, again, *try* to arm ourselves with suitable instruments at the lodging of Marla, the mad sorceress, if we can find her, and persuade her not to kill us or eat us, or both. Our last stop will be the most difficult. A smuggler named Nanok is known to camp and travel along the road from the marshlands to the Rising Coast, which is where we are going. I will not conceal from you that he despises me, and he has my gradation stones. I don't want to talk about why he has them or how he came by them, or how I lost them, but I will tell you why I need them. Why *we* need them.

"Konjo, you are my conscript. At any moment of my choosing, I can return you to the Titan. While I respect you and assume your compliance on the grounds that I have already given you everything you wanted in the world, the return of your beautiful beloved, of course we all understand that one practical purpose of this power is leverage. Like you, I find such means to be distasteful and I prefer not to exercise my gifts in such a nefarious and heavy handed manner. More useful, and I suspect, agreeable, is the implied capacity to rescue my conscripts, and under the circumstances, my own skin, from unexpected and imminent peril. If anything should happen to us along the way, so long as there is breath in my body and I am conscious, I can return us all to the Titan.

"As you are probably aware, the number of times I can do this is limited. The gradation stones will not change that fact, but they will allow me to conserve my power by enabling me to change the moment to which we return, and therefore increase the number of times I can reset our position. There were once a hundred stones. Nanok, if he hasn't lost or sold or traded them, possesses twenty four of them. I suspect he still has them for two reasons. One, because they are of no use to anyone left alive in Omnia but myself. The lot of them wouldn't fetch him half a decanter of *roua*. The second reason is that they are of no use to anyone left alive in Omnia but myself. Nanok would not easily relinquish the stones because without them, I would never have to see him again. And of course, he would be right. But it is not the stones he wants. It is my life he wants, and with the stones he is impervious to my power. That is use enough. He is formidable, and will not be peacefully persuaded.

"We have two days, three missions, and a lot of ground to cover if we are to reach the Rising Coasts before the *Marvu* weighs anchor and departs the piers at the mouth of the Injha. We must secure passage aboard that ship and convince its pilot to carry us to the Kalama Temple, where we must find and recruit a creature named *Ursal*. She dwells beneath the sea, many leagues from the shores of Omnia, where the waters are deep and home to many forgotten things, some wonderful, some quite treacherous. *Ursal* is both. She is Kalamaii, the revered deity of the Kalama, the monks who reside in her temple and offer their sacrifices and rituals. She is their protector, and in exchange for their fealty, she fills their nets with her bounty and drives intruders and pirates and strangers away from the temple. Over her, I have no power whatsoever, but I must gain her trust and plead for her aid.

"Konjo, you are to be the ambassador of your people. Brinka, you are to be the ambassador of mine. My lifeforce is nearly spent, and there is less time ahead of me than behind. Your Konjo is the strongest and most courageous of all the Kenjah; of this I am sure you have no doubt. But you Brinka, you are special. And you are special to me. I beg your patience. If I explained this to you now, it would make no sense at all. There will be a time and a place for that conversation. *Ursal* will be the ambassador for the island folk, if we can persuade her to join us. We will need a representative of the Viermah as well, but I do not yet know who it will be or where to find them. The five of us must ascend the Dab and invoke the ancient Council of Lavaris."

Here, Talthielle trailed off into an uncertain silence.

"Look down along the road we have traveled, Konjo." There was sadness in Talthielle's voice. "See those men down there, following the same path from the Titan, now just passing the place where we camped. In the version of your life in which I do not find you in time, you leave the Titan and sleep in the same place we slept. When the crow calls, you do not awaken. These men stumble upon you and catch you as we now speak. You flee and they pursue, and they overtake you here, where we now stand. At first, you refuse to fight. You are the color of stone, until at the very last, you see the horror in your *kinja*'s eyes. You become starlight, and you take many of your attackers with you, but it is too late, and there are too many of them. Konjo, my dear friend, you die here today, right where I now stand. And the worst thing about it isn't that it is completely pointless and vulgar and unprovoked. The worst thing isn't just the hatred and prejudice in the black hearts of these empty souls, drunk on *roua* and numb to their own shallow contempt. The worst thing is that those of them who fall by your hand here in this place become martyrs to that bigotry that animates them.

"The others return to their homes and neighbors with their tales of heroism and indignation. They say they were attacked on the road by radical, lunatic mountain trash. They say that you drooled and sneered and cursed them like an animal as you ambushed them from the morning shadows. They say that they ran and you chased them and slew them without mercy or restraint. They say that their dead must be avenged, and that the Kenjah must be destroyed, once and for all. And they are heard and believed. Konjo, these hateful men will bend their forked tongues around a terrible lie and rally their own to the altars of their false gods. Your death would have been the first rolling stone of an avalanche of abysmal villainy and bloodshed. They will hunt your people once again, and be hunted by them. I have seen these things come to pass, as sure as you see me now. Their callous barbarism will become contagion, and not a whole season will pass before they are hunting the Viermah and the Kalama.

"All of Omnia will be at war. And no one alive will remember that Konjo was the name of the first casualty. They leave you here to rot in the sun, while their lies cover the world in unspeakable darkness. My friend, we do not embark on a noble adventure to save the world. I have already saved it, by saving you. I have surrendered nearly all of my remaining strength to return to you your beloved Brinka. Like yourself, she is made of starlight, and is eternal. But Brinka, it is my own life force that extracts your form from the realm of the *kinja*. Konjo, your beloved, is Kenjah. You, my dear soul, are *Epozia*. I and my kin have been but humble servants of the seasons. Of our kind, only I remain. When my last breath is drawn, fair friend, you will become the Queen of the Epochs.

Your children will bend time itself, just as easily as you and your brethren bend starlight. They will bring peace and serenity to Omnia.

"The Council of Lavaris can only be convened by a Kenjah, a Viermah, a Kalama, an Epozia, and Lavaris himself. The old ghost of the Dab, patriarch of the *kinja*, the Lord of the Departed. He will not reveal himself at the mountain's crest unless an ambassador from each lore agrees to enjoin a quorum. This has not occurred in Omnia in ages, since even the Epozia were very young. So much of the history of this strange and magnificent place has been lost to the diaspora and dissipation of goodwill between our houses. We used to celebrate the annual council with festivals and feasts. You wouldn't believe it now if you saw it, but the mountainside in those days was covered in a sea of travelers and revelers from every walk of life, from every corner of Omnia. There were songs and contests and markets, and at night the spirits of our ancestors would walk amongst us and share their wisdom. But as our numbers grew, so too grew the spirits in our wake, and Omnia grew smaller. Our sight shortened. We did not see that the Men we grew in our various gardens, once childlike and curious and benign, would someday spoil like fallen fruit, and hunt us all to extinction.

"I want to gather the best and brightest of what remains of each of our lores, the starlight of the Kenjah, the golden wings of the Viermah, the eyes of the Kalama, and myself, the last of the Epozia, and appeal to Lavaris to reopen the gates to his kingdom. The spirits of our ancestors have forsaken us as we have abandoned them. Their memories, their truths, lost to civilization for a parade of lifetimes, must be restored. Men have taught themselves to fear the starlight, to resent the glory of the sky, to suspect the mystery of the sea, and to take time itself for granted. They hate us because our beauty is rare and inaccessible to them. They do not possess light or command the air or rule the deep or bend moments to their will. They eat and they kill and they consume. Their gods are wicked and wretched and wasteful. The men must be taught to love, or at least tolerate what remains of our kind, or they must be forced to live with the spirits of those whom they abuse and destroy. If something doesn't change, each of our lores will fade out into myth and legend, and then superstition and fairy tale, and then vanish into the void of infinite nothing. Men will inherit Omnia. Can you imagine a more pitiable or vacuous outcome?

"So that is everything, I think. I have not withheld anything, at least not purposefully. I have no intention of stringing you along or feeding you crumbs and morsels. This is my entire plan. I am telling you everything now, not only because it is not a cause I can bind you to merely with the leverage of resetting your lives, but also because if something happens to me along the way, in my weakened condition, it will fall to you to find *Ursal* and go amongst the Viermah in the Verdant and persuade the most noble among them to ascend the Dab and convene the council. I cannot know what perils we may face in this quest, or whether or not I can keep us all alive long enough to pull it off. What I do know is this. We must make it aboard the *Marvu* at all costs. We will need provisions for the journey. We will need arms to defend ourselves. And we will need those stones if we are going to find *Ursal,* let alone convince her to join us. That part alone is flat out going to take more than one try. And if we have to keep starting over at the damned Titan, my strength is going to be spent long before we reach the Viermah, and we won't get one without *Ursal.*

"If we fail to persuade the Kalamaii and the Viermah to join us before the snows fall, none of us will survive the winter."

Konjo and Brinka were the color of sinana vines, and daylight covered the face of Dab. The men from the Titan were leagues behind them, all of them alive and oblivious, and most of them by now quite unconscious as well. Talthielle had told the Kanjah his plan, or as much of it as he safely could. What little he withheld he did not conceal without reason. The only versions of this journey in which they all reached the *Marvu* safely were the ones in which Konjo and Brinka trusted Talthielle. If he told them what Lavaris was going to want in return, at any moment in this journey before the one in which Lavaris told them himself, his conscripts would rebel in horror and disgust. To complicate matters, one or both of the Kenjah was eventually going to ask. Talthielle would have to dodge the question or lie. To him, this inevitable moment was represented by a large and obstinate stone against which the waves in his crystalline sea of consciousness broke and scattered, like one's reflection in shattered glass. He had no idea which choice he would make, let alone how the Kenjah would respond to either the truth or the lie.

The Kenjah were honest creatures by nature. They were sensitive to dishonesty, and resented fraud as an overt attempt to constrain their freedom of choice. One supposes all creatures are basically this way. Without Brinka's restoration, Konjo would never have permitted himself to be conscripted, no matter how stubborn or cunning the clocksmith. Reunited, however, their debt to Talthielle was virtually insoluble, ironically, as it were, just so long as Talthielle told them anything but the truth.

Only three things would persuade Lavaris to reopen his kingdom: the skin of a Kenjah, the golden wing of a Viermah, and the all-seeing eye of a Kalamaii. The Council of Lavaris did not require the opinions of its constituents. It required their obedient sacrifice. It required their powers. And unlike their effort to persuade *Ursal,* Talthielle was certain he was only going to get one try with the old ghost of the Dab, the patron of the *kinja*, the Lord of the Departed.

(Brinka)

The Kenjah were no longer walking. Konjo and Brinka were the color of autumn leaves. Talthielle took a breath and a sip and contemplated the distance to the river Injha while a thousand new questions formed in the Kenjahs' eyes.

"Queen of the Epochs, Brinka!" Konjo broke the silence at last. "We're going to find a Kalamaii and a Viermah *swelu* and meet a witch and you're the Queen of the Epochs! I don't know what in Dab any of it means my beloved, but I am calling you the Queen of the Epochs for the rest of my life and no one will stop me!" The Kenjah faded into the color of choral and erupted into hysteria. Talthielle sighed and eyed the road ahead.

"And you, my KING! King Konjo! Bearer of the Boulder's Crown! I would have it no other way, my Konjo!" Brinka coughed and wiped tears from her eyes as Konjo knelt before her, shoulders and chin high, eyes wild with mischief. Brinka spun a silver shawl around Konjo's brow and rolled it tight. Konjo made a grand and sweeping display of proffering his blades, hilt first of course, "to the matriarch of time and starlight! I wonder if he'll let us start on those children of yours soon?"

"Yes, he must, Konjo! He simply must! Peace in Omnia, Konjo! Did you hear him? And at what a price!"

"It is a bargain my love! A BARGAIN! I would bathe this world in peace for generations upon generations. I find these terms exceptionally agreeable! Talthielle! If it is peace we must have, and this is how we get--" Konjo and Brinka found Talthielle unamused, and their words stuck in their throats. A guilty hush fell over the Kenjah.

"Come on, Kenjah. We have a long way to go and very little time." Talthielle shook his head and turned his feet toward the mountain, putting his conscripts and their furrowed brows behind him. "Yes, Konjo. Queen of the Epochs. So keep a sharp eye on her. As if you could do otherwise." Talthielle shrugged and said nothing. The road wound on beneath six sandaled feet in silence for a league. The trail from the Titan to their camp had been mostly wide dirt between hewn pine. From the camp to the place behind them where Talthielle said Konjo was lynched, the wide dirt narrowed into weeds and stones as the land rumbled into foothills and rock formations. Dab, far away and occasionally straight ahead, spawned little ridges and croppings of lesser ranges, through which the mighty Injha cut from its headwaters in the eastern shoulder between the mountain and the setting coast, south through the lower peaks and higher valleys before turning eastward on its course through the marshlands, which descended some distance south from the river before leveling off into dense, flat plains.

Beyond the marshlands the Injha fed the Verdant, the bulk of which extended north at the foot of the Dab's sloping salients. The forest above the river was home to huge and ancient sinana and poliana clusters, some two and three times as big around as the wingspan of a full grown Viermah. The forest below, into which the sprawling marshlands jutted, was thick with knotted pine. Carriages could roll clumsily between the giant sinana and poliana. There were places in the pine where only bugs and rills could cross on foot. Talthielle and the Kenjah would find Jorgan's cottage shop at the end of the trail they followed when the foothills broke against the Injha basin. They would find Marla south of the river where the marshlands mingled with the larger, older pine. They would have to cross the river into the Verdant at the foot of the Dab's southernmost shins to find Nanok, and they would have to search for him, find him, placate him, and beat rocks to make the piers by nightfall of the second day. The Kenjah could be somber or they could be bellicose. Talthielle would pay no mind, so long as they weren't standing still or moving in the opposite direction. They did not have to believe him to honor their word. And believing him wouldn't change the fact that they were conscripts of a determined clocksmith. Of this, neither of them had any illusions.

Konjo was the next to break the silence of the march. "How will we deal with this Jorgan fellow, when we find him?"

Brinka answered. "We'll get old Talthielle here to put the surly merchant under his spell when we see him and then we'll grab him by the arms and legs and play tug until one snaps. Before the foolish pilferer becomes midnight and expires, old Talthielle here will flash him back to first sight, and then we'll just ask the fellow politely for what rations he can spare." Brinka was the color of citrus and trying not to giggle. Konjo put up no fight at all.

"I suppose we can just handle Marla and Nanok the same way? I suggest we approach the Kalama differently. The Viermah? I'm on the fence..." Brinka was the color of the

Injha at dawn. She cupped her hand over her smile and snuck a wink at Konjo over Talthielle's shoulder.

"As far as Jorgan is concerned, I have no objections. Marla, on the other hand... Of everyone we meet, Marla is perhaps the one you should approach with reverence and caution in equal measure. If we can help it, Nanok we will not approach at all. He is treacherous and will require treachery in kind. *Ursal,* well, if we are lucky, she'll approach us."

"What if we are unlucky?" Brinka stifled her laughter with a nervous note.

"If we are unlucky, my dear Brinka," Talthielle spoke slowly, "we won't see her coming when she does." This seemed to stifle the levity in both Kenjah. Brinka pressed.

"And the Viermah? I suppose we shouldn't be planning to quarter an avian none of us have even met yet, and who it seems we are going to need. But I have met some Viermah I wouldn't mind quartering." Brinka saw Konjo nod in agreement and fell silent.

The Kenjah were the color of tumbleweed, and Talthielle let the rhetorical echo away into the sounds of footfall. The Viermah was an unsolved variable, but the Viermah was a long way off. There would be plenty of challenges just making the piers, and plenty more negotiating with the Kalamaii, who would very likely know exactly what Lavaris wanted without having to be told. Talthielle and his conscripts made their way through the rest of the morning, withholding their questions and comments. They held hands and kept pace with the old tramp, whose long legs and wiry agility put even Kenjah to test. From time to time, Brinka would sight berries in the bushes and vines that dotted the hillside. As the river drew nearer, the land and air around them became pungent with foliage and recent rains. Clouds simmered in from the west, beginning to fill the sky, but the rain and thunder would not come until the sun began to set behind them later in the day. The Kenjah could smell it in the air; the rains would come.

As the hillside broke, Waterside spread out beneath them. A smattering of crisscrossing roads led away from the banks of the opposing Injha at its widest point, where the waters were deep enough to form a natural harbor where skiffs and small boys could tie off into traversable rafts. There were no lodges at Waterside, and little trade was conducted ashore. The residents of the ancient river city were comparatively few, and often less than the populations of the rafts which anchored, for historically practical reasons, just out of reach of a stone's throw from the docks. Some would come ashore from time to time for leatherworks and medicines and food. By these means, the people of Waterside supported themselves and, with reticence, sustained their usefulness to the perennial sailing community. The rafts were never empty, and what they couldn't get from the landed, they bargained for amongst themselves. Each night, some would untie and ship out for the Rising Coast and points between, or, if inland bound, would scuttle their way back up towards the western ranges and the icy headwaters north of Dab and the old mountain forts and mining caves along the way.

While Konjo had lived most of his life hunting and hiking with his kin in the Dab's western ranges, Brinka's people lived many leagues north of the headwaters. Rarely had either of them ventured this far south of the Injha. Neither had ever passed the marshlands into Viermah country, and neither had ever seen a Kalama in person, let alone the fabled Kalamaii. Both had had their fill of menfolk who farmed in the southern plains or huddled in their brick huts in the deserts of the far west. They doubted they would see many Kenjah on their journey east. But neither of them would have gambled on meeting a clocksmith anywhere in the wide world, the Titan perhaps notwithstanding.

The closest thing to a tavern in Waterside, they all knew well, was the Barrel, so called for the large wooden kegs of *roua* tied to the docks beside the larger clapboard cottage with the grassfed lighthouse fire burning in a bell chamber above its rafters. The sailors did not refer to the location of the adjacent raft community as the ports at Waterside. They just called this whole place the Barrel, and on their maps Waterside was merely designated with a tiny little sketch of the clapboard cottage itself. The Barrel was set apart at some distance from the rest of the cottages housing the inhabitants of Waterside, and this was obviously by design. Sailors were more easily discouraged by large fields of untrodden tallgrass than by large fences or printed signs.

Waterside was accessible, if that was the right word, to the floaters (a word most Watersiders readily agreed was correct), by a much smaller dock which rode up into a small heart of trees nearer the residential proper. The trees broke the sightlines between the raft and the town, and afforded its inhabitants some sense of cover from their ever present visitors. If a Watersider had wares for market, they would gather them up and lay them out on stone tables between the tree line and the river, so that they could be seen from the rafts, and so that sailors would not need to wander into the neighborhoods knocking on doors. Jorgan, the sour and surly merchant, lived in one of these cottages, Talthielle knew. And the last thing in Omnia he would be expecting was a knock at the door by an old scheming tramp and some rainbow flavored mountain trash. When that knock came, and there was no loud shouting or disgruntled epithets, or any answer at all, Talthielle very quietly turned the knob to Jorgan's door and pushed it open. Konjo grunted and Brinka shrieked. Talthielle, for his part, was mortified. Konjo turned away and Brinka buried her face in his chest, clutching him close.

There Jorgan lay, in a pool of blood on the floor in his parlor.

His arms and legs were torn off. Jorgan was dead, and had not been dead for very long.

***

Talthielle and Konjo stood speechless and still, and when the mangled corpse on the floor finally released their eyes, they both turned to Brinka, whose own eyes lingered longer on the atrocity before them. After a moment, Brinka forced herself to turn away to found them both staring at her in stunned disbelief. Talthielle's disbelief, she privately observed, was tinctured with something extra. Konjo's disbelief stung her a little as she comprehended the thought which had possessed her companions. "What?" *Why are you both looking at me that way?*

Konjo answered her mind with his mouth. "Brinka, it's just like you said. He's been... *quartered*?" Konjo struggled to force the word past his lips. Brinka struggled not to hear it and failed.

"Okay, I said it. I get it. I said we might play a little game of tug with the guy. But I also said we'd reset his round before he--" Brinka's eyes fell back to Jorgan, prostrate and violated in such a vulgar way. "Talthielle! Konjo! Obviously I didn't do this. Somebody say something that makes sense. Please! Don't just leave me dangling out here by myself. I'm pretty freaked out too."

"Brinka." Talthielle's voice was a nervous calm. Konjo was the color of the mountain. Brinka was the color of the sea at twilight, and shimmering. "Brinka?" Talthielle regained his wits and spun his head around to take in their surroundings, of which he had completely lost awareness in the moment, until the shock of the gruesome scene attenuated into conscientious confusion and alarm. "We must flee! If we are found here, no one will believe us. An old vagabond and two half-naked mood stones standing over a carcass in a town full of backwards peasants who hate everybody. Kenjah, we have to leave here, now!" Talthielle was stern, and the Kenjah coalesced into shades of burgundy.

"What about supplies?" Brinka would not have spoken the words if she had thought them first. Ever practical, clearly to a fault. Konjo's eyes widened in disbelief before she could catch herself. But Talthielle's eyes were sharp. Konjo opened his mouth to protest a thought which Brinka had already internally repudiated before she could open her mouth to concede its absurdity, but Talthielle's tongue was faster.

"No Konjo, she's right. We need supplies. We can't do without them, but we need to be on the other side of the Barrel and marching hard for cover in the next ten minutes or we will be discovered. We cannot be seen. I need a moment to plot the routes, and we can't just stand here gawking. We haven't been seen yet. Everyone inside!" Konjo and Brinka pulsated with conflicting and contrasting vibrancy, but did not move or speak. All four eyes were saucers. He couldn't be--

"By Dab, I am serious! GET INSIDE." Jolted, the Kenjah swiftly complied and Talthielle closed the door behind them. looking both ways down the path and along the tree line before bolting the wood into it's frame from the inside.

"Konjo, blades up my lad. Search the house, quickly and quietly, and make noise if you see anything or anyone.

Brinka, Jorgan's stores are all along that far wall. Stay away from the windows. Fill a bag with what we need. No one make a sound."

Konjo and Brinka were on the case, and Talthielle laid both hands on the door of Jorgan's cabin and closed his eyes. No one approached the body. Konjo stooped his head and followed a narrow hallway into the rear of the home, blades up and feet quiet. The door to Jorgan's bedroom was opened. His bed was unmade, his effects somewhat dishevelled. Jorgan plainly lived alone, Konjo observed. but nothing looked thrown or turned. If anything had been stolen, it would not have required thieves to search for it. Konjo checked his corners, cautiously, and decided not to touch anything.

Brinka, for her part, was laying hands on anything and everything of use she could find. She filled a canvas rice bag with thick cloaks, rolled and stuffed to form a stable bottom which held the bag more widely open. Into this space she put pounds of dried roast wrapped in salt leaves, a few small bottles of ointment, long candles, some basic utensils, a shiny compass and a pad of parchment with a small bottle of ink. No Kenjah worthy of color needed matches to start a fire, but she took some anyway. She found a length of tomi, wrapped around a rod thick enough to serve as a walking stick. For this, she tossed in a thatch of hooks and lures. For their cloaks, she selected a few fine broaches shaped like sinana leaves, each carved of petrified whitewood with silver inlay and emeralds. In the farthest corner, she spotted a garden blade in a sling, and made herself step carefully over two pieces of Jorgan to retrieve it. She sinched and tied her satchel with a foot of tomi and returned to Talthielle's side shortly after Konjo returned from his inspection.

If each was curious to hear of the other's observations, neither could hold the thought while watching

Talthielle in his trance, shaking and gurgling with his eyes rolled back. Somewhat aware of his conscripts, Talthielle broke himself loose and disregarded the mix of impressed skepticism in the Kenjahs' expressions. No one spoke, or counted the moments. Talthielle rested his hand on the bolt of the door and lowered his eyes, taking deep and calmly deliberate breaths. No one counted these either. At length, the clocksmith's moment came and he unbolted the door, pulled it narrowly ajar, drank a deep breath and held it. Konjo and Brinka followed him out of Jorgan's home into a breakneck sprint towards the tallgrass. A loud horn blew from the rafts right at the same time, and in the moment, the town's occupants cast their obligatory and instinctive glance toward the river, collectively ignoring the fields behind them as a wiry old tramp and two colorful beasts high-stepped into a rolling dive when they reached the fields between Waterside proper and the Barrel.

All three, on all-fours, scrambled through the grass as slowly as possible, until nearing the farside Talthielle signalled a halt. Konjo, in the rear, dragging Brinka's spoils and trying not to mow an obvious row in the tallgrass with his brutish, oversized frame, could see little more than Brinka ahead of him, crawling along with a measure of effortless grace and balance, and Konjo thought she cut a fine figure for the circumstances. There are good reasons why Kenjah always gave ground to their mates. More than occasionally, the view was one. The three came to a still crouch in the dense brush, a quarter league from the rear walls and stables of the Barrel. When they emerged, they would have to break for a tree line and disappear from the road for several leagues, until Waterside and its gross mysteries were far enough behind. Again, Talthielle lowered his eyes, controlled his breath, and said nothing. His palms were flat on the soil. Brinka stole a knowing glance back at Konjo, who blushed at her little half smile. Konjo also controlled his breathing, and Brinka suppressed a little chuckle so as not to have to explain her lapse of bearing to Talthielle. Instead, she put her serious face on and watched Talthielle like a hawk, but she couldn't resist a little shimmy at the waist. Konjo suppressed a longing groan.

Talthielle put one hand in the air and held it suspended for a breath, and then motioned. The three of them scrambled out of the brush into a dash, all eyes forward. Now was no time to stumble. If they made the cover of the treeline, the could look back to judge whether they had made it unseen. But when they reached the line Talthielle did not slow, let alone stop. The three blitzed their way through branch and weed, following the glade within rough sight of the road to their left, with the river behind it, now and then lurching to a halt behind Talthielle's raised fist, and pausing for some straggling foot traffic to pass along, sufficiently oblivious. After a time, they all heard the muted noise of another blast of that horn from the raft, now quite a ways behind them, bleating out a staccato.

"Jorgan has been found. We must not be seen or heard before reaching the marshes. Lift your feet Kenjah, or we are to be hunted!" The clocksmith and his conscripts raged through the wood, ducking and dodging the low hanging bows, until the high sun began to drift its way down toward the western prairies. Twice, Brinka nearly fell, but Konjo had arms beneath her before she could even lose her step. Talthielle, not quite as tall and nearly half as wide, had an easier time dipping through and under obstacles which he had the corresponding advantage of seeing first and far enough away to navigate. Many times he would easily evade a branch which Brinka and Konjo had less than half the time to see coming and twice the mass to maneuver around it. None would emerge from this gauntlet unscratched.

They ran for hours until the clay beneath them began to pepper with peat and moss and become damp and sludgy. When they made the marshlands, the sun was already sinking fast. They slowed, mercifully, and began inching their way back toward the road, looking for enough hard ground bare enough for anything but standing. Finding something nearly suitable, they all bent down and doubled over and drank from their casks, which they had not bothered to refill. Konjo quietly set his burdens down and laid flat beside them. Brinka collapsed alongside, her head on Konjo's heaving chest. The shadows around them were elongating, and the twilight was setting in. Nothing about this day had gone the way Talthielle had envisioned it, and his troubles were many. One question burned his mind, and he was sure it wasn't far from theirs' either.

"Brinka."

"I don't know. By Dab, I truly do not know. I was just making a joke. I've never even met Jorgan. Talthielle, what is happening? What in all of Omnia was *that* about? I've never seen anyone quartered before. I was just hungry and the talk about Viermah made me think about dinner fowl. I get that that's not a great answer. I just. I shouldn't. I don't understand, Talthielle. Why would someone do such a terrible thing to someone?"

Talthielle, himself on hands and knees, brought his eyes to meet Brinka's and said nothing for many breaths. His face was puzzled and worried. The Kenjah had known him for less than a day, but puzzled and worried both seemed very out of place and unexpected on the face of their friend, the clocksmith. The servant of the seasons. The mysterious and singular being who had indentured two Kenjah and resurrected one of them. Or, in a way, both of them. But one of them for sure, in a very real and impossible way. And none of them had left each other's sight, though two of them had slept. But even Talthielle could not have made the journey to Waterside and back to camp to awaken them before the crow's call. Haphazard and helpless thoughts raced through all of their minds, struggling to form sensible questions around a senseless premise: Had Brinka spoken Jorgan's horrible death into being? Had she obliviously glimpsed a vision and mistaken it for a passing thought, just morbid enough for a laugh? The how and the why and plenty of other questions that hung on these dry speculations were enough to overwhelm the mind. But if *neither* of these things were true... Then what?

Then *what*?

Talthielle had no answers, but an inkling gnawed at his gut, yet unformed and weightless. Brinka was, in fact, *Epozia*. Talthielle could not dismiss this inescapable fact as unrelated, but for all his long days he had no clue what to make of that detail. Brinka was *Epozia*. An interesting footnote which answered exactly zero questions and shined no light at all. Talthielle was an ancient and powerful clocksmith, but nothing in his repertoire accounted for the prospect of speaking someone's death into being, from any distance, or for witnessing the death of a complete stranger who was not a conscript. Brinka was no youngling, as Kenjah go, but in this form she had been imbued with Talthielle's magic for less than a day. While such a thing as resurrection was rare even among the most gifted *Epozia*, it was not unheard of. But nothing in Talthielle's memory of the old traditions or his own dealings over the ages offered any reasonable corollary, let alone an explanation, or an example, for what had occurred between Brinka's words and Jorgan's fate. Talthielle and Brinka searched each other's eyes for answers neither possessed.

Konjo, grasping intuitively that a mystery was afoot, but that no one present was going to solve it any time soon, held his beloved with both arms and closed his eyes and waited for his captor and his queen to work out the next move. Konjo and Brinka were many colors at once.

***

The disquiet engendered inertia, and all parties felt the burden of wanting to drop an undroppable subject for absence of any satisfying alternative. Brinka sat up and opened her makeshift satchel; the others watched with an aura of reticence as she unloaded her ill-gotten gains. The party may not have killed Jorgan, but they had willfully robbed a dead man, and then left him there to rot. Brinka reached into the bottom of the sack and produced their rolled cloaks and ornate broaches. She tossed one, sort of *at,* each of her companions, and rose to drape her naked form in the twilight. She clasped her broach and drew her hood over her head.

"Get up, the both of you. Let's go. We still have to find Talthielle's witch, and I'd rather find her with more light in the sky than less. I'm going to say this out loud. I really hope we find her alive and in one piece." With this, Brinka replaced the contents of her satchel and slung it over her shoulder. Her robe was the color of lambswool. Konjo, the obedient, lifted himself in silent compliance, wrapping his bones and covering his head. Brinka took his broach and set its clasp, looking woefully into Konjo's eyes. There was a shared thought between them. Both of them wondered if Brinka would be shade again if Talthielle was forced to reset the round before they located his gradation stones. Neither of them wanted to ask the question out loud. And neither of them fully trusted their strange new friend the way they had this morning when the crow called. The thought they shared was that this paradoxical contradiction was the price of their second chance.

Talthielle, taken aback by Brinka's assumption of leadership, was nevertheless somewhat grateful, and perhaps impressed. Kenjah can be tenacious, when they are not brooding in isolation or enraptured by one another. Any fool could sense the sincerity of the unbreakable bond between Konjo and Brinka. They wore that on their sleeves. Talthielle's interest in the dynamic between them was suddenly piqued. Though Konjo possessed the clear advantage in size and physical strength, he did not project any sense of the corresponding confidence. Talthielle knew it would be a profound mistake to believe Konjo to be simple of mind or dull of wit, or in anyway lacking the substance of courage. But he had to wonder if Brinka wasn't the brains of the operation, and if so, was it because she was smarter or quicker? or because Konjo would simply never fail to obey her every command and indulge her every whim?

What would Brinka have to do or say for Konjo to resist, let alone rebel? Was Konjo's Brinka even capable of imagining such deeds or words? If she was, was there a part of her that considered Konjo's limits before presenting a course of action? Or were these two curious lovers simply resonating at all times to the same chord. Talthielle had only observed a single moment between them when their colors diverged. It had been the moment when they both comprehended and responded to the implication of Jorgan's unfortunate circumstance. Brinka had the full version of that experience by herself, and Konjo could only ascertain her feeling vicariously. Brinka was *Epozia* now. Talthielle could not shake the thought. She was starlight, and with training and practice and development, she would someday govern Time itself. Konjo was no more or less the same Konjo right now than he had ever been or would ever be. But their colors were always the same, so long as they were together. Except for that one single moment, when both of them saw Jorgan's mangled remains and recalled Brinka's fateful words in the context of witnessing them manifest. Was that momentary divergence strictly a result of the structural difference between the Kenjahs' perspectives in that moment? Or was there another explanation?

Talthielle robed himself, trying to think of something to say. The Kenjah let him attend to his own clasp. He surveilled his robed conscripts. "The most beautiful and honest creatures in the world. And I must transport them in anonymity. If these lamentable circumstances are not sufficient evidence that Omnia begs to be rescued from its own wickedness, then no more plausible case can be made. We will return to the road. The only people we are likely to encounter at night will be villains, and who may care what they see or think. I only pity them who take us for easy prey in the dark." Talthielle helped himself to the gardener's blade in Brinka's satchel, and produced the dried roast. The blade he tied to his leg beneath his cloak; the meat he proffered to Konjo. "Tear me off a reasonable piece, and share the rest between yourselves as we walk. When the night is high, we will detour to the river and refill out skins. A sliver moon will rise tonight, and tomorrow night will be moonless. Let us hope we lose as little time as possible. The *Marvu* will not wait."

They reached the road as the last shadows fell across the face of the Dab. The slim crescent of a fading moon hung low over the horizon ahead of them. They put the marshlands to their right and set forth with speed, eating and talking in turns, until the food was gone and the sounds of a night in the swamps of Omnia filled the air with chirping and buzzing symphonies. Hours passed this way until Talthielle turned and motioned them down a narrow hill where the river drew closer to the road. As they dipped their skins alongside a shallow brook, Konjo ventured a question.

"Talthielle, how did you know what happened to Brinka?"

Talthielle filled his skin and tied it closed, gazed up at his conscripts, and sat back in a deep sigh. When he spoke, there was sadness on his lips and in his eyes. "I was with you in the town of Flask. I witnessed the whole grotesque spectacle. I was helpless to intervene, but the terrible event persuaded me that-- it was then that I understood what I had to do. What we have to do. Konjo, I have been following you and your beloved for some time. Tracking Kenjah through the open plains is no easy task. When I found you, I did not know I was looking for two Kenjah. I was searching for the poor soul whose slaughter had precipitated such unforgivable events in my own world. I have seen visions of the wars and massacres and feuds and catastrophes that were to beset Omnia upon your death. I have spent considerable power trying to look forward for answers to where these conflicts began. It was only by chance that I discovered the events which followed your murder and realized that this was where all the fighting truly began.

But you were alone when they found you and set upon you. I traced your path backwards from there, to Flask, to the night they took your Brinka and forced you to flee. I have never seen such callous brutality, but I have long felt that with each new season, Omnia's aspect has seemed to darken more and more. We have all seen and survived troubling times. But what they did to Brinka was unspeakable, and unprecedented. I considered coming to you sooner, Konjo. But my power has limits. It had to be the Titan, especially if I was going to exert myself to bring your beloved across the barrier between our realm and the next. I cannot express the depth with which I regret prolonging your suffering, dear Kenjah, please understand and believe. But if we are forced to return to the beginning of our journey by some unforeseeable calamity, so much less time and energy are wasted if we return to the Titan. Returning to Flask would have been, in practical terms, out of the question. This is also why it is so important that we find Nanok and regain my gradation stones. After today, the thought of having to start again at the Titan should revolt everyone present. As for myself, dear Brinka, I have also never seen anyone-- *quartered*, as you put it. If I live a thousand seasons more, I hope to never see again anything like what happened to you, or to your Konjo, or to that poor obnoxious merchant in Waterside.

"I wish I understood what evil and cynical spirits have possessed this land and its inhabitants. I would change it, if I can. If it takes everything I have left, I would see peace restored to the heart of Omnia." Talthielle fell silent again. Brinka and Konjo followed him back to the road, absorbing his explanation and commiserating. When they cleared the short climb from the bank of the river and spied the road for strangers, they all spotted the same stranger at once, and each of the three jerked themselves down into a crouch and froze there. A lone shadow of a statuesque silhouette, standing perfectly still in the eerie midnight glow of the swamp beneath a fingernail moon. Watching them cower in shock and fear behind a mound on the side of the road. No one spoke or moved for several breaths, and then the figure vanished into nothing just as quickly as it had appeared.

Talthielle stood first, and clamored back onto the road with his conscripts trailing close behind.

"Who was that, Talthielle? Was that your witch?" Konjo asked with a hint of worry in his voice.

"I really hope that was your witch, Talthielle. Because it would mean she hasn't been--"

"Quiet! Both of you." Talthielle looked up and down the road in all directions, and studied the marshlands and the river bank by turns. "Stay close and don't speak. It was most definitely Marla. I don't know what happens next, but she has clearly seen us, and we would do well to remember that we are in her domain now. Konjo, take the rear, and keep your eyes and ears peeled. Brinka, stow your blades. I promise, they won't help you here." Brinka groaned with a sprinkle of insolence, but sheathed her blades just the same. "If we see her again, let us hope it is from ahead. If she comes from behind, she means us harm. Brinka, take off your robe, and walk ahead of me. I need you to shine, Brinka. If she is watching us, and she most certainly is watching us, she needs to see that we are not road men. Brinka, I need you to be starlight, or as close to it as you can be without endangering your friends. Konjo muttered something in the way of sly approval, and Brinka shot him a coy look and peeled away her cloak. Brinka's starlight was stunning, and even Talthielle struggled to retain a respectfully modest eye. Kenjah had no word in their own language for bashful. The irony was not lost on Talthielle that only a short time ago he had mourned the urgency of anonymity. Airtight plans were for the unprepared.

(Marla)

Unprepared was Konjo, when he heard the giggling
witch behind him. When he spun around to find nothing
there. When he spun again and realized that his companions
had heard nothing at all. When he whirled back again at the
sound of footsteps falling at his very heels but saw only empty
space. When he looked back at his oblivious companions and
tried to croak a sound through the knot in his throat.
Unprepared was Konjo when no sound would come from
within, and when a scream at his neck spun him around again
to find himself face to face with a horrid, wide eyed creature
with hard features and a web of scars. Konjo stumbled over
his own feet and tried not to fall backwards. As his hands
rose, to balance himself, to protect his face, or just to release
the involuntary stress of shock that ran through his limbs, he
felt her grip his wrists with fingers like brass wire, and before
Konjo could even squeak, he was flying through the air and
landing on the side of the road in a dazed heap.

Talthielle, sensing the commotion unfolding behind
him before actually hearing it, turned on his heels, and in the
blink he saw Marla's palm flash against his forehead, and then
an unconscious paralysis overcame him and he slumped to
the ground, decommissioned.

Only Brinka saw Marla's full form, bathed in starlight, without scars or burns or smeared peat from the swamp. Before Brinka, Marla stopped and was still, head cocked to the side in curiosity and wonder, as if she had not even noticed Konjo or Talthielle, let alone disposed of them only breaths ago. Marla seemed momentarily preoccupied with the spectacle of a glowing Kenjah maiden, as beautiful as she was vulnerable and ignorant. As if sleepwalking, Marla took small, cautious steps to close the short distance, clearly lost in an oblivious trance. Brinka watched the creature's gentle approach while trying to process the pile of Konjo on the side of the road and the pile of Talthielle just behind the witch. Brinka reclaimed her starlight, and was the color of emeralds under a waning moon. This seemed to shake the witch loose of her trance, and for an instant Brinka wondered if she had blundered. But when Marla's own candlelight returned, Brinka saw what seemed like a slow wave of recognition wash across the witch's face, followed by flashes of fear and horror. Marla screamed a blood-curdling scream at Brinka and fell backwards, as Konjo had, hands high in reflexive defense. She cried out and tried to catch her breath and bearings at once; whatever had amused her when she snuck up on Konjo was now apparently very far away from her thoughts. What Brinka saw was terror in the witch's eyes.

Marla's scream had roused Konjo from his own surprize and lifted him to his feet. He hadn't seen Brinka withdraw her light, but he watched the witch fall away. He hadn't time to understand what was happening or why. He lunged towards the witch and grabbed her by her elbows from behind, expecting her to thrash and reel in protest, but she only sagged and surrendered. She was fixated on Brinka, and didn't even turn to see who had grabbed her. Later, Konjo would have time to reason that she probably assumed it was him, because Talthielle was very seriously unconscious. By Konjo's slightly resentful calculus, this meant that she had identified Talthielle's smaller form as the greater threat even while cloaked. By the time he would find himself the luxury of being able to ponder such things, Konjo had learned enough about Marla to not be surprized by anything.

The witch trembled in Konjo's hands and tried to possess herself. A wave of palpable calm washed over her hysterical face and, with assistance, she rose and straightened herself, absently brushing away the dust from the road, apparently not yet willing to raise her eyes. Konjo saw a flash of empathy in Brinka's expression as she nodded her head, and with a degree of hesitation, he released his fare. Konjo respectfully took a wide step away from Marla and stood alongside his beloved, somewhat bemused, but completely without any clue as to what to make of what was apparently unfolding before him. From Marla, he turned to Brinka with questions in his color, but Brinka was fixed on the witch, the shadowy and statuesque stranger who had only moments ago tossed aside her tree trunk of a mate like old linens from a drawer, the same one who had seemingly incapacitated a totally suspecting clocksmith, by surprize and without effort. Brinka had questions of her own. As she struggled to breathe form into a disordered list of impulsive queries, Marla was reading the scene, and opted to preempt an interrogation.

"You are Brinka and Konjo. You are on a mystic quest* to save the world from itself. I know that this is Talthielle, servant of the seasons. I humbly beg all of your pardons. I-- I mistook you for someone you could not possibly have been. I mistook your companions for captors. It is not safe for Kenjah east of the basin. I cannot answer your questions, but I will help you. You will find others on your path who know you are coming. There are those among them who will have no intention of helping you. Your road is long and your time is short." With this, Marla gazed back at at Talthielle, unconscious where he fell, and something of a sad chuckle escaped her core. "Time is a candle burning."

"How did you do it? Who are you?" Konjo hadn't exactly hit the ground softly, and wasn't sure how to feel about himself or his prospects with this strange creature, now seemingly timid and capitulatory, offering help and withholding explanations. Konjo pressed, but with nervous silence.

Marla appraised the stifled flickers of starlight in the obsidian Kenjah with an air of nostalgia and heartbreak that did not make Konjo feel any better about the moment. "Konjo. Your captor will not awaken until the sun's light touches the Dab. Until then, you are immensely vulnerable. You must both come with me. Pick him up and carry him Kenjah. My home is about a league from the road, through the shallow marshes. Mind your feet!" Marla turned to Brinka with what must have been a compelling expression of urgency, and in service, Brinka restrained a flood of her own inquiries. "Come!"

The four of them, Marla and Brinka at shoulder's breadth, with Konjo trailing under his burden, mushed through the slog under the sagging moonlight. Marla held Brinka's shoulder in an absurdly familiar way, as if Marla wasn't the only being on this trail that didn't need light or a crutch to navigate. Brinka's steps were twice as cautious, but she held Marla's elbow in a similarly sororal fashion as they traipsed. Konjo, bearing the full and dead weight of a limp and lifeless carcass, to which he was himself indentured, involuntarily, as it were, could well grasp the humor in the situation, but pushed the thought aside to concentrate on staying close enough to Brinka to see where he was putting his feet. Each step seemed to sink a little deeper into the muddy peat and soon they were all but wading through a dense bog.

Marla's thatched hut was simple, and entirely earthen, but both of the Kenjah marveled at what they could make out of the woven pylons of sinana and whitewood, the seams of which were sealed with dried brackish and wrapped at the cornices and joists with thick nomi leaves, which did not whither or permit moisture to permeate its membranes. The space was larger within than the structure, which could have passed for a tangled logjam from above or behind, appeared on approach. The perpetually wet floor stooped inwards from the landing, and all but Marla had to duck to enter, but after a few steps, all could stand abreast, if Konjo relinquished his load onto a divan beside an impossibly ornate fire place. When all were inside, Marla asked Brinka if she had any matches, explaining that such things were a commodity in the marshes, and difficult to come by. Brinka realised she was still holding Marla's elbow and withdrew her hand. She was sure Marla knew what was in her bag already, but that was just another question. She acknowledged Konjo's unspoken concurrence as the thought passed between them, and dutifully reached into her sack with performative uncertainty before *discovering* that she did indeed have matches.

Marla lit a modest fire in the damp hearth on her first try with a single match, which impressed even Konjo. As light filled the space, the Kenjah could see where the thatch above gave way to wider, deeper walls of stone, dug into and carved out of the ground around them to form an impressive hollow, lined with framed drawings and little carved tokens representing local and exotic flora and fauna and historical scenes. Shelves beyond the hearth contained bound volumes of ancient texts and jars packed with all manner of curio. But with all the scene revealed, the Kenjah found each other mutually captivated by their hostess. Marla was not old and haggard and scarred, as Konjo had seen her. In the soft glow of the firelight, the witch was exquisite. Her smooth skin and pale eyes and soft hair seemed to radiate youth and vitality. But Marla was somber.

"You are my honored guests. Beyond the curtain at the rear of my parlor you will find a barrel of clean water and a place for washing. You will find a jar of lyptus berries beside my bed. They will ease your mind and grant you rest. Above my bed, you will find a lever which will draw open a portal and let the sounds of the swamp into my chamber." Marla curled a bit of a smile. "I trust you will find them sufficiently deafening. But you must try to sleep for a few hours. Behind my vanity you will find a door that leads to a long tunnel with other doors on either side. You will take the sixth on the left, and you will emerge on dry land nearer the road than we are now. I will wake you in time to reach the Silver Bridges by dawn. Go now, my weary friends. I have much work to do if I am to outfit you before it is time to leave, and I must work alone and without distraction, so let us hope the song of the rills is high enough to cover the sounds Kenjah lovers make in darkness.

"Brinka, you have not spoken. I know that if you started now you wouldn't stop. Take your Konjo instead, whom any fool can see you desire more than answers. For you, I will forge an Enigma Blade. It will draw upon and focus your starlight without depleting it. It will contain a single deathblow. If you are to be struck down in combat, the sword in your hands will find the angle and parry, but only once. If you take a single life with it, it will disintegrate in your hands when your foe's final breath expires. Between these two extremes, you will find it serves you well. Just remember, if you should come to blows, aim to maim, and not to kill, especially if you are outnumbered.

"Konjo, bearer of the Boulder's Crown, consort of the Queen. You will take your beloved's blades. I will enchant them so that if she is lost in darkness, you may but cross them, one over the other, and they will lead you to your Brinka, no matter how near or far, they will reveal your path. When your captor awakens, he will find a single gradation stone in his cloak. You must demand it of him before you cross the bridge. Under no circumstances should you permit him to defer. When he gives you the stone, bury it in the hilt of one of your beloved's blades, whichever you unsheath with your right hand. Remember these instructions Kenjah, and keep them.

"As for your stupid clocksmith, I will tear a branch off of a tree outside and present him with a walking stick. I may put some decorative quarts in the crest and carve his name in it or something. Tell him it is magical, and that I send my regards." Marla spoke and the Kenjah listened. Here, she became very stern. "Listen to me Kenjah. You have set out upon this path and you must see it through. There are so many things I wish I could tell you, but there isn't time, and I cannot predict how my words will affect your choices, let alone your circumstances. Your journey will be hard. Trust this clocksmith of yours only so far. He is not who he seems to be, but you must follow him, as far to the end as you can. Tell him nothing of what I have said to you. Promise me Kenjah. Show me your colors and swear to me upon each other's lives that you will not breathe a word of what I have said to him."

Konjo and Brinka searched each other's eyes for doubt or reservations. Brinka nodded to Konjo, and they were the color of roses. "We agree to your discretion."

"Good. Brinka, you must reach Lavaris, at all costs. With your Konjo, or without. With your Talthielle, or without. If you fail to reach Lavaris, you will lose your Konjo forever. Konjo. What I say is even truer for you. Look at me Kenjah. Look in my eyes and hear my words. Your Brinka must reach Lavaris. Do you understand, Konjo? If she does not reach Lavaris, the whole world will descend into an incomprehensible darkness. You must trust her instincts, as you always have. A moment will come when you have reason to doubt her. Your colors will diverge, and you will want to beg her to hear reason. Konjo, hear my words. When that moment comes, you close that big dumb face of yours and *yield*. Do you hear me Konjo? You must YIELD. Trust your Brinka."

"Marla? When we met, you seemed, for an instant, terrified of me. Who did you think I was? Why were you so scared of me?" Brinka had waited and listened and restrained herself long enough. Marla was right. Brinka would trade a whole raft of answers for a wash and a moment of privacy with her beloved Konjo, who had already been lost to her once, only a single day ago. A comfy bed and a few hours sleep made the bargain irresistible. But her mind was drawn to Waterside, and Jorgan, and the fearful look of confusion on Talthielle's face. There was something hidden. And she was sure that Marla knew exactly what it was, just as she had known that Brinka packed matches she would never need. Perhaps Marla even knew *why* she packed those matches. But this was more important.

Marla, for her part, only turned to Brinka with a look of longing melancholy. After a few passing breaths, she said "Brinka. I did not mistake you for anyone once you withdrew your light. It was *you* I was scared of my dear Kenjah. I knew exactly who you were. When I saw you on the road, I mistook you for anyone else in the Omnia but yourself, because I could not have imagined it would be you. You were the last soul in the world I expected to find on my road this night, wandering with your living beloved and his scheming captor. No more questions. Go Kenjah. Be off with you."

The Kenjah very willfully resigned themselves against protest as Marla led them across her parlor and through the drapery, drawing the partition closed behind them. As soon as it was closed, Konjo and Brinka were alone for the first time in their new lives together. Not a breath passed between them, nor did any thought of anything else in the wide world intrude. They washed each other as they kissed, and their lips did not part until they fed each other lyptus berries. Brinka clumsily pulled the lever above Marla's bed, only managing to open it halfway as they collapsed into the woolen down, tangled in starlight. They melted together in darkness, bathed in starlight. The sound of the swamp was deafening.

***

The Kenjah were the color of chrysanthemum and tangled like sinana branches when they were awakened by Marla's call. But when they arose and pulled the curtains, they saw they were alone in the parlor. Marla's arms were laid out beside the divan where Talthielle lay motionless in the same position he was in when Konjo laid him down. They both shared a quiet wish that they had had some of whatever sleep magic she had put on their so-called captor, but in all fairness they felt rested enough. The lyptus berries had lent an additional measure of rapture to their embraces, and patiently lowered them into a gentle, heaving sleep when their exchange was consummated. Konjo picked up Brinka's blades and turned away from her, crossing one over the other, and nearly sliced his finger off when the leading edge slashed around on its fulcrum to point at Brinka. Konjo was convinced. Brinka picked up her Enigma Blade and marvelled at its exquisite craftsmanship. As she sheathed it across her bare leg and threw her cloak around her shoulders, she picked up her sack and found it heavy with cheeses, berries, and little glowing vials with labels like "farsight" and "stealth" and "cramps." She chuckled at the unabashed tenacity of the swamp witch and made a made a private vow to return to this place some day and hug the breath out of the curious old hermit.

Konjo picked up Talthielle's walking stick, finding no quartz and only the rune for the letter "T" carved, almost haphazardly, into an awkward spot near the crest. A single nomi leaf was wrapped and tied around the grip. "I really don't think she likes him as much as he likes her." Konjo and Brinka shared a smile as he hoisted his own sack of wiry meat and brittle bones over his shoulders and they set out through the little door behind Marla's mirror at the rear of her parlor. "I really hope show knows we like her as much as she likes us. I want to come back here someday, when this is all over, to thank her for her hospitality, and for her bed." With his free hand, he took Brinka's, and they held onto each other as they counted the oddly set doors. Brinka kissed his cheek with a twinkle, and squeezed his hand until it hurt. The Kenjah were the color of orchids.

The tunnel was just that. It was long, low, narrow, and winding. The walls were dark and the ceiling was just a mesh of roots and sod. The doors were made of whitewood, framed at uneven intervals in little stout circles with brass latches. They counted six doors on the left, and when they emerged, they were not surprized to find even, level, dry cobble beneath their feet. Konjo went through first, setting his load down behind him and then dragging it through the tiny hatch by the feet in an unceremonious manner. When he looked around and gave the all-clear, Brinka shuffled through with her sack. Both stood upright and stretched. Through a natural break in the clearing, they spied the hulking spire of the Dab, and followed it back to the riverside road, turning east once again as the crow called morning. Sunlight crept in overhead and dispelled the morning shadows. As the Silver Bridges came into view, true to Marla's word, Konjo's heavy corpse began to stir and groan. Konjo set him down, this time with gracious and deliberate care, and the Kenjah watched Talthielle struggle to regain consciousness and awaken.

"Konjo? Brinka? What has happ-- where am I? Oh, by Dab I feel as if I've been run over by plow beasts." Talthielle looked about in a daze, trying to piece together his own jumbled memories.

"We met your witch. She gave you this. She said it was magical, and she sends her regards." Brinka handed Talthielle his stick, and watched the *Epozia* study it with wonder and admiration. "We are near the Silver Bridges, and are ready to cross into the Verdant and try to find your Nanok. Morning has come. We persuaded her to give us a sword and some food. Otherwise, our night on the road has been long and uneventful. Looks like you got some rest. She didn't have anything particularly useful to say." Konjo and Brinka mustered similar shades of peony and violet, and stamped their feet impatiently.

"That's Marla, alright. I'm ashamed to say she must have caught me off guard. Wily little tart. If I had gotten my hands on her first, we might have gotten some answers. She can be very obstinate with strangers. We will just have to make due. I'm sorry that our second stop was not more productive. I suppose it was at least better than the first. Brinka, I don't know what happened to Jorgan, but I owe you an apology. I brought you both on this journey, and you are my responsibility."

"Don't worry about it Talthielle. She said she mistook you both for road men and me for your captive. That's why she attacked us on the road. Once she discovered who we were, she begged our forgiveness and gave us what she had on her. She pleaded with Konjo to not let you be angry with her. She gave you her own personal staff as a token of her sincere regret."

Talthielle watched Brinka with a visible sense of satisfaction and Konjo watched Brinka struggle to hold her colors until the moment passed and the three were up and moving again. As he fell into the rear guard, Konjo smiled to himself. If they made it aboard the *Marvu* and were fortunate enough to get their own cabin, he resolved to tease her mercilessly. He also recorded a private observation: others do not perceive the variants in a Kenjah's hue as carefully as do Kenjah themselves. For the first time ever, Konjo knew exactly what Brinka looked like when she was lying. He wanted to laugh out loud so badly, but mustered all his strength to constrain it to a few quiet quivers between his chest and shoulders. Their captor wanted desperately for them to see him as he saw himself. Such things are forgivable, thought Konjo. It was just refreshing to sense a little vulnerability in their impenetrable and all-seeing captor. Many such thoughts are better unspoken.

"One more thing." Konjo put his hand on Talthielle's shoulder before they came to the first bridge. "She said she put something in your cloak, and insisted that we were not to cross this bridge until you gave it to me. She was very adamant on this point. She said you would know what it was."

Talthielle reached into his cloak and felt around until his hand found the stone Marla had promised. When he pulled it out and realized what it was, he stared in disbelief. "Are you both very sure she didn't say anything else?" The Kenjah held their colors and their tongues. "This is a gradation stone! I wonder how she came by it. You said she insisted that i give this to you here?" Talthielle's question was rhetorical. He was too distracted by the workings of his own mind to require a reply or notice that one was not forthcoming. He looked upon his conscript and his beloved queen, and upon the stone, with mixed feelings of disbelief and hesitation. "Marla is both cunning and wise. Oh how I regret not getting the chance to speak to her. Between you and me, I think she rather fancies me. Oh well, Konjo, you have apparently been carrying me on your shoulders for many leagues in the dark. I supposed I have put you through enough for one day. Here you go old chum. Your day has been reset, and if anything happens, I am sure we will all be grateful to have put at least one very stressful and taxing day behind us. We shall return to the bridge, then. My dear sweet Marla. She never fails to surprize me. I only wish you could have gotten a chance to meet her under better circumstances, but good fortune has brought us forth, nonetheless."

Talthielle handed Konjo the stone, and then looked on quizzically as Konjo produced one of Brinka's blades and set the stone in its hilt, as he had been instructed, and then sheathed the blade as if there was nothing conspicuous about the procedure at all. The Kenjah were clearly hiding something, thought the clocksmith. They had probably dumped him in the shadows somewhere along the way and stolen a few well-deserved moments of intimacy. Such simple creatures, of course. Talthielle would begrudge them a few innocent diversions. If anyone in Omnia had earned a little confidence, it was these two. "Come Kenjah, we are about to cross the Injha and enter the Verdant. We must find Nanok as soon as possible, and then make haste for the piers of the Rising Coast if we are to reach the sea by nightfall. Nanok aside, this part of the journey should be relatively simple, compared to what you've been through so far. We must be cautious. The Viermah in these woods are not exactly lawless, but they are not exactly neutral either. Keep your eyes and ears open. Don't forget to look up from time to time. There are almost always eyes in the trees, looking down."

As Konjo and Brinka fell in behind their captor, they took hands again, and paused at the foot of the bridge to look backwards, out over the marshlands behind them, not, they hoped, for the last time. *Thank you Marla,* they whispered between themselves. Somewhere, off in the distance, another crow cawed. The witch's welcome. The Kenjah crossed the bridge, hand in hand. Neither had ever been across the river on this side of the Dab. Both were excited to visit the Verdant for the first time, but rather apprehensive about the dubious prospect of encountering the quarrelsome and tedious Viermah in their own dominion. *Come what may*, the Kenjah thought.

We already have everything we need. Come what may.

(Nanok)

Talthielle led the Kenjah across the Injha in peaceful silence as dawn crept over their shoulders and kissed the murmuring waters running beneath the Silver Bridges. Ancient lore proclaims that these bridges, byproducts of a bygone era, were built before the great floods came and turned all the old mines into farmland. The Injha, now wide and in foul weather sometimes roaring, had long ago been only a narrow stream as it crossed through these lands beneath the Dab on its meandering course to the sea. Legends tell of a time when the banks of the slender Injha glistened with diamonds and gold and silver and many precious stones. Omnia's many peoples and lores all have their own epic tales about how this or that heroic explorer from their respective castes had discovered this magical and beautiful wonderland and decided to plant the Verdant above it, in service of Omnia's first mining colony. Farms to the south, fish to the west, and laying in the shadow of the great Dab, this had once been an idyllic place for treasure hunters and merchants and travelers from far and wide. They scraped the banks of the Injha all the way to Waterside in the west, and to the fabled city of Call, the jewel at Injha's end, to the east.

The wealth, it had seemed, was inexhaustible. The first wave of settlers dug and drilled enormous shafts into the ground beneath the slender river, and extracted precious metals and stones by the cart load. They decorated their temples with huge diamonds, carving them into prisms which scattered light in the mornings and evenings and bathed their altars and their faithful in every shade imaginable. They smithed much of their gold into ornate jewelry and magnificently sculpted artifice, and traded the rest. The silver, being the most plentiful, they used for tools and weapons and cookware. They had so much left over that they began using it for construction. They dug out the banks of the Injha, widening the river more and more each season, until its mass and current would no longer permit foot or shallowboard ferry travel from one side to the other. The bridges, in those days, had been the most ambitious civil engineering projects ever conceived. Twenty could walk abreast from one end of of each of five of the six bridges to the other. The sixth, due to a gross miscalculation in the original plans, and aggravated by several seasons of torrential floods (predictable, as it were, only in retrospect) which widened the river even further, was half the width of the rest, but slightly longer as it bridged a portion of the river where the banks had not yet been retained with petrified sinana trunks, themselves carved into great interlocking beams and thrust deep into the mantle.

All of these bridges were still standing, and though rust and vines had reclaimed much of their aesthetic, they were all still very solid. But of these, only the sixth still received any traffic. Sometimes the farmers and merchants traveling to or from the northerly towns will drive their carts over one of the larger bridges, but the perennial complaint among pedestrians is that only the sixth allows an unimpeded view of the river flowing beneath on either side. Travellers are eternally enchanted by the glimmering auras refracting from the dense layers of residual dust of shaved gemstones and milled ore that virtually coats the riverbed. Not even centuries of silt deposit and other kinds of headwater runoff could completely obscure the nuanced majesty of a literal reflection of Omnia's long lost prosperity.

Over time, the mines ran dry and the spoils of a fading age were carried off by conquest from without and conflict from within. Each of Omnia's lores proclaimed ancestral rights to dominion over this area and its material wealth and complex internecine political machinations. It wasn't long until succeeding generations grew resentful and entitled and boisterous. When the floods came, the peoples dissipated and went their separate ways. The Kenjah returned to the mountains. The men took south for the farmland and west for the distance. The Viermah retired into the high boughs of the Verdant above the Injha, and the Kalama drifted east, toward Call and the Rising Coast. Beyond this grim diaspora, history records only in brushstrokes a dark and treacherous era of mutual contempt and callous villainy. Omnia's lores have existed perilously alongside one another ever since, in disintegration and distrust. Trade goes on, and the old feuds are less pervasive, but the broken peace has never healed. The city of Call, on the eastern sea, is the last gasping echo of any kind of cosmopolitan community, where the lores walk freely amon each other and interact as sovereign peers. Much of what is north of Dab is frozen tundra, but those glacial climes are not as frigid as the relations between the lores everywhere else in Omnia. The piers to which Talthielle and his conscripts travel are several leagues south of the city of Call.

Talthielle and his Kenjah indulged the obligatory pause upon the arch in the middle of the bridge to surveil the scenery. None spoke. Brinka held Konjo's waist and Konjo held Brinka's shoulders as they contemplated the spectacle. Talthielle closed his eyes and tried to see ahead, but his mind was clouded. He had hoped to receive news and perspectives from Marla. He was pestered by the inexplicable fate of Jorgan. He would encounter Nanok in the blind, with too many growing mysteries vying for his focus, which was strained. He placed both palms upon the nomi leaf of his staff and held its crown to his own, eyes closed, and tried in vain to still the frothing ripples in his consciousness. Talthielle was nervous. His honest Kenjah were concealing their thoughts, and likely more. His first day on this journey had been beset by bad luck and unaccountable misfortune, and he still had Nanok to locate, let alone deal with, and hoped to have done so before sundown. At length, he relinquished the fruitless effort at foresight and contented himself to lean against the rails with his conscripts and try to just appreciate the moment. A growing and uncertain sense of urgency prevailed upon his patience, and he resolved to draw his Kenjah away from their quiet sublimity and press on. Unwilling to break the river's spell, he merely found Konjo's eye, and nodded respectfully.

As they reached the far side of the bridge and approached the line of the Verdant, the road quickly spent the last of its cobble and became a matted and narrow trail through low weeds and lichen. The morning air was thick with birdsong and the sound of wind through the swaying canopies above. They had not ventured a league when Konjo and Brinka abruptly stopped in their tracks. Talthielle, with studious faith in the senses of Omnia's best pathfinders, watched their eyes sharpen and their hands move, unconsciously it seemed, to the hilts of their weapons. Talthielle felt the sudden tension between them and understood. The clocksmith and his companions were no longer alone. Konjo and Brinka perked their ears and looked around at various points ahead, behind, and besides, but could not mark a soul. Talthielle recognized the implication immediately. They were surrounded by unseen, stalking Viermah, and that was never a good place to be.

"You know, Talthielle, for a clocksmith I would have imagined you better at seeing these things coming." Konjo's tone was irreverent, and a touch impatient.

"Konjo, be still and be quiet. Kenjah, you would do well to keep your hands off of your weapons. It would seem that we are expected." Talthielle raised his hands like a wizard and stepped forward, still looking about to spot the hiding places from which the ambush would spring. Only when a moment's silence revealed nothing concealed behind the trees or bushes did Talthielle remember to cock his head back. He felt foolish, but before the words could form, a whistling arrow sailed down from the canopy and embedded half of its shaft in the dirt at Talthielle's feet. The Kenjah, comprehending, looked to the branches and found themselves covered from enough angles to count themselves properly and sufficiently so.

"In fairness, Konjo, he did remind us to look up." Brinka shifted herself to Konjo's six, shoulders back and eyes sharp. "How many, Konjo? This looks like plenty. What do you say Talthielle, think we ought to go ahead and burn that stone now?"

"I said to be Still and Quiet, Kenjah."

"We should have gotten sheilds. Brinka, did Marla have sh-"

"Quiet! Don't mention the witch here, or Jorgan or the Titan or Flask or any of it. Both of you, be silent!" Talthielle took a cautious and respectful step backward from the arrow, which had nearly grazed the hem of his cloak, and he kept both of his own hands high as he called out, "We mean you no harm. We are travellers, beating east to the Rising Coast. We crossed the Silver Bridge because we are looking for someone with whom we have business. "Please do not fear us!" Another arrow hit the ground, this one more generally in front of the three, rather than Talthielle specifically, and graciously, a few feet further away.

"Yeah, I don't think that's quite it exactly, Talthielle..." Konjo and Brinka were the color of honey and beginning to shine. The Kenjah were having none of this. A stern voice, if slightly screeching, called down from the boughs above. Someone, at least, was in charge here. What was said was imperceptible against a sudden rustling in the limbs all around, and promptly, a flock of armed Viermah drifted down from their perches and landed softly in a half circle around the trio, bows drawn and talons bared. The last among them, and the largest, touched down in their midst, carrying a figure bound and hooded and in restraints. It was another Viermah, with its wings clipped. It was skinny, and raw from what appeared to be a fresh beating, most likely at the hands of the Viermah captain towing it down.

"You are Talthielle, the servant of the seasons, and these are your Kenjah conscripts. We have been expecting you, as you surely observe. You have come to find Nanok and your gradation stones. Well, here he is." The captain shoved his captive down with contempt, and bent down, yanking off the prisoner's hood in a rough manner. The captain took a small pouch from his belt and threw it on the ground at Talthielle's feet. Some glinty stones spilled out of it, and

Talthielle was nearly speechless. The Kenjah looked on, for once, perfectly still and quiet. They had had just enough time to count at least twenty arrows, all leveled in a generally even distribution between the three faces of the intruding travelers. Talthielle looked from Nanok to the captain and back again at Nanok, trying to comprehend too many unexpected variables at once.

"Why is he in restraints? What has he done? How did you know we were-"

"He has done nothing Talthielle. He is in restraints because he could be compelled to go with you no other way. We know that you are on your way to the Kalama to fetch your water whore and bring her back here, to help you choose which of us is worthy of your little quest. Well, we have all taken a vote and chosen. Forgive us for saving you the trouble, clocksmith. We have chosen your dear friend Nanok, here. If anyone here *believes* he is the best and brightest among us, it has always been Nanok. You need a Viermah? Well, here he is. And you will get no better offer on this day or any other, not from us. And if you don't accept him, well." The circling Viermah tightened their bowstrings. "You're not leaving here otherwise. Not until you've come around. So what say you, Talthielle?"

"Well, captain, gracious am I for your patience. I'm not foolish enough to, um" Talthielle coughed a little, stalling, "not foolish enough to contend with the wisdom and thoughtful considerations of... so many... strong and brave... I, um, I suppose I should just be honest and share the first couple of thoughts that come to mind, mind you, not they're your uh, problems, of course, I just... Well. Captain, as you may or may not know, this um, this Viermah, in particular, has only sworn an oath on the blood of his family and clan to um, well, to kill me on sight. I suppose, of course, as I say,

that's for us to worry about. But, well, I say, we can't--"
Talthielle was groping for the obvious. "I mean, we can't
exactly just escort a clipped, half-beaten, half-clothed
Viermah to the sea in shackles. It would seem, um, improper.
Do you see what I mean?" Talthielle wasted no time as he
spoke, kneeling to gather up his stones, and exchanging a
rather complicated look between himself and Nanok, who
seemed almost relieved at the dubious prospect, considering
the alternative, but the enmity in his eyes remained unmoved
by these unpredicated circumstances.

Mischief sparkled in the Viermah captain's eyes, "Ahh
yes, I see the problem exactly. No, you're right Talthielle, how
thoughtless of me." With a theatrical flourish he bent and cut
Nanok's ropes with the razor edge of one of his talons, and in
the same breath, Talthielle, comprehending with the speed of
instinct, pulled the gardener's blade from his hip and held the
point to Nanok's throat the instant his hands were free.
Nanok flashed hate and anger at Talthielle, but made no
abrupt movement. The Captain, for his part, flashed a
satisfied amusement. *Yes, this will do just fine.* The thought
was as plain as the feathers on his face. This will do just fine.
"Well then, it seems you have everything you need from us
Talthielle, and everything under control, as always. We will
see you depart the Verdant then, the way you came? And we
shall presume that if we see you in our forest again, it will be
because you have reconsidered our hospitality?" The warning
in the captain's voice was clear. Talthielle did not misconstrue
the message.

The Kenjah, watching and listening and waiting,
understood that the important part of the conversation had
transpired, and the thing to do now was to relieve their hosts
of their presence with some sense of haste and propriety.
Konjo, however, found the moment, and indeed, the clear

lesson, irresistible. "Excuse me, sir?" Konjo pretended not to notice the look Talthielle shot him. "Yes, I am terribly sorry to interrupt. But we seem to have neglected some criticals when packing for our journey." Talthielle kept the blade sharp at Nanok's throat, but winced as he heard the question coming. None of the Viermah had lowered their bows. "Could we trouble you for a couple of good shields? In retrospect, we probably should have-"

The captain surprized all present with a bellowing belly laugh. "Kenjah, carrying Viermah aegises? Whoever heard of such a thing? Why sure Kenjah, and in fact, I do see your point quite clearly." The Viermah surveyed his soldiers and the precarious position of their prey with a sense of irony. "Your clocksmith has brought you ill-prepared!" He unlatched his own buckler from his waist and presented it to Konjo, as one professional to another. He took another, smaller buckler from one of his archers, a lady, and her expression when he did so made it clear she was his wife. She did not protest in the moment, but he would hear of it soon; her expression was unmistakable. The captain turned to face Brinka, and a gentle seriousness possessed him, noticed by all. "This is for you, fair Kenjah maiden. May it serve you well. When your quest is over, we will happily welcome you and yours here in our lands, and we will celebrate your success, or we will drink to your misfortune. Please leave your time teller behind, of course. I am sure in due course you will understand why he is not welcome here. In the meanwhile, we wish you luck. Bring our Nanok home to us in one piece. Go now Kenjah. Go and save the world from itself." The captain held Brinka by the shoulders until he finished speaking, and then laid the buckler at her feet. When he stood, he shot a brief and dismissive glance at Talthielle, and in a fluttering flash, the Viermah posse took flight and were gone without a trace.

"Ugh." Nanok was not pleased. Talthielle was downright bewildered, but not quite ready to lower his gardener's blade. "Well, Talthielle, are you going to let me up or are you going to *prune* me right here in the Verdant. What in Dab is that thing anyway? Did you steal it from a child?" Nanok looked up at the Kenjah, who were now the color of the river and clearly ready to leave.

"Hello Nanok, I am Brinka, and this is my Konjo. At your service, of course. We see you have met our clocksmith already. He seems to make an impression on people, we are learning. We are curious though, how did you know we were coming?" Brinka was inspecting her buckler and fastening it to her belt as Konjo was lifting his rice sack over his shoulder. Talthielle was silent, and as curious to know the answer. Nanok looked again upon the meager blade and up at the mute clocksmith wielding such an unlikely weapon, and rose to his feet uninvited, brushing off the dust and pretending to ignore his captor.

"How did we know you were coming? Are you kidding? We could hear you two in the marshes." Konjo and Brinka shared a chastened expression of mild embarrassment. *Fair enough, Viermah.* "You two are not exactly inconspicuous creatures. But you're right to ask. That's not how we knew. Our eyes and ears are keen, Kenjah. Very keen. Nanok turned to face Talthielle squarely. The Viermah was tall, even for his kind, but stood nearly level with the clocksmith. "You've got some stones, *Epozia*. And I don't mean the ones in that pouch."

"Brinka. Please tell me again, what did Marla say to you before she sent you on your way last night? Something very strange is going on and I sure would like to be in on the joke." Talthielle reluctantly lowered his blade, but was in no hurry to set it in its sheath. Nanok cut him off.

"Keep your secrets Kenjah. You can be sure your captor here guards many of his own, and jealously. Tell me, Talthielle, have you told them? The *whole* truth?" There was restraint in Nanok's voice, but not fear. Talthielle's blade returned to the Viermah's throat, daring him to speak again. Nanok had his answer, and shook his head. "You never change, clocksmith." Talthielle sighed and stowed his blade. "Well then. Konjo, Brinka? I am Nanok. Talthielle and I go way back. Shall we?" Nanok set off towards the line of the Verdant, and the Kenjah fell in behind him, feeling like the road had been a much more hospitable environment, all things considered. Talthielle stood, absently, watching his conscripts fall in behind a mortal enemy in such a casual way. He looked down at the little pouch full of gradation stones in his hand, with a numb feeling of astonishment. He had shared his plan with no one but the Kenjah. But Talthielle felt like the only soul left in Omnia who didn't know what was going to happen next. He took up his staff, and thought of Marla.

"Brinka. What did Marla say to you?"

Brinka called out over Konjo's shoulder. "She said she sends her best, Talthielle."

Nanok laughed at this out loud. Talthielle studied the staff the witch had sent along, quizzically. He had his doubts. Nevertheless, he took a deep breath, and set his feet on the path back toward the road. Konjo kissed his Brinka's face and called out over her shoulder. "Don't worry, old Talthielle, old pal. Konjo and Brinka still like you just fine."

Four souls emerged from the Verdant where three had entered. Talthielle had his stones, and required only one more soul for his quorum at the crest of Dab, to invoke the

ghost father Lavaris and persuade him to open his gates to the
world, once again, that all souls might live and walk together
as they had when old souls were few and Talthielle's seasons
were fewer. Nanok and his Kenjah conscripts took the road
when the Silver Bridges were behind them. This time, it was
they who ignored their moment at the summit of the sixth
bridge, but as Talthielle lagged behind, puzzling over the
events of the last day, and watching those impetuous youths
storming off to save the world from itself, it was he who
found himself momentarily ensorcelled by the ages of lost
and neglected history glimmering up from the sediment in
the Injha. He could tell that in spite of all the grim odds, in
spite of the sheer absurdity of the whole affair, Nanok and the
Kenjah were fast friends. So it goes with the young.

They talked and chattered like children on the road
east, readily touching ground on their mutual, if suspended,
distrust of Talthielle. The Kenjah were not bitter or biting;
against the impossible satisfaction of their impossible
reunion, the Kenjah's loyalty to their clocksmith would never
budge. They meant what they said. If he had been a crazed
and cynical villain with bloodstains on his face and viscera in
his fingernails, he could have still persuaded them. If he told
Konjo to pick up a spade and move the whole colossal
mountain of Dab one foot to the left, he would have done it
for Brinka. And Brinka would have torn out a battalion of
throats if they stood between herself and her beloved. The
prospect of ducking a bad scene and taking a sea cruise with a
hardheaded old stranger wasn't a tough sell, in the scheme of
things. *Ursal* would adore them. And Nanok would make her
laugh, and probably blush. The Kenjah were the only reliably
controlled variable in the clocksmith's plans. Nanok was a full
flush of wildcards.

Nanok's words were barbed and serrated. His tone was irreverent; but he really did take to the Kenjah. But while the Kenjah humored him in good nature, if at Talthielle's expense, it was a demonstration of their own mock rebellion. They could count their freedom of speech as evidence of the truth of their conscientiously voluntary enlistment as Talthielle's conscripts. Konjo and Brinka were starlight. Konjo had literally thrown Talthielle over a bar by the throat. Talthielle wielded no real control over them beyond the compulsions of their own gratitude. His prerogative was to lead. The Kenjah only permitted themselves to be led, and it only ever worked with two of them, if one had been lost. Talthielle might never tell them about Flask. But he wondered there, at the top of that Silver Bridge, gazing into the ripples, if he never told them the truth, would that only prove Nanok was right? He let them drift ahead as he straggled, already forming predestined and inevitable friendships that would transcend what their progeny would someday recall as history.

He appreciated the moment.

Talthielle wrapped his hand around the nomi leaf on his staff and thought of Marla as he crossed to the road and fell in a comfortable distance behind the Viermah and the Kenjah he was supposedly leading, just far enough behind them for the wind and river to drown out some of their more pointed exchanges. He wanted Nanok to know the truth, and would tell him, if not only to ease the young Viermah's pain, but perhaps to regain his trust. But he would let the Kenjah believe a calloused lie unto the very end, because he needed them, and would compel them no other way. But on a clear day on a calm internal sea, Talthielle could listen to Nanok and Brinka telling their grandchildren campfire stories about the great and powerful clocksmith that had brought them all together to save Omnia from a terrible fate. This was the version of Talthielle's life he had chosen, and it was every Epozia's right to choose their own idyllic end. The best possible outcome.

Talthielle knew that Marla's staff did nothing. The nomi leaf was soft on his hands for climbing and long hikes. As haphazardly affixed as it seemed, it was tied at the perfect height, and the staff weighted to Talthielle's lean gate as faithfully as a prosthesis. It would shift some of the stress away from his knees and spine. The rune she had inscribed, the first letter of his name, was the Epozia glyph for *Ratesc,* change over time. She didn't put quartz in it, though she might have, but in this case, Talthielle's companions were walking torchlight. He would not be hindered by darkness so long as a he kept them both close and safe. Marla's staff did nothing, and yet its magic was undeniable.

When the Viermah captain had embarrassed them in the Verdant, Talthielle privately observed, he said he could hear them from the marshes. That could only have meant that Marla had taken them home and given them her bed. And if that were true, then Brinka was undoubtedly with child. Marla had rescued them from the road, plied them with her night fruit, and sent them down for a few hours so she could meditate over her lost and found (and occasionally pilfered) armory of edged artifice in need of a new home and a sometimes clumsy orange tint, or a signature of her flavor of magic (this dichotomy is hotly debated between them, Marla and Talthielle). Marla, a capable witch, obtained pleasant company, some conversation and news of the world, and some space on a few of her her shelves, just by giving Talthielle an involuntary nap he needed anyway and wouldn't take otherwise. For the price of just a few extra berries which her gardens will never fail to yield by the bushel, she created

life and changed the course of a civilization. The House of
Konjo and Brinka. What Marla could accomplish by doing
nearly nothing, Talthielle marvelled.

Would that his own ends were so readily accessible.

Marla lived in isolation. Not really, of course, but in
the general sense, Marla lived a solitary life, a league from the
road in a proverbial hovel in a dense and dreary bog
(excepting dawn and dusk and midnight, full or moonless,
when its majesty was undeniable). Hers was a life of self
sufficiency in the context of profound vulnerability. Marla's
ideal outcome in most interactions she was likely to
encounter was that in which she never *had* to do anything.
That she could exist free of external compulsion, and derive
the most profitable, or least offensive yield from a
proportional investment of her own consensual time or
energy. The magic of not needing magic was all the more
magical. Marla was not often well regarded or taken seriously
by her contemporaries on account of her eccentric lifestyle
and theatrical disposition, but Talthielle shuddered to think
what would probably happen to anyone who ever *forced*
Marla to demonstrate the full range of her power.

The House of Konjo, Talthielle thought. The Queen
of Epochs. The Champion of the Verdant. Children of Dab,
one and all. Talthielle was going to have do better than this to
persuade the Kalamaii, he supposed. *Ursal* was notoriously
vain, demagogic by default, and pathologically preoccupied
with herself. And at some point, Talthielle reflected, she
would have to surrender her eyes. Unlike these children of
Dab before him, she would already know that. She would
probably know it the instant she witnessed Talthielle standing
on the bow of a hijacked ship with two and a half nervous
Kenjah and clipped and surly Viermah, waving a petrified
staff with a waterproof handle and a white strip of race sack at

the top of it, begging her not to make him waste his stones in the stormy drink. And she would know that Brinka was with child, or Talthielle simply would not dare put himself in a flimsy floating prison above her home. If Marla's magic was passive, the magic of the seabourn Kalamaii was most decidedly not. And truthfully, most of Omnia's problems couldn't swim.

She doesn't particularly need anything from Talthielle, and is unlikely to be moved by an appeal to the concerns of most of Omnia's self-inflicted conditions. So Talthielle was bringing her Nanok. Epozia play the cards, but they never gamble. The game, presently afoot, was to prevent the dryly contemptuous Viermah from running away or cutting Talthielle's throat, and to keep both of the Kenjah on the road long enough to reach the piers intact.

Konjo broke the silence, roughly an hour after the silence suppressed the idle chatter of younglings on a lonely road. "Well, Talthielle. You predicted we would spend half the day chasing down your stones and persuading our new friend to relinquish them-"

"I would never have done so." Nanok was terse, but demonstrating his own restraint.

"Of course, of course. My point, clocksmith, is that if our formerly feathered friend here can keep up at pace, we should make the Rising Coasts well before the golden hour, maybe even in time to visit Call." Konjo turned his voice up at the end to signify his observation was a question.

"Out of the question." Talthielle spoke with paternal firmness. Nanok was open for any opportunity to duel, and spun on his talons.

"I would very much like to visit Call, Talthielle." Nanok always looked Talthielle squarely in the eyes when they spoke, with a burning intensity that suggested there was much more being said which words could not effectively convey, and some shared sense of propriety persuaded them to conceal. Brinka also wanted to visit Call, though she understood Konjo's apprehension intuitively. From his point of view, and in a way, from hers as well, they were oh-and-two for well populated areas. Waterside had been a shock, but Flask had been an unmitigated disaster. The Kenjah were naturally suspicious on their best day of the supposedly cosmopolitan dispositions of the seafaring crowd, and there would likely be very few fellow mountain monsters among them. He would not willingly deny his Brinka a tour through the shops and spectacles of the salt life, but he would not be able to hear a word over the racing drum of his own nervous and pounding heart. Brinka turned to Talthielle, but held her tongue.

Talthielle tabulated the petty mutiny forming before him, but held his ground.

"Talthielle, I am absolutely not getting onboard that ship without a proper cloak and a bow."

Talthielle said nothing for a breath, and then pulled the pin in the clasp on his broach and unsheathed his blade as he flung his cloak to Nanok. "Brinka, please fetch Nanok a lyptus branch, about your height, and no bigger around than the hole between your thumb and little finger. Konjo, if Marla didn't send you all along with a length of her twine then I am the king of caught fish. Will you please look in your luggage there and see?" Talthielle would not raise his blade to Nanok if Nanok did not press the issue. Brinka shrugged and obeyed, scurrying off to the line of trees in the fading marsh opposite the Injha, below the road. Konjo unflung his rice sack and rummaged for twine, chuckling a warm memory of the witch when he found it. Nanok was frozen solid, staring sternly at Talthielle's chest.

"A hairshirt, clocksmith? Really? For whom do the *Epozia* suffer but themselves alone? Or did you scheme that thing from some already luckless whelp who happened to be in your-"

"Enough, Nanok!" Talthielle did not want to do this here. Konjo was right; they were making excellent time, and the road had already given them enough surprises. Talthielle would avoid spoiling their advantageous momentum if he could help it. He had quite forgotten about the hairshirt, having entered the marshes cloaked. Too many things on his mind. Too many things. Nanok would not be dissuaded. Talthielle would have had better luck begging Nanok to ask, rather than forbidding him.

"Where did you get that, Talthielle. No. You tell me. If you, of all the souls in Omnia, tell me that you have a guilty conscience, then I've got a mountain of pine coins taller than the Dab, and I'm the king of fish catchers. Let's hear it, clocksmith. I'm just dying to know who made you feel guilty so I can find them and buy them a week's worth of *roua*." Nanok would not budge. So it goes. Talthielle knew the moment the Viermah captain pulled the hood from his captive's brow that he would have to deal with this. He took in all his breath, tightened his grip on the gardener's hilt, and turned his eyes to Konjo rather than to the ground.

"Your mother made it for me."

Anger and hatred flashed red in Nanok's eyes. "You LIE! Don't you dare speak of her, I'll kill you, you traitorous wretch!" Nanok lunged forward, only to find his throat once again at the tip of Talthielle's meager blade, where he stopped short and permitted reason to return. Konjo put a gentle hand on the Viermah's shoulder. Nanok found his composure, and smiled his violent oaths inaudibly into Talthielle's eyes. "Liar." And nothing else.

"Your mother made it for me when you were born, Nanok. When I gave her the last of my stones and swore my retirement. And begged her forgiveness." Talthielle finished in a whispering sigh, lowering his blade and walking past Nanok, turning his back around a cold shoulder. Konjo liked Nanok, and understood something yet unshaped about the tension between the Viermah and the clocksmith. He could tell by the puzzled and chastened expression Talthielle left Nanok standing beneath, Talthielle had just torn down some kind of wall between them. Konjo sighed, and turned, and fell wordlessly in behind Talthielle. Brinka returned to the road with a knotty lyptus branch and huffed, realising she had missed something important. Her eyes found Konjo and Talthielle moving onward, and a pitiful looking Viermah standing still, holding a fine cloak in one hand and a white-knuckled fist in the other.

"Come on, Nanok. Let's go." Brinka's voice was friendly and neutral. It was the voice of a friend, and distinct in this way from any voice Nanok had heard in seasons. When he looked up at her, at last, there was sadness in him, and she would not judge him for that. Nanok would not follow that scheming clocksmith, but he had nothing but disgrace to return to in the Verdant if he did not pay his own debts. He couldn't fly in this condition, clipped and beaten, and he would not survive long in Omnia alone, no matter which other direction he chose. He would follow Konjo and Brinka, even knowing in advance the traps and misfortunes into which they were surely being led. Brinka put a calm hand on his shoulder.

"You know he's lying to both of you. He's lying to me. You get that, right Brinka?"

Brinka knew he was right, and had no context or clue to point to, but when she looked up the road to Konjo, who seemed to feel her eyes and turn and float a simple smile as she did, Brinka knew it didn't matter. "It doesn't really matter, Nanok. Everyone in Omnia has their secrets. Everyone but the Kenjah. We only have each other." Brinka was the color of morning glories. "Talthielle has his secrets, we know full well. And so did Marla, and so do you. But you've also got something else now Nanok."

Nanok wanted so badly not to let his anger fall away. He begged himself to keep the jagged edge on his lips as he spoke, even though he and Brinka both knew she was not who he wished his words would cut. "Oh yeah, Brinka?" Nanok managed the last bit of passive aggressive venom he could muster. "Tell me, what have I got? You've got your Konjo. Talthielle's got his secrets. I've been kicked out of my home, clipped and smeared by my kith and kin, and conscripted into a fool's service. Tell me, Brinka. What in Dab have I got?" Nanok flushed. It all sounded even worse when he said it out loud than when he said it in his mind, as he had been doing for the last several leagues before Konjo spoke up about going to visit Call.

Brinka took his venom and pacified it. She smiled a gentle smile and spoke softly as she turned down the trail towards her captor and her beloved.

"You've got us, Nanok."

Nanok stood there, thoughts racing and skin crawling and shoulders tight like bricks. He hated Talthielle, and he hated that arrogant captain, and he would probably hate the Kalama too. But he knew he already loved Konjo and Brinka. He turned, at last, and set his feet to sullenly drag behind in silence until the sun set. "Liar." He whispered it to himself, and to no one in particular. "Damn you, Talthielle." And down the road he went.

(The *Marvu*)

Out of the question. That's the phrase that was bouncing around in Talthielle's brain as the giddy Kenjah and the defiant Viermah were entering the gates of the great city of Call. The closer they got to the coasts, the more vocal Brinka had become about what a shame it was that they had all this time and would come all this way just to miss *just a little peek,* in her best singsong voice she would say it, at the shops and wares in the legendary port town. When Konjo sensed the game afoot and began egging her on, pretending to argue on Talthielle's behalf but proffering only the easiest contentions to rebut, a little twinkling of a mischievous smile in his eyes, Talthielle had repeated himself even more firmly. In the end, it was Nanok, who also sensed a contest of wills and eagerly interjected on Brinka's behalf, who finally wore Talthielle down and extracted his exasperated concession. Nanok needed a leather helm and arrows, or at least a reasonable supply of points. Sticks he could find, and feathers...well. Brinka had readily accepted her willing ally, and pivoted to press her own advocacy for the case of their poor, defenseless indentured friend. At long last, Talthielle finally caved. They would permit his escape from this cyclical nuisance no other way. And Konjo was right, they had a little time to spare.

Talthielle agreed, only on the condition that they visit the piers first to verify their vessel was indeed moored there. The *Marvu* only sailed at night, when the last of its weary passengers straggled in from their various points unknown. The ship always waited, however long it had to remain in port to do so, until the new moon rose over the Rising Coasts, to get underway. This was less a mystical ritual than a practical one. There was much in Omnia that operated in conjunction with the lunar phases, there being no other rational calendar which any of the lores could agree upon. The Kenjah calendar had four seasons. The Viermah calendar had eight. The men of the plains scheduled their annual cycle around the harvest, which shifted wildly between cycles due to the nature of Omnia's orientation with respect to its own celestial bodies. The *Epozia* regarded calendars the way scribes regard pencil shavings. And the Kalamaii had no real use for calendars at all. Their seasons were described by the warm sea currents they followed around the width and breadth of Omnia. This was the equivalent of at least a lifetime for a clocksmith, and several lifetimes for a Kenjah or Viermah. So the *Marvu* and many other ships scheduled their port visits and departures around the phases of the moon, because the moon was visible and common to all.

Of course, there were plenty of good mystical reasons as well. Foremost among them being that the Kalamaii were widely believed to only hunt near the shores of Omnia when the light of the moon illuminates the shallows. This is mystical, or at least mythical, because no ship has been attacked at sea by the Kalamaii in ages, but superstitions persist even when their origins become obscured by the telescoping sights of passing time.

Ages past, the Kalama had sailed out into the deep and built a massive floating temple to the Kalamaii and prostrated themselves in negotiation for the safe passage of Omnia's sailing class. They received annual provisions from the landed lores as tribute in return for a lasting peace, and they also took in their share of gossip and news of the regions. Sometimes they took in prisoners whose sins were too egregious to remunerate, and these often found themselves made tribute to hungry Kalamaii as well. These were the "caught fish" Talthielle had referred to himself as king of earlier in the day. It had been a grim joke, considering where he was going with his own prisoners in tow. There was no relevant corollary colloquialism referenced in Nanok's response. Nanok just wanted the last word.

The sun's light was meandering its way up the Dab, pursued by the creeping shadows of an oncoming moonless night, when the party's path from the piers led them up to the city of Call and through its wrought silver gates. Talthielle had wanted nothing more than to climb aboard that ship, negotiate his party's cabins, and bury himself in ship's wool for a whole night of quiet rest and contemplation. But Nanok and the prospect of visiting Call had taken the Kenjahs' minds off of Jorgan's gruesome fate, and Talthielle could justify a kindly gesture in the spirit of magnanimity. Konjo and Brinka, and Nanok as well, had all been through some pretty serious ordeals in recent days. A little carnivale, a few souveniers, and some exotic food might lift their spirits and improve Talthielle's odds of negotiating the coming days at sea, with what would inevitably become a quietly resentful sea captain and an openly hostile crew, with a surly and dangerous Viermah bastard and two amorous and distracted Kenjah, and with the prattling band of seaborn monks and zealots and their very troublesome and belligerent ocean goddess lying in wait beyond.

Hovering over the tall silver archway through which inlanders enter the city of Call was a great salt-bitten portcullis, ornamented with two golden orbs, bolted within its thick metal grating, representing the sun and moon. The structure was rounded, and would roll upward from the ground along its tracks to permit entry by day, wherein the sun would rotate over the moon and stand above it. Soon after the twilight hour, the thing would spin down along its axis and the moon would surmount the sun, signifying evening closure. Each diurnal event would be preceded by concurrent horn blasts from the watches in the flanking battlements. One was not trapped in the city, by any means, when the evening horns blew. In the old days, one would be forced to cross to the east end of Call and either wade or swim, depending on the tide, around the jetties and beachbound tourists to reach the exterior. An old stone wall in the shape of a crescent moon had once stood over the city, but nowadays all that was left of its once loftily stacked merlons and spacious crenels were occasional heaps of broken rubble over which most children and some adults could climb with little effort. In some places, only the hard-stamped imprints in the suppressed weeds and grass recalled the blocks which had long ago been carried away or repurposed.

Talthielle debated handing out gradation stones, but preferred to wait until all present were safely aboard the *Marvu* and the arduous day was concluded. Call was not a hostile place, but the mystical old Gunship* surely would be. They just had to stay together and not antagonize the locals. The Kenjah and the Viermah brat were cloaked and would draw few eyes amidst the frenetic spectacle that accompanies seaside life in a merchant port. Tramps like Talthielle would abound.

Even Nanok seemed to brighten a little as the first scenes unfolded. Konjo and Brinka walked abreast between the gates behind him and Brinka gasped and grabbed Konjo's waist with both hands. The scent of smoked coney and fried cod drifted along on the sounds of lutes and lyres and bells. Lit candles in brass censers hung from strings between two and three story shops along the main road, which straddled the mouth of the Injha and led from the western gates to the sea in a nearly straight line. Besetting this main drag on either side were tenements and storehouses and administrative offices, a seedily reputable red light district frequented by sailors and drunks, a very immodest library of sorts, an arena where games and shows and rallies were held, and an perennially empty jail. At the northern and southern fringes there were little plots of farm land on either side of the broken walls. Going south from the jetties along the shoreline there was a well traveled road above a seawall, with dozens of long hewnwood piers jutting out for quarter leagues into the tide to where the shelf vanished and the shallows gave way to the deep.

The boardwalk was presently alive with the patronage of a harvester's bazaar, and a busy cross-section of Omnia's lores were tending to tables and baskets of goods underneath banners advertizing wares and prices. There were jewels and trinkets and journals and portraits, and row upon row of scented oil candles. One could find common sundries and ointments for all manner of ailments. For a pine coin, in a handful of booths one could get a pint of *roua* and listen to wild adventure stories from an elder scribe or some old wayfaring mage. Some were true, some were fanciful, and often the best tales belonged somewhere in between. There were clearing houses and lenders and brokers of all stripes, some with tables, and others running endless loops between, negotiating futures and sorting inbound cargo for the various territories.

But the pulse of the town was surely the dancers, whirling like dervishes in and out of the throng, to the delight of all. These wore flowing gowns of every color of the rainbow, with frills and boas and painted faces. They would hypnotise the uninitiated and draw them hither and thither, laughing and clapping and oblivious, and then vanish suddenly into the thicker crowds where they could not be as easily pursued, leaving their entranced subjects forlorn, and often quite literally lost somewhere in the middle where it could be unclear to strangers which way was which. Sure enough, these were the first to greet Nanok and the Kenjah, spinning inward from some unseen periphery, drawn by the new blood smell of newcomers. Konjo was holding Brinka tightly by the waist and Brinka was beaming and giggling and jumping up and down on the balls of her feet. Nanok was grinning from ear to ear, in spite of himself, as the writhing performers weaved in and around them and each other in measured choreography. The music in the streets rose just above the din, and both were intensely penetrating. Dusk approaching, the city became a living spectacle.

Even Talthielle felt a twinge of regret that he had considered skipping Call, let lone stubbornly pretended to prefer skipping it and depriving his young wards of such a delightful experience. But time could be most elusive, he knew, in a place like this. He studied the position and pace of the sun carefully as they set foot onto the main drag, and gave his instructions as precisely as he could.

"We have an hour here, and we will make the most of it. But we must not part from each other under any circumstances or get lost or otherwise detained. If something happens, we all agree to make haste straight for the *Marvu*. I will not reset the day until we have reached our berthings safely, so if calamity strikes us here, we'll all walk another day's worth of leagues before we can rest again, and we will be short a round for the rest of our journey, which I tell you, has still yet to even begin in earnest. We will get food and eat as we walk. We will take in the sights and sounds on our way through a few tables and shops, and then we will leave. Are we all agreed?" Talthielle had barely taken a breath when he realized that Nanok and the Kenjah were already scampering off in a nearly aimless fashion without him. He sighed deeply and hung his head, trying vainly to scan the ripples in a sea of chaos. And then he set his feet to follow, once again, the souls he had resolved to lead. "Hey, don't wait for me or anything!" He was starting to understand why Lavaris might require a quorum of the most stubborn and impetuous creatures in Omnia. Herding these hardheaded heathens was the kind of challenge that required nothing less than the tedious commitment of very serious people.

"Hey! I said wait for me!"

Talthille lumbered along behind his eager conscripts and his birthright nemesis into a flood of chaos and frivolity, trying to keep three and a half impetuous tourists in one eye and the rapidly setting sun in the other. Nanok led them to the first food vendor he could find, ordering a round of kabobs (mostly everything in Call was served on skewers, and it was no secret that most of these were retrieved and washed and reused from the previous night's refuse, and so on). Talthielle laughed in spite of his own impatience with the whole debacle, when the three of them spun on their heels and stared at him when the vendor called the price, and he obediently produced a few pine coins from the pouch on his hip. The kabobs were a rainbow of baked salmon, turnips and squash cubes boiled in lard, and fried coney, with bell berries and bree. The price was reasonable* and the food was infallibly delectable. Brinka and Nanok darted away as if being chased, but Konjo leaned in and whispered gratitude on behalf of all, winking at a slightly nostalgic clocksmith as he fell in behind his comrades. Talthielle tore a crispy chunk of cheese from his kabob and whispered "you're welcome," to no one in particular.

Brinka stopped short in the middle of the boardwalk and grabbed Nanok's arm for support as she stood on her toes to peer over the fray. After a breath or two, she dropped back to her feet with a big grin and pulled Nanok through the crowd towards an armorer's tent. Talthielle and Konjo strode along behind in high spirits, both knowing neither were in charge.

"Konjo, she really is delightful. Such a charming creature. You are truly blessed, my lad."

Konjo didn't need a breath. "She is Queen, Talthielle. Queen of the Epochs. And may all the epochs pass before I lose her again. Talthielle, I never really-"

"And you'll never have to Konjo. What happened was unconscionable. I could not live with myself if I let it stand. The world would be a wretched place without her light."

Konjo took his captor's measure and saw kindness. With kind eyes of his own, he said nothing.

"Konjo, I want you to know I have not given you back your Brinka as the price offered for your services. I meant it when I said I cannot do this without you both. And having spent a few days with you, my magnificent Kenjah conscripts, I have only persuaded myself of what at first I could only dimly suspect and dared to hope for. I'm glad it's *you two*. I've been thinking about the last couple of days,

Konjo, and I think I've begun to grasp some of the strange and... unpredictable things that have been happening on this journey so far. The trouble is Konjo, and I beg you to understand me even if you don't completely understand me, the trouble is that if I am right, I cannot tell either of you what I think is happening. And if I'm wrong, Konjo, it just doesn't matter anyway and telling you would only complicate matters immensely for no clear purpose."

Konjo chewed his coney and berries and his thoughts for a few as they found the periphery of the crowd around the armorer's table. Brinka and Nanok had slithered their way to the fore and already laid out a hand full of points and shafts and were now trying on helms, trading commentary about the defensive capabilities of this one or that one and the fashionable aesthetics of the day. The argument thus constructed, it became clear that neither would settle for anything less than the finest (and most expensive) cap in the store. The armorer, following the arc of this dialectic exchange, had properly and respectfully diverted his attention to the two gleeful and obviously sophisticated customers now plying him with questions about custom embroidery and options for an inset for enchanted jewels (or at least, flossy ones), questions with which the merchant engaged with matching levity and enthusiasm. All things were possible in the city of Call.

Konjo had digested Talthielle's words while watching the charade unfold, and finally leaned into Talthielle's ear and said "Talthielle, you see the future. To speak candidly and without restraint about everything you see would unalterably change that future in myriad ways which are beyond our comprehension or control. I think I understand you perfectly. I only ask you this, is this a good thing, so far as you can tell, or a bad thing?" Konjo was satisfied with his formulation and

left the question hanging in the air. He read a mixture of
ambiguity and trouble in his captor's eyes as Brinka appeared
before them, dragging a handsomely crested Viermah in one
hand and a bellowing armorer, a stocky, bearded brute in a
longish red robe, in the other. Brinka prompted the merchant
to state his terms and then stared with doe eyes at Talthielle.
Konjo chuckled and Talthielle grunted.

"Konjo, I take back everything I said about her. I'm
pretty sure I'm going to drown her before we reach the
Marvu."

When Nanok followed Brinka's example and mocked
big doe eyes of his own, Konjo erupted and nearly fell to the
ground clutching his stomach trying to breathe between
laughs. To this, Talthielle just hung his head and sighed the
sighs of the dead. "I'm going to drown both of them." Once
again, he produced his pouch from his waist, gave it a sad
little shake and a forlorn look, as if farewelling a dear friend at
a funeral, and began counting out pine coins. As he
approached the bottom, Konjo had a moment of clarity, and
interjected his genius contribution to the evening's memory.
Talthielle would fondly remember the moment countless
times and always count it fortuitous.

"Talthielle, will we have enough left over for *roua*?"

At this, a wave of serious contemplation washed over
the crowd. A grave sobriety subdued Brinka and Nanok, and
sensing the fragile nature of the circumstance, the shrewd
merchant quickly appraised the situation and proposed a
hipshot solution without even taking a breath.

"My dear friends, I can tell you are all fine souls and I
would not have my best customers do without. This is my
finest helm. You would not have need of it if you were not
embarking on some great and perilous adventure. You are
clearly heroes, one and all, and heroes are terrific for business.

I am Rali, and you heroes would honor my name and show the world the quality of my craftsmanship if you choose this helm. So I'll tell you what, if you buy from me, I will fill you with as much *roua* as you can swill before your ship departs. What say you, my dear friends?" Rali flashed a big toothy smile and held his hands up in the air, as if wizardry might close the deal. Now, Rali, Brinka, Konjo, and Nanok were all standing in a halfmoon, staring doe-eyed at Talthielle and waiting with practiced patience. It was a fine helm indeed, and Nanok had not been wearing it in any of the visions in which Talthielle awoke to find his throat being torn out. Talthielle sucked his teeth and stared blankly above them all as he filed the coins back into his pouch and tossed the whole thing to the merchant, who promptly exalted them all as canonically deified.

    Moments later, after the jubilant merchant barked a handful of obvious orders to his already overwhelmed and baffled assistant to carry on and hold down the store, the five of them were gathered around the stauncheons of a small tent across the boardwalk from the armorer's tables. Their host, a buxom mistress with silver hair and wild eyes, readily comprehended Rali's instructions. The two shared a block and were regular intimates when it came to the imbibing of festive spirits. Rali had simply told her to pour until the "kindly old codger" called the time. Talthielle abandoned his reticence and accepted the only remaining perk associated with his involuntarily reified status. He stepped promptly to the front of the line and was handed a frothy mug of cinnamon ale, and when his companions had all been served, he raised it to the sky and blessed the night. A circle formed around them, and for a delicious moment in time, the heroes themselves transcended spectacle in the city of Call, as onlookers perceived the noble ritual of Chug was afoot.

"To *starlight*!" Talthielle called, and chug they did. Nanok and Konjo stood eye to eye, mugs in hand, and turned them back. Nanok knew he could not beat Konjo at this sport, and Konjo beamed as he intuitively understood Nanok's calculus, that he could only win by trying. By natural capacity, the rounds were consumed in the order of each of these characters' appearance in this story. Konjo emptied his mug before Brinka, who drained her *roua* just a breath quicker than Talthielle and Nanok, who were quickly followed by the merchant, himself all too happy to lose at his favorite sport to these lucrative heroes. Between Konjo and Rali, an intense hush fell over the crowd; though most of them accurately predicted the round, all held their breath with deference to the contestants. When Rali's mug was drained, they all erupted into laughter and cheers and hoots, and Bola, the barmaid, commenced to pouring.

"Chug, chug, chug!" the whole crowd chanted, and chug, chug, chug, the heroes obliged. This time, Nanok rounded the turn on Brinka and clacked his mug to Konjo's in solidarity. Second place between Kenjah was no laughing matter. Talthielle and Rali finished last, and the crowd was roaring. Talthielle eyed the sun for a moment, and Konjo and Brinka and Nanok and Rali and Bola and dozens of well-spirited strangers all eyed Talthielle, who, after a breath, failed to disappoint. Bola poured, and Rali cheered, and the heroes drank. Not to be out done, when their third round was gone, Bola jumped into their midst with the last of her decanter and turned it bottom over top until it was empty. The onlookers exploded with approval, and as Talthielle tried to give the signal, all other parties present fell into spontaneous unison, yelling "one more! One More! ONE MORE!" At this, Talthielle raised his hands to protest, sighting the sun touching the sea and the shadows creeping up the Dab, but the mob would not relent. "One More! One More!"

Talthielle looked at his conscripts, and they looked at him, and Talthielle raised his mug once more to Bola. As she dove into her tent for a fresh decanter, the other patrons reached the height of their hysteria. Rali grasped Talthielle's shoulder and smiled a sincere benediction, and the two old souls shared a moment of mutual satisfaction upon which great stories are built and lasting friendships are born. "I don't know where you are going, my dear friend, but I wish you well, and when you make it back, I hope you'll all come and visit me with tales of your adventures."

Talthielle shifted his staff to his shoulder and shook Rali's hand. "We will most certainly do that. You have my thanks, old man!" Bola reappeared and poured them all another round. This time, Nanok and Konjo took the foreground for one last battle. Serious eyes between them commanded the din to silence, and Talthielle assumed the roll of referee. He stood between them with his mug in hand, and held the breaths of everyone hostage for several tense seconds, and then raised his staff high in his other hand to give the start. Konjo and Nanok turned their mugs to the sky and chugged with gusto while silence pressed from all directions. Talthielle and Brinka and Rali pulled hard enough at their own draughts, but the contest between the Kenjah and the Viermah was in ernest, and few would have bet that Nanok and Konjo would *tie!* But when they did, everyone in the city of Call turned to hear the shouts and cries the crowd let out around Bola's tent. Konjo took Nanok's hand and raised it to the sky in solidarity. Pride notwithstanding, he secretly hoped he wasn't going to have to carry the Viermah *and* the rice sack to the ship. He whispered something to that effect to Nanok,

under the cover of the roar, and Nanok just twinkled and
shrugged a grinning uncertainty right back at him.

Just as Konjo was thinking of his rice sack, Rali was
proffering him a proper leather pack which he had ducked
away to retrieve, as if he had heard Konjo's thoughts. Konjo
tried to wave it away with humility, but the slushed armorer
would have none of Konjo's silly protests. Bola appeared
beside him, and bid them keep their mugs and handed Nanok
the nearly full decanter she had just opened, all for the road.
Talthielle drained his mug and shouted, trying to pretend
stern against the levity and failing in affect, but getting his
point across none the less. The heroes hugged Bola and shook
Rali's hand and waved triumphantly to a chorus of applause.
Rali slipped Talthielle's empty pouch back to him as a
professional courtesy. Talthielle took the limp satchel and
laughed. *Totally worth it.* Konjo tried to gently dump the
whole rice sack into Rali's leather pack, and resolved he would
explore the pockets and compartments and organize
everything later on. He held the bag open for everyone's
mugs, fine souveniers indeed, and likely signifying
complimentary refills if any of them survived long enough to
come back to Call under less pressing constraints, and then
sinched it up and slung it over his shoulder, feeling the
difference in his neck and back immediately.

"Let us fly! Thank you all and goodnight!" Talthielle
fell in behind Brinka, with Konjo and Nanok bringing up the
rear and supporting each other (and themselves) with hands
on shoulders as they all ran to the sea road through gaps in
the city wall and dashed towards their pier, where they could
see the *Marvu* had not yet raised its flags or its anchors, but
that crewmen seemed to be drifting towards their stations.
The four of them bolted through nearly a league, waving and
hailing the quartermaster at the gangplank until he noticed

them. Such sights were common in the city of Call, and patiently indulged. The quartermaster would welcome them aboard without grief or grumbling. But they would be the last riders to board for the night; the piers were otherwise empty and no other riders appeared to be coming.

Talthielle and his conscripts were winded from running and laughing and yelling when they reached their pier. The salty sea air was crisp, and a steady wind blew along the open shore. Everyone stopped shy of the *Marvu* to compose and contain themselves before going aboard. Nanok passed the decanter around, offering it to Talthielle first, assuming correctly that Talthielle would feel obliged to comply with the token of amicable neutrality. Talthielle accepted the ritual armistice with a smile, pulled hard, and passed it along to Brinka before Konjo, as is customary with Kenjah. Talthielle spoke in congratulatory tones.

"We have made it. Look at her! The majestic old *Marvu*. This ship was keeled before any of you were born. Isn't she beautiful?" The four of them took in the length and breadth of the worthy craft, its huge cannons on rotating mounts, two large guns fore and aft, and two smaller each port and stern, midships. The masts rose high over a central tower, a crow's nest above the captain's chambers and the pilot's cabin, and these above the quarterdeck on the first level, where the Officer of the Deck watched four nearly late stragglers haul themselves up the lashed wooden gangplank and present themselves for passage.

"I am Talto, sir. And these are my companions, Konos, Brinna, and Paunch. We request passage aboard your fine vessel until it returns to this port, and we are hoping you have cabins available. One for my nephew and I," Talthielle could see Nanok's quizzical little grimace, even if the OOD missed it, "and one for my betrothed Kenjah companions, who are in the family way and are to be wed at sea." Talthielle held the officer's attention while Konjo and Brinka exchanged a hastily concealed look of surprise with Nanok.

"Permission to come aboard, dear sir?"

The OOD inspected the last few prospective passengers, noting their arms and their luggage and their generally familiar condition of spirit, and found nothing overtly objectionable about them, excepting to some small degree, the smell. "Permission granted, Talto, Konos, Brinna, and Paunch. Your names will be added to the passenger list, and this seaman will see you to your cabins. I am certain we can find you adjoining accommodations, as only a few passengers will be joining us for this voyage. It's the slow season, you understand. You will all be expected to attend muster in the mornings and evenings, to assist with field day and laundry responsibilities in rotation, of course. The Captain will take breakfast with all hands in the morning, and if you have any other needs or questions, please address them to the officer on the watch at this station. I am Officer Nabul, the night watch in port. I will have the day watch at sea and you will find me with the helmsman on the bow. The name of the Captain is Bran. He is a sharp and courageous fellow. Our course is still being laid out at this moment, but for the first few weeks, we will be traveling out to fishing depth and taking in nets for our stores. We are slated to provision the Temple of Kalama, and have taken on substantial cargo to that effect. You will of course be expected to assist with the offloading, but if you have never visited the Temple, I trust that you find the experience... unique. Have you any questions?"

Talto shook the officer's hand, and assured him he had none at all at this time, and thanked him on behalf of four new shipmates. Konos and Brinna shook the *swelu's* hand by turns, followed by Paunch. The crewmen were now pulling the gangplank aboard behind them. When the sun finally set and left the world in quiet darkness, soft bells would inform them that the flags were being raised and the anchor weighed. A polite seaman led them below deck through narrow passageways and stooping hatches to the berthings until he found two cabins adjacent, and marked their assignments in his log.

Konos, Brinna, Talto, and Paunch were now officially crewmembers and guests aboard the *Marvu*, and Talto sank into his staff in a deep sigh of relief. They had made it to the sea safely and on time. He would think about what came next on the morrow. For now, he invited the Kenjah into his and Paunch's cabin for a few closing words and a nightcap, and three well earned stones.

Soon, the *Marvu* rocked gently beneath its bells and unfurled its sails. Konos and Brinna held hands and watched Omnia and the Rising Coasts drift away through the portal in their quarters. When nothing but stars and darkness could be seen, they drew their heavy curtains and turned their attentions to each other at last.

(Red Sky By Morning)

Paunch was no longer so sure that he hated the old tramp the way he always supposed he would when the fates inevitably crossed their paths. The two shared an uncomfortable silence in their cabin after the enamoured Kenjah departed, but the silence was soon broken by many awkward sounds which the bulkhead between cabins could only muffle. Talto and Paunch made mutually heroic efforts to find random spots to stare at without making eye contact or acknowledging the situation, but when Brinna cried out in a piercing wail from next door, the blood feuding nemeses lost their forced composure and buckled into respectfully stifled hysteria. Paunch, feeling his *roua* and watching the cabin spin on multiple axes, found Talto's twinkling eyes and passed him the decanter he had been clutching like a liferaft. It was a deliberate gesture, made possible perhaps only by the cinnamon ale, but the shared moment was pregnant with conciliation and relief. Talto accepted the decanter in the spirit offered, though his own head already swam like a school of startled fish.

"Talto, what in Dab are we really doing here?"

Talto swilled his *roua* and passed the decanter back. He understood that Paunch was posing many questions at once, and he clenched his eyes to steady his nerves and order his thoughts. Paunch let the question hang until Talto could compose his answer. Konnos could be heard grunting like a wild boar. Paunch clenched his own eyes and shook his head, trying not to giggle, hoping Talto would speak sooner rather than later.

"Until yesterday, I was sure I knew. I have an explanation, of course, but I am no longer sure it explains anything. Can I ask you something first? How did the Viermah know we were coming? If you can tell me that, it might shine a lot of light on some very unexpected developments. I want to answer you, but something is happening and I can't see it. You may understand when I say that to *Epozia*, that's the equivalent of saying there is a strong wind blowing and I can't fly."

Paunch sighed and shook his head. "All I know is that my kith and kin barged into my nest in the middle of the night and put that dreadful hood over my head and handled me very roughly. I overheard some loose-lipped cadets gossiping about a mysterious visitor while they were massing for your ambush, but whoever it was hadn't come to talk to cadets. This interloping stranger appeared in our wood and parleyed with that malingering captain in private for over an hour, and then vanished in a frightful hurry. That's all I know. Talto, someone knows what you're trying to do. But from what I can tell, they don't seem to be moving against you. I know my captain, and you know my people. We could have held you in the Verdant for as long as we wanted. My captain very clearly wanted you out of there as quickly as possible, and was obviously prepared to give you anything you wanted to get you gone. That he gave the Kenjah those bucklers, without even the slightest hesitation, is unheard of. But I think it illustrates the point."

Talto grimaced and shook his head. "It doesn't make any sense, but it rings true. Noone but the Kenjah could know my plans, because I haven't told anyone but them. I didn't even know, really, what it was I had to do until I saw them in Flask. What happened to Brinka... It's a long story. But everything about our journey so far makes a little more sense in light of what you say, and what I have only dimly suspected, though I can't explain any of it yet. Someone knows what we're up to. And if they wanted to stop me, well, they have had plenty of chances. They clearly have me at a disadvantage, which is no small feat for any but the *Epozia*... Talto trailed off as his eyes narrowed and the lines in his forehead furrowed. "For anyone but the *Epozia*... But until I reached the Titan and found Konjo, I was the only *Epozia* left in Omnia. Until I brought Brinka back from the dead."

Talto stood up sharply and began pacing around the cabin in a feverish struggle to supplant the *roua* and steady his mind. Paunch watched him with glazed eyes and wished he would sit down again, and after a moment, Talto conceded to the *roua* and slumped back down on his cot.

"I just don't understand it. I thought we would never make it aboard the *Marvu* in time, but for two whole days it has seemed that the whole of Omnia has conspired to keep us moving. Everyone hates the clocksmith because noone wants to surrender control of their own lives to anyone else, and this much I totally understand." Talto's eyes became stern and serious. "But when I tell you I've never really known what that feels like until..."

Talthielle sat up straight and pulled hard from the decanter, resigning himself to recall as much of the last two days as the *roua* would permit as he handed it back to Paunch, who listened in an an enraptured trance as Talto told him everything, from Flask to the Titan, to Waterside, and from Marla in the marshes to the Silver Bridges and the Viermah ambush in the Verdant. The two nemeses traded pulls from the decanter as the one listened and the other spoke. The *Marvu* heaved in darkness. Talto finished in the wee hours, and the two sat in silence while Paunch took it all in.

"I knew Jorgan. That's pretty gruesome, but I can't say I feel sorry for him. He was a first-class *pircka*, and I am one hundred percent certain he would have made trouble for all of you. That's an interesting clue, Talto. I can see why you're puzzled by it. If he were going to hinder you, who else but the *Epozia* could have known it? Who else but you?"

"Someone had to have known that. I guessed it, but when I reached ahead, I could never see past Waterside. I couldn't see Jorgan at all. I know, or knew, I suppose, that Jorgan was a hard case. I just figured he would be an obnoxious haggler and try to overcharge us for everything. That was his way. But after yesterday morning, I have struggled to see even more than a few moments ahead with any kind of clarity. I don't know what is going to happen next, and that is a very unfamiliar and anxious feeling."

"Well, Talto, that's pretty much how it is for all the rest of us all the time, you know. I suppose you'll just have to get used to it. It's all so odd to contemplate. Never in a millions moons would I have predicted I'd be dragged out of bed, beaten, hooded, and *clipped* by my own kind and handed over, to *you* of all people..." Paunch shrugged and lowered his eyes for a moment. "But the odd thing is that after tonight I couldn't imagine myself anywhere else in the world but here. All sense of control has abandoned me, and yet somehow I'm strangely comfortable with it. The Kenjah are delightful. Call was a blast. I've never been at sea before. And for the first time in my entire life, having hated you every minute of every day, having met you, you're not at all what I expected. It's your turn, Talto. I have a question for you, and I think you know what it is."

Talto accepted the decanter graciously and pulled softly. "Ask me, Nanok, and I'll answer."

"Why did my father kill himself?"

Talto's heart shattered and he wept abruptly.

"That's not what happened Nanok. I've heard that story too, and it's terrible. If I could change anything in Omnia... I wish with all my heart that you did not have to grow up thinking that. You had every right to hate me, and I could never tell you what really happened. Your father did not kill himself. Nanok, your father was a hero. He saved the world for you. In fact, he saved it *because* of you. Nanok, what I am trying to do now, I tried once before. Your father helped me. At first, he refused, that much is true. He was young and brash, and we *Epozia* are rarely well received, even under the best of circumstances. He told me I was a foolish old schemer and I let him go. He lived a full life, into middle age, until you were born. Your mother was sick, and she passed away giving birth to you. When he saw you, he told me everything changed in that moment. He said he finally understood why I had chosen him, and that he had to help me. He begged me to spare your mother from her illness, if it was in my power to do so, and said that if he could trade his life for hers, he would follow me into hell if it meant that you both would live. And follow me he did. Nanok, your father gave his life trying to help me, and I failed him. I tried to explain what happened to your mother, but she would hear none of it. She cursed my name and my kind and all my days. I fell to my knees, begging her forgiveness. I gave her what remained of my stones, and she gave me this hair shirt. I have worn it ever since."

The two sat in silence for a time. Paunch was weeping too. He knew Talto was telling him the truth. No one can cry while lying.

"What did you tell him? What did you ask of him?"

Talto gathered himself and wiped his eyes with his sleeve. "I told him that when the wars came, the Verdant would burn. The men would gather at its edge with torches, and no one would escape their fury. Together, we stopped the wars before they started. The hard thing about my life, Paunch, is that when I succeed, no one ever knows it. All the things that never happen leave no witnesses. When I've done my job well, it's as if I was never there at all. If we succeed here, though, the whole of Omnia will know it. We are going to persuade Lavaris to open his gates and let the spirits roam as they did in antiquity. The lores must learn to live with the consequences of their petty vendettas. Now it is only the victims, of this blind rage that steals across the land, who are ever haunted by the loss and wanton destruction. If the men who murdered Konjo knew he would torment them into their own graves, they would have just as soon let him be. It wasn't always this way."

"Why did Lavaris close his gates in the first place then?"

Talto gazed into Paunch's eyes for a long time before he finally spoke. "I don't know Nanok. No one but Lavaris knows. The lores lived in peace for ages. The way things are now, one can take a life and evade justice. But noone could evade the spirits of the fallen. When Lavaris let the spirits wander Omnia in peace, the lores were at peace with one another. One day, the whole world awoke to find all their loved ones departed, and over time, new spirits swarmed into his kingdom, abandoning ours.

"Brinka haunted Konjo, when her own tragic fate befell her. Her love for her betrothed was strong enough to defy death itself. It is a part of why I chose them. She is special, you know. Of course, he knows, and none could persuade him otherwise. Kenjah are honest creatures by nature. Their starlight shifts in shades and unfailingly shows the world who they are. But even Brinka's starlight is unique. She can bend her shades at will, and with practice, she can conceal herself like a shadow at midnight and evade even the most scrutinizing eyes. I am hoping to work with her to develop this skill while we are aboard the *Marvu*, where everything is awash in greys and browns; this environment is ideal for such training."

The two shipmates fell silent once again as Paunch pondered all that Talto had told him. At length, another question grew in Paunch's belly and burned to find breath of its own. "How did you save my mother? Why isn't she *Epozia*, like Brinna? Or," Paunch hung his head, "why wasn't she?"

Talto looked up at Paunch, as if startled by new information. "Paunch? Nanok? What happened to your mother? I hadn't asked you about her, or even thought to; we've been so preoccupied with everything else, I--"

"Her sickness returned a few winters ago, and she passed. She gave me your stones, and told me what she knew, which I supposed was not nearly as much as she believed, or maybe it's the other way around, because she believed very little of any of it I guess. She never forgave either of you for leaving us alone in the Verdant, a disgraced widow and a bastard youngling, draped in awful rumors and terrible speculation. She said you told her my father had died to save the world. Save the world, from what? You say the Verdant would have burned, and I guess I am inclined to believe you, maybe because the Kenjah believe you now. Maybe because I really just wish to remember my father some other way, or to remember him at all. But you haven't answered me Talth-, Talto. How did you save her? Could you have done it again? If..." Paunch was holding back tears now, and the *roua* was gone. He nursed his clipped wings, and Talto knew the youngling had been made to suffer for a clocksmith's sins, too many times for Talto to forgive himself. "If she would have listened to you. Could you have saved her again?"

"Nanok, I didn't save her. Marla did. Your Viermah are stubborn and superstitious, and they don't trust conjurers or apothecaries, or clocksmiths either, for that matter. Her condition, when I knew her, believe it or not, should never have been fatal in the first place. But your Viermah shun the ways of the outside world. Marla's remedy was a simple concoction of herbs from her own garden. Your father was desperate, and permitted himself to be persuaded to give it to her when she became pregnant with you and her first symptoms appeared. I am so sorry to hear of your loss, and I don't know what finally overcame her, in the end, but if it was the same thing, then by all rights, I suspect the answer is yes. We could have helped her. Nanok, I have made such a mess of things. You can't know how sorry I am. I am trying to help, on my stones I swear I am. But this world just fights me at every turn. Konos and Brinna had already abandoned the mercenary trade for each other, and would have lived their whole lives without ever inconveniencing a rill, if only the men had left them alone. Omnia is a tinder box. Call is perhaps the only place left in the world that hasn't been touched by this sickness of heart and mind. Let us hope beyond hope that the Kalama and their idols have retained some sense of propriety in their isolation."

Breaths passed.

"Talto, you can sleep if you want. I forgive you, and I will follow you. No harm will come to you tonight. The Kenjah would never forgive me anyway, and I can live with this hate no longer. On my father's behalf, thank you for helping my mother." Nanok arose and offered his hand. Talthielle stood and took it firmly.

The cabin adjacent had fallen quiet. The *Marvu* heaved gently on its keel, and the morning hour was not far off. Talto knew the captain would serve a late breakfast on the first day of a new voyage, not only for the sake of the straggling revelers, but for most of his crew as well, returning from shore leave, as reliably well spent as earned. Breakfast would be their last fine meal before settling in on ship's rations for much of the duration. The day's duties would be light; everything on board was already polished and scrubbed raw. There would be a little work in the scullery, and watch rotations forward and aft for a few days, until they sounded depths for nets and hauling. No one was chasing them now, but the danger had not yet passed. In a few weeks, the *Marvu* would approach the Kalama Temple and begin offloading its annual tribute at the floating docks opposite the Temple. It would be then that Talto would have to persuade Bran, one way or another, to venture farther out, past the Temple, into the vast trenches where the Kalamaii abide. From these tempestuous waters, at the whims and mercies of colossal leviathans, shipwrecks are never recovered. Bran would not be easily persuaded, and neither would be his crew.

And if *Ursal* agreed? If she came aboard? Well, by tradition, as mythical and obscure as any known, Bran would no longer command his own vessel. It would surely be this to which he objected most emphatically. But this was the way it had to be. If the Kalamaii refused, all was lost, and the mission might end abruptly. Very abruptly. Talto was sure that no living soul aboard, except himself, had ever seen the Kalamaii in the flesh. This was the way the Kalamaii preferred things. And they would continue to prefer things this way. Bran would know this much, at the very least.

***

Brinka swung the Enigma Blade wildly in the darkness, aiming for nothing and nowhere all at once. Blind darkness was a new and unfamiliar kind of horror. The Kenjah's starlight would not shine in this place. Whatever hunted her in this lightless void would not bare its fangs. It would not breathe or scratch the ground when it stepped, this way or that, deftly eluding Brinka's panicked swing. Her skin was cold and her limbs were lazy, as if she was under water. When the thought occurred to her, her head swooned and she consciously tried to breathe, but couldn't. The blade would protect her when the deathblow came. If she could hold it fast and wait, the sudden loss of control would tell her which direction the beast had chosen, and give her the chance to counter. But how long could she go without breathing? Did this thing in the darkness need to breathe? Could it smell her? Brinka could smell nothing. She thought if she tried to breathe in, she would surely drown, and this nefarious thing would have her.

When Brinka held her breath, she could hear her heart thundering in her chest, and wondered if the thing could hear it too. The more she swung the blade, the more the pounding of her drum intensified. The thing was close. She could only sense it with her senseless fear. It was stalking her. If she turned and ran, it would pounce. But there was nowhere to run in this formless abyss. No homes or huts or tents or trees. No walls, no floor, no ceiling, and no light. No north or south or east or west, or up or down. She could muster forwards and backwards, and could still comprehend left and right, but only because she was still alive enough to exist at the center of her own reality. Just alive enough to know that hers was a dead star in an empty universe. But she was not alone here. What was this thing?

Brinka suddenly felt a sharp jolt from the blade in her hands as it leaped above her head, nearly yanking itself from her grip. With the last remaining spark of instinct she possessed, she held tight to the Enigma Blade and thought of nothing else. In the span of a breath she wished she could take, she thought the blade would connect and parry, and she tried to focus on that moment, because the moment would be the only chance she got to strike a deathblow of her own. There would be no aiming to maim this time. But the blade found no parry. Instead, it lifted Brinka toward whatever direction was straight up from wherever she was. Brinka felt the pressure closing in around her temples as her lungs and heart protested with vigor. As she ascended beneath her blade, the pressure grew intolerable, and she felt as if her chest would explode. She felt her speed increasing, as if she was being pulled into space. She wanted to scream, but couldn't. She didn't look down to see if the thing was pursuing. She fixed her eyes on the hilt of her blade and tried to force every other thought from her mind, but her thoughts were many and her mind was full and pregnant and pressing just as hard against the hostility of the outside world as the outside world was pressing inward on her skull.

As Brinka lost consciousness, her last thought was of a single stone, set in the hilt of her blade. In the darkness, it suddenly flickered on and began to shine, and with it, the blade, and with the blade, so too shone Brinka.

"Brinka! Brinka! Brinka, wake up," Konjo was shouting. The *Marvu* was riding tumultuous waves, tossing about and listing hard to starboard against the furious winds. All but one brave little candle, evidently one of Marla's contributions and not Jorgan's, had blown out. Konjo's face was just another blurred shadow in a disorienting sea of darkness. Talthielle and Nanok stood over Konjo's shoulder, each wearing expressions of worry and alarm. As her nightmare dream reluctantly released her mind, the chaos of the scene flooded in abruptly, overwhelming Brinka all ar once, until she finally remembered to breathe. As she filled her lungs, her back arched and her arms flew up to shield her face from blows. Talthielle held Nanok's shoulder, and Nanok held a bulkhead against the heaving tide. Konjo at once enfolded Brinka in his arms and drew her into himself tightly, against the tide and against her own sleep-blind thrashing. "Brinka! It's okay! It's me!" The Kenjah were the color of storm clouds, and lightning shimmered in Brinka's skin until her fright subsided and she realized that she was alive, and awake, and still aboard the *Marvu.*

"Konjo?" Brinka squeaked at first, still afraid to release her breath for any other use but breathing. Then, all at once, she sagged and collapsed into Konjo, gratefully sucking in as much sweet sea air as she could steal from a breathless room. "Oh, my Konjo! Konjo, did you see it? Oh Konjo, it was horrible!" Brinka sobbed into Konjo's neck and wrapped her arms around him, squeezing even tighter than she had held that blade. "Konjo, it was horrible. I think I just died, again. Only this time it was so much worse. Oh, Konjo! Oh I am so glad you're here. Please don't let me go."

Talthielle and Nanok exchanged quizzical glances tinged with relief and puzzlement. At last, they also remembered to breathe, and both of them collapsed onto the rack beside the Kenjah, exasperated. "Well, good morning everyone!" The four of them startled and looked about for the origin of the voice which didn't match any of their own. All at once, their attention turned to the hatch, where stood a tall, wiry man with a young face and old eyes. His hair was blonde and neatly cropped, and his face was clean shaven. His skin was tan from years at sea, and his arms were lean and tight. He had one gold tooth flashing in a momentarily bewildered, but disarmingly friendly grin. Beside him stood a stout troll of a man with glassy eyes, which were somehow both hard and twinkling, and a wild beard, which grew at angles in every direction from his leathery face. A brief silence hung in the air as all parties present tried to take in what they were seeing, and the *Marvu* heaved on its keel.

Talto was the first to seize the initiative and speak. "Captain Bran, I presume! We are terribly sorry for the disturbance; our lady friend was having a spell of night terrors. Sir, this is Brinna and her mate, Konos. And this is my, er, umm, *adopted* nephew, Paunch. At this, Paunch restrained a glare, barely, shook his head and shrugged his acceptance of the status quo as he stood to shake the captain's hand properly, looking Bran squarely in the eye and squeezing firmly, without pretense, as he had been instructed in his youth. Konos hesitated for a moment, unsure of how to divide his attentions, but felt Brinna shift in his arms and they both tried to stand together as the deck rolled from port to starboard and back again. "And I am Talto, a traveling mage and a soothsayer. Paunch is Viermah, from the Verdant, and as you can see, our companions are Kenjah, from the hills west of Dab. We have come to see the Kalama and to seek adventure!"

Bran listened and watched and said nothing, until he had shaken the hands of all the new passengers in the room. As another silence hung in the air, and the *Marvu* swam against an aggressive morning squall, Bran took in the scene, trying to commit the obviously made-up names to memory, and reminded himself to address it at some more opportune moment in the future. As he scanned the new faces, his attention came to the young Kenjah maiden, only moments ago captive to her own hysteria. Some vague sense of recognition washed over him, and his eyes narrowed and became suddenly very stern and serious. "Brinna?"

The captain became oblivious to everyone and everything else in the cabin, and stepped forward with a palpable urgency in his bearing. "Young lady. They said you were having night terrors. I must beg your pardon for my indiscretion, but I need you to tell me exactly what you saw."

The captain's forgotten first mate drifted into the room and became a spectator with the rest of the audience. He turned gingerly to Talto and whispered "Hi, I'm Hinds. Welcome aboard," and took Talto's hand and shook it firmly.

"Nice to meet you Hinds; call me Talto."

"Yeah, sure thing!" Hinds quietly nodded and shook with Paunch and Konjo, and then stood quietly among them as the scene unfolded.

Brinna found the intense captain captivating, and soon heard herself babbling an unconstructed account of a disjointed dream which was already slithering out of reach of conscious memory. She stopped herself and tried to compose, and began again. The captain and her shipmates seemed to lean in as they listened. She could tell by the worry in Konos' face that he *had not* shared this dream, and she reminded herself to address it at some more opportune moment in the future. She could not tell by Bran's reaction if she was making sense or not, and she was halfway through what she could remember when it dawned on her that his concern was not only genuine, its impetus had nothing to do with her at all. He really did need to know exactly what she saw. Brinna wondered at this observation, but tried not to let herself become distracted by it. Bran seemed to be following every word with growing interest, and perhaps growing alarm as well. As she finished, Bran's eyes told her that something was indeed very wrong. Even Hinds' demeanor had changed as she said her part. Konos, Talto, and Paunch all seemed very worried for her and confused by the imagery. Bran and Hinds were clearly very disturbed by something else entirely, and the nervous looks they exchanged said as much. Yet another uncomfortable silence hung in the air. This one didn't last nearly as long.

"Garrison! M-A, get in here! Now! Hinds, get topside and tell Troy to bring the ship about and point the prow back toward the shelf and ride the wind with all sails, on the DOUBLE, heard?"

"Heard!" Hinds vanished and a bear of a man appeared in the hatch behind him, stooping to enter the space. The man looked as if he would have had to stoop everywhere aboard ship except topside. As the Master at Arms entered the cabin, he seemed to be taken by a lot of different details at once, and for a moment, couldn't quite absorb them all. Bran preempted Garrison's effort and gave him clear and specific orders as the captain stood to dash away on some grave compulsion.

"All parties present are hereby confined to quarters until further notice. If anyone tries to leave before I clear this order, you are to punch them in the face. Heard?"

Garrison caught Konos' eyes and his doubts about the dubious prospect were felt, but after an extra heartbeat he sighed and shrugged. "Heard."

Paunch was the first to protest. "Hey, wait! What did we do?" But Bran was gone. The bulking Master at Arms hung nervously beneath an awkward silence of his own.

"I-- I don't know. What *did* you guys do?" No one else had heard the captain give him an explanation either, so he didn't feel particularly pressed to provide one. His eyes returned to Konos, and his shaken ladyfriend. Garrison was trying to read the room for any indication that he might actually have to engage his orders, but could sense no overt hostility, only diffuse confusion, and a touch of impatience in the clipped and hungover Viermah. Talto, the old tramp in his woolen robe and hair shirt, was the only one in the room preoccupied by something other than unexposited captivity. When Paunch turned to him for an explanation he obviously didn't have, he ignored Paunch entirely.

Talto was fixated on Brinna.

"Brinna, you said you saw something at the end of your dream? You said you saw--"

"A stone, Talto. I saw a glowing stone set in the hilt of my sword. It was the only thing in the whole dream that I actually did see. Until it turned itself on, I couldn't see anything at all. Not my skin, not my sword, not the... the thing I was trying to fight. And as soon as I saw it shine I blacked out in the dream and woke up here. I couldn't even see the ground." Brinka turned inward for a moment, and then turned back to Konos and slid her arms beneath his as he held her. Konos, for his part, said nothing, and watched Talto carefully. Talto asked Brinna to produce her sword. Garrison shifted anxiously in his boots, but looked on. Brinna reached beneath her robes at the foot of her rack and proffered Talto the Enigma Blade that Marla had fashioned for her only two nights prior, hilt first, as is customary.

Talto had not stopped between the Silver Bridges and the *Marvu* to take the time to examine any of Marla's contributions. When he took the sword from Brinna, the stone he had been ordered to give to Konos before the crossed into the Verdant flashed in his mind. There was no stone in the Enigma Blade, of course, but he noticed a small concavity in the pommel. *An exact fit.* Marla's capacity to surprize him was unmatched. Garrison, mindfully *un*present, observed the fine quality from over Talto's shoulder, and recognized the craftsmanship immediately, as had Talto. Both of them held the thought in private. The Kalama had not bourne arms in ages, not since the days of the pirates and the historically short lived Kalamaii hunting expeditions, when the Temple was first being constructed and many of Omnias' best and brightest had not yet fully grasped, let alone embraced, the paradigm shift in seagoing politics which was then in full swing.

Viermah blades, when they used them, had feathered shoulders. Kenjah blades were usually just blades they had taken from whomever was foolish enough to attack them with blades. Men's blades were shorter and inornate. At sea, blades tended to be thin, long, curved, razor sharp, and without shoulders or guards. A rather curious and rare innovation had taken root amongst a conspicuously hearty band of island monks, who inlaid dense cork around the stock of the grip and wove it into the spiral pommels, the novel effect of which was that when one dropped a sword in the water, it would not sink to the bottom. Even more curious, the genius adaptation never seemed to catch on amongst the landed antagonists and venture sailors who harassed the Kalama at sea, and were always losing their own weapons in the drink.

"Konos. Do you have the stone I gave you at the Silver Bridge? The one Marla put in my cloak? Let me see it, please." Garrison noted another familiar element which seemed to be a pretty big clue about the quarantined passengers. He made it a point to remind himself to address these things with Bran at some more opportune moment in the future.

"What is it Talto? What are you thinking?" Paunch found himself caught up in the dramatic show of arms and briefly forgot that he was meant to be protesting his unexposited captivity. Talto acknowledged him with uncertainty, and Konos pulled one of Brinna's short blades out of his own rumpled cloak where Brinna's sword had lain. He thumbed loose Marla's stone and held it aloft.

"Don't give it back to me, just hold it in the light. Brinna, is this the stone you saw?"

Brinna squinted in the dim light and craned forward for closer inspection, but in as many breaths a new sense of perplexity gripped her. "Yes, Talto. It was one of your stones? This one is different from the one you gave us when we embarked."

Fourteen yellow; six are blue.* Talto thought hard. A picture was forming in his mind, which he could not see the edges of. Questions flooded in, half formed in broken columns. Talto suddenly noticed that the Kenjah were the color of nomi leaves, and the stone had shifted to a dull green. Was this one of his after all? He had never conscripted Kenjah before, and hadn't thought to look at Konos' stone after he gave it to him. It didn't really even matter if Konos had kept the stone or lost it, or if he carried it or stowed it away in a cigar box in a drawer beneath his rack and forgot about it. If Talto called them all back to a prior moment in time, it would be to the moment when the stone changed hands, from *Epozia* to conscript. Whatever happened to it after that was inconsequential, because when Talto called them back, the stone and the future it inhabited would cease to exist at once. An idea formed. Whether it was the right one or the wrong one was a question of its own, *an enigma.* Talto tried to do the math while two Kenjah, one Viermah, and a performatively indifferent M-A gawked at him, waiting for an explanation with arched eyebrows and blank tension.

Garrison clocked the enigmatic jewel, and held his tongue. Strange things were afoot aboard the heaving *Marvu*.*

Paunch interjected, drumming his talons to the beat of the throbbing sound of his pulse in his hungover crest. "Hey, Garrison, right? So, he said we're confined to quarters until further notice, right? Can we, perhaps confine ourselves to our own quarters? And also, I'm really very hungry. Do we still get to eat breakfast with everyone, or...? And why are we turning around?"

"Paunch," Talto rescued Garrison, who had answers to exactly none of these questions, but might have to punch the punchy Paunch in the face if that disappointing nonanswer was not otherwise sufficient. "We are turning around because the headwinds are too strong for the *Marvu*. The captain put the rudder to the temple to drive us toward the shore. He won't turn back, he'll use the storm to follow a long curve which will eventually point the ship back toward the Kalama Temple at a quicker clip, on a leeward approach. In the meantime, we're all going to stay right here until Bran returns. I have every confidence that he will explain himself in due course, when his shipmates aren't barrelassing into a melee with mother nature. As for your middle question..." Talto turned from the stone to Paunch and from Paunch to the Master at Arms, who stooped slightly in the cabin and had thus far kept himself pretty successfully uninvolved, while also keeping everyone in the space, as ordered. Garrison acknowledged Talto, but kept a sharp eye on the giant Kenjah with the enchanted antiques and the big sword. Garrison did cringe a little when Talto suggested the *Marvu* couldn't handle the headwinds. But he withheld correction of impropriety on the basis of propriety, which was a skill he noticed the landed folk rarely honed.

"I'm a hundred percent with him on that one *swelu*, I was really looking forward to the breakfast part, if I'm honest. The uh, lady, here, is with child, we should mention. In all the wonderful stories I've heard about this fine ship, some of which I've actually been in, mind you, the hospitality abord this vessel has never been impugned." Talto tried to rise gently to his feet just as the rudder order was conveyed and the jib tacked its counter angle, hefting everything onboard that wasn't nailed down or braced for hard pitch sharply to the starboard, and for a moment, most hands aboard could stand and walk abreast on the bulkhead, if they were careful, and many were. Everyone in the cabin lurched and grabbed ahold of any stretch of vertical-qua-horizontal plating that would support their weight. Garrison caught a tumbling Veirmah just shy of smashing the protruding dog on the hatch behind him with his vaguely punchable face. Konos and Brinna sat on their pillows the wrong way, while Talto was jostled head over foot across three corners of the room in a humiliating spectacle.

A final moment of heavy silence hung over the cabin as everyone present processed what they witnessed. For a full breath, no one moved. Talto lay crumpled in a ball at Garrison's feet, groaning loudly. The Master at Arms had picked up plenty of land dwellers off of the deck in his career, and in a flash, his own muscle memory kicked in, grabbing Talto under the shoulders and standing him up to see if could stay that way on this own. That was the *swelu* way. In another breath, Talto was on his feet again, with a steadying hand on Garrison's shoulder. Brinka broke next.

"TALTO! Are you? Wow man! Hey, are you okay? That was wild!"

Paunch was still trying to wrap his mind around having just narrowly escaped a similar fate, and was also holding one of Garrison's shoulders. The Master at Arms had been ordered to punch any one of them in the face if they tried to escape. How many moments had passed before he became responsible for their collective ability to just stand up safely. For a moment, he felt like a coat rack. The time to discuss boundaries was fast approaching. He wished Bran would come back soon.

Garrison also wanted breakfast.

(The Epochal Matriarchy)

Konos had set Marla's stone in one of Brinna's blades, according you her instructions, prior to crossing the Silver Bridges into the Verdant. He reset the stone when Talto's examination seemed to prove fruitless for the clocksmith. He gripped each of the short blades tightly and held the jeweled edge over the other, facing away from Brinna, and much more carefully demonstrated how the blade would spin on it's fulcrum until it pointed directly at his betrothed. Paunch cooed and even Garrison seemed to nod in approval. The Viermah had little knowledge of the enchanted world, but no sailor worth his salt would receive a commission aboard a vessel like the *Marvu* without having obtained substantial experience with the numinous and paranormal. The landed folk may live on without their ghosts and spirits, but the ethereal haunts of the mysterious deep would never permit themselves to be so easily dismissed and discarded. Garrison supposed that much of what was magical in Omnia probably arrived by sea and migrated inland. But here was charming and authentic craft originating ashore and finding its way to the sea. Talto was no soothsayer or traveling mage. These Kenjah were outfitted as mercenaries and loaded for some preternatural conquest. And the vaguely punchable Viermah clipling was clearly in way over his feathers.

Talto did not coo, or contemplate the origins of this novel parlor trick. "Pathfinder," he explained, and all present listened on as though the explanation would continue, but it did not. Talto slumped down on the deck and rested his wounded back against the bulkhead. He shouldn't have needed the gift of foresight to know the ship was going to heave hard on its keel when the rudder order was passed on to the navigator. But Talto had the gift of foresight and inexplicably failed to see it coming. He had been tossed about the cabin like a plaything, rolling across one bulkhead to the next and the next like a bouncing ball. Garrison had stood him, gracefully, as it were, and Talto tried to present himself as well enough for Paunch to finally chuckle a little at the spectacle. But Talto felt every glancing blow reverberating in most of the bones of his body. Thankfully, the cloak would conceal the bruises, but he would walk with a limp, he could already tell. And his hair and face were even more dishevelled than usual. His eyes watered a little, if not for the pain, then at least for the solid blow across his temple which had set him dizzy after he hit the deck at Garrison's feet.

Nothing in the last two days had shown itself to Talto. He had been caught off guard in Waterside, in the marshes, and again in the Verdant. And here was the stone of another *Epozia,* which Talto had carried unwittingly through the morning of the previous day, and he even reset the day with it for Konos at the bridges. This was not one of Talto's stones, after all. He knew that Marla was not *Epozia,* so *whose* stone was this? Talto chose silence in the moment, because silence was safe. He had to think very carefully about what he said next, and now very much more carefully indeed about the nature of this mission. Thinking carefully about a thing is made much more difficult by a sudden and unexpected barrage of bodily harm. Talto thought to himself that this is how Konos must have felt the night he found him sulking in the Titan. Covered in welts and sore from head to toe.

Time is a jealous mistress. When all the *Epozia* still lived, they rarely convened beyond the annual festivals, except to discuss events of grave significance. They strictly observed a very rigidly implemented system of spheres of influence. The journeys of their conscripts could not be permitted to overlap. One perfectly obvious reason for this was the implicit potential for utter chaos in the continuum. A conscript's rounds are to be expended based upon the circumstances and conditions which are unique to his or her own path. If the ripples in the mental sea upon which a clocksmith operates are colliding with someone else's water, which is to say, one's conscript's experiences are being modified by those of another's conscript, the potentialities exponentialize and the game simply becomes broken and unmanageable. The second good reason is that all this confusion and chaos simply wastes the power lifeforce of an *Epozia*. It is not only an inefficient practice; it is literally a health hazard. As Talto was the only servant of the seasons who remained alive and in business in Omnia, he had long since abandoned the consideration of competing influences. Talto was on his own, for better or worse, and the only person left alive who could overcomplicate his own life's work was himself.

But by Dab, that just wasn't true anymore. *Brinka is Epozia now.* Talto found himself watching Brinna quietly. She and Konos had settled somewhere between giving up on any more useful information from their half-mangled captor and openly challenging the Master at Arms to violence for a few hundred extra meters of freedom to move about the ship freely. Instead of pressing either of these, they had set

themselves busy about inventorying the contents of the rice
bag and repacking their spoils in Rali's fine leather satchel.
Talto watched as the Kenjah worked almost wordlessly.
Paunch, finding his sealegs, was sidling up to the M-A and
studying his bearing and boots in a peculiarly absent way, as if
Garrison had been waxwork in a museum, rather than wide
awake and watching his own ward inspect his uniform,
jawline, and laces. Paunch was unfamiliar with every single
thing he had or would encounter after traversing the
gangplank, and this stoic soldier of the sea remained at his
post with the dubious responsibility of punching a Viermah,
a Kenjah, or an *Epozia* in the face, as if that was just a normal
day's duty. Paunch was reluctantly concluding to himself that
there was some merit in the superficially absurd prospect: he
conceded, privately, that he indeed did not want to be
punched in the face by the stooping hulk of *swelu*. Talto
ignored Paunch's obnoxious comedy, but remained alert to
the mild tension it was generating. Garrison was a
professional, that much was sure.

  Brinna and Konos worked in tandem. First, each had
cleared everyone off of their rack with shooing gestures
instead of verbal commands. Each rounded a side and found
the edges of their sheets and ship's wool, gripping both
corners in each hand and pulling as they lifted and recentered
them perfectly. They smiled at each other as each found their
topside corners and turned them in, fluffing and placing their
down pillows beside each other at the turn, and tucking in
the drape from head to foot. In spite of Paunch's
boundary-averse curiosity, Garrison did observe and approve
the nearly inspection ready result and made some internal
modification to his assessment of the fundamental character
of the Kenjah, as individuals, as a couple, and as a lore. He
decided he liked them, one and all.

Brinna and Konos next retrieved their cloaks and shook them out, standing next to one another at the foot of their rack and holding them out, gripping them at each shoulder, turning in right over left, and then neatly rolling them into tight bundles on the rack, sinching them with tomi and fastening their broaches over the seam. These they place beneath each of their pillows. Brinna picked up the rice sack and set it at the foot, and began pulling out the items one by one and handing them to Konos, who then arranged them in a kind of ordered grid, with larger items towards the cloaks, and smaller items in rows and columns spreading downward, according to kind. They had a system. They shared an unspoken language of intuition, communicating with simple motions of the eye and chin. Konos would be uncertain about the exact arrangement of this item or that, and would just pause for a second looking at Brinna, who would instinctively comprehend the nature and validity of his hesitation. She would squint a little as she worked on the problem, and then just bend her head a little, this way or that. Konos would decipher this ambiguous response immediately and nod his concurrence with her infallible calculus, and there the thing would go.

Talto knew the Kenjah were special. The problem, he thought to himself, is that he had no way to measure or define just exactly how special they were. In one particular version of the world, their conspicuous and consecutive deaths would precipitate a global conflict of untold proportions. But until he found them, Talto had really only contemplated their significance in this external context. They were strangers to him otherwise. It was only over the last two very strange and frenetic days that Talto had begun to discern the novel nobility of their own individual natures, and the quality of love that bound them together in life and death alike. Even among Kenjah, these Kenjah were unique. They *had been* unique, even before Talto decided to impose his own life upon them and press them into his service. But Talto had brought Brinna back from the other side. He had imbued her with his own life force, and in considerable measure. There had never been a Kenjah *Epozia*. No servant of the seasons had ever wielded starlight. His kin would never have permitted such a being to live. But Talto had to make his own decisions. It was Talto's will that these Kenjah survive. Konos trusted Brinna, as Brinna trusted Konos. Something about that one certainty seemed to sufficiently satisfy Talto that, together, these two honest creatures would always polish and purify the impulses of the other.

Too much power for one was perhaps more safely and equitably shared by two such as these.

Paunch had completed his inspection of Garrison and was now sitting against the bulkhead beside uncle Talto, watching the Kenjah arrange their wares. The *Marvu* moved high and swift on it's keel as the worst of the winds retreated towards the storm's center. The Gunship rocked on the waves, but the pitch and roll had become manageable. The Kenjah, having emptied and folded their rice sack, now sat opposite each other on the rack, sorting and examining the items. These somewhat naturally fell into two categories-- those from Jorgan and those from Marla.

In Jorgan's section, Talto saw hooks and lures, a bundle of matches, ink and parchment, some ointments, some long candles, and a rather gaudy compass, all demarcated by a handroll of twine. Brinna unwrapped the salted meat and tore off a shred for the grateful but grumbling stomachs of her shipmates. Garrison was happy to taste any meat that had been packed in salt rather than died swimming in it. Talto and Paunch were only slightly less enthused. As Brinna and Konos split the rest and nibbled quietly, their attention turned to Marla's contributions.

Marla had sent mainly food and medicine. Garrison politely refused the berries, and Paunch politely refused the cheeses. No one refused a modest tug from the skinbound bottle of port which had gone unnoticed in the rice sack until now. The Kenjah nibbled and inspected Marla's potions. She showed Konjo "cramps" and they shared a little venerating chuckle. Konjo held up "recover" and nodded both to Talto and Paunch. Brinna chewed on the suggestion for a moment and shrugged.

"Na.. Paunch, come sit in front of me, facing-- Talto." Paunch looked skeptical, but was inclined to oblige. To protest required too much energy. He crossed the cabin, acknowledging Garrison as he passed in tight quarters, and folded his legs on the floor at the foot of the Kenjah's rack. Brinka poured a little bit of the gold liquid out of the vile onto her hands and proceeded to rub it into Paunch's shoulders and arms in the places where feathers had once grown. The scent of earth and honey filled the cabin, and was sharp, but pleasant. Paunch had clearly not expected whatever sensations to balm produced, but his eyes widened and then narrowed as his body tensed in abrupt protest and then sagged in raptured compliance. When Brinna finished, Paunch was a puddle. She smelled her hands and held them up to Konos, who breathed deeply and concurred with her approval. She closed the vial and proffered it to Talto, who accepted graciously and made no notice of the inherent implication that he was to apply it himself, on his own time.

Brinna then picked up the remaining potions, one by one, calling them out by their scrawled labels to her companions, so everyone would be apprized of the party's stock. Talto did his best to fill in the gaps, but his experience with Marla's concoctions was as limited as was his need for them.

"Stealth?"

Paunch shrugged a general approval. Konos nodded, making note.

"Stealth will dampen the sound of your breath and feet for about an hour or so, depending on how much you drink. For Kenjah, I suspect it might also have some effect on your colors. For Viermah, perhaps it inhibits the jaws and tongue." Paunch leered at Talto, and Garrison nodded in approval.

"Speed? Makes you run fast, I suppose?"

Talto nodded, hoping there weren't too many complicated explanations in Marla's repertoire.

Brinna held the next one aloft, struggling to read the symbols, and Konos squinted against the dim candlelight. "Smoke?" The bottle was a little bigger and heavier than the rest, but the glass was thinner, and there were little stones jostling around at the bottom of the purple fluid.

"You throw it on the ground if you need cover to fight or to flee." Simple enough.

"Farsight?"

Talto's ears perked up. *Thank you Marla.* "I'll take that one, Brinna, if you please. At this point, I'll take all the help I can get." Brinna reached over a pile of Paunch and handed the little green vial to Talto, who shook it in front of his face and watched it fizz and bubble and glow.

"There are a couple here that say Antidote. This one just says Dream." Brinna handed down Paunch's bundle of shafts and points from Rali's shop, and Paunch took them eagerly, having nearly forgotten Rali's shop entirely on account of Bola's *roua*. Brinna handed him a length of tomi roughly his height. It didn't have to be exact. The last item to be inventoried was a little black cloth, folded over itself in several layers. Brinna unfolded this on the rack between herself and Konos, and gasped when its contents were revealed. There were two large silver rings, a beautiful necklace of shells and charms, and a white jewel shaped like a talon. These had all been packed with a fair chunk of carved quartz. The rings were obviously meant for the Kenjah, as no other fingers would fit them. Brinna handed the quartz down to Talto, another obvious conclusion. Paunch received the jewel and after staring at it for a moment, he decided it belonged in his helm, and thought it would look rather sharp.

"By process of elimination, and because of the little squid pendant, I'm guessing the necklace is for *her?*"

Talto adopted the Kenjah's method of pantomime and narrowed his eyes to instruct Brinna to speak with discretion. Brinna comprehended and said no more, but Garrison had already gleaned enough to comprehend the significance of the remark, and interjected accordingly.

"Her? Is there someone in your party who is not here now?" At this, Paunch, Konos, and Brinna all turned to Talto for the appropriate response. For his part, Talto just sighed and did his best.

"Not aboard, if that's what you're asking, no. But yes, we are hoping to persuade a fifth member to join our adventure. An old friend of mine lives and serves at the Temple. She may ride back to Omnia with us if we can convince her."

Garrison wasted no breaths. "The Kalama do not leave the Temple for any reason. Certainly not to go to ashore." His voice was not exactly confrontational, but he did not varnish his skepticism with shy tones. Talto had no desire to have this conversation now, and made a valiant attempt to defer. Garrison himself was visibly unpersuaded, but

restrained himself for the sake of bearing. No one was trying
to leave, and Bran had not returned. Best to avoid prickly
entanglements. All riders had their secrets, and the same was
true for the crew, and perhaps doubly so for their captain.
The sea was no place for anyone's objective concept of truth.
The *Epozia*'s stones, the Kalama relics, the witch's brews, and
the prospect of an unlikely and unidentified passenger were
all curious details in an incomplete puzzle Garrison had not
been ordered to assemble. The M-A had been ordered to
secure the passengers until his captain returned with further
instructions, or, at the very least, a relief watch, or some
breakfast. Bran would appreciate and consider all these useful
details, and might know what to make of them, but until
then, Garrison could see no good reason to rock the
proverbial boat. So he just shrugged and stood his watch in
silence.

Brinna and Konos stowed their gear in Rali's satchel,
marveling at the buttons and hidden pockets, and trying to
make good use of them. They tied their weapons to the pack
and secured it to a bulkhead beneath a small protruding
writing desk beside their rack, on the side of the cabin
opposite Garrison and the dogged hatch. Brinna took Konos'
hand and the Kenjah reclined patiently on their made bed.
Paunch was fast asleep at the foot, and Talto found himself
dozing as well. The space fell quiet, and the *Marvu* found
and tacked the leeward arm of the storm and its course
steadied against a port wind. Gradually, the rain outside the
ship began to intensify, but the keel held steady and
comfortably balanced on its vector. The Gunship was
tracking back out to the deeper seas to ride the maelstrom on
its own terms.

The Master at Arms reflected to himself that he
would have almost rather his wards had tried to escape rather

than all fallen asleep at once. Between the rain, the steady rhythm of the ship's roll, and the silence in the space, Garrison began to fight a succession of yawns. Fortunately, no one else was awake to see when a yawn got the better of him. Every *swelu* knew from experience that the best way to summon their captain was to let the yawns win during a watch. Garrison would not be caught sleeping, under any circumstances, but his desire for Bran's expeditious return grew, as Bran's return grew less and less expeditious.

As Talto drifted off, the word *Pathfinder* drifted silently from his lips once more.

***

Captain Bran, his navigator Troy, and his first mate Hinds, spoke in hushed tones at the helm of the *Marvu*. They had put the storm to their port bow and were making a valiant run to avoid getting pinched between the hostile winds and the craggy shores of Omnia. Hinds was quietly recounting a recent and widespread wave of strange dreams among sleepless crew. Troy was nodding along and making note of familiar elements in common with his own dreams. Bran was shaking his head and listening in grim silence.

"Pelton says hes's seen the Kenjah and their companions drowning each other in the waters near the Kalama temple. Offey told me he's seen everyone on board the ship diving into the frigid deep in the middle of the night. Says it gave him hot terrors and now he thinks about it every night and can't sleep a wink. Bad news captain. These passengers are just plain bad news." Hinds was shaking his head with Bran, concurring with the bad omens. Troy interjected.

"Tell him what Stilver told us this morning, Hinds. About the monster!" Troy trailed off into a cautious whisper. Bran looked sharply at them both, expressing intrigue, but not knowing what to make of anything either of them were saying.

"Stilver says he awoke this morning covered in sweat and shaking, Cap. Says he saw the Leviathan herself; says she rose up out of the water like the Dab, howling and wailing and flailing about with all her limbs awhirl. Eyes black as coal and furious as the wind itself. Skin like dark leather, he says. Says she lifted the *Marvu* out of the drink like a child's toy, held the thing aloft in front of her face, just screaming and hateful and wicked, says he woke up right as she was flinging the ship away from the temple. Says he felt his guts in his throat flying through the air, clinging to the railing for dear life but knowing he was surefire dead as soon as the thing landed. Says he saw all of us just sliding and tumbling head over holes off the deck and into the broiling froth. And Stilver ain't no wog either Cap. We both go way back, and we've both seen some crazy things in our day, but he says he ain't never seen anything like what he saw in that dream, and swears he can't shake it. I can't remember the last time I seen ol' Stilver scared of anything at all, you know? A man like that you gotta take serious, Cap."

"Stilver ain't no wog Cap, that's for sure. I seen her too, Cap. Just this last night before we pulled the moorings. Only what I saw didn't make no sense. I saw the same creature, I'm sure I did. I could feel it in my bones-- it was her! But she wasn't the size of no mountain. I watched her slither aboard the ship and take the form of a woman. Naked as a brass hook and twice as sharp, Cap. Only way you could tell was those eyes. But the weird part Cap, she took the form of a Kenjah girl. Skin glowing all different colors and everything. I could tell she wasn't no Kenjah, though. It was like she was heavy. The deckboards creaked and splintered under her steps, and when she was all the way aboard it seemed like the whole ship just sort of leaned under her, until the waterline was almost up to the rails. My last thought was that we was going under for sure."

Bran's brow furrowed. There were no two men in the world whose judgement he trusted more. He remembered Garrison coming on his watch looking red eyed and ghost bitten, but Bran had figured his M-A and the boys had just gotten the better end of the taps while they were ashore. If Garrison had had strange dreams, he might as likely have not mentioned them at all without knowing or hearing of anyone else onboard having similar stories. Garrison was not easily shaken by anything, and frankly, he wasn't the type of mate to be easily bested by the pisswater they pour in Call. Troy and Hinds waited for Bran to speak, and Bran was trying to decide what, if anything at this particular moment, he might should say about his own night terrors.

"What about the old tramp or the birdling? Anyone mentioned seeing them? I wonder how they fit into all this."

"Nothing much on them, Cap. Nabul says he figures they all gave him fake names last night, by the way the Kenjah and the birdling exchanged their little glances when the old tramp introduced them. Says he didn't really think anything of it. Lots of folks travel under aliases for lots of reasons. Says it weren't his business and they all seemed harmless enough. Arms not withstanding, sir, of course." Hinds and Troy shared each other's blank skepticism, and Hinds had nothing further to add.

Bran eventually shrugged. "Well boys, on the one hand, I got sixty three souls aboard to look out for and a timetable to keep. We've got a year of stores and provisions for the Kalama, and if they don't get 'em, every ship at sea might be in danger of the consequences. We've got a sacred truce to abide. On the other hand, these folks are guests on

my ship and so far, they've done us no wrong. Their business
with the Kalama, whatever it may be, is their business and not
ours. These things are tricky, you know. Dreams... Dreams are
only ever pieces and fragments. We don't know one way or
the other, the way I see it. I don't want to provoke an
encounter with the Kalamaii if I can help it, but how can I
know whether it might be them or us that brings it about?
Say we mistreat these folks, unjustly, as it were, and that's the
reason things go sour on us? Or maybe we were all just
doomed the moment they came aboard? No way to tell. Old
man says he's a soothsayer and a traveling mage. Doubtful
story, maybe, but how do I know? He does seem a bit odd, I'll
grant."

Hinds and Troy dutifully concurred with the
captain's analysis of his quandary, and could not improve
upon it. Bran thought hard about what he knew and what he
had heard, and finally made his judgement. "Give 'em all a
wide berth and keep 'em happy. I'll corner the old man when
the time is right. We'll see if we can get the whole story out of
him, and if we can't, well? Boys, we're just gonna have to sail
straight and keep our bearing until the puzzle pieces put
themselves together. Garrison has been down there with
them for a little while. He's got sharp eyes; we'll see if he's
picked up any useful clues. Troy, stay focused on keeping us
alongside this storm and out of the hairy parts. Hinds, put
word around to the men to keep the loose talk of bad dreams
and strange omens secured. Our best odds probably follow
our best manners. Let's show these folks some good old
fashioned *Marvu* hospitality and see if we're not better off
keeping odd friends than making odd enemies. Heard?"

"Heard!" the men rejoined, and resumed their posts.
Bran made his way down to the galley to check on the
morning meal, and then climbed below decks to the

berthings to check on his newest shipmates. *Talto, Konos, Brinna, and Paunch.* Made up names, of course. But so far, that seemed like the least unusual thing about them. Talto seemed the senior rank in the party, so Talto was where he would focus his efforts.

When he arrived at the Kenjah's cabin, he gave a soft double-rap on the hatch to alert Garrison of his arrival, and Garrison promptly turned the dogs and granted entrance. Bran grinned at Garrison when he entered the space, and chuckled at the old tramp, the birdling, and the snoring Kenjah, all fast asleep and seemingly without a care in the world. Bran immediately noticed the sharp corners on the made rack, and approved. Little things like this were significant at sea. Garrison looked relieved to be relieved, but seemed otherwise undisturbed. Bran decided not to wake the riders until breakfast was served. He nodded a pantomime to Garrison, who comprehended. Both of them exited the space noiselessly, and left the sleeping passengers in peace, unattended.

"What do you make of them Garrison? Hinds and Troy tell me the whole ship is awash with strange dreams about sea monsters. You had any strange dreams lately?"

Garrison was a naturally quiet fellow, and Bran waited with customary patience for his M-A to construct his response carefully. "The old fellow is a clocksmith sir. I think the Kenjah are his conscripts. One of them is armed with enchanted Kalama relics. The birdling is rather obnoxious, but basically harmless, as Viermah go anyway. As for me, sir, I've had some trouble sleeping in general lately. But if I've had any strange dreams I can't remember them."

"Well, M-A, that's a relief. From the sound of it, if you'd had any of the kinds of dreams I've been hearing about, I think you'd remember. Do me a favor, will you? If you have any strange dreams, or if you notice anything odd or out of place, don't be shy about it. There are some strange things afoot on this voyage Gary, and I'd like to be kept abreast of things, whether they seem silly or strange or significant, I'll be the judge. Heard?"

"Heard, Captain. Will do."

"A clocksmith, you say? Can you be sure?"

"I'm never really sure of anything Cap, but they all made a big fuss over this odd little stone the brute had in one of his short swords. The old one gave it to him on the way here, apparently at the behest of that old swamp witch, which is where they're coming from. I can't say why exactly, sir, but I suspect they've been having some pretty strange experiences themselves. What are we going to do about them? I take it you're lifting the confinement order, or I'd still be stuck in there watching them all sleep the day away. Do you think they're dangerous?"

Bran was searching his mind for anything and everything he knew about... about the *Epozia*, which was not very much. He had heard plenty of good sea stories and got the basic gist, but he'd never heard any stories about clocksmiths coming *to sea*. "I don't rightly know yet, Gary. I assume everyone's dangerous in a corner, so for now, we're gonna try to make them comfy and avoid antagonizing them. We've got a storm to beat, nets to cast when we beat it if we're to eat, and quite a bit of cargo to deliver to the temple before the next new moon. Let's be friendly, and accommodating, as we would be with any other riders, and we'll wait for them to play their own hand and see how they play it. Heard?"

Garrison gave himself a moment to consider his instructions, and then snapped his affirmative and was dismissed.

Bran lagged behind as his M-A departed the berthings, and he took one last baleful look at the cabins where his mysterious new riders would reside for the season. He had decided to withhold his own bothersome dreams, for now anyway.

A *clocksmith* aboard the *Marvu*. Bran smiled to himself and shrugged, parsing from a vague sense of ill-defined trepidation just a novel little twinge of pride. Sometimes, the *Marvu* sought adventure. Sometimes, adventure sought the *Marvu*. Something about the improbability of it all just made it all the more believable. Bran shook his head and shrugged again, to no one in particular, and decided to conduct a few spot checks throughout the ship before breakfast. The morning had barely begun, and already the day felt hectic and long. The *Marvu* sped along, riding high upon its keel in the coriolis wind, heaving gently toward uncertainty and peril. Finally, some excitement!

***

Paunch was the first to stir. The rumbling had moved from his head to his stomach, but his attention quickly turned to the tiny little feathers already beginning to sprout along his shoulders and arms. "Would you look at that!" It had not yet occurred to him that he was the only one awake, and in the moment, he had quite forgotten anyone else was in the cabin. Talto's eyes popped open, and as soon as they did he felt the groans converging from every joint and tendon in his body and erupting from his lips unrestrained. This mournful sound drew Konos and Brinna back to the waking world around them.

"It looks like we've lost our warden. I suppose that means we're no longer confined?" Brinna and Konos shared a loving embrace and a long yawn before scrambling to their feet and donning the largest sets of shipboard linens Garrison or Bran or somebody could have produced for them. On Brinna, all quietly agreed that they were tight enough to be rather flattering. On Konos, all readily agreed they looked absurd, and the sleeves tore before he could even pull them all the way on. Talto found his own issue hung a little loosely for his tastes, but he was thrilled at the prospect of removing the hairshirt for the first time in ages, and replacing it with something so much more airy and soft. Shipboard linens are washed in bulk and redistributed randomly by size and by nothing else. They are well made and durable, but they see extensive service, and the constant exposure to the salty sea water renders them threadbare and translucent over time. The Kenjah were the color of brine, and not bothered by this at all, apparently, but Talto felt somewhat exposed, and this feeling was readily confirmed by the bashful smirk on Paunch's face as Paunch watched them all don their uniforms.

Paunch conceded to the trousers, but decided against the shirt so that his mottled natal down could come in uninhibited. Viermah naturally spend a considerable portion of their lives with their backs to the sun, and Paunch supposed himself reasonably well suited for that aspect of topside life. He stowed his helm, for the time being, in the Kenjah's satchel, neatly folded and stuffed into a pocket behind where Konos had sinched their blades. The four of them pulled each themselves and each other to their feet and steadied their legs against the motions of the *Marvu*, and looked each other over.

Sailors now, one and all.

"Talto, I'm guessing you're the only one here who's been aboard a ship before. What are they going to require of us here? And what happens next, you suppose?" Paunch's footing was a little unsure, and he took to instinctively bracing himself against whatever happened to be fast and within reach. "I wonder if they'll let me drive!" At this, the Kenjah giggled a little in spite of themselves, and Talto shrugged.

"Paunch, if you find yourself driving this ship, I would imagine the circumstances to be such that we all simply have no other choice."

"You know, *Talto.* I think I would have preferred to have been consulted on *Paunch* before you settled on it, incidentally."

"Paunch, there's a lot about this trip so far I wish I'd been in on prior to its coming to be. We don't always get what we want. Unless we're these two here, I guess. Enjoy your luxury cruise kids!" Talto winked and poked Konos in a familiar way, and the gesture was warmly received. "As for your duties, *Paunchy* my lad, I expect it to be mostly housekeeping and such. Bran, if he's the sort of man I expect he is, will likely wash the whole ship from buttons to boom at least once every other day. Half the crew will rotate on those shifts, and they'll likely split us all up, so look for that probably once or twice a week, depending on your rotation. It's not hard work, and it's usually how you get a bath of your own around here. If we ever make it ashore again, you'll smell like lemon oil and wood soap for the rest of your life.

"Then there's food and laundry. If any of you can cook, I strongly suggest you mention your love of laundry out loud in front of someone who looks important before the day is out. If none of you can cook, I would ask you all please to consider remaining silent on either issue either way. Anyway, Hinds will likely have these broken up by thirds or fourths, but you'll all likely get one or the other once every day or so, depending on how he does it.

"If the wind abandons us, we'll all wind up down in the galley pulling the long oars, and frankly folks, I'd advise you all to consider saying a little prayer once or twice a day for favorable winds. You'll occasionally hear every other sailor on board mumbling these to themselves at some point or other. Gunships carrying annual provisions with skeleton crews tend to be rather cumbersome at long stretches, as I'm sure you can all imagine. You'll find many of the traditions out here seem borne of myth and legend, but are indeed deeply rooted in the practical. The lords of these seas may not feel obliged to answer your prayers, it is said, but they do love hearing them.

"As far as the business of rigging and sailing and driving the ship, I believe the crew itself will retain those responsibilities, generally speaking, unless someone is injured or otherwise incapacitated. In which case, one or more of us are likely to receive crash courses in whatever job was occupied by whomever was reassigned to fill the vacancy. Duty and hierarchy are inextricably bound together in the organization of labor at sea. Everyone moves one notch forward, with the hindmost bringing in the slack. You are all the 'hindmost'.

"As I am old, and weary and infirm and brittle and so on... I will likely wind up walking around the ship trying to amuse the captain with whatever fanciful tales of the landed folk he can stand. And I suspect the sun will not set before Mr. Bran corners me with quite a few very delicate questions about myself and all of you, and where we're going and so forth. While we're on the subject, we're going to the Kalama Temple, and the thereafter is our business. Sailors are curious creatures, but are not nosey by nature. If you are up to nefarious purposes, they will sniff you out in myriad other ways, but otherwise, they will tend to leave you to your own.

"When your work is done, obviously you'll be expected to stay out from underfoot by those whose work is not, but otherwise, you'll have plenty of time to your own ends. When I was last aboard this vessel, there was a fine library below decks, with books on a fascinating array of subjects. I suspect it remains. Bran's bearing and meter strike me as having a delightfully literary bent. If there was a library to curate, I'd wager Rali's purse of my pine coins Bran is the type to demand the job. If you can't find me, that's probably where I'll be. And if you still can't find me, I would kindly request you begin a more urgent inquiry into my whereabouts as soon as possible. Which brings me to an important point. If no one *sees* you go in, no one is going to *hear* you go in. Understand? If you're by yourself, anywhere at any time, please do yourself the enormous favor of steering clear of the rails.

"I suspect we'll outrun this storm and clear the midshelves by a quarter moon or so. We'll drop nets for three days and for those three days folks, this ship will be a madhouse. No one will sleep. No one will rest. And nothing with gills that we can stuff in a cargo hold has a prayer of reaching any other destination. Since we're fishing for the Kalama, it is a near certainty that we will have perfect weather, calm waters, and nets sagging with every conceivable waterborne creature that won't break the ropes. It's the only expedition you'll see all year 'round at sea where the nets go unmolested by those waterborne creatures that *can* break the nets. The haul will be enough to feed the Kalama and compensate the *Marvu* until next cycle's cold season. Then the *Marvu* will go on again fending for itself as it always has, and some other ship out of the city of Moan, probably an ice cutter, will break its way out through the northern seas to find the tides towing in the Temple.

You'll understand that part when you see it, but if you didn't know, the Temple isn't fixed or anchored. It moves about Omnia on the warm currents, which the Kalamaii spend their lives following. It will look like an island, and you have to remind yourself that the whole thing was *built.* And not just built, but built in a time when the lores would still work together on such projects. Every part of it was hewn out of some region of Omnia and carted to the western seas, loaded onto great raft ships, which have since gone out of fashion, and assembled on location. Really, just a spectacular example of architecture, craftsmanship, and ingenuity, but of the power of cooperation most of all. You will see, my friends, that my words simply do not do it justice. You will remind yourselves daily that the thing did not just spring up out of the ocean on its own. If you fail to remind yourself, I think, you really will miss something very important about where you are. When our nets and holds can hold no more, and the sea laps at our rails for the weight of the *Marvu* under its load, the captain will direct the navigator to direct the pilot to tack the rudder towards the Temple.

"If we can make it that far, my friends, I will administer stones before we reach the Kalama. We're not going to get many chances to get this right, and *Ursal* must be persuaded. We will have to be prepared to offer her *more* than she actually wants or needs, and we'll have to give it to her just the same." As Talto trailed off, the Kenjah were zeroed in, hanging on every word and nodding in time when they understood, glancing at each other for synchronicity and concurrence, and committing his every word to memory.

Paunch was, again, fast asleep.

Talto leaned into his conscripts and spoke softly.

"Konjo, while we are at sea, if anything should happen, if we are attacked or if there is some kind of unexpected crisis, I want you to give Marla's stone to Brinka. I don't know what to make of your dream, my dear Brinka, but the stone might save your life. Set the thing in your pommel, and whatever you do, don't lose your blade. Konjo, this is important my lad. You'll hear bells throughout the ship. Loud, staccato bells, ringing in a repetitive rhythm. A bell will strike the hour, Konjo. A couple of bells signal a ship approaching. A few bells for reveille and taps. A few good hard rings, always twice, means the captain wants all hands on deck, usually for an announcement or for a holiday gathering or something like that. But if you hear the fellow just start wailing on those bells like they deserve the beating, you get yourselves armed and fight the ship wherever you're called. But make sure you give her that stone, Konjo!"

"I want a stone for my bow!" Paunch was awake and listening intently. "What does it do anyway? What's so special about Marla's stone?"

A light tap at the hatch startled everyone just a little, and Bran sort of leaned into the space, bracing himself on a dog with one arm and holding open the hatch with the other. The *Marvu* was rocking a bit more tenaciously now as the navigator began steering into the storm to keep his sails full.

"Welcome folks. Feeling better young lady? I apologize for locking you guys down this morning like I did, I promise it was nothing personal. In truth, I have kind of been waiting for all of you, but I didn't know I was waiting for you until I found you all aboard my ship this morning. I'll come straight to the point, if you all don't mind. I think the thing in your dream, Brinna, is the thing you guys are going to try to bring aboard my ship. Now, I can't make much sense of that, personally, but I'm sure our soothesaying friend here will manage to convince me in time that this is a sensible course of action. May I register my humble protest in advance? I suppose we'll enter that harbor when we approach it. For now, I suppose I should tell you that I'm happy to see you. I worried that you wouldn't come, that you were just a figment of my own fever dreams of late. I'll permit you all to reveal yourselves in your own way on your own time, and for now, I suppose I'll keep my own secrets as well.

"I am Bran, your captain, of course. The grizzly fellow with me earlier is my first mate, and he'll be responsible for your needs and obligations while you're aboard my ship. The brute I left in here with you earlier is my Master at Arms. He's in charge of punching you if I need him to, so let's all agree to give that fellow there an uneventful ride. I'm sure we all find that to be a reasonable enough request, but if there should be any contentions on those grounds, I should mention, Gary's also in charge of throwing people off my ship if I need him too, and he'll have plenty of good help.

"You may have occasion to meet my navigator. If something happens to me, or if I am not aboard this vessel for any reason, you will kindly defer to his authority in all matters. You will find his judgement sound and his spine resolute."

Bran had made it through his indoc, and looked his riders over one good time. "Talto, Paunch, Konos. And Brinna. Inlanders in search of adventure, you say. I suspect that much is true enough. For now."

Bran took a breath, slouched a little, and smiled in an honest way.

"Who wants breakfast?"

(Splinter)

Talto and his conscripts ate in peace with the crew that morning. The captain and his officers were in high spirits but said little. Nabul and the nightwatch were served first, and by the time the rest of the crew and riders were seated, the nightwatch was already gone to their berthings to sleep the day away. The navigator's helmsman ate with them and returned to relieve the navigator, who sat with the captain at the middle of a long table surrounded by enlisted men. Hinds ate with the riders, and Garrison ate by the hatch to the mess, alone. Of the riders, there were comparatively few this morning, as Nabul had suggested there would be.

Two older gentlemen politely identified themselves as merchants when Talto sat down beside them. These two explained that their function was to coordinate and supervise the annual provision of the Kalama Temple. By all rights, the bulk of the *Marvu's* cargo was effectively under their charge until it was safely offloaded to the island. A young woman sat opposite them, alternating between her utensils and her stylus and parchment. She looked up gingerly enough, and acknowledged those around her as they arrived, but whatever words she had were shared exclusively with the thick dusty journal beside her plate. She seemed attentive to her surroundings, however preoccupied, and one could tell that she was listening to every word anyone said around her, but she contributed none of her own. She pecked at her food somewhat absently, between inspired paragraphs.

A man and a woman with two small children also sat with the riders. The lady explained at some length that they were inclined to show their children the world. The children seemed less enthusiastic about the prospect, and were already restless and bored, finding little of interest on their plates, but very curious about the sailors and their strange clothes and tongues. The last of the riders was a small band of traveling musicians whom the captain had personally invited along as entertainment for the crew. Musicians in Omnia will take any gig that affords them shelter and board for any length of time. With cooks and crew and officers and riders in attendance, there were roughly forty or so patrons in the mess. Conversation was slow between them this morning. Most were nursing hangovers from shore leave, and nearly all were hunched over their plates shoveling food into their faces with their elbows floating just off of the table.

Talto savored what he properly understood would be his last good hot meal for awhile. The Kenjah ate voraciously, while Paunch was somewhere in between. He was just as hungry, but the menu was a little exotic and offputting for his tastes. The grilled pork and butter biscuits, together with the cheese and fruit and syrup drenched cakes were appetizing enough, if somewhat foreign by themselves, but the lineman had served him a full scoop of poached eggs without even the courtesy of a second glance. Pauch poked at these with mixed sentiments. At some point, the silent comedy of this affair set itself on the minds of all parties observing, and Talto eventually leaned to assure Paunch that, while the pork and cakes and most of the cheeses and berries would soon vanish from the menu, the poached eggs would remain a consistent staple throughout most of the voyage. A little salt goes a long way.

Shared moments like these have a way of bonding indifferent strangers, and Paunch was very much aware of a little respectful chuckle at his expense that drifted from one end of the table to the other and formed virtually everyone's first good-natured impression of himself. Viermah did not habitually go to sea. Nor did Kenjah, for that matter, but hungry Kenjah will eat anything, it is said. After an internal battle with his own sense of propriety, Paunch found his resolve, and picked up a large spoonful of eggs, held it up in a kind of dry salute to his shipmates and new friends, looked around to make sure everyone was watching, and just swallowed the mouthful without any further hesitation. He would work it out privately in his soul later on, with a full stomach and a settled mind.

When the captain finished his breakfast, he left his seat with the crew and sat with the riders, all of whom had already received similar indoc speeches this morning. He had already committed all their names to memory, and set himself about introducing them all to one another, beginning with the young lady, who seemed to be a personal acquaintance of his own.

"Lua, my love! My muse! It is my pleasure to introduce you to Mond and Kamar, my accountants. This wonderful couple are Kuska and Deni, and their little ones are Piko and Paka, aren't they lovely! This is Talto and his adopted nephew Paunch, and these two fine souls are Konos and Brinna, who I am told are with child as well! And of course you know Batiste and the boys down there, hiyoo fellas!"

Lua beamed and dropped her utensils and her stylus and stood up to embrace Bran as long lost friends would do. None failed to note the obvious chemistry between them. Piko and Paka toiled disinterestedly with their eggs. Talto and his conscripts respectfully stood as well, not quite sure what else to do. Bran quickly waved them at ease and bid them be seated and enjoy their meal. Mond and Kamar, clearly old hands, proffered their sincere smiles to all in between bites and didn't bother with any formalities at all. Bran made it clear, without being explicit on this point, that his crew would abide by well-established traditions of shipboard etiquette, but the riders were to be treated as guests and would be mercifully spared from much of the professional protocol of shipboard life. If Bran still had it on his mind that Talto and his mysterious conscripts were all probably going to get everyone else on the ship killed and eaten by a mythical leviathan deity, he betrayed no sense of this in his bright eyes and bubbly nature. Bran and his crew were all plainly excited about this voyage for its own merits. The odds of another ship having been chosen for this year's provision were practically null, but the relative odds of any crew being alive in the right place at the right time to receive the honor of provisioning the great Kalama Temple were also comparatively low.

Lua greeted everyone as the captain made his polite introductions, and then set herself to gathering her pen and journal back into her satchel and made ready to depart with him when his own greetings were concluded.

"Folks, Hinds here will work out the duty roster this afternoon and will send a man around this evening around twilight to give your stations and assignments. I trust you'll all be responsible for the condition of your own living spaces and the surrounding areas as a general rule, but otherwise you

are all welcome guests aboard the *Marvu* and will have plenty
of leisure time to relax, explore the ship, make friends as you
will, and enjoy the ride. You will have the balance of this day
to yourselves to get your sea legs and orient yourselves. If you
have a question or a concern or need something specific, every
crewman aboard my ship has explicit instructions to make
themselves as available and hospitable as their duties will
permit, so please do not hesitate to come to anyone you see
with anything you have. If you need me for something, please
see either Hinds or Garrison, and they will make appropriate
arrangements, of course. Under no circumstances is my
navigator to be approached for any reason. He is not an
antisocial man, by any means, in fact you will find him quite
amusing and outgoing when his duties permit him to
socialize. But the plain and simple fact is that his first and
only priority is the safe conduct of this vessel and its crew. For
urgent matters, you will find at all times a deck officer at the
bow and stern of the ship."

The riders listened and nodded and 'yessired' the
captain as he proceeded through his speech, and when Bran
was sure everyone had heard and understood him to their
own satisfaction, he took Lua's free hand and bid them all a
safe and pleasant voyage. Before he turned to go, he found
Talto's gaze and addressed the old mage directly.

"If you have the *time*, my good sir, I would very much
like to address a few additional matters with you when you're
done here. Will you be so kind as to find your way to one of
my officers when you're ready and they will escort you to my
cabin or to wherever I may be at the time? Excellent! Thank
you all very much enjoy your breakfast! Lua, my love, will you
join me for a little stroll about the ship? Lua, everyone!"

As Lua waved to depart, Hinds stood first, in
adherence to the custom of noble men, looked her in the eyes,

and shook her hand firmly and respectfully. Konos had instinctively stood with him, though he had to kind of lean awkwardly over the table to reach her hand. Following their example, the rest of the men at the table arose to do the same. They all waited until Lua and the captain had made their way out of the mess before retaking their seats.

When they were all settled and picking at their food again, Hinds sat back down and addressed them all at once. Hinds was a grizzly sort of fellow with hard eyes and wild hair, and a tattoo which covered almost half of his face, but he spoke with a genteel patience that was effectively disarming. This, Talto privately observed, indicated years of practise in managing the needs and obligations of his rambunctious crew. Here was a man who had competently earned the trust and loyalty of all with whom he served. Where the captain had been somewhat brisk in speech, however friendly in tone, Hinds spoke slowly and calmly, and would pause to wait for his own words to form. He smiled with his eyes and talked with this hands. He slouched a little, in a familiar way, and would lean towards whomever he addressed, conveying a deeply personal intensity that marked his character and style.

"Well folks, I think Bran hit all the high notes there. I would like to second his point about everyone on this ship making themselves readily available, so again, please don't hesitate. My guys are good guys, and they all know this ship like the lines on their own mothers' faces. If we haven't met, I'm Hinds. I'm the First Mate aboard the *Marvu,* and as such, the crew and its riders are my responsibility. I will make it a point to try to check on all of you individually at least once a day, as I'm able. Or I'll send a man around if I'm not.

"Laundry is located aft, near the back of the ship. There is a lovely little library beside it that serves coffee until about midday, and tea from sunup to sundown. You'll all work as you're able, and so that you leave the ship with no more or less money than you came with, you'll be awarded credits for your shifts. The little library also serves as a kind of ship's store where you can get a little smoke and bitters, as our supplies permit, and toiletries and other things you might have need of. Once a week or so, the captain will gather the crew and riders together on the bow for some recreation. These musicians here will master the ceremonies, so if you like to drink and dance and mingle, you are sure to have a memorable time. If you can sing or tell stories, you will not find a more gracious or attentive audience anywhere in the world. Don't be shy, and don't be stingy with your gifts either. Entertainment is precious to us out here, you understand. Anything that takes our minds off of the monotony and danger of sea life is welcome and certainly well received. On a long enough voyage, stories are pretty much how we all get to know each other.

"If I've missed anything, I'm sure I'll remember it as soon as we've all parted ways. For now, I'd like to know if any of you, other than Mond and Kamar here, have been to sea before? And do any of you have any particular preferences regarding your duty assignments?"

Talto was the only one who spoke up on the first point. "Talto, good sir. Pleased, of course! I have spent considerable time at sea in my long days. In fact, I rode the *Marvu* under Captain Pike, many years ago. I'm happy to help wherever you might find me useful."

Hinds smiled again at Talto, approvingly, and shook his hand.

The Kenjah promptly seized the moment, as they had been instructed to do. "We're Brinna and Konos, and we're both very good at doing laundry, sir." Talto stifled a chuckle, but Hinds didn't miss it, and curved a little knowing grin back at Talto in return.

"Roger that, shipmates. Roger that!"

Paunch, who was now getting something a little bit like jaundice around the eyes and ears, was holding on to the table against the motion of the *Marvu* and also trying to physically hold the breakfast in his stomach with the other hand, merely squeaked.

"I have never been to sea, sir. I am terrified you may find me useless."

Hinds nodded, gently. "No one is useless at sea my dear Viermah. We'll get those legs under you in no time!" Paunch's expression betrayed a wave of uncomfortable and unfamiliar sensations.

'Convinced' was not among them.

Hinds had already made up his mind. The old mage would be given the library for the duration of the voyage. The Kenjah would work together in shifts in the galley, cooking for the crew. Paunch would clear the tables and wash about a million dishes. The husband and wife with the children would work the laundry. Mond and Kamar would naturally be exempt from the duty rotations, according to their seniority and status as envoys for the Kalama. And the band would have plenty of work of their own cut out for them, when they weren't doing laundry or washing dishes with the seasick birdling who was, presently, now running earnestly toward the nearest bin to return his eggs. The crew were always on alert for inevitable moments like these on every voyage, and they all gave in to amused cheers of satisfaction and approval. Paunch felt as though he'd received enough attention for one day, but steadfastly wiped his chin and stood proudly, cupping his hands together and shaking them over both shoulders to indicate his happiness to be of service to these adoring new fans. Then he threw up again and ran out of the mess.

At this point, a general and spontaneous consensus formed amongst the remaining riders that breakfast was effectively concluded. Utensils dropped onto plates, benches screeched backwards across the deck away from the adjoined tables, nods and smiles and mutual salutations were exchanged as crewmen appeared to clear the trays, and Talto and his conscripts politely made their way out of the mess to follow Paunch, with the other riders straggling out behind them on their various paths. The sailors were not so easily dissuaded, and went back to their own plates with unabated enthusiasm.

Talto decided to go and find the captain directly, and to bring the Kenjah with him. He had some sense of the conversations they were all going to need to have, and his assessment of Bran as a captain had persuaded him that the best course of action would be to meet these matters head on, and to be as truthful and upfront about their business with the Kalamaii as prudence and propriety would permit. He intuited that the young lady Lua was Bran's scribe and would not be so uncouth as to speculate beyond that point, but upon grasping the fact, Talto figured Bran would probably want Lua to listen in just the same. Best to do a little aimless dawdling on their way about the ship to give Bran and his friend an appropriate amount of time to catch up, but to try to catch them both before they parted ways. Talto had shaped a thought in his mind as he watched the young lady working through breakfast. He was thinking about the last few days and all that had happened when the thought came.

Someone really ought to be writing all of this down.

They found Bran and Lua on the bow after wandering around and touring the ship to kill some time.

The *Marvu* tacked along the outer edge of a mammoth storm, and the rainslogged wind was furious. The captain and his consort held tight to the railing to support themselves against the roiling tide, but they both seemed otherwise unmoved and undisturbed. Talto approached on sore and unsteady legs, holding the rails as well and nearly climbing, with Paunch and the Kenjah climbing along behind him. The skies to the port bow were black and raging, even in midday. All of them were drenched to the core, their linens accomplishing little more than highlighting everything that they meant to conceal. The air was electric, and little flashes of lightning routinely danced and sparked across the silver rods buried in the taller masts. A flurry of seamen received shouted orders and passed them along as they busied themselves fighting the booms and lines. The Kenjah were the color of snowcaps, and Paunch was just green from helm to spur.

"Captain!" Talto shouted, and Bran turned to see the spectacle of inlanders clinging to the rails for dear life with a little satisfied twinkle curving the edge of his lips and eyes. Lua arched an eyebrow in a friendly but bemused way, and as Talto and his conscripts reached the bow at last, they pulled alongside the captain to take in the breathless view of the tempest, each of them shaking the captain's hand and greeting his companion with deference, but in the chaos of wind and rain, reaching for and finding little else to say in the way of proceeding. "I suppose this washer will make landfall around sundown. Do you think it will break when it hits the shelves? I'd hate to be in Call tonight if it doesn't!"

"I don't think it's going to land, my friend. This is no ordinary storm. This is a pusher! The Kalamaii kicked it up to drive us toward the Temple. You see, we don't actually know where it is. It's always moving, following a sort of migratory pattern around Omnia, you understand. In this way, the Kalamaii protect their followers and attendants from marauders and nefarious interests; no one ever knows for sure exactly what course to chart if they wanted to find the island. We are instructed to steer into its edge and just hold full sail, and the Kalamaii direct the storm across the surface, basically towing us in whatever direction they choose. It's never a straight line, on the one hand because of the centrifugal arc we follow, but also so we can't plot the stars and record their position. I'm told we'll see a few days of sunshine when they bring us to where we are to sink our nets. Otherwise, get used to the rain folks!"

Paunch and the Kenjah knew none of these things, and each of them wondered whether or not Talto knew, or if he was just making conversation. Either way, they all turned their attention back to the storm with a new sense of awe and admiration. One must appreciate the irony: a big ship with an able crew going to drop their nets to catch their quarry, but the ship itself and her crew were all already ensnared and subject to the whims of something much larger and more powerful. The great *Marvu* was mere quarry in its own right, to the Kalamaii. None had heretofore considered the scope of their errand in light of this newfound perspective. *This* was the work of the creature they were going to try to persuade. Talto was not immune to the collective shudder that ran through his conscripts as these thoughts dawned upon them, and it was only by contemplation of this asymmetry that the captain's concern with their objective could be properly understood. Agreeing to let the Kalamaii drive his ship via hurricane was quite enough of a dubious proposal, thank you very much. Surrendering his own command to a Kalamaii was another proposition altogether.

Talto understood in his bones that Bran had already directed the course of their conversation in a consciously deliberate way. He didn't want to talk about the weather. He wanted to talk about *Ursal*. Talto did not need his premonitory prowess to sense that Bran already knew a great deal more than Talto might have believed when they came aboard. Bran confirmed this immediately, when he leaned in and whispered on the wind what only Talto could hear.

"Does she already know you're here, Talthielle?"

Talto folded. He was in no position to insult his captain's intelligence.

"I don't know, Captain. I assume so. Apparently, she wouldn't be the only one. I've been on the road for days now, and for some reason, everyone seems to know we're coming before we arrive. Everyone except Call, that is. A peculiar clue I'm still wrestling with, among many other questions without answers. How did you know?"

"I might have guessed, you know?" Bran was a natural born brinksman.

"Yes, I suppose you might have. Your security chief spent enough time with us this morning. I'm sure he picked up enough basic details for you to put a coherent picture together."

Bran nodded and looked out upon the amorphous horizon, volunteering nothing yet. Talthielle admired the diplomatic bearing and the seductive restraint. But he wasn't fooled.

"But you didn't guess, Captain. Did you?"

Bran looked Talthielle in the eye and smiled a friendly smile, and shook his head quietly, and winked, and looked out to sea again. After a few more moments of reverence, Lua punched Bran in the ribs and cocked her head toward the tower. Bran nodded his head obediently, and suggested they all reconvene on the Bridge, which was two levels above the main deck in the tower. They climbed their way along the port rails towards the midship, and then hustled themselves indoors by timing their dash with the heaving starboard list of the *Marvu*. Paunch trailed with Talto and helped him from the rails across the deck and inside the oh-one, where the enlisted ranks stored a vast array of spare cables and folded sails and other impermanent components related to their various occupations. Up a spiraling ladder into the oh-two, which was full of maps and logs and served as a conference room for the officers, as well as a kind of unofficial break room. There were a few chairs bolted into the bulkhead, and a couple of long wooden tables in the middle with charts and plottings tacked or gummed to their surfaces in meticulous arrangements. The oh-three was the Bridge, where the navigator and the first mate were stationed when they were not on watch or roving.

Bran, Lua, Talto, Konos, Brinna, and Paunch crowded into a cramped space stilted beneath the oh-four on all sides to permit an unobstructed view in all directions, and protected from the elements by dazzlingly ingenious feats of angular carpentry and structural design. The oh-four was just an overhead platform on top of the tower, which served as the colors station and as a general observatory, and common area when the sea wasn't actively trying to drown the crew. This is called a crow's nest, and every great ship has some version of one. From the Bridge, looking forward and aft, one can see the whole wide panorama of creation, from just below the respective gunmounts all the way out past the horizon and up to the carved overhang extending several feet out in all directions from the deck of the crow's nest. It is this gently sloping overhang which keeps the Bridge dry in inclement weather. From the Bridge, the captain and his officers can observe all conditions topside and shout orders to crewmen below, called runners, who would swiftly relay those to the pilot and his helmsmen, the boatswains, and the deckhands.

The *Marvu* carried two large cannons, which mounted forward and aft beneath the tower, and were stored on the keel decks in the bow and stern compartments and serve as weight distributing stabilizers during peace time. What remained topside of the cannon assembly was the base ring and the carriage, which resembled two jutting tuning fork structures on a sturdy round swivel. If the order to battle stations was given, four hands each would scramble below decks to haul up the barrels and mount them on the carriage. The forward interior of the main deck had sections of false planking which, when removed, permitted access to the ships armory of balls, fuses, and powder. Understandably, smoking aboard ship was emphatically restricted to the stern. Hinds drilled his crew down to a three minute mount in the aft station, and nearly four and half minutes forward.

On its present course, the *Marvu* fielded no cannons and flew no colors. It didn't require signals or designators or identifiers, because it would encounter no other ships on this mission. It didn't need its cannons because even if it did, they wouldn't do any good. Still, Bran kept his armory fully stocked, and Hinds kept his men well drilled and ready. Cannons might not do much good against whatever they might have to confront out here, but at least cannons would at least make them feel like they tried. The *Marvu* and her crew would never concede helplessness or surrender in a fight, no matter how overwhelming the odds.

After a brief and wind-beaten tour of the Bridge, Bran led his friends and riders back down to the oh-two and out and down through a rear hatch which opened into a rather cozy little saddlebag at the base of the tower behind the aft mount. This was the Captain's cabin, where he slept, washed, studied, wrote, and entertained. Three sides of the cabin were bounded by tables and couches and pocked with little shaded portholes. The fourth side abutted the crewman's area of the oh-one, and on the captain's side of this bulkhead there hung a sprawling and faded map of Omnia, with nautical lines and the ancient names of ancient towns and cities labeled in ancient languages. Beneath this was a spartan cot and a small wash basin, each with retractable drawers built into their frames beneath for secure storage of his personal effects. From a trunk at the foot of his cot he produced several rolls of ship's wool, which he distributed to his grateful guests. They all wrapped themselves and plopped down on the furniture. The cabin was comparatively warm and the couches were plush and comfortable. Bran retrieved a wineskin from his personal stash, popped the cork and passed it around.

Lua took the first draught, then Paunch and the Kenjah. As Lua handed the skin to Talto, Bran was asking them in a congenial way about their real intentions with the Kalama and their deity.

When Talto's hand touched Lua's, however, his vision abruptly went black just as a ball of lightning peeled across the walls of Bran's cabin. Talto swam in the abyssal void of splintering consciousness and disorientation for what felt like an eternal heartbeat, before his senses returned. When they did, Talto was stunned to find only himself, Brinna, Lua, and the captain in the space. His jaw locked and his heart raced, but no one seemed to notice his struggle right away. Brinna was speaking in sour tones, and Konos and Paunch were nowhere to be seen, and only Talto seemed to notice.

"It was all that bastard Jorgan's fault. That scum! I knew I hated him on sight, but Talthielle here said we would be okay." Brinna's words were contemptuous, and only added to Talto's confusion. "He was surly and rude as soon as he opened the door. He clearly hated strangers in general, and seemed to have a special hatred for Konjo and me. We just wanted to buy some food and some supplies and be on our way. But no! This waste of human skin and bones was just so aggressively confrontational and disrespectful. We weren't there more than a few minutes before he became so intolerable and nasty that my poor beloved had had enough and just laid him right out. If only we'd known that wouldn't be the end of it, we'd have just as soon torn that bastard's limbs off. I swear if we ever make it back to that town, I will find him and finish the job!" Brinna was seething.

"So we took what we needed, and we left a stack of pine coins to pay for it, and we just left. But we weren't on the road for more than a couple of leagues when this guy appears on the road behind us with a whole screeching mob of fanatics with clubs and swords, screaming about how we broke into his shop and waylaid him and robbed him. So we ran! What else could we do? We ran through the night until they finally gave up and turned away, or at least we thought they did. We went into the marshes and made camp for the night, mud slogged and exhausted. But we were awakened in the middle of the night by Jorgan and a band of blood thirsty trappers." Brinna's tones began to sink from rage to mourning, and as Talto began to put the pieces together, his heart sank as well. "My Konjo fought them all. Full starlight and wrath. But they were ready for him. My poor Konjo! I hate them! I HATE them! Talthielle and I barely got away while Konjo held them off. He was screaming for us to run! I wanted to go back and fight, but I panicked and listened to this monster instead. And now we're here, on this stinking ship with you, and my Konjo is gone! We fled and left him behind. And now I'm stuck here with this delusional old conjurer, as if I'm supposed to be grateful. I got one more day with my Konjo I wouldn't have gotten otherwise, maybe. But I would rather have just stayed dead. At least my Konjo might still be alive. I could have lived with that. I still think his lonely shade is still out there, wandering around the marshland trying to find me. Lavaris himself couldn't have dragged my Konjo through his gates without me."

Brinna was now weeping and unconsolable. But for all the confusion of the moment, Talto only began to feel his own perception breaking when he slowly turned his head to see what no one else in the cabin could see. As Brinna cupped her face in her hands and Lua put her hand on Brinna's shoulder in sympathy, and Bran looked on with growing suspicion and disapproval at Talto, Talto turned away to find...

Konjo's shade. Just sitting there, invisible to everyone but Talto. Just sitting there, staring at Talto with sadness in his eyes, silent and motionless. This was more than Talto could process. The circuits in his own mind frittered and sparked and fizzled. Talto's heart beat like a heard of ox hooves, and a sharp pain raced between his temples so furiously that his eyes watered and protested the dim candle light. He tried to resist the seemingly imminent collapse of his faculties, and reached out for some kind of comprehension, in vain.

"Brinna? Where is Paunch?" Talto's voice was feeble and cracking. Brinna's response was terse and angry.

"Talthielle! My name is Brinka! What in Dab is wrong with you? Who the hell is Paunch?"

Unbearable. Talto could make no sense of any of it. Nothing he had ever experienced in his lifetime prepared him for the sheer shock and helplessness he felt in that moment.

"Nanok? Brinna, what happened to Nanok?"

Brinna ignored him. "You see captain? He's been like this since we came aboard. He just speaks nonsense and gibberish. He's useless! And I'm stuck with him now. I feel so alone." Brinna was weeping openly now, and nearly hysterical. "You stupid old fool! Nanok? Your so-called nemesis? How am I supposed to know where he is? If he even exists, he's lucky to be as far from you as possible! I hate you! I wish you'd just left us on our own. My Konjo might still be alive if he hadn't listened to you! Damn you Talthielle! Damn you forever!"

But it was too late. Talto could hear nothing over the sound of his own thundering pulse, until the ship's bells began to ring out in alarm. Bran jumped to his feet and excused himself awkwardly, and Lua and Brinna arose to follow him, leaving Talto there alone, reeling in paralysis with Konjo's voiceless shade hovering beside him, judging him without a shred of pity or doubt in his countenance. Brinna turned and spat when she reached the hatch to follow Bran and his consort towards whatever emergency was unfolding. "Damn you. You miserable old fool." And then she was gone, slamming the hatch as she went.

So this is what it feels like.

When Talto awoke again, he was sprawled out on the deck with the captain, his scribe, one Viermah, and *two* Kenjah standing over him, all looking very startled and concerned. Talto was still clutching the open wineskin with white knuckles, and some of it had spilled onto his trousers. He opened his eyes and tried to blink. His body hurt worse than it had this morning when the sharp turn of the rudder had sent him glancing across the Kenjah's cabin. Whatever was in Marla's potion had seemed to work relative wonders before, but now it had apparently vanished without a trace.

"Talto? Talto! Are you okay? Can you hear us? Lua, fetch the ship's medic, fast!"

"No need." Talto's voice was a cracked whisper forcing itself between two dry lips. "I'm here. I think. I'm...alive? What happened? Why am I on the floor?" Talto knew what happened, and he knew why he was on the floor. He simply could not condense the flood of thoughts racing through his pounding skull into anything like a coherent explanation of his own. Talto was rattled, and everyone could see it.

"You seem to have had a seizure of some kind? You coughed and sputtered and choked on your wine and then just went down, flopping like a live fish on a hot skillet. You've only been out for a few minutes, but there for a few of those minutes we thought you might have died. Your heart stopped beating and you stopped breathing Talto. You ok mate? You sure you don't want a medic?"

Talto didn't know what he wanted. He wanted to lay down, but he was terrified of closing his eyes again. He wanted to be alone, but he didn't want to let Paunch or the Kenjah out of his sight again. Talto did not know if he was okay, and suspected quite rationally that he was not.

Paunch looked scared. Something about that gave Talto some kind of vague glimmer of undefineable comfort. Paunch was alive, and still with them, and actually cared if Talto was okay. In some unspeakable way, Talto recognised that this was important. And Konos was just as alive, and just as worried. And Brinna, too. His conscripts-- his *friends* were all still alive and with him. Talto had no words to express the gravity of his relief, and fewer words still to express the *why* of what he was grateful for. He had seen something, now only addled fragments already trying to flutter away from him like broken dreams at dawn's light. He grasped the moments he had witnessed, and could frame their context, but a shroud in his memory was already closing in around the scene and dissolving it into an inaccessible sequence of jumbled flashes. He could remember the cruelty in Jorgan's face. He could hear Konjo screaming for them to run. But none of these things had happened.

"Should we help him up? Should we not move him? What do we do? Talto, what should we do?" Paunch had forgotten his unsettled stomach and the dizzy feeling of being so mercilessly thrown about by the waves.

"Let him lie, Paunch. He took quite a spill this morning. His injuries may have been worse than we thought. He's a tough old bird, make no mistake. Let's give him some space and let him gather himself. He looks pretty dazed." Konos and Brinna were the color of ichor, and Konos was holding Talto's hand. Brinna was holding Talto's head off the deck. Bran and Lua were holding back a litany of questions. Paunch was holding Konos' shoulder, in solidarity, but also partly against the motion of the sea. Talto was still holding the wineskin when he heard the bells.

The bells sounding a ship wide alarm.

Bran's priorities shifted on instinct. He would have to get his answers another time.

"You all stay with him, and stay here. I'll go see what's happening and I'll send someone down to check on you if I am unable to return." He gave Talto one last puzzled and skeptical look, and then turned and shuffled out of his own cabin with Lua in tow, leaving a pile of Talto and his bewildered conscripts alone with one crisis while he rushed away to attend to another. Too many things were happening at once. But the safety of the *Marvu* took precedence over all other matters. This was the first day of their voyage, and already it was proving to be a fiasco.

In the cabin, Talto tried to quiet his thoughts and quell the throbbing in his back and shoulders long enough to summon his strength and sit up. Even with the Kenjah supporting his weight and trying to help him, he felt like they might as well have been sitting on his chest. Every little movement of any muscle between his ankles and his eyebrows felt like a beating. He struggled to breathe, let alone speak words anyone could make any sense of. The simple act of sitting up was a gauntlet of sharp, jarring pains, but at last he managed, or thought he did. Because after only a moment, Talto's eyes rolled back in his head and his body went limp. He was unconscious. But at least this time he wasn't flopping around like a live fish on a hot skillet. His heart was beating, and Brinna could feel his breath at his lips and nostrils. Talto had surrendered to the shock and passed out cold.

"Well what do we do now?" Paunch asked, and the Kenjah just blankly shrugged.

***

On deck, the wind ripped at the sails and the linemen shouted at one another in urgency. Bran climbed to the Bridge and found Hinds and Garrison already there waiting for him, and Troy was climbing the ladder behind Bran as soon as he arrived.

He was about to open his mouth to ask what was happening when his eyes found the point on the horizon everyone else was staring at, and he no longer needed to finish the question. There, mark forward from the prow, less than a league out, was a huge mass rising up out of the tumultuous waves. His words died on his lips, and the four of them stood their with their jaws hanging open in disbelief.

The men had heard wild stories about the cephalopods at sea. But none of those tales ever spoke of such an encounter within a day's ride of the shoreline. The giant squids and octopi were creatures of the deep, who travelled in open water and rarely surfaced for any reason. Some giant squids could live for hundreds of years and grew to lengths comparable to ships like the *Marvu*. These were the creatures of old legends, pitched battles with colossal beasts who would sometimes wrap themselves around doomed ships and drag them below the surface, the stuff of every sailor's nightmares.

This was no giant squid.

This creature had fins on all sides of its head, and before its black eyes even broke the surface of the water, even from this distance, it obviously dwarfed the *Marvu*. Slowly it rose above the sea and lifted itself like a mountain until its full breadth and terrifying scale could be seen in whole by Bran and his crew. To their credit, the men aboard the ship did not panic and flee their posts, but they did all but freeze in silence as they watched the impossible creature heave itself up on dozens of legs and spread itself across the horizon like a vision of the raging storm itself.

On the Bridge, no one spoke, but everyone tried to. Eventually, each one composed themselves enough to offer their own suggestion. Troy was first,

"Should we turn and try to run, cap?"

Garrison spoke next, "Should we mount the guns?"

Hinds did not have a question. "It's *her*, Bran. You know it's her. If it isn't... Well, it might as well be."

Bran rebuked himself for his own paralysis in the moment, and again for having accepted the charge of the Kalama provisions. But there would be no running, and no fighting. Hinds was right.

"The Kalamaii." he whispered, as if she might hear him otherwise. "No Troy. Keep the rudder locked, but have the men take in the sails. Garrison, our guns won't save us here. Get aloft and raise the white flag. We'll set dead in the water and wait to see what happens next. We've got a year's worth of food and supplies for her people. She won't sink us here. I hope." His hope was an open question.

Troy and Garrison rushed from the space to carry his orders. Hinds remained at his side, almost dumbstruck. "We haven't even cleared the midshelf yet, cap. She is *standing up.* Unbelievable. What does she want, I wonder? And how are we supposed to figure it out? I can't imagine they speak the language."

"I think I know what she wants, Hinds. And when she's ready, I suspect she'll make her intentions very clear."

The creature in the distance continued pulling itself up out of the drink as the wind whipped and the rain stung the skin of the hands below. Words fail to convey the enormity of what they all witnessed. The creature's fins and head and enormous eyes lifted higher and higher until they reached the cloud line. The arches of its bent arms rose and writhed around it on all sides, protruding in obscene arcs and sinking again as it shifted its footing on the sea floor for balance and heft. What rose from the sea that day was so much bigger than the *Marvu* that the ship could have spent most of a day just trying to sail far enough around the thing to return to its starting position. Bran was right. The guns would only provoke certain death. Their best course was to maintain the present uncertainty of what was perhaps still only a probable death.

It rose, and rose, and rose. And when it seemed it could rise no more, it rose again, until its whole form could be seen from skyline to surface. When Bran and Hinds could no longer see the part of it that rose above the overhanging weather guard of the oh-four, they scrambled down to the main deck for a better view. As they pulled themselves along the railing past the gunmounts, they could see the whole thing it all its breathtaking magnitude. It seemed to dominate the whole horizon, and against it, the *Marvu* was a bug. As the thing reached its full height, it began to lift its arms out of the sea, one after the other, on either side, until it seemed to be standing up on its last two. These flailed and flared out above and along the surface of the sea, nearly trebling the immensity of the creature's full measure.

Hinds succinctly expressed aloud what everyone else was privately thinking.

"Oh, come on!"

And then, as the *Marvu* came to an ambivalent halt on windtossed seas and signalled its unconditional surrender, everyone watched, and waited.

(The Waterline)

Bran, Lua, Garrison, Hinds, and Troy stood at the prow of the *Marvu,* speechless and reverent. When the last of the sails were furled and latched, the wind died and the rain stopped, and a permeable silence draped the ship. All at once, the frothing waters became still as clean glass. Not so much as a ripple disturbed the zen calm of the surface. The ship stood motionless, like a child's toy on a level shelf. Nearly fully laden with crew and cargo, the *Marvu's* high waterline rested about ten to fifteen feet below the railing. In calm waters, with the remainder of its bays filled with the bounty of a full catch when the nets were to be cast in a few days, that waterline would probably rise another ten feet or so, the most the *Marvu* could displace without risking going under. One could hang over the rails by the hands and dip their feet in the water. Bran's understanding was that they would not have to travel far or long after that to reach the Temple. That had been the *plan.*

Neither Mond or Kamar had mentioned anything about an unscheduled open confrontation with a mammoth sea goddess in dead water on the first day. Bran remembered something Talto had said, less than an hour ago, standing in this very spot, about failing to see important developments coming in advance, and felt now as though he understood exactly what the old mage had meant by that. Bran instructed Hinds to fetch the Kalama ambassadors, and Hinds rushed away to find them.

Back in Bran's cabin, Paunch and the Kenjah observed the sudden stillness of the ship, and Paunch was especially grateful for this, but each of them were curious about what was happening above. Brinna and Konos lifted Talto's nearly lifeless carcass onto Bran's bed and covered him with ship's wool, tucking in the edges to hold him in place if the winds returned. They turned the dogs of the hatch and filed out onto the deck, not having to look around for long to discover the central subject of the ship's alarm, and as plausible of an explanation for the sudden change in weather as was likely to be found.

"Is that her?" Brinna whispered cautiously.

"I think so. Incredible." Konos and Brinna were at a loss for anything else to say about the overwhelming spectacle watching them from the distance.

"Nope. Not interested. I'm going to stay with Talto. Good luck Kenjah!" Paunch was mortified, and wasted no time in idle staring vacantly at certain death in the distance. He turned right around and hastily scuttled back into Bran's cabin, and turned every dog behind himself with expert mechanical precision.

Konos was as befuddled by the sheer scope and scale of the sea monster as everyone else, and was relieved, as was everyone else, not to be the only one who could see it. But he couldn't help being also a little amused by Paunch's flat rejection of the scene entirely and guttural refusal to endure it beyond his first glance. "Champion of the Verdant right there!"

The Kenjah held hands and held the rails as they worked their way back to the prow to join Bran and his acceptably incredulous officers. Bran thought to remind the Kenjah that his orders were to stay put, and dismissed the thought. Shortly thereafter, Hinds materialised on deck with two slightly agitated liaisons, prematurely roused from solid midday naps. They emerged from below grumbling and groaning about unnecessary disturbances and the importance of rest for old men, but they trailed off when they saw the Kalamaii, and both of them immediately fell to their knees and pressed their faces to the deck, muttering inaudible nonsense in a foreign language.

Garrison glared at them, "I don't think they're going to be very useful."

Bran just shrugged and shook his head and turned away from them in mild disgust. The Kenjah seemed to have plenty of salt of their own, and Brinna had wonderment in her eyes, and no trace of fear. Garrison and Hinds stood holding the prow railing opposite the captain and Lua, and Troy rejoined them as well. After a few quiet moments, they all sensed a commotion behind them, and turned to see Paunch lumbering out onto the weather deck, loaded down with his bow, the Kenjah's blades, and Talto's quartz tipped staff all bundled under one arm, and a semi-conscious Talto draped over his other shoulder. Talto took his staff and nodded his gratitude to the Viermah as he attempted to gain his own footing. Soon, Bran and his officers and his scribe, and Talto and his conscripts were all gathered together at the prow. With the sails in and the winds gone, the sailors and linemen were standing at their posts, equally captivated by the scene they would never forget. The nightwatch had been stirred from their bunks by the battle station bells and were all groggily mustering at the forward mount, many of them trying very hard to discern if they were all actually awake, or just collectively sharing a fever dream.

No one spoke. Talto tore a length of linen from his trousers, and with some difficulty, managed to tie it to the top of his staff. With profound solemnity and Bran's reluctant nod of consent, he raised his makeshift white flag as high above his head as he could, and knelt on one knee with his eyes lowered. His friends and Lua and the captain and his officers all respectfully stood aside and gave Talto the center stage, and all present wondered at the sight, and tried to imagine what would happen next.

A gentle wind began to blow from the stern, and a great albatross suddenly fluttered down onto the rails in front of Talto. At this, Mond and Kamar let out stifled peels of amazement and sat back on their folded legs with their hands on their thighs behind Talto, who pulled himself by the staff until he was standing eye to eye with the creature. Both of them seemed caught in each other's trancelike gaze, until the bird lowered its own crown to Talto and turned around on its talons, kneeling again to the leviathan on the horizon, and everyone aboard watched the thing slowly lower itself back into the sea and vanish from sight. When it was gone, the albatross turned around and beat its wings at Bran and Troy, and spun again, side stepping a few degrees off of the centerline toward the starboard railing, and then very deliberately folded its magnificent wings behind itself and pointed, roughly in parallel with the growing breeze. Troy found Bran's eyes and both of them nodded their understanding. Troy turned and started yelling orders to the sailors and linemen, who in turn began yelling to each other in a frenetic and hurried sequence of motions. Soon, the sails were unfurled again and full of wind, and Troy gave the command to angle the rudder towards the track indicated by the bird perched on the prow like an old figurehead. The *Marvu* was moving once again.

"Lua, my love, it would seem your passage on this voyage is fortuitous. I suspect you're going to get some pretty great copy out of this journey. Boys, have you ever seen anything like it? Talto? I've spent my whole life at sea. I've never seen anything like this." Bran was generally spare on the rhetorical, but in the present moment, everyone already knew what they had just witnessed was a once in a lifetime spectacle that none of them would have ever believed if anyone else alive had tried to persuade them it really happened. But it did happen, and the crew and riders of the *Marvu* would never forget.

"Somebody remember to feed the bird." And Bran and his scribe just turned and walked away.

"Bran?" Even Talto's voice hurt.

Bran turned to Talto, the old wandering mage and soothsayer, and saw for the first time the ancient *Epozia* with clear eyes, welling with an uncertain mixture of respect and concern and curiosity and resolve. "Yes, Talthielle?"

"I will come and see you in a little while. I need to rest and think."

"That will do just fine."

"And Bran? I am sorry for putting all of you in this position. In my heart I truly believe I have no other choice. For whatever that's worth."

"Talthielle, you didn't put us in this position. We were already in it, and I suspect you wouldn't be here if we weren't. Sometimes, the stars just align how they align. Get some rest. We'll sort it all out."

Bran and Lua went back to his cabin, and Garrison and Hinds returned to their duties as well. Paunch and Talto and the Kenjah lingered there with the bird, who now

ignored them and focused intently on straddling by
incremental degrees to the port and the starboard like the
needle of a living compass. The winds would carry the *Marvu*
along now, but the storms would not return. The overcast sky
would continue to obscure the stars at nightfall. Talto and his
conscripts quietly agreed to return to their own cabins for dry
clothes and some congenial reflection on their shared
experiences thus far.

At length, Hinds did eventually send a man around
to check on them and give them their duty schedules. Paunch
got the scullery, and the Kenjah got the galley line. They were
told their shifts would rotate, one off and one on, so they
could help each other if they just wanted the company or
something to do, but they would not be required to do so.
Talto was somewhat surprized to be assigned to the library,
but guessed that Hinds had already assumed he would spend
most of his time there anyway, and why waste a hand just to
have someone else there for him to pester? Paunch teased
him, reminding the great and powerful servant of the seasons
that he was now just a glorified barista. The Kenjah decided
they would make the best of cooking for the crew, and were
not a little relieved at dodging laundry duty, which did not
seem at all preferable to kitchen work.

"Don't eat all the food, Kenjah. Hinds made it very
clear I was supposed to tell you that," the man had said.
"Don't eat all the food!"

"Well, we do have to taste the food to make sure it's
prepared correctly, of course," was Brinna's prompt reply.

"Of course..." It was clear the man had not been
instructed to permit himself to be drawn into a semantic
debate about appropriate rations, and had no personal
burning desire to argue with hungry Kenjah about food. One
does not argue with the cooks. Every *swelu* knows that. The

man also informed them that they would all stand staggered watches, balls-to-four, fore and aft, staggered two-on and one-off, and that all they had to do was stay awake and give a shout if they spotted anything other than water, "...you know, like..." But he didn't finish the thought. To this, they all agreed, and with a brief pause of nervous skepticism as the man looked them all over, an old man, a clipped birdling, and two colorful giants, the man bid them all safe journeys and politely excused himself to carry similar orders to the remaining passengers.

"I need some rest, and I suspect you all could use a little yourselves. Come and find me this evening before supper. I'll be settling into the library and, um, I guess trying my hand at a proper tea for the first time since I was a lad. For your sake, wish me luck!" As Talto scurried off to his new quarters, Paunch was pleased to piece together having inherited a cabin to himself, and decided some good rest sounded just fine.

"You two, you know... could you, *keep it down?* You know?"

Konos and Brinna blushed a full rouge and chuckled at this. "We will do our best Nanok. But we promise nothing!"

Paunch, feeling a bit like the man who had just come around with their assignments, decided he would take what he could get from the Kenjah, and just sighed deeply and smiled. "Fair enough, Kenjah. Pleasant dreams. If you get that far..." And he bowed low and deep with exaggerated deference, and was fast asleep within moments of dogging his hatch and hitting his rack. The Kenjah, for their part, did *eventually* get that far, and for once in three long days, their dreams were actually pleasant.

***

Brinka wailed and moaned in her cabin beside Talthielle's. Bitter visions of sea terror and old age and loneliness plagued her mind, and she was sleepless. She had witnessed horror heaped upon horror, and it just kept coming. First, in Flask, horrors upon herself in a previous life she could not outlive. Then in the hills above Titan, watching the horrors they heaped upon her Konjo. Then the marshes, where he suffered and died for her sins, for the second time. Talthielle had spared his life for a single day with little more than a bit of treacherous timing. She suspected now that this was how he had spared hers. He had let her watch her Konjo meet his first end that fateful morning after the Titan, alone and helpless and outnumbered, and already broken before anyone cast the first stone. He said she could save him. He said he could save them both.

Stupid clocksmith. Stupid Kenjah.

One day. What is the value of one more day with the missing piece of your own soul if in the end you just have to watch the world rip it out of you again? She could never have said no. Even if she'd known, she'd have agreed anyway. She knew now. Stupid Kenjah.

And now, somewhere out there, not more than a league from the port bow, an incomprehensible horror she could not fit into her mind. A monster. A hellish leviathan, a Kalamaii. Black and cold and fearful. The thing had been as big as a hundred Gunships, as wide as one half of the horizon, and sprawled against the black noonday sky like, like nothing she'd ever seen. If the thick, low hanging storm clouds had not blotted out the sun, the thing would have done so on its own. The ship stood dead in the water. The crew was petrified. And Talthielle lay half dead in a freak coma next door. And the thing out there just waited in a deadly silence. There was no wind. No birds. The crew languished in paralysis, and no one would speak. All the candles and torches onboard the Marvu had been ordered extinguished. The captain and his condescending officers were trapped on their Bridge and clueless about what to do.

Brinka knew what it wanted.

It wanted Talthielle. She could feel it in her bones. The whole ship was doomed because of him, just like she was, just like Konjo, and this Nanok Talthielle had asked about, and probably just like everyone and everything else he ever touched. It wanted Talthielle, and who could know why? What damage had he managed, even way out here in the deep, far away from everything Brinka had ever known or cared about?. What absurd grievance did this creature have with the so-called servant of the seasons? What morbid carnage had he wreaked upon this impossible thing's life? That it would stalk and menace a ship full of strangers, with children onboard...

Brinka couldn't close her eyes without seeing their frantic faces whither beneath the waves as they cried out and clawed at the infinite nothing. She saw the piers and beams break and splinter beneath them as the thing tore the ship apart like so much wet paper. She saw their little fingers disappear beneath the waves, forever.

Brinka sat up in her bed, clutching the ship's wool around her, feeling her mind begin to slip away. She had run out of tears, but wept endlessly. Her head hurt, and her stomach was tied in knots. Her own breath burned her throat like razors. Anxiety, grief, and dread were her only companions. Talthielle had brought her here, and would not tell her why. He would not tell the captain. She wondered if he even knew himself. What could that puny little tramp hope to accomplish in the face of the primordial tyranny out there right now, lording over the ship like a child's toy? He was going to get them all killed. Brinka knew it was true, and couldn't shake the *thought. Talthielle had somehow broken the world around her, and everyone in it would suffer. And he had broken her, and broken her Konjo. Whatever suffering he endured next door in his pathetic pile of incontinence, she knew it could never be enough to atone for his sins. For his incompetence and lies. Brinka couldn't shake the thought, or shake the nagging idea on its heels. Brinka could stop Talthielle. And maybe she could spare the crew and its riders and those two little children from the consequences of Talthielle's folly. Brinka was sitting up in her bed, wrapped in ship's wool, and clutching her two short blades. Souvenirs from a previous life as well, just like the scars they'd earned her before she met her Konjo. Brinka was sobbing. Brinka was seething.*

When Brinka appeared on the main deck of the Marvu, *the entire crew was mustered in ranks down the port and starboard railing. The Deck Officer did not give a shout or a whisper. Thousand yard stares from one end of the ship to the other. All hands standing at attention. Bran and Hinds, likewise, on the prow. Troy and Garrison on the helm. No wind, no birds, no sound. No speeches. No questions. Brinka carried Talthielle's body like a doll. Blood trickled from his throat and wrists, staining the dry wood.*

Talthielle always leaves a mark.

As Brinka marched her funeral march, an albatross appeared on the railing beside Bran and Hinds, and they were startled by it. Bran tried to wave it away, and it beat its wings at him aggressively until Hinds restrained him and advised against antagonizing the creature. Brinka could see the sweat furrowed into the stress lines on Bran's weary and nervous face. He was doing everything he could to hold it together, and only barely succeeding. Both men forced themselves to regain their bearing, and the bird seemed to forgive them their petulance, or rather, it seemed to just ignore them altogether, because it was staring at Brinka and her offering. The king of caught fish. A worthy tribute to the Kalamaii, and one less malingering trouble maker in Omnia.

Brinka approached the prow, refusing to look in the bird's eyes, or Bran's or Hinds' or anyone else's. Brinka's whole being was locked on the creature in the distance. Brinka and the Kalamaii were the color of the midnight sea. Talthielle was a fading pale, tinged with jaundice and smeared with crimson. Bran and his men were the color of their beaten sails, and now everyone was looking down at their own boots. Not the Kenjah, or her burden. Not their captain. Not the leviathan in the distance. No one saw her throw him in the sea. The splash was the first sound many of them had heard in hours. Somewhere, way up high in the sky, a waxing fingernail moon pierced the firmament between two clouds, and somewhere down below, upon a tiny ship in the eastern seas of Omnia, a small breath of wind began to stir.

***

Talto found the ship's library empty, but had only just arrived when Lua appeared behind him. Her demeanor had been passive and preoccupied since this morning. Talto wasn't sure he'd heard her speak a single word since Bran had introduced her at breakfast. Bookworms tended to be timid creatures, but the creature that appeared before him now was anything but. Her soft eyes had hardened, and her diffident quietude had been a facade. She slung her satchel down on a countertop and briskly dogged the hatch and turned to him with iron in her posture. Talto remembered Konjo's words in the Verdant. *I would have figured you'd be better at seeing these things coming.* Talto was growing weary of the unexpected.

"What are you going to tell him Talthielle?" Lua's tone was rhetorical. Talto instinctively refrained from saying anything in haste, and wore his genuine and sincere confusion like a losing card player. "You aren't going to tell him the truth, obviously. Have you even told them?"

This time she let the question hang in the air.

At length, Talto accepted at least that he was, for the moment, cornered. He relented.

"I'm sorry, ma'am. You seem to have me at a disadvantage. It's a feeling to which I am begrudgingly growing accustomed. What, may I ask, do you mean by Truth, and how do you assume I haven't told them?" Best he could do, under the circumstances. Buy time.

"Don't be obtuse, darling. It doesn't suit you at all. We both know you haven't told them. You can see it on their faces. An *Epozia,* two Kenjah, and a Viermah, traveling to meet the Kalamaii. You're going to try to bargain with Lavaris. You were going to have to tell them at some point; Lavaris would never accept an involuntary quorum. You haven't told them. Or those two dough-eyed turtle doves wouldn't be walking around the ship giggling and holding hands. The clipped birdling wouldn't be worried about the bad food and gravity. They'd be stone faced and somber and quiet as a mausoleum."

"Honestly, you make a great argument for telling them." Talto was essentially and effectively stunned, and tried to push his own eyes back into the recesses of his skull through their clenched lids with his thumb and fingers, pinching the Bridge of his nose and trying to make the pain go away. He sighed from the gut and slumped down onto the nearest piece of soft furniture that would hold him. "I'm impressed, I suppose. I do love people who love books. Clearly, I'm in good company. What do you want from me?"

"What do you think I want from you?"

"Well, I'm really hoping you want to be my biographer. I've been thinking someone should be writing all this down.

Finding the captain's scribe on board has been, well, until a few moments ago, I suppose, a pleasant surprize. My lady, if that's not it, you're just going to have to tell me. I am injured, tired, drained, and clearly behind. I can't see five minutes into the future, and haven't had clear sight for nearly three days. I can sense that you want some kind of explanation from me. Well, I sure wish someone alive would graciously provide me with the same. What are you doing here anyway?"

"Captain's scribe? Is that what you--" Lua rolled her eyes and groaned her own impatience. "No Talthielle. Not even close. You know, for a clocksmith-"

"Please, I beg of you, don't say it. I will throw up and pass out if you say it. I swear on the Dab I will."

Lua harumphed in a mildly contemptuous way and shook her head in disappointment, but she didn't say it. Instead, she opened her satchel and took out the weathered old book she had been writing in this morning, opened it to her last entry, and thrust it at him forcefully, making him flinch. Talto looked up at her with puzzled boredom and irritation, but she just gave him a cold hard stare and thrust the open book at him more forcefully, and so he took it.

"You're already in a library, Talthielle. You might as well enjoy a good read."

Talto sighed his surrender and turned his attention to Lua's entry, and squinted against the dim candle light to read her tiny print. As he made out the first few words, he shuddered and slapped the book closed, holding the place with his thumb as he craned his neck to the overhead light and tried in vain to capture a whole lung full of air. Lua narrowed her eyes and plopped herself down across from him, putting her feet on a small table and spreading her arms out over the top of the couch. "Read it."

"How did you get this? Lua, I can't read this! You know I can't read this. If you know anything at all, you know-"

"READ IT, TALTHIELLE."

Talto sank into himself, exhausted and aching, and complied. When he closed the book and set it down on the table between them, he said nothing, and Lua waited.

The silence between them became stifling and oppressive. Talto was filled with an inexplicable sense of shame and remorse. He was overwhelmed. The pain from his bruises surged through his body and condensed in the space between his temples. His mind was a thick and impenetrable fog and he could retrieve nothing useful from it without immense difficulty and strain. His hands were shaking, and he was fighting tears for a future that did not even seem to exist.

"Who wrote this, Lua?"

"You did. Last time you were here." Lua didn't blink or wince. Her level eyes were burning holes in Talto's face.

"Last. Time. I. Was... No. No, Lua, it isn't possible. I don't understand what you're telling me."

Lua sprang to her feet in a rage, "Somebody should be writing all this down!" That's what you said, Talthielle. That's what you've said every single time. Somebody should be writing this down! Talthielle, I am not Bran's scribe, you gnarly old fool. I'm *yours!*"

"Lua. I've never made it this far. I don't understand what you mean. I have no idea who you are. I have no memory of being murdered and thrown overboard by my own conscript. This is some kind of bad dream you've written down. This is some kind of jo-"

"Your conscript?" Lua erupted in a peel of sardonic laughter. "*Your* conscript, Talthielle? You think Brinka is your conscript? Konjo was your conscript. And he died, over and over and over again. Each time, you blind old menace, you failed to see it coming. You were helpless to stop it, and you were lost after it happened. Blathering and incoherent and dazed. Sometimes they don't even let you on the ship because they think you're too stone drunk to be anything but a liability. Your conscript. I've heard everything now." Lua threw her hands up in disgust and frustration.

Talto stared at the book on the table and tried to comprehend nonsense from a stranger.

"What else is in that book?"

"Do you want to read it? Go ahead! It's yours anyway. Open it up, Talthielle. Look upon your works and tremble, ye mighty."*

"No. No I don't really want to do that, I don't think. I think I've seen enough of my works for one day. I'm assuming you've read it. Indulge me, would you? You say you're my scribe. I'm assuming I would not have indentured someone who already hated me for such a task. You must have found me persuasive at least once. Wait, *you're* not one of my conscripts are you?"

Lua closed her eyes and shook her head in disbelief. "Wow man, you really are a wreck, aren't you? How far back can you remember? It's a pretty big book; maybe help me narrow it down a little?"

Talto, until that moment, would have thought he could remember his entire life. He could still see flashes and fragments of familiar faces and important moments, and there was a sort of threadbare continuity that held it all together, but when he really closed and eyes and focused, he was stunned to realize that he could not remember anything about his life very clearly... before Flask.

"I saw what they did to Brinka. I watched her die."

Lua did not soften, exactly, but for the first time since she had stormed into the ship's library and began interrogating him, she seemed caught off guard. "And then what.?"

"I followed Konjo and his *kinja* to the Titan and conscripted him. I brought Brinka back from the dead as his payment in advance for services rendered."

"Did you now? Interesting. Go on." Lua knew something he didn't know and it was driving him mad trying to skirt the central issue in this exchange to pacify her, but her scorn lines had migrated across her brow and become intrigue and curiosity. Talto decided less stress was better, and proceeded without reservation. He was himself well stocked with plenty of budding curiosity of his own.

"We travelled north, to Waterside,"

"Why did you conscript Konjo, Talthielle?" Lua's open frustration either subsided or suppressed, now a more casual bedside manner. Something about not being shouted at in riddles and insinuations reduced the pressure in his skull to a manageably dull throbbing. He wondered if there was anything left in Marla's little vile.

"To save the world."

"No, Talthielle. That's not why you did it. It's not why you returned his Brinka to him either. Why did you conscript Konjo, Talthielle? Why did you do it? Think, Talthielle. Why?"

Talto tried to order the slack sequence of broken images and bits of conversation and purpose and pulses of dull throbbing ache in his head. He saw Brinka suffer. He saw her shade. He saw Konjo suffer. He saw Omnia set in flames and chaos. He saw all three bulkheads of the Kenjah's cabin he had slammed into this morning. He saw Konjo in the Titan, toppling a mean bartender with a ragdoll clocksmith.

He saw Konjo on the hill, unreachable. He saw the Kenjah's restless sleep in each other's arms beneath the clear stars on what might have been their last night together in any form, ethereal or otherwise, anywhere in Omnia, forever.

"To save Konjo."

"Why did you want to save Konjo, Talthielle?"

"Because he has a soul. And I do too! I don't understand what you're asking me! Why wouldn't I?" Talthielle tried to feign incredulous, but he was slowly beginning to understand where Lua was going with this.

"All this, Talthielle? Just to keep two doomed Kenjah alive for one or two more days?" Lua picked up the book and dropped it on the table with an emphatic thud. "All this?"

Talto pondered Lua.

"I don't know how to tell you how long you've been stuck in this loop Talthielle. Or how to measure how much of your life force you have wasted getting here. But I'll tell you a few things you might find useful. Until last night, Konjo had never set foot aboard the *Marvu*. He's never made it past the Verdant. Not one time. But that's not even the really strange thing, Talthielle. You want to hear it? Can you guess?"

"Nanok."

"Nanok."

Talto saw the flashes. A bloody fistfight beneath a weeping willow. A botched attempt at home invasion. Aimless searches and precious hours wasted in the wilderness looking for nothing at all and finding it.

"We never found him. We didn't find him, I mean. He was delivered to us in restraints and a hood. We were ambushed in the Verdant by a squadron of Viermah who were very persuasively eager that we be on our way. For the record, I did not clip him. They did that, apparently. What a gruesome thing. I was surprised by everything about it except his willingness to go with us rather than stay there. He and the Kenjah were almost immediately inseparable. Lua, it is as if someone has been one step ahead of me every step of the way."

"And who do you think that is?"

Talto grimaced and grunted his impatience. "Lua, how can I know that? What do you want from me? Don't you hear me? Aren't you listening? Do you understand what I'm trying to tell you, that for the last three days I haven't understood a single thing about what was happening around me? Lua, I am *Epozia*." Talthielle was mustering a little bit of salt. Lua was unmoved.

"I've seen the wars that tear those people apart. I've seen generations into the future. I've crawled over a thousand threads trying to find the one thing, the one piece of the puzzle that holds the whole horrible story together, just to try to write a different fate for the people of this world. I found it in Konjo, in those two poor doomed souls out there, and the little one to come. Lua, if I can save them, I can save the world. You would not have me do other than try!"

"And Lavaris?"

Talto grasped for a breath and then stopped, and sunk into his couch again, deflated.

"And Lavaris. Lavaris isn't who I have to worry about right now."

Lua smirked and shoved a chuckle back into her chest.

"Most sense you've made in a very long time. So what is your plan, you know, for *her*? Besides getting your Kenjah and all the rest of us killed and eaten? Were you just going to wait and let *her* explain it to them? Or did you let Konjo go every single time, just to try to convince a grieving Brinka that you might be able to bring him back if she helped you? Just like you brought her back for Konjo? What did you think she would do when she figured out you couldn't do it twice? Your starlight wielding *Epozia* initiate. And who in Omnia did you think you would recruit from the Viermah, Talthielle? Why did you really want to find Nanok?"

"I don't like this. Nanok had my stones. I never in a million cycles thought he'd wind up on board the ship with us, let alone that he'd ever have forgiven me for depriving him of a father. I didn't know who we'd get. I didn't figure it would be harder than persuading the Kalamaii, and if we'd persuaded the Kalamaii, finding a Champion in the Verdant seemed like it should have been pretty straight forward."

"You're not getting the point, Talthielle. How many Kenjah do you need for a quorum?"

"Gross. I don't like this. I want you to stop."

"How many do you need, Talthielle?"

"STOP IT, LUA! Please."

"How many?"

Talto slammed his open palm on the book. Lua didn't flinch.

"One."

That's right, Talthielle. One. One Kenjah."

"Stop."

"One Viermah, and one Kalamaii."

Talto reeled. "And one *Epozia*."

"One representative of each lore."

Talthielle was speechless. It had been right in front of him the whole time. He had never tried to look beyond his own ideal outcome. He assumed Omnia would just have to get along without the clocksmiths as best as it could. It had never occurred to him that his own ideal outcome was too far in the future to matter. That if he succeeded in saving Omnia, he might never make it that far. He might not live to enjoy it.

"Sometimes you have to consider the possibility that you can't save the world, Talthielle. That that responsibility might correctly belong to others. Sometimes you have to consider the possibility that your best chance is to make sure someone else succeeds."

Lua stood up and picked up her book and stowed it away in her satchel.

"We've got a long ride, Talthielle. And plenty of time to talk, if that thing out there doesn't drown us all in the middle of the night, that is. Or if your Kenjah clocksmith doesn't slash your wrists and throat in your sleep. I've also been assigned to the library. Get some rest, clocksmith. See you in the galley." And Lua was gone.

"See you there, Lua."

Talto wanted nothing else in the world more than a nap. He was afraid that if he closed his eyes, he would just see Brinka throwing his lifeless corpse over the rails, or Konjo being wrestled to the ground by trappers. He wished he could see what really happened to Jorgan. He wished Lua had left the book, but he was relieved that she didn't. Talto closed his eyes.

(Quarry)

Dinner aboard the *Marvu* that evening was uneventful and quiet. The collective urge to confront the awesome scene which everyone present had witnessed in the afternoon was stifled by a universal inability to form words and phrases that would serve any purpose. Everyone was still alive, and no one would take that fact for granted again on this voyage. There was a dense air of solemnity and introspection in the galley. Bran and his officers ate together in silence, surrounded by their crewmen. The riders picked at their food and chewed with apathy.

Only Kuska and Deni and their children seemed to be unaffected, as yet. They had already heard plenty of the encounter, but had not been obligated to muster with the crew when the battle station bells had sounded because of their priority obligation to their little ones. Bran had been firm with them on this point, even though both of them had insisted that at least one of them should be obligated to fight the ship if the need arise, and that either of them could stay behind with the children. Bran would hear nothing of it. So they had not witnessed the Kalamaii, and though the stories they had already heard were wild, they had not really gotten a sense of just how profoundly impactful the experience had been on the rest of the crew, until now. The crew had been jovial and energetic this morning. Now all that could be heard in the galley was the sound of utensils scratching the plates and the plates shifting on trays. Piko and Paka occasionally cooed and squirmed, but even they sensed the impenetrable quiet and were not inclined to violate its sanctity.

Bran watched the children as he ate. He was lost in his thoughts as well. He had been cornered by Mond and Kamar after the day's spectacle, and they had more questions of their own than answers. They seemed to gather from Talto's performance that their own authority and centrality in such matters had been challenged and found somewhat wanting. Bran did not know what to tell them, and assured them that the mission would continue on, and that he had the highest confidence in his crew's ability to meet whatever challenges they might face along the way. He had not felt especially persuasive, and the envoys had graciously conceded the urge to press him further, though they did share some muted grumblings between themselves as they went away.

He had asked Lua her thoughts on the matter, and she had been a bit guarded on the subject. "I don't really know what happens next, Bran. But it would seem that so far as anyone else in the world is concerned, I might as well be writing fiction from this point on, because no one who didn't see it today will ever believe a word of it. I think we're going to be okay though. Whatever that was between the old man and the bird was peculiar, but it did seem encouraging I suppose." *Encouraging* was a word Bran knew he was going to have to keep as close to the forefront of his mind going forward. The mission to provision the Kalama now seemed relegated to something like pretext on the part of the fates themselves. He had read plenty about the voyages of previous ships and crews billeted for this task, and had read nothing of anyone ever witnessing an actual Kalamaii in the full flesh, let alone anything about old tramps communing with mystical sea fowl for permission to proceed. Peculiar just didn't seem to do the exchange justice. That bird was still out there, perched on the prow and shifting now and then a little port or starboard on the railing, guiding the helmsman's rudder by pantomime.

Lua ate beside him, and watched the riders, as did Garrison and Troy. Hinds seemed to be the only officer not preoccupied with the black calamity out there towing the ship to sea, or with the old clocksmith and his entourage, or anything but his sausage and bread. Whatever was out there waiting for them certainly would not require empty stomachs. Some very practical people are not so easily moved by the supernatural, and Hinds had seen plenty of strange things at sea and lived to lie about it. He had served on board the *Marvu* the longest, and had been Pike's navigator on some hairy treks. What his crew needed from him was a calm head and plenty of energy.

Talto ate greedily, finishing even before his Kenjah. Paunch, for his part, took his time and resolved to finish his food and leave none of it in the bin this time, either from his plate or otherwise. The musicians had been the last to muster, and had not witnessed the entire scene, but had caught enough of the tail end of it to be awed. They were good enough at reading the room to abide the silence. Mond and Kamar attended the galley as a matter of course, but had mutually agreed to begin fasting in celebration of their devotion to the Kalamaii. They ate their bread, but touched nothing else. Paka poked her brother and giggled as he squirmed and tried to brush her hand away. Piko grinned and held a stubby little finger out at his sister and tried to poke her back. Paka shrieked with laughter and wrapped herself in a defensive posture. Deni smiled nervously at Kuska, who shushed the children and smiled back. Bran could restrain himself no more.

"Attention on deck!"

Utensils dropped and a general shuffling of chairs and stools and benches brought the crew to its feet for orders. Bran stood and walked to the forward end of the galley to address all hands, still trying to put the words together even as his lips began to move. A sea goddess was pushing his ship. A strange bird was driving it. And they had all been unwittingly indentured to whatever end or errand had brought the clocksmith and his conscripts. Bran would do he level best to pretend he was still in charge, and was grateful at least that the albatross was not inclined to give motivational speeches. And since the bird didn't appear ready to answer any of a complex of pressing questions, Bran decided it was high time someone else did.

"*Marvu,* you did well today. Honestly, I don't really know what else to say at this point. You held your wits and stayed your stations. For those of you who don't know, that thing out there today was a Kalamaii, the Kalama deity revered by the people we are sailing to supply. The point is, if we do our jobs, and conduct ourselves with dignity and poise, we have nothing to fear. We are all out here in service of her people, and she is the one essentially driving the ship right now. We are alive by her grace and good will, and I think we can all agree, after seeing what we have seen, that we'd all be very happy to keep it that way.

"But, my good men, as it turns out, we are also on a different mission as well. We are carrying a handful of riders on a quest of their own to go and parley with that creature out there, for reasons which have not yet been made entirely clear to me. We have all had strange dreams lately, and I think that this is the reason why. And since we are all in their service now, as well, for better or worse, I think the time has come for our new friends to speak on their own behalf about what has brought them aboard, and what their intentions are. I don't know what they will say, but I will tell you I know this much. That thing out there is expecting them, which means that thing out there is expecting *us* to bring them to her safely. I am sure that they would very much also like to arrive there safely, and so would we as well. So whatever happens, *Marvu*, I expect each and everyone of you to comport yourselves with the character and efficiency which marks this ship's great and storied reputation. We will see this thing through, together, to the end, no matter what. *Heard*?"

The crew answered promptly with a resounding "Heard!" and remained at attention.

"Outstanding. Ok *Marvu*, it is my pleasure to introduce you to Talthielle and his companions. I will let him tell you their names, because as of yet, they have not told me themselves. I want you all to listen carefully to what he says. You cannot be expected to perform at your full potential if you are kept in the dark about what your mission objectives are, or if you do not understand what the plan is, or the risks involved. Talthielle, my friend, I know you were not expecting this tonight, but after today, I am sure you understand."

Talto had indeed not been expecting to provide an impromptu account of his business to the crew of the *Marvu*, and had been making a very self conscious effort to move his food around on his plate as the captain spoke, until he heard his own name spoken. Paunch smirked at him, and the Kenjah gave him some encouraging eyes as well. The musicians, not exactly anticipating the gravity of what Talthielle would have to say, awkwardly led the crew into a

blind alley of inappropriately cued applause, as if the old
tramp was about to take the stage for a sea shanty. Talthielle
cringed. Paunch immediately grasped the comedy in the
tension between reality and perception, and was already on
his feet pounding his hands together and shouting like a fan
of the show. Talthielle covertly shot him daggers from
beneath his bushy eyebrows as he finally stood up and
approached the captain. The Kenjah were also on their feet in
solidarity. Talthielle knew Bran was right. But he would have
preferred a chance to prepare. But then, he supposed, so too
would have Bran. Fair enough.

    "Fair enough." Talthielle began.

    "Hello everyone. My name is Talthielle."

    He saw Garrison shrug absently. One made up name
was as good as another.

    "I am Talthielle. I am *Epozia*." Some older crewman
seemed to lean in.

    "I am *Epozia,* and I and my friends are on a mission of
our own to..." Talthielle stumbled. Saying it out loud was
much more difficult than thinking the words and not talking
about them, as he and the Kenjah had privately, but mutually,
agreed to deal with the subject for the last few days. "We are
on a mission to persuade the Kalamaii to return with us to
Omnia." Puzzled looks from the crew. Bran lowered his eyes,
mustering his resolve. Lua mouthed a phrase to Talthielle and
looked on supportively.

    The Truth.

    The truth, Talthielle thought. The truth is a trash
can.*

    "We are going to try to persuade Lavaris to open his
gates and release the spirits to walk amongst us again, as they
once did, ages ago." Talthielle gave pause for the wave of

murmuring chatter that washed over the crew. Bran cleared his throat, and the crew regained their bearing and fell silent.

"I am Talthielle. The two Kenjah are Konjo and Brinka. The Viermah is called Nanok. Konjo and Brinka are from the mountains, and Nanok lives in the Verdant." Talthielle trailed off, stalling for time to think about what he said next. *The Truth.* Lua nodded to him when he found her eyes again. Bran did not miss this exchange. Talthielle took a deep breath, and continued.

"A few days ago, Konjo was murdered by bandits outside the Titan, south of Waterside. Not long before that, Brinka was murdered by a vicious mob in an unspeakable and unprovoked attack in the city of Flask, south of the Titan. I have expended most of what was left of my life force to rescue them both from these awful fates. It is not just that neither of these wonderful souls, of whom I have grown very fond lately, deserved what happened to them. I have rescued them because what happened to them would have set off a chain of events that would have set all of Omnia at war with itself. The consequences of this conflict would have been endless carnage and chaos and suffering and destruction." Talthielle was rambling, but he had the rapt attention of everyone present.

"The creature out there is called *Ursal.* She is as likely to eat us as to help us, but I suspect that my friends and I are the only ones aboard who should have to concern ourselves with such undesirable outcomes. As your captain suggested, you are all already in her service, and there are people out there on that island who are depending on you. I honestly don't think any harm will come to you. It is not our intention to put anyone in danger but ourselves. She knows we are coming, and I think she knows full well what we are coming to ask of her. I believe she has indicated a willingness to hear us out, at least, and that should be no small comfort."

Talthielle saw mixed reactions from a somber and sober crew. He imagined trying to give a speech like this to the patrons of the Titan, and was grateful for the discipline and bearing of the crew of the *Marvu*. "It is no secret that Omnia has lost its way. It is a sad state of affairs when people who just want to live safe and normal lives have to go to sea to find them." A general wave of recognition informed Talthielle that he had found his proper course. "Our people have forgotten the wisdom of our ancestors. They have forgotten that we all used to live and work together, and they fail to appreciate that which we accomplished when we did. If you have never seen the Kalama temple, as I suspect few of you have, when you see it, you will understand what the people of Omnia could build when they cooperated with each other for a common cause. Now, all we all seem to be capable of is tearing things down and fighting over the pieces. The Kenjah and the Viermah isolate themselves from the world, and the Kalamaii could not have gone farther away from it. I am the last of my kind, and this will be the last of my works. We all go to give ourselves to Lavaris in exchange for the return of our forebears. We go to the Kalamaii, because we cannot go to Lavaris without her. The lores must enjoin a quorum to treat with Lavaris."

Talthielle looked at Lua, and then at Brinka, and closed his eyes. "We will offer Lavaris our lives. If we fail, I believe that the wars will come to Omnia, and the world we as we know it will burn. We can no longer survive with our common heritage buried away in the past. The spirits of our ancestors must walk among us again, to guide us and to judge us."

Lua was not entirely satisfied, but shrugged a 'good enough' at Talthielle, and he welcomed the opportunity to finish his speech and relinquish the limelight. "We are all very grateful to you for your hospitality and your fidelity to your ship and its mission. We will do our best to be useful to you all while we are aboard, and to not get in your way. For whatever its worth, I am told that the Kenjah will be serving the line in the galley when it is their shift, so you all at least have the silver lining of Kenjah cooking to look forward to." Talthielle only need a few nods of approving compromise, and got them. "Conversely, you'll all be happy to know that the Viermah will not be cooking anything at all." Talthielle received a heavier barrage of approving nods and a little bit of tension breaking laughter, and even Nanok seemed to shrug his own approval of the arrangement. Konjo and Brinka smiled at Talthielle, and it gave him comfort. "I'll be in the ship's library when I'm obligated to not be anywhere else, so I look forward to being of service to you all, and to the chance to get to know my shipmates while we are here. I beg your forgiveness for the quality of the coffee in advance. My skillset is not without its natural limits. Thank you all, and good evening."

An awkward moment of silence trailed Talthielle's closing remarks; he wouldn't have preferred a round of applause when he took the stage, but since he'd had one, now that he was done...

Nanok followed Talthielle's predicament with a mischievous eye and decided this time he'd rescue Talthielle from his own ineptitude. Nanok gave a hoop and a holler and started beating his hands together, and within seconds, the whole galley erupted in a semi-voluntary and slightly confused volley of pavlovian applause. Talthielle permitted himself to smile gratefully, and as he turned to run away, he found Nanok giving him a salute and a little bow, as if to say "you're welcome." Bran and his officers all shared a more subdued expression with each other, and only with each other, before they all stood up as well, to clap apprehensively and give their best impression of unforced smiles.

No one really noticed Lua get up and leave until she was already gone.

Talthielle rejoined his conscripts and the rest of the bemused and slightly befuddled riders at the table, and in a few moments, the rest of the crew was seated again to finish what remained of their meals. A calm sense of order was gradually restored. The captain and his officers picked at their plates with a vague sense of preoccupied indifference as they mulled over Talthielle's absurd revelations. Talthielle waited for some indication from Konjo and Brinka that they had heard him. *We intend to give our lives.* It occurred to him rather suddenly, neither of them had responded to his announcement on the quarterdeck that they were in the family way. He supposed they had already known this, and assumed he had just guessed. Talthielle looked around for Lua and discovered she was no longer in the galley, though he hadn't seen her leave. Finally, he found the Kenjah's eyes. He did not see shock or awe or alarm. He saw their gentle resignation. Had they already known? While stories of the antics and adventures of the *Epozia* abounded in Omnia, very little was known, generally speaking, about the old man of the mountain. And much of that was apocryphal.

Nanok was quite another story indeed. Talthielle had not planned on conscripting Nanok, let alone having him forcefully thrust into the clocksmith's service by his own kind. Talthielle had planned on going back to the Verdant with the Kalamaii to recruit an actual champion. He knew he could not oblige anyone present to sacrifice their lives for a halfcocked hypothetical. The Kenjah knew they had already gotten everything either of them ever wanted in the world when they were returned to each other against impossible odds. Talthielle supposed they knew they were already living on borrowed time, and were of such character and fearlessness together that they might even prefer to have such a noble end, at least over the despicable end of which they had been spared. Nanok was leaning in with a serious look on his face, clearly prepared to press the issue if Talthielle didn't address it on his own. What would Lua say?

"Nanok, will you be the Champion of the Verdant and offer to Lavaris your life with ours, to entreat for the salvation of Omnia?" The Kenjah, and not a few riders, turned to Nanok, as if the clipped green birdling should have an answer at the ready. Talthielle could still go to the Verdant if need be, and he still didn't have a Kalamaii, so there was technically no good reason to try to browbeat the Viermah out of his own better judgment. Nanok was free to say no. Nanok was looking at the Kenjah and saying nothing. No better time, Talthielle supposed, than the present. He wished Lua had stuck around, if not to hear whatever came next, then at least to know Talthielle had finally relinquished his penchant for impermeable intrigue. The clocksmith did concede, inwardly, that a heavy weight had been lifted from his soul. The truth seemed so much easier when it was on the table. Fine then, let the Viermah make his own decision.

Talthielle thought of Nanok's father, and of his bereaved beloved. He almost wished Nanok would say no. Talthielle could not bear to think of sacrificing an entire lineage, let alone that of a friend, even for such a noble cause. But then, what of Konjo and Brinka and the youngling they carried? Not for the first time, Talthielle wished he could see another way through the storm in his mind. But time was no longer a luxury he could afford to waste. They all still had a long way to go, and Talthielle would spend his very last breath trying to get the Kenjah queen to the top of that mountain, if that's what was required of him to see this through. Nanok turned from the Kenjah to their captor.

A day and a half ago, the young birdling might just as well have torn out Talthielle's throat if he had had the chance.

Nanok stood up and planted his hands on the table beside his half eaten supper, and looked hard into Talthielle's eyes. His face was as serious and as full of purpose as Talthielle had ever seen it. "Talthielle! You crazy old scheming degenerate! I've got just one thing to say to you." The Viermah was causing a scene. A hushed silence fell over the galley as everyone turned on instinct to see what was happening. There was a sudden and pervasive mood of concern, and Bran and his officers were now watching, as though a fight might break out. Konjo looked at Brinka out of the corner of his eyes, and she elbowed him in the ribs. His eyebrows arched and he turned back to Nanok, feeling the vibrations in the galley shift in unpredictable ways.

Nanok became aware of the sensation one has when everyone in the room is watching. He took a deep breath and looked around at all the riders and crew and officers, and at the Kenjah, and back at the clocksmith. Talthielle waited, for anything, for something, and it seemed as if time itself had slowed to a crawl. He could read nothing in Nanok's narrow eyes. He wanted to look away, but didn't dare. Entire futures were written or erased by moments like these, and Talthielle could not see beyond the choices that others had not yet made. Nanok stared him down like prey, with hard eyes and a scowling grin. He could almost hear the sound of the clocksmith's heart beating. The Kenjah, if Talthielle had bothered to look, were lapping up the theatrical airs from their Viermah companion.

"Talthielle, you just try and stop me!"

***

The Marvu *stalked through the midnight sea on a leisurely wind. When Talthielle went under, the crew quietly filed out of ranks with worried expressions and no words to convey them. Bran motioned his officers dismissed, and lingered behind with Brinka on the prow. He stared at the deck planking and his boots and said nothing. He had just stood idly by and watched a murder being committed in the presence of all of his hands, and yet somehow he knew everyone aboard understood, even if they didn't really understand, that a morbid sacrifice had been made for the preservation of their own lives. Bran knew he didn't really understand, but could not break the silence to form a question, even if he'd known what to ask. He sensed that the dark, glimmering Kenjah had no answers to give. And he could not ignore the apparent pacification of certain death out there on the coal black horizon. The thing might have held them all there indefinitely. It might have never volunteered to disclose what it required for the* Marvu *to continue on its journey. Somehow, the Kenjah had known what it wanted, and she gave it willingly. Talthielle had been made tribute. What other choice could there have been?*

Brinka fell to her knees and wept. Bran lowered himself to the deck and slumped against the rails, and continued to say nothing. He would not interfere or interject, and she would not be alone. The poor creature had lost everything now, and had suffered endlessly for the price of losing. Hinds would remove her from the duty roster, as is customary for the bereaved. Bran wished Troy had stayed behind; he was better at this type of thing. But Troy had a ship to drive, and Hinds a crew to manage. Garrison had perceived that his services would not be required for this particular-- whatever this was, and had made himself scarce after a long day's watch. Garrison's domain was shipboard threats, and from this moment on, Bran supposed, Brinka was no threat to anyone but herself. No. She was his responsibility, and he didn't have to be a soothsayer to stay with her, whether she needed him or not, even if he had no other solace or consolation to offer. What does one say in moments like these? What could he say?

And then Bran was rescued by a most unexpected turn. He heard her footsteps first, and turned to see the ship's librarian and his closest friend approaching. Lua nodded at him in a silent instruction to leave the two of them alone. Bran knew better than to argue with Lua, and wouldn't have tried anyway. He was ill-equipped to deal with tears, and welcomed his relief. With great caution and the softest touch he could manage, he laid a hand on Brinka's shoulder and told her he would be there if she needed him, and that he was truly sorry for her loss. As Lua plopped herself down on the deck, he rose to go. Brinka looked up at him with too many muddled emotions in her eyes and sobbed something like gratitude.

Lua sat with Brinka until the tears dried up. The two had been briefly introduced at breakfast, but had not exchanged words otherwise. When Brinka finally wiped her eyes and sat back on her haunches and stared blankly at the dim and clouded moonlight, Lua opened her satchel and retrieved an old, tattered book. Brinka didn't know which horrible possibility she dreaded worse, that this stranger would try to placate her with some absurdly timed fairy tale, or that she was about to be cornered for some kind of judicially predicated postmortem interview. She wanted desperately to change the subject before either eventually could come to pass. And honestly, she really just wanted to be left alone with her sorrows.

Lua knew she was intruding, and held off as long as her own dwindling patience would permit, but she knew she was never getting off of this accursed ship unless something changed, and the sad, grief-stricken and prostrate creature before her was the only one left who could rewrite this passage in the Book of Konjo. Lua had been moved by Talthielle's grotesque end, the first half-dozen times she'd been forced to live through it. Now she didn't even come topside to watch anymore. Tonight was the first time in too many resets to count that she had finally decided to come topside after it was over. She had no taste for the gruesome mellodrama, and no more reason to abide the protocols which had been so rigidly established by her own captor. She was tired of living in quiet passivity while this poor creature's world was torn apart over and over again. Something had to change, and Lua was likely the only person left alive who could see.

"There's a version of this story in which Konjo lives, Brinka."

Lua waited patiently for a response she knew she would not get. Brinka stared off into the distance in absent dispair, and tried in vain to ignore this new nonsensical treachery from another stranger. Lua could empathise with this pathetic creature, but would not pity her, and would indulge this nerve wracking circle of clumsily bundled madness no longer.

"Look, I know you're having a tough go of things right now, and the last thing in the world you want is another round of rarified false hope. I get it." Lua gestured in the abstract at the place off the prow where Talthielle had been sent to his watery grave, though the Marvu had already travelled several leagues from that ceremoniously unmarked patch of deep sea and darkness. "Talthielle was a complicated character. He lied to you. Over and over again, he lied to you. And he's brought upon you incomprehensible suffering. From your point of view, and I expect, from his as well, under the circumstances, Talthielle failed you. But that thing out there did not want and did not ask for a tribute. And that clocksmith you just murdered and surrendered to the deep was a friend of mine.

I've watched you murder him over and over and over again.
And I won't watch you do it any more."

Brinka could no longer pretend to ignore the brass and
timbre on the girl beside her, whom she had apparently
mistaken for a rather timid and mousey bystander. The words
"over and over and over again" were too pregnant with
indelible incongruence to let pass unaddressed. Brinka was the
color of the shadows of stormclouds. At last, she turned and
faced Lua directly, making clear that she would listen if she
didn't have to speak, or pretend to believe it, or pretend to care.
Brinka wanted to dive into the sea and race Talthielle to the
bottom and win. What was one more stupid story from another
interloping stranger, other than visibly unbearable. She felt, as
Konjo once felt, as if she were being asked to sanction the picking
of her own pockets.

"And that clocksmith you threw overboard, who you
think took everything you ever loved away from you and left
you here, a helpless sobbing mess, pressed into service aboard a
ship you'd probably rather throw yourself off of right about now,
that clocksmith has already redeemed you. Both of you. From
your point of view, Kenjah, this has all been one big singular
nightmare. But you're just a page in a story he's been writing
and rewriting and editing and revising every day of his own
life for as long as you've been alive. He is lost in this loop, and
he is failing every single time for one simple reason. One reason,
Brinka! It's because he doesn't trust you. And it's not even really
that he doesn't trust you, it's that he's convinced he has to be the
only one among you who is capable of pulling this thing off. It's
not a question of whether or not you can succeed without him,
Brinka, it's that he thinks he has too much at stake to permit
anyone else to bear responsibility for failure. He's not afraid of
losing you or Konjo or of either of you slashing his throat and
throwing him overboard, do you understand? He's afraid of

martyring your mortal soul to a lost cause if it doesn't work. So he can't see past his own choices, just like he can't see past anyone else's. For an Epozia, *Brinka, that is basically a level of impotence equivalent to two broken legs. He doesn't want credit for saving the world, Kenjah. He wants to spare you the eternal gnawing guilt of watching it crumble in your fingers. And he doesn't believe he has the right to thrust that choice upon you. Kenjah, I'm telling you that from his point of view, this awful fate you're living through was somehow preferable to another one so much more profoundly worse that this one had to be the right choice."*

Brinka measured her words as carefully as the knot in her stomach and the lump in her throat would allow. She felt sick. Her head was spinning, and she wished this infernal ship would just be still.

"I don't feel redeemed. You say you've watched this whole thing happen before? What makes this time different? Why are you here, and why are you telling me these things? What is it you think I'm supposed to do? And if he couldn't do it, what in Omnia makes you think I can? I don't care about Talthielle. I don't care about his quest or his pride or his ego. I don't particularly care to ever hear his name again, if we're being honest. I want my Konjo. Whichever version of this story he survives is the right one, and clearly it isn't this version. So who in Dab are you, and what in Dab do you want from me? I need you to start making sense and get to the point or I need you to leave me alone here so I can muster up the courage to find my own spot out there on the sea floor where I can finally get some peace and quiet."

"I am Lua. I am a conscript, just like your Konjo."

"So Talthielle rooked you into this stupid loop with me, and you're just stuck here? I don't get it? If he's dead, then you're free. What's the problem? You can throw that book over *the rails and consider yourself emancipated. What does any of this have to do with my Konjo?"*

"That's the problem, Brinka. I am not Talthielle's conscript."

Brinka had no energy for riddles. She just sighed an exasperated sigh, shaking her head and shrugging. "Okay Lua, I give up. Whose conscript are you? I thought he was the last one?"

"I am Lua, First Conscript of the Queen of Epochs. I'm your conscript, Brinka. You put me here."

Lightning peeled across the sky, and Brinka's sight fractured into a thousand rippling shards.

(Uncle Talto and the Suicide Cult)

"The terms of our agreement have clearly changed, Talthielle." Brinka and Konjo were shades of flax and linseed. Their demeanor was calm, but their backs were straight and their eyes glistened in the candlelight. They were in the library with no interest in reading. Nanok well sensed a conversation which would involve him soon enough, but his instincts predicted a number of preliminary points which would not involve him just yet, so he made himself look busy perusing old shelves lined with older volumes on the many lores of Omnia. Talthielle was struggling with coffee at midnight,* and was as tightly wound as he could manage to remain in the gauntlet of corners he kept finding himself in. The *Marvu* had seemed like an idyllic reprieve from the chaotic vibes and barbed surprizes of the mainland. Now it was beginning to feel like all of Omnia's problems were just being condensed into a smaller space. Ten gallons of piss in a five gallon drum.

"Konjo and Brinka indentured themselves into your noble service in exchange for the miracle of our reunion. Our hearts and minds are aligned with our feet and fists on this matter, Talthielle, please make no mistake. We will follow you to Lavaris. If it is to be as you say, then we will give our lives to Lavaris. If this will restore peace and balance to Omnia, then it is our quest just as much as it is yours." Brinka paused. Her hand was in Konjo's, and where they touched, little pulses of lilac and hyacinth swirled in particles and waves, radiating outward over their skin. She bit her lip and looked at Konjo with uncertainty, and he understood.

"Brinka and Konjo don't know how you knew we were with child. We supposed you knew Marla well enough to speculate about her motives in ways which, frankly, you understand, we probably would not have thought twice about. The berries, the window, the very spacious bed." Nanok coughed over a worn copy of something unintelligible to him. Konjo noted Nanok's reminder of his own presence and reframed the construction of his point. "What you may also know, Talthielle, is that we didn't know we were with child until you mentioned it to that deck officer when we embarked. So, you see, clocksmith..."

Talthielle was holding a pitcher of boiling water over a nomi full of grounds, trying to steady his aim against the rhythm of the swaying *Marvu*. He was not oblivious, nor was he trying to pretend to be. He was, in fact, concentrating very hard. He just wasn't looking the Kenjah in the eyes.

"Nanok! Second partition aft, portside, row three, seventh book from your left." Talthielle dribbled a bit of hottish water on his opposing thumb and swore under his breath, but finally emptied the pitcher. Coffee, for better or worse, was ready to serve. Nanok looked wildly from left to right, forward and backwards, up and down, trying to do advanced calculus in his head. "Aft is that side, Nanok." Nanok was prepared to take the correction to heart, rather than chafe at the critical tone, because when he turned around and looked where the clocksmith pointed, for a brief moment, the whole width and breadth of the *Marvu* suddenly made sense to him, as if he were flying overhead and seeing it below for all its layered decks and crisscrossing passageways and cramped, candlelit spaces.

A moment later, feeling the scrutinizing eyes of the Kenjah and the gambling twinkle on Talthielle's muck, Nanok surprized them all with a sudden flourish of deliberate steps and pointing motions culminating in the retrieval of a manuscript from the seventh space on the third row of the second partition, portside.

"Bring it here, Nanok."

Nanok grinned at the Kenjah, who saluted his prowess over beams of their own, and strutted into the middle of the library, a kind of rounded or bulbous space accessible by opposing hatches, port and starboard, and flanked by flags of partitions full of books, forward and aft, for roughly twice the area of the middle part. This middle area was considered common, and was furnished by a few couches and chairs, bolted to the deck beside and between little varnished wooden tables carved out with cup holders and candelabras. At the absolute retinal center of the library from overhead, the way Nanok would perceive the space, were two adjoined halfmoon countertops with a few stools mounted on risers around the outside. This was Talthielle's new post during his stay aboard the *Marvu*, and one which he was already utterly thrilled to serve, coffee notwithstanding.

When Nanok's last foot cleared the aft flag, there was a loud clatter, which stunned the Kenjah speechless and nearly killed the Viermah, and all present but Talthielle gave loud, startled shrieks when the whole aft flag suddenly collapsed into the deck below, revealing a nearly empty space of equal size, but beset on all sides with leather beams and canvas bags of various sizes on ropes. The entire flooring was a two inch pad of woven nomi. Where one half of a library had been, all but Talthielle were hang-jawed and frozen in shock to discover a completely different space had appeared from above. Talthielle, for his part, poured his fourth cup of a hottish and dubiously titled coffee like substance, without spilling a drop.

"A fine selection, Nanok. I think you'll find it a fascinating read."

"A sparring chamber!" Brinka had managed to forget herself even as she consciously tried to avoid forgetting herself in another one of Talthielle's diversions. It was, in fact, a sparring chamber.

"Nanok, it is customary to read on deck watch, and it is not frowned upon. Technically, you're not supposed to read at work-"

"Talthielle! It's a sparring chamber!" Brinka would not be deterred.

"...but I'm not sure if laundry qualifies as exceptional. Here's your coffee everyone. Please be kind, but be honest. I promise I'll learn. You know, I'm rather certain that galleywork is not conducive to reading, and as a point of fact, does not qualify as exceptional. But they won't throw Kenjah off the ship for reading I think, at least not after they've tasted what I am hoping will do justice to the as yet hypothetical reputation of... said Kenjah."

"Talthielle, we can cook. As a point of fact, Talthieeeeeelle, Konjo and Brinka *can also fight.* I'm sure you'd love a spectacle, but"

"Brinka, my dearest darling warrior queen. I have given serious thought to the matter of your child." Talthielle was now looking both Kenjah in their eyes as emphatically as he could. "What I'm about to say is gross, but the moment has come for it to be said. No one is going to like it, one way or the other. In fact, quite literally, one way or the other."

Talthielle stood and clasped his hands and closed his eyes. Brinka shook her head dismissively and poked Konjo in the ribs and pointed, *sparring chamber!*, and Konjo grinned and poked her back. Nanok had already accustomed himself to rolling his eyes at Talthielle's parloresque flair for the dramatic. They soon found Talthielle again, when a softer voice appeared from the shadows of the forward flag behind him.

"He's going to tell you all it has to be an *Epozia* and a Kenjah, presuming the birdling-"

"I was clipped." Nanok interjected.

"...presuming the Viermah and the sea monster will go along. So it will be Talthielle and Konjo. Because it cannot be Brinka. Or it will be Brinka, because it cannot be Konjo and Talthielle. Which is why he, and within very few moments, he and Konjo, will begin trying very hard to persuade you very energetically that it must clearly be Talthielle and Konjo."

"It will be Konjo and Talthielle." The Kenjah did not need time to hear Talthielle's argument. Suddenly, he and Brinka pulsated a wide differential between crimson and amber. The other Kenjah would hear nothing further from anyone.

"Everyone stop. No one say a word."

Everyone stopped. No one said a word. Talthielle cringed and seemed very much like he wanted to say quite a few words. Lua gave him hard eyes as she appeared at his side, and he bit his lip, hard.

"Lua? the scribe? Hi, hello Lua, I'm Brinka, nice to meet you, we we're just *discussing-*"

"Shut up, Kenjah. It's not a question. It has to be Talthielle and Konjo. It's already happened. It's already happening. It's not a debate."

"Now you listen here, bookworm!" Starlight flashed in Brinka's eyes as she stood up and squared off. "And that goes for all of you-"

"Shut UP Kenjah! And SIT down!"

Brinka went dumb and stood fast. *The brass on this wench...*

Lua strolled around the bar and found the stool beside a glowering Brinka and a very nervous Konjo. Nanok and Talthielle took stools opposing. The space between them all was both empty and rife all at once. When Lua sat down beside her, Brinka sat down beside Lua and went vaguely crimson again. Konjo lingered in his indigo, and could sense a gulf forming between points of view and feeling something very much like a knot in his stomach. Deliberate hints of Brinka's starlight remained, but she waited for Lua to continue. Talthielle, having already received hard eyes from everyone present, reluctantly conceded an entire prepared speech to circumstance, and yielded Lua the floor. He poured her the last of a fifth cup, which seemed to distract her. She cast a woeful eye on the cup Talthielle offered, and looked up at him hopelessly.

"Talthielle, your coffee is terrible." She took the cup away from him, rather than from him, and she returned to the inner area and dashed it down a deep sink.

"This coffee IS terrible, Talthielle." Nanok relinquished his cup to the brassy librarian lady with a grateful smile.

"Yes. I would like to know when Nanok pissed in my coffee." Konjo gave up his cup, and Brinka's. Brinka ignored yet another distraction, and pinched the top portion of her nose where the stress ball was being born.

Lua rinsed all of their dishes and retrieved a small array of measuring cups from a drawer beneath the aft counter, and began administering a fresh pitcher of boiling water. As she weighed out a portion of the grounds into a small bulb of nomi, she began to speak.

"The Queen of the Epochs must live, Brinka. And that's not even the part you're not going to like."

"I already don't li-"

"It isn't only that you must live, Brinka. It's that you can't even go. You have to stay behind with the Kalama. You have to raise the House of Konjo."

"It makes sense." Nanok was the first to speak after a long pause, shared by all.

"And you can't go either, Nanok. You have to stay out here with Brinka and the monks. It has to be Talthielle and Konjo. And the Kalamaii. Nanok, whether you want to be here or not, you were taken against your will. You cannot proceed on this quest and form a quorum. Another champion of your lore must be chosen." Talthielle's eyes narrowed at this, but he held his tongue. Lua poured boiling water over a nomi bulb full of grounds, and spilled nothing.

"Again. You'll just have to try and stop me." Nanok would not be roused, and still sensed that other arguments were currently in contention. He would let them all wear themselves out, and then he would be heard. Nanok yielded patiently.

"If Brinka stays, Konjo stays." Konjo's voice was firm and decisive.

A ring of contention was rapidly forming. Lua poured four cups of coffee, spilling only a slight amount down the side of Nanok's hand. He pretended not to notice, but she apologized anyway and offered him a bar towel. She would not surrender another moment to any of Talthielle's prepared speeches. His detached expression suggested at this point he was happy to leave her occupying the ground she had chosen. An impasse had formed on multiple fronts, a circumstance Talthielle associated with migraines. He offered Lua a shrug. Lua rolled her eyes, and proceeded.

"If the Kenjah don't go, then there is no mission. There's no Lavaris. We don't need the Kalamaii, and no one has to stay with the Kalama." Nanok was piecing the the thoughts together as he spoke them, and Talthielle was growing visibly restless.

"And if there is no mission, at least half of you never make it aboard this ship. I'm telling you, it's already happened, and it is happening right now. This is it. This is the closest any of you have ever or will ever get to pulling this off. You'll never get another audience with the Kalamaii. And *great* sacrifice has been made to get the four of you this far. Brinka has to live. Everyone else here is expendable. If Konjo stays, we have to find another Kenjah, and that's not going to happen. Bran is not going to turn this ship around, and we're not pointed at Omnia, as I'm sure you've all noticed. We're all locked in, and there's no way around this decision. It has to be Konjo and Talthielle."

Nanok was the only one with questions. The Kenjah were trying to find the center of their palette before either of them spoke again. Talthielle was staring at a fixed point on the bulkhead and waiting. His migraine was a fully formed hammer beating against his temples.

"What if we just don't go, *yet?*"

Lua hung her head. She was not being heard.

"What if we all stay with the Kalama until the child is born? We'll ride back in to Moat next cycle on an icecutter. It's easier to scale the Dab from the east anyway, and my northern kin in the Upper Verdant are still very hospitable folk. The child will be safe. We won't have to deal with the trappers or try to trek back through waterside with a sea goddess to ferry across to the southern passes. What if we stayed, Talthielle? You said Konjo lived, and we've averted the great conflict his death would have precipitated. What's the rush, Talthielle?"

The Kenjah leaned into Talthielle, sensing the prospect of a conciliatory moment. Nanok's formulation sounded plausible to them. Lua sighed until she was deflated, and pushed herself up off the ground with her arms until she was sitting on the bar itself. She gave Talthielle a long, hard look, and then cradled her head in her hands. Talthielle was no longer visibly restless. He suddenly understood what Lua meant. What she was trying to say. A tear came to his eye, and suddenly he felt very quiet and still, and small. Far away voices murmured in his mind as the ripples cleared and the fragments and shards became a single, unmuddied panorama of lucidity and self awareness. The air in the room hung upon his brow. He tried to form the words, and heard his own voice cracking as they came out.

"If we wait, then it will have to be Brinka and Konjo. And that cannot be. It simply cannot be. I would rather raise all of Omnia to the ground myself than pay such a price. Lua is right."

Lua had raised her head on Talthielle's third word, and a sad but thoughtful smile had formed well before his last three. *Finally, Talthielle.*

Nanok and the Kenjah were not far behind Lua now, and sobriety overcame them as they comprehended the meaning of what they heard.

"It has to be Konjo and Talthielle." The clocksmith's voice rang flat, and silence engulfed the library until the evening bells tolled taps. The diurnal watch and post rotation aboard the *Marvu* was underway. Bran and his officers would be relieved, and some combination of them would inevitably be meandering on down to the library, hoping to find one or more of exactly everyone who was already here. Talthielle found himself considering that he'd inadvertently managed to put the captain off all day long, and realizing he was very likely about to find himself cornered once again.

"I won't live another cycle, Kenjah. Brinka was my last miracle. I bet most of my lifeforce on her mountain's majesty, the Kenjah queen of starlight and time. My dear Kenjah. I don't even think I've got the strength left to reset the day, even if I had to. We have to persuade the Kalamaii, at all costs, and we have to find Lavaris while I am alive. He will accept Nanok, because we are not his captors. We are his friends. Brinka, you will have to say good bye to all of us, and Lua is right. You should stay with the Kalama. There can be no safer place in the world for your child."

Eventually, Nanok broke the silence.

"How come the ship's librarian knows so mu- nope, never mind. I heard myself say it. My apologies ma'am." Nanok fell silent again.

A breath passed, and a forlorn looking Konjo burst into laughter. After a vain and brief attempt to stifle it, Brinka erupted as well. Nanok phhhhhhhhed and accepted it. Lua tried to shake her head in a serious way, but the chuckles forced their way through. Talthielle drank in the scene and smiled, to them, and to himself. Konjo chortled,

"Hey Talthielle, all this fuss about Konjo and Brinka or Konjo or Brinka, are you really sure Lavaris will take *this* guy?" Brinka doubled over, and Lua laughed out loud. Nanok flicked a finger's worth of cold coffee on the Kenjah and sneered. Suddenly, Lua bolted upright.

"Oh Konjo, that reminds me! Nanok! Fourth partition forward, starboard side, fourth row from the overhead, eighteenth position from the centerline."

"Talthielle, I distinctly heard the man say that *you* were the confounded librarian."

"Nanok, I don't remember the confounded part, but I assure you I agree with it."

The Kenjah were already working out the calculus in their head, and Brinka was on her feet before Nanok could finish equivocating. Sensing a race, he abandoned his protest and dashed around the bar to try to outrun her, but she was already stooped down and counting before he even reached the forward flag, and was barely rounding the partition when she shouted,

"Got it!" and darted past a good-naturedly furious Viermah, dropping the book in his hands and winking at him as the two victorious Kenjah bumped fists and toasted their coffee. Nanok bowed in defeat, graciously and deep, saluting the spry Kenjah matriarch in exaggerated deference. After a moment, his eyes found the title of the book, and a visible wave of distraction overcame him. He frowned, puzzled, and read it again as comprehension washed over him. He looked up at Talthielle, and saw interest in the old clocksmith's face, but it was clear he didn't know any more than the now curious Kenjah. Nanok looked to Lua, who clearly knew, and was just smiling her saddish kind of gentle smile.

"Is this?"

"Your father's. The world is full of strange and curious coincidences, Nanok. But I suspect this is not one of them."

Nanok was a rare shade of speechless. He looked down over the worn spine and the smooth leather, and tried to muster the wits to dare himself to open it. Gradually, it dawned on Talthielle what Nanok was holding, and why it was Lua that found it. "It can't be?" Talthielle knew that it was, but just could not bring himself to imagine the odds of it winding up here. "The Book of Valishnok! Lua. Who wrote this? I don't understand. There was no Book of Valishnok. I would have moved the Dab ten leagues to the left with my bare hands to retrieve such a chronicle. Nanok, if I could have given your mother *that* book, I could have kept my stones. You would have known him as I did. But that *book* was never written. Valishnok and I travelled alone, and well beyond the reach of the Order of Tranquility."

Lua felt the midnight hour approaching as she appraised Talthielle anew. The morbid thought occurred to her that if Brinka had just let him live long enough to sleep off his bad day, Talthielle might very well have figured it all out before breakfast the next day. But then, if things had been permitted to proceed that way, Konjo would have never made it aboard this time. And if that book had been Talthielle's to give, he wouldn't have given up his stones. His answer, Lua considered, was right in front of him, he just couldn't see it from the right perspective. If he had kept his stones, Konjo and Brinka might never have found themselves among Talthielle's last, best, and brightest hope.

"I wrote it, Talthielle. I wrote the book of Valishnok."

"Young lady, you weren't *born* for the-"

The clocksmith felt as though his head might explode if one more slithering shadow of a half clue tried to shove its way in. He couldn't stop himself from turning to the Kenjah with a dumb, halfcooked expression on his face. Puzzled looks greeted him, and he looked back to Lua with genuine confusion in his eyes.

"Lua, you're not my scribe."

"I am very much your scribe, Talthielle."

"Lua, you are not my conscript. How can you be my scribe if you are not reliving my days with me? How do you come by these works?"

"You are correct, Talthielle. I am not your conscript. But I am your scribe. I am not reliving your days with you. I have been living most of my days without you, in fact, until this one. But I've been living *these days*, with or without you, for quite a bit longer. I've been recording your days for you, because this isn't your loop. It's hers."

The Kenjah had been paying attention, quite attentively in fact, but were slow to process the implied cue Lua left hanging in the air. The Kenjah were the color of the western skies and setting fast, and even Brinka needed a moment to recall that she was the only other 'hers' in the space. Safely assumed, neither of the Kenjah were aware of having a loop, let alone having anyone else in it, for that matter. They and Nanok all felt the exchange between the brassy librarian and the exhausted clocksmith to have taken a somewhat inaccessible turn, which, on the one hand, seemed to involve the Kenjah directly, but also, on the other hand, seemed to have nothing to do with the Kenjah, whatsoever, in this particular rhetorical mode.

Talthielle looked as though he finally glimpsed the final missing piece of a grand tapestry of a puzzle, and discovered that the piece itself was just the hole where a piece might have just as well belonged. He understood the language. He understood the mechanical architecture of *Epozia* constructs. He understood, in theoretical terms, what Lua was suggesting. But he could make no practical, linear sense of what Lua's suggestion implied. To complicate matters, he also understood that here and now, in the conclusion of what had evolved into a very open and forcefully honest discussion of shared circumstances, a new incentive had arrived to guard carefully against careless speech. If Brinka, in the here and now, was living in the contrived shadow of her own future construct, then Lua had already been too reckless with her words.

For *Epozia,* there is a fine line between constructive honesty and catastrophic confusion. Knowledge of the future requires an intuitive grace and the capacity for abstraction. For the uninitiated, genuine and severe danger accompanied the mistaken impulse to confuse a sense of knowledge of the future with a sense of certainty. If some version of Brinka had already lived long enough to contrive at this level of discretion and sophistication, and to go back and reshape her own past and the fates of her companions, it certainly wasn't the version of Brinka sitting here now, three days fresh from her own shallow grave, on a ship being driven on the winds of a sea monster and steered by a magical bird, and only just coming to terms with the prospect of motherhood, in the context of a noble quest of kamikaze altruism. If *this* was the version of herself Brinka had chosen to succeed, then this version of Brinka had to make her own decisions, unencumbered by any misguided sense of cosmic determinism. If Lua was who she said she was, and who she seemed to be, she should well know better than to interfere so haphazardly in the contrivance of her own captor.

Suddenly, the details mattered, and Talthielle could see the moving pieces. Some version of Brinka had survived one of the disastrous loops Lua had recorded in the Book of Konjo, and had gone on to master her own powers, but had done so without Talthielle's tutelage. Being *Epozia,* Brinka would no longer be constrained to the linear framework through which all other life in Omnia perceives the passage of time. Talthielle could not change the past. Somehow, Brinka had managed to do the impossible.

Dear reader, if you would pause to consider a body of still water in a basin, and in your mind's eye, imagine gazing upon it in bright light as you would your own reflection, and seeing the whole course of your own life reflected instead. If you touch the water with your finger, you will see a little ripple spread out in all directions until the wave has reached its own natural barrier in the periphery. If you touch the water again, a second later, you will see the same rippling wave follow its predecessor, but never touch it before it breaks. Now imagine you touch the water, gently, and send the first wave rippling out, and then you punch the water a second later, one can envision the second wave traveling with enough force to overtake the first. Finally, imagine touching the surface of the pool in three places, evenly spaced, and with precise timing. There will be a place where all three waves intersect and break against each other.

In this metaphor, dear reader, the waves are the consequences of decisions, or of changes to those decisions, in the realm of time and space in which a clocksmith intends to contrive. Talthielle can only alter a segment of a conscript's life with respect to the sequence of consecutive events which compose that segment. The one thing affects the next, and so on, but never the other way around. The second wave never overtakes the first. Within the constraints of this metaphor, only a colossal and destructive force could produce such a consequence. The kind of thing Talthielle might have warned Brinka to avoid if he had been permitted to live long enough to have the chance. In the second example, when one touches the pool in three places and three waves intersect, it would be possible, Talthielle speculated, as did his own kin in their day, to change something behind you by changing something in front of you, without having to reset the day. But it would require two *Epozia* to be operating at once, in overlapping spheres of influence.

This, dear reader, is what Lua meant when she said she was keeping Talthielle's days because this was not his loop. Brinka had managed to conscript someone in Talthielle's path, and contrive a point somewhere along in which to begin her own loop, so that while Talthielle labored over and over again to get Konjo safely aboard the *Marvu,* he did so without knowing it or having to reset the day himself, because at some point in his own journey, he ceased to be the clocksmith in control of the initiative. She just kept resetting him herself, over and over again, until he made it aboard the ship with both Kenjah in tow. From his own point of view, this version of events which have been so laboriously presented to you, would naturally be the only version he was conscious of. He just didn't understand how it could be Lua. Or why. Brinka's point of departure would have necessarily been somewhere between the Titan and Waterside, if she were to get to Jorgan before they did, and conspire with Marla, and bargain with the Viermah. Had Brinka even won over Rali, in Call, before they arrived last night? Was Brinka near by? Were there two Brinkas aboard the *Marvu?*

Talthielle's head began to swim. A vision of multiple waves breaking against one another in a clever choreography of theoretical heresy can seem overmuch like a beautiful and poetic expression of grace and talent. In practice, what results is a chaotic and disorienting cascade of broken waves and discordant breaks that covers the face of the surface in confusion and contradiction. Again, something Talthielle would have happily warned her about, if she'd given him the chance. Now, his own conscript had become his captor. He had given Brinka back her life, and in turn, she had assumed control of his. And then he thought of it.

"The Pathfinder," he whispered, with a sense of awe and admiration. He would have burst into laughter, but it occurred to Talthielle that in the short span of time in which he had been musing his way through the mathematics of Lua's impossible assertion, Nanok and the Kenjah were staring at him dumbly, obviously waiting for an explanation and convincing themselves that he was using this space to construct some reasonable explanation, when in fact, he wasn't. Brinka and Konjo knew nothing of the mechanical architecture of *Epozia* contrivance. And while they waited for him to explain, Talthielle was coming to realise, as Lua should have, that he would now have to be very judicious about what kind of explanation he could construct for the Brinka sitting before him that would not impinge upon the designs of the Brinka, somewhere out there, pulling the strings. Obviously, the word 'Pathfinder' did not satisfy anyone's desire for clarity.

Talthielle was cornered, once again.

He looked from Lua to Brinka, and to Konjo and Nanok, and tried to appreciate the irony of no longer being in control, but still somehow being in charge. Brinka had corrected Talthielle's mistakes, and though he had many unanswered questions of his own, he could be sure of one thing: Brinka was entrusting him with the safety and guidance and wellbeing of this version of herself and her beloved. Now, more than ever, Talthielle could feel the gravity and urgency in the compulsion to tread softly and think and speak with focused caution. But *now* was minutes after midnight, following a long and arduous day marked by an incomprehensible sequence of calamitous crises, conspicuously having begun on the restless legs of a sleep deprived hangover.

He thought of Brinka's dream, and of the tumultuous wave that had sent him spinning around the Kenjah's cabin like a ragdoll. He remembered the Viermah's breakfast going into the bin, and remembered collapsing into a fevered nightmare hallucination in Bran's cabin just before the leviathan sea goddess revealed herself and seared a terrifying memory in the heart of everyone aboard who laid eyes on her. He recalled his confrontation with Lua before dinner, right here in this space, just hours ago. His body was sore, and he was tired. He didn't know what to say to Brinka and the boys right now, and wanted time to consider his position.

"That's enough for one night, my friends, I think. You were right, Lua. We have a long ride ahead of us, and we'll have plenty of time to give these questions the attention they deserve. I am weary, Kenjah. And my mind is full. I bid you all retire for the night, before Bran and his officers arrive and casually trap us in this conversation into the wee hours. Try not to trouble yourselves about these things. We are all here, and we are all safe, for the time being, and apparently, unbeknownst to myself, this has been accomplished against great odds, and with, as Lua says, great sacrifice. I believe it is up to us to decide what we do next, and how we do it. We will do it together, in good faith and in good humor and high spirits. But we won't do it tonight. Good night, my friends, and get some rest. Tomorrow, we will make *swelus* out of all of you. To the *Marvu*!" Talthielle toasted high, and retired.

***

In the black distance, the albatross watched a single point of brilliant light that no one aboard could see. The *Marvu* advanced along a northerly path into deep and frigid waters. The wise old bird shook its feathers against the cold winds that began to blow. The ship was still being driven by the centrifugal event horizon of a wailing storm several leagues off the port bow, too far off to menace the crew, but close enough to be heard rumbling over the frothing waves.

Below, many fathoms down, the midshelf gave way to vast webs of ancient and craggy trenches, reaching abysmal depths, well beyond the reach of Omnia's mortal lores or those men who set out to conquer the sea. In the bottom waters, which have never seen the sun or the moon or the stars, *Ursal*, the Kalamaii, waited, watched, and listened to every word spoken aboard the *Marvu*. She could hear Bran breathing as he lingered behind on the Bridge with his officers, appreciating the peaceful and quiet moments of internal deliberation.

Troy followed the bird on the prow with a sharp eye, and occasionally whispered his rudder commands to the pilot, trying to keep the creature pointed straight ahead, and hastily scribbling these into his log to try to plot out and make sense of the trek. *Ursal* knew that a capable navigator could rough out his or her ship's course with careful enough attention to this sequence of rudder commands. It was not necessarily a question of any dishonest attempt to discover the location of the Kalama temple. It was a question of mutual respect, and she made no effort to confuse him or corrupt his log. *Ursal* understood that Troy had his own people to protect. If she chose to abandon them in the middle of nowhere and maroon them in the wilderness, Troy would be negligent in his duties if he was not able to make some reasonable guess as to which way to point the ship to return to Omnia. The navigator would trust his Kalamaii host and her vector finding friend insofar as she did not eat his friends and tear his ship apart. He would not abandon responsibility for the lives of his shipmates to blind trust. So the bird shifted back and forth across the centerline to point the way, and Troy whispered his instructions and wrote them in his log. Everyone involved understood that she could spin that ship around and around until she got bored or tired, and just bathe it in such an impenetrable fog that it would sail in circles until everyone aboard died of starvation and exposure, and it would never see a stretch of land. Mortals cling to the illusion of control, even if they know it is an illusion.

She could hear Garrison and Hinds finding Talthielle in bedclothes in the antechamber of the ship's library, and curtly instructing the weary clocksmith to report to the Bridge, and volunteering, in no uncertain terms, to escort him there personally. She could hear his defeated sigh of acquiescence, and the sound his enchanted staff made when it scratched and tapped the deck of the ship between oddly spaced footfalls. He was injured, and favoring his limbs. Garrison and Hinds were friendly, but serious. They had been ordered to maintain a few feet of personal distance from the *Epozia* rider, as a general precaution-- a 'respectful distance,' Bran had said. *Just out of arm's reach* of the clocksmith. She could tell by his lagging gait that he still had no idea what he would say to Bran once their final moment of truth arrived. Talthielle had commandeered an entire ship, its mission, and its crew, and would be held to account with as much diplomacy and tact as any *swelu* could muster. But he would be held to account, nonetheless. And he would have to do better with Bran than he was doing so far with everyone else.

Ursal could hear the Kenjah, pawing and purring softly and refusing to sleep, but trying much harder to be mindful of the lonely and seasick birdling next door. They knew more than they let on about Talthielle and the fate of Omnia, and most importantly, they knew that she could hear every word and every breath and every step. In their private moments, they moved little and said less, but spared nothing on the breathing, of which there was plenty. She could hear Nanok tossing and turning and scratching at his mottled down. The Champion of the Verdant, so ill handled by his friends and warmly received by his enemies. *Ursal* could feel change moving in the riptides. The end of an epoch was approaching, accompanied by the birth of another. She had listened as he turned the pages in an old book until his eyes fell heavy and he drifted into restless dreams.

High above *Ursal*, on the calm surface still far from the storms which drove the *Marvu*, there rested a monumental structure, the Kalama temple, floating under clear skies and a fingernail moon. Aloft in a watchtower, a Kenjah queen looked out over the tranquil seas. She was whithered and gray, and ancient to behold, yet never quite frail. She was the color of dying stars, but still very much alive, and shining brightly, a brilliant point of light in the infinite darkness. In her mind, she spoke to Vaullus, her nocturnal pet, and thanked the winged creature for helping the *Marvu* find its way safely in the icy tempest.

Like *Ursal* below her, Brinka watched, and waited, and listened.

(Shadows in the Mirror)

"I've had unspeakable dreams, Talthielle."

Bran appeared as tired and restless as Talthielle felt. He was pouring over arcane charts and drawings in the oh-two. Hinds and Garrison politely bid them both pleasant dreams and happily made themselves scarce. Troy had already been ordered to relinquish his watch to Stilver, a less capable, but eminently earnest navigator who understood the risks of failure or negligence, though a reluctant and grumbling Troy spared no breath in reminding him before finally conceding his captain's command. Bran was following the projected courses which previous provisioners had estimated during their similarly blinded voyages, and trying to ascertain some common patterns in the deviations those courses followed.

Some of it was elementary. The Kalama Temple was necessarily never beyond a two week's journey from the shores of Omnia, notwithstanding the two or three day fishing excursions each ship would endure along the way. There was always a set of corresponding arcs, one outbound and tending towards a port rudder. The inbound arc was generally shorter, but more intense, and would deposit the ship somewhere in the middle of the waters it had crossed when the skies finally cleared and the navigators could plot the stars to steer the ship back to port. By then, the position of the temple would have been well enough obscured to protect its inhabitants, and in any case, the temple itself would be long gone by then, and no ship would be fast enough to double back and catch up with it, let alone foolish enough to try. In this way, these missions tended to be consistently successful, to the point of being rather uneventful.

There were very detailed logs of the festivities and celebrations held by the monks, who received their provisions with immense gratitude and deference. If Mond's projections were accurate, the *Marvu* would reach the temple by the full moon, adjourn for three nights and two days, and then depart for the trek home on the final evening. There would be long tables covered with a dazzling array of exotic food, laid out each morning and evening by their hosts, and in between, the crew would participate in an assortment of games and contests. The musicians aboard the *Marvu* would play for the monks, and the tales of wild dances and merriment lasting well into the wee hours abounded in every log Bran could find. But the most enticing element of the whole experience was what was ubiquitously only ever referred to as *the ritual*.

Neither the monks, nor anyone else in Omnia for that matter, had any concept of genetic stock, but they understood well that it had to be regularly replenished and supplemented with the help of willing and worthy outsiders. Bran's crew possessed an ample supply of willingness, and would compete valiantly to prove their worth in the contests and dances, after which the eligible monk maidens would deliberate and make their own selections. It was considered among the sailing class to be the highest imaginable honor any salty *swelu* might ever receive.

Generations of this ritual had allegedly rendered profound benefits among the Kalama, whom the tales claimed had essentially evolved into an extraordinary race of graceful and intelligent devotees, beautiful to behold, and moreso, many speculated, as the years went on. One ship's captain trying to wrap his mind around this ancient tradition famously supposed that each new ship that visited this island would find its inhabitants more excellent in every way than had the last, and therefore, every new voyage to provision the Kalama temple would necessarily be the greatest voyage any *swelu* had ever made. None of the logs, however, mentioned a single word about witnessing the kind of spectacle the *Marvu* had witnessed today. Curiously, though the logs were replete with much ado about the hospitality and frivolity of the Kalama, there was very little mention of the Kalamaii in any of the logs, and nothing really of substance at all. Bran was, in all senses of the phrase, venturing into completely uncharted waters, and this prospect filled him with trepidation for which there was no remedy but forward motion.

What he knew he would not find in these logs, which were themselves the accumulated testimonies of ships which inevitably survived, were the testimonies of ships which did not. Pike, his predecessor, had once told him a grim tale of a ship, whose name he would not utter if his feet were not squarely on dry land, which had unwittingly carried a small band of foolish would-be assassins and looters who planned to raid the island for its treasures, and mutiny against the captain and her crew. Some of the crewman conspired with them, and when they reached the island, as the story goes, they assaulted the monks and attempted to mishandle their women. There was a furious battle, and the monks, whom they discovered they had sorely underestimated, drove them all back aboard their ship and away from the island, where many of them met a terrible fate.

According to the legend, a handful of crewman, who had been appalled by the behavior of their shipmates and riders, had joined with the monks and fought furiously to protect them, and some of these even gave their lives in the conflagration in defense of the Kalama. Those among them that did survive, told unbelievable stories of how their ship was lifted out of the water in a dead wind, and crushed like so many leaves beneath a boot. The survivors, a fortunate and worthy few, had been chained to gallows below decks and beaten by their captors and punished for their defiance, but when the ship was torn apart and taken under, a mysterious force had broken their chains and rescued them, setting them adrift on the floating wreckage and pushing them home on a gentle wave.

Pike had been a walking repository of wonderful stories like these, but Bran suspected that even Pike would have been incredulous if he'd lived long enough to hear this one. What a first day!

Bran abandoned his fruitless pursuits when Talthielle arrived, and found a seat to deposit his addled bones. Talthielle approached the curious drawings which had held Bran's attention and studied a few of them with some casual interest, and found a place to sit beside the captain.

"Speak of your dreams, my friend. There seems to be a lot of that going around."

"Tell me about it. I suppose I'm happy to hear my officers and crew aren't the only ones. I don't have to tell you, we have all been very excited about this trip since we learned our ship had been chosen by the Kalama. I'm very proud of my men, and I'm sure you understand me when I say there is no line I will not cross to protect them. I'm sure you understand what I mean."

"Loud and clear, captain. Loud and clear. I don't believe we will come to that. And I have not the words to express my gratitude for this... indulgence. It is not our intention to endanger anyone but ourselves. What we are going to try to do, so far as I know, has never been attempted, not since Lavaris closed his gates. I would be dishonest if I claimed to fully understand the implications or the risks involved, but it seems reasonable to presume that the Kalamaii will not arbitrarily break the truce. She had ample opportunity to do so today; in fact, I think that the whole spectacle may have been meant as a clear reminder of her unopposable ability to do so, and of her decision to refrain. She is an unusual character, vain and pretentious and flamboyant. But she is also wise beyond measure, and both just and gentle in spirit, once you get past her somewhat abrasive personality. Her superiority is, to her, merely a fact of her existence. This truce, frail and fragile and tenuous as it may sometimes seem, we must remember, was her idea. I'm sure you can imagine, after what you have seen today, that nothing in Omnia is capable of imposing its own will upon her."

"Nothing but you, apparently."

"Oh no captain, I have no such delusions of grandeur. I will seek her audience, plead my case, and make my request. If she agrees, we may all have a chance to save Omnia from itself. If she refuses, on the other hand, and you may mark my words, captain, I will back away very slowly and thank her for her audience as profusely and with as much humility as is possible."

"And then what?"

Talthielle sighed from the gut and closed his eyes, trying to ward off the images in his mind.

"I will have done all I can for Omnia, captain. What else can there be?"

Bran seemed unconvinced, but equally uncompelled to challenge Talthielle's reasoning. He simply shrugged absently and said nothing. There was much to consider, and little else to say, and apparently less to be done about any of it.

"I am curious about your dreams, captain. I myself cannot remember the last time I slept long enough to dream. I know that the Kenjah have had some strange dreams, and I suppose Nanok will have a few himself this evening."

"No, Talthielle. Another time maybe. My sense is that the time is not yet ripe for such discussions. We have both had some long days, and longer nights, it would seem, and I have detained you long enough. I think I am about done for one day, and I suspect I am going to need my wits about me, and probably so will you. Good night clocksmith, and for what it's worth, I wish you luck. I know about as much about the Kalamaii as I know about Lavaris, and it isn't much either way. Maybe this all makes sense to you and yours. Who am I to judge? We are at your service."

"Thank you Bran. And good night to you as well."

***

A few moments after Talthielle clambered down out of the oh-two and found his way back to his quarters, the aft hatch of the space quietly opened, and the ship's librarian quietly entered. Bran looked up at her with heavy, but loving eyes. He spun his legs down as she sat beside him. Neither of them spoke for a time. She had listened from Bran's cabin while Talthielle talked, but they both knew he'd revealed nothing new. Lua, Bran knew, had been very selective about what she would disclose about her business with the clocksmith and his conscripts, but he could see the concern in her eyes that she either would not, or could not conceal. Something had changed in her demeanor since this morning; he was sure of it, but he knew not how to ask or what to ask if he did. Sometimes Bran got the feeling that Lua was even more guarded than the *Epozia*. She knew something, or had discovered something, which no one else involved had yet discovered. And they all seemed to know more than Bran, so he did not beat his own brow against the bulkhead trying to guess at the mysteries they kept even amongst themselves. He was not one to be easily deceived, but was not one to press the point either. People revealed themselves in their own ways, all in due time. Lua was about to give him some new piece of the truth just now, he suspected, and a carefully curated version of it at that. He would save his questions until he knew what they were, and he would save his strange dreams until he knew what they meant.

"I don't think they know what happens next." Lua broke the silence with reservation in her soft voice.

"Well, they're not alone. You know, I half suppose I remembered inviting you aboard to chronicle our voyage. I'm beginning to wonder if that's why you really took the job. There's something between you and these mysterious riders. Look, I know I'm the captain, but I'm also your friend, and I really do hope you know that I don't mean to intrude. I'm not jealous of them, Lua, on my soul I'm not. It's just... I've got a lot of people's lives to look after, and when I saw that thing today--"

"You felt as though control of your life had been suddenly ripped away from you. Believe me, Bran, I can relate. I'm sorry. It was not my intention to conceal anything from you. Honestly, I don't really know what I can tell you, other than this." Lua took a deep breath and measured her words. "So far as they all know, from their point of view, they really do mean what they say."

"They mean to convince that...thing, out there, to come back with them to Omnia to offer themselves to Lavaris, in some vaguely defined quest to set all the ghosts free and save the world."

Lua hated hearing it out loud. She hated being the only person aboard the *Marvu* who at least pretended to understand it. She hated having to walk the careful line between conceding its absurdity and defending its merit. She knew. She knew in her bones, she knew. They all had to proceed. And if *that thing* didn't come back with them, she knew she would never leave this ship alive. To see Konjo live, Brinka would repeat this process forever, or until her own lifeforce was finally spent.

"They have to make it to that island, Bran. Me, you, your crew, this ship, we are all expendable. As strange as this may seem, that thing out there is the least of your troubles. It can simply be no other way. I don't know what happens when they get there. I truly don't. On my soul, as you say. I just know that there is no future onboard this ship but theirs. As soon as those Kenjah set foot on the gangplank for the first time, we all became conscripts. And there is *nothing* we can do about it."

An indifferent expression of disbelief glanced over Bran's brow.

"No, Bran. I need you to hear me when I say this. There is NOTHING anyone aboard this ship can do about it. You have no agency here. I'm going to be very specific, so that I am not misunderstood." Lua's tone became very grave and stern. "I can hear the list of potential options running through your head right now. I can see it in your face. I need you very much to understand this. You have no agency. This is not your ship. Those are not your officers. This crew no longer belongs to you. Whether that *thing* out there ever comes aboard your ship or not, it's immaterial. Even if it did, and you were obliged by the old customs to stand relieved. Even then, Bran, it would only be a redundant formality. If you sincerely want to protect the lives of your men, if you really want to see the other side of this thing, whatever that may mean, you have to understand what I am telling you. You can't kill them. You can't throw them over. You can't turn this ship around." Lua was pensive, and still trying to curate her version of the truth. Bran could see that much in her eyes, but the urgency on her lips was compelling and real. "You would only doom everyone aboard to a horrible fate."

"Even you?" Bran asked.

Lua shivered into something somewhere between laughter and tears.

"Especially me, Bran. Especially me."

Bran accepted Lua's best effort to navigate constraints he knew he could not comprehend and she could not transgress. For better or worse, Lua was someone he trusted without question, and he could tell by the strain in her voice that her intentions were sincere, even if her thoughts remained guarded. At length, he just shrugged and shook his head. He didn't have to like it. But Lua was telling him what she knew *he* needed to understand.

"Are we in danger, Lua?"

"Yes."

"And if those Kenjah make it to the island, are we still in danger?"

"Yes."

"What do I do, Lua?"

Lua shifted her weight in the cushion and turned to face him. He'd never seen her this way.

"When the time comes, Bran, you stand relieved." She touched his face, and stood, and left.

Bran sat with his thoughts. He tried to inventory the circumstances like items on a manifest. His mind craved order amid a sea of details. Sixty three souls. Sixty four, if he counted his own. An injured old tramp who claims to control time. Two predestined mountain folk who can't take their eyes off of each other or they might actually suffocate. A clipped Viermah, who seemed to be having a difficult go of things just being alive. Two nearly senile old zealots, nominally in charge, but with nothing useful to contribute. A pleasantly naive young couple with two small children. A swarthy band of pickers and crooners who drank heavily, but mostly kept to themselves. Four officers, four alternates, and forty crewman. And a bird, whom Bran supposed, might be the only soul onboard the ship who has any idea what in Dab was actually happening around here.

Suddenly, Bran had an idea so stupid it nearly made him laugh out loud.

"I should just go talk to the stupid bird. Not having an awful lot of luck with any-"

And then Bran fell silent, thought for a moment, and then stood up and rushed down to the main deck. There it was, tailfeathers and beak on a perfectly stooped plane, pointing the way forward like a wooden lady bolted to the bow. As Bran approached, the creature pretended to ignore him at first, but when Bran lingered with a sense of purpose, the bird slowly turned around with an inquisitive look in it's big, nictating eyes, as if Bran were the thing about this situation that was out of place. It was a look Bran decided he didn't really care for, honestly, but he put it out of his mind.

"Garrison!"

Garrison immediately appeared on the main deck, as if from nowhere, and tried to process the makings of another spectacle as he crossed the weather deck.

"Sir!"

"Nightwatchman." The forward deck officer hadn't needed to be called; Bran and the bird already had his full attention.

"Nightwatchman. I'm going for a swim. You are to carry on as ordered. Understood?"

Of course not. What an absurd question.

"Understood. No. Wait, WHAT!?"

"Captain? What do you mean! That water is freezing!"

"Garrison, nothing gets ON or OFF of this ship while I'm gone. Heard?

Garrison bit his tongue, and his eyes drifted from Bran to a distant spot of black nothing in the distance, and back to Bran.

"HEARD?" Bran's eyes were gleaming with intensity and impatience. He was already pulling off his boots and shirt.

"Heard, captain. Nothing on, or off. Captain?"

"Yes, Garrison?"

"Be careful out there mate."

Bran would promise him nothing. The ship's captain gave one last look at the mystified bird, and shouted under pursed eyebrows.

"Ursal! I think it's time you and I had a chat!"

The albatross ruffled its feathers and hunched its head back in its neck and studied Bran the way one looks at a polynomial equation after three pints of sour. Bran did not wait for the bird to reply. He looked out to the horizon and shouted again. "You hear me, Ursal? I'm coming in!" And with that, Bran dove head first off of the prow and hit the water already breaststroking as if he had somewhere to be.

Garrison and the nightwatchman stood there speechless in the dark with their jaws hanging open until the deck officer finally managed to squeak out a piece of a syllable, almost inaudible against the distant thunder and the sound of the wind in the sails.

"Sss... Sir?"

Garrison closed his mouth and narrowed his eyes at the watch. "You're relieved. Go wake the officers. Now!"

"Heard!" and the bewildered officer dashed away.

***

Bran felt the frigid plunge for only the first few seconds before his body went into shock and refused to convey the stimulus to his overwhelmed mind. He was numb from neck to heel before he'd covered half a league. The ship was already a memory buried in the darkness behind him. He swam, arm over arm, and kicked his feet to the rhythm. He wouldn't turn back now even if he knew which way it was. He could see nothing in any direction but clouds above and the sea below, and the shadows and fog between. He grimaced against the froth and tried not to swallow as he turned his head left and right between his strokes. The salt stung his eyes, and his hair lapped against the sides of his face. He had angled himself in line with the direction the albatross had pointed the ship, and he only focused on holding that tack. Swim straight, and swim hard. He had no idea what he would find ahead of him, but he had suddenly realized one thing while standing there, staring at that bird. And only one thing for certain. She was not going to let him die out here. And because there was now nothing else out here but her between certain death and himself, she was going to have to save him.

This thought pounded his mind between the thuds of his booming pulse. Insane? Maybe. Desperate? Probably. But for the first time since he'd stumbled into that cabin this morning to find that Kenjah Queen lost in her nightterrors, Bran had reclaimed a sense of control over his life, and he would not relinquish it now. Not to her, and not to the bottomless fathoms below.

"Force of Nature?" he shouted against the wind, "Meet Force of Will! I am no one's quarry! You will either speak to me... Or drown me! What's it gonna be Ursal!" Nothing answered him but the wind and the waves, but he would not doubt himself. He just kept stroking and kicking and pushing the tides, feeling his overworked heart pumping less and less heat to his freezing extremities, which sent none back. "URSAL!" he shouted, not with anger, but with fury. He lost track of time and space and distance, and soon he could feel nothing but his hands and feet slapping the water. He was slowing down. He was running out of breath. The waves were swelling, and soon he slowed to an aggressive dog paddle, and was essentially swimming in place, in the middle of black nowhere, alone, and losing consciousness. "URRRSSAAAAAAAALLLLLLLLL!"

And then his answer came. He felt the first constricting sensation around his waste, and then another, and then his feet were bound, and at last, another tentacle came up out of the water beneath his face and wrapped itself around his neck. Bran felt himself lifted out of the drink and held aloft, and then he saw her form, rising out of the sea before him like the Dab itself, and twice as wide. She squeezed him as if she were wringing out a rag, and lifted him up until he was twice as high as the sails on the *Marvu*, and he saw her black eyes, and heard a deafening voice beyond his own comprehension.

"Fool! Who are you that you would dare to summon me?"

Bran retched, trying to squeeze wind through his throat past her iron grip, and she loosened it ever so slightly, just enough to let him whisper his raspy pleas. But Bran had no pleas.

"I want to go somewhere we can talk." Bran didn't know which eye to stare her down in, so eventually he just picked one and tried to ignore the rest. The sound of her laughter was the sound of boulders rolling down a mountainside, mixed with the hellish sound of a thousand children screaming.

"Somewhere we can talk? Suit yourself, sailor."

And then Bran was flying in the air, tumbling head over heels. She tossed him up like candy, opened her gaping maw, and ate him whole.

***

"What do you MEAN he just jumped in and swam away!" Troy was shouting at the nightwatchman and the security officer. Hinds was behind him, yawning and trying to rub the sleep out of his tired eyes and replace them with an appropriate measure of concern. He was not entirely sure he was awake. One's captain does not merely leap from the prow of his own ship and swim away in the freezing black waters in the middle of the night. But then again, one does not often question these things in a dream.

Garrison, obviously, would answer for the equally incredulous officer, though he was sure he had no better explanation of his own. Troy was furious and confused at the same time, and Garrison knew, somehow, that Bran was not going to just suddenly reappear any time soon, and worried whether he would reappear at all. He estimated that even a capable man such as the captain could survive probably no more than an hour in those waters. "He said something about *Ursal* before he went in. Told us to carry on, and said nothing gets on or off the ship until he returns. And then he just... jumped in and swam away. I don't know man. Should we call Man Overboard?"

Troy blinked at Garrison several times with blank confusion.

"Hinds! Have the men haul in the sails and drop anchor. Go!"

Hinds immediately bolted away, shouting at the linemen who were already clustered in a conspiratorial clot at the hatch of the oh-one, trying to make sense of the senseless and grateful for something else to make sense of. They sprang into action, pulling lines and drawing in the sails, and passing the order on to the aft watchmen to release the anchor pins at once.

Troy turned to Garrison, still shouting. "Get those Kenjah out here and up to the crow's nest, and tell them we need every bit of starlight they can muster. We need light to see, and Bran, if he's still out there, is going to need it too."

Garrison understood and concurred and complied without hesitation. "Heard!" he shouted, and vanished below decks. Troy stayed behind, ordering the nightwatchman to post lookouts on the rails at every stanchion. As the crewmen bustled about their orders behind him with marked urgency, Troy briefly found himself alone with the bird. Troy looked at the thing as if he was about to demand an explanation and might bash its brains in if it didn't come up with a really good one. The bird looked up at him, just as clearly confused by the situation as Troy, and took a few nervous steps out of Troy's space, just in case the exhausted navigator's better nature failed him. Troy almost laughed at the bird's trepidatious attempt to make itself invisible, and instead of bashing its face in, he took the hint and tried to regain control of his wits and think clearly. This, whatever it was, was not the bird's fault, and Troy was quickly coming around to the realization which had already set in on Garrison: no one was getting any sleep tonight.

Within a few moments, the lookouts were posted, and Garrison was emerging with two half-clothed and very concerned looking Kenjah.

"I need one on the prow and one aloft! I don't care which!"

Konjo and Brinka exchanged nervous glances, and seemed to share a thought between themselves, as one looked aloft and the other nodded. Brinka shone the brightest, or at least was incapable of persuading Konjo otherwise, so she went aloft, and Konjo joined Troy and the baffled looking bird. The crewmen and officers beheld the spectacle of two of their riders peeling off what remained of what they wore, and taking their positions above and below as lightning and fire crawled from their sinewy muscles, soon illuminating the night sky. Konjo and Brinka were the color of falling meteorite. At first, only Troy noticed the bird suddenly fix on the Kenjah in the crow's nest and fall into a kind of dull-eyed trance, but then it shook its wings and shrieked, and jumped up and down on the railing, nodding and shaking its head in a frenzy, before it leapt from the railing and flew to Brinka's shoulder, cawing like a feral child.

An even more curious spectacle followed, when the bird lit on her shoulder. Even Brinka was startled by the bird's inexplicable impulse, and wasn't sure herself if it meant her harm as it beat the wind to reach her. But when it landed, everyone aboard saw a brief flash of light ripple through her body that was somehow every color at once, and also colorless at the same time. For the space of a heartbeat, many would later recount amongst themselves and to others, it was if they had all witnessed, for the first and last time, a completely new color they'd never seen before.

Even from the weather deck, what Troy could see that no one else saw, is that for several moments, Brinka seemed to have fallen into that same dull-eyed trance he'd seen on the bird. Everyone saw her strange reaction, but none had seen the bird do the same thing. Some vague memory or association came into Troy's mind, and he turned to look at Konjo, whom no one else was paying any attention to in the moment. Konjo had gone the color of starstuff, and had fallen into the same trance as his beloved. The thought occurred to Troy all at once that he had no point of reference whatsoever for anything happening right now. Bran was in the water. The Kenjah were filling the air with light. The sails were in, the anchor away, and the lookouts posted. And his strange avian compass needle had completely abdicated its post. What in Omnia could he do now but wait, and hope?

Garrison and the Kenjah had awakened Nanok, who in turn rushed to the library, retaining exactly one half of the jumbled and hasty explanation the Master at Arms had given the Kenjah. After his equally hasty and jumbled recitation, Talthielle was sure he understood less than half of that. Nevertheless, his first instinct was to find Lua and wake her. Whatever was happening, he was sure she wouldn't want to miss it, especially if it was happening to Bran himself. But also, Talthielle supposed she was probably the only one left aboard who might make any sense of it. Talthielle was sore and burnt, and half-jokingly considered resetting the day just so he could just go back to sleep. Only half-joking, of course, because if Bran didn't return to the ship within the hour, Talthielle might be the only one aboard who could stop him from having jumped in in the first place. By the time he reached the weatherdeck with Lua and Nanok, the very serious thought of having to relive this entire day over again just to save the captain's life was becoming a gnawing kind of calculus he was too tired to work out. When he saw the Kenjah in the breadth of their splendor, and all the lookouts posted, he quickly gathered, as had the rest of the officers and crew by now, that no one was getting any sleep tonight.

Troy met Talthielle on the forward deck without speaking, and intimated that Talthielle should not speak either. All hands had been ordered by conveyance of hand signals to maintain utter silence for the duration. This was partly to ensure that Bran might be heard if he called out for help, but it was also intended to abate the inevitable spread of rumor and panic among the crew and its riders. Troy could not know that his order had also deprived *Ursal* any further information about what was happening aboard the *Marvu*, though she already knew it was standing dead in the water. Troy motioned to the empty prow, and then directed Talthielle's attention to the albatross perched Brinka's shoulders, which he had not yet observed himself. One would struggle to look directly at a Kenjah in full starlight, though many of the awestruck crewmen could not help but try.

Talthielle followed Troy's motions and saw the bird perched on Brinka's shoulder in the crow's nest. The navigator drew no reassurance from the clocksmith's puzzled shrug. He turned his own gaze back out toward the stretch of seawater where the nightwatchman had pointed. It was an oblivious and futile guess. Many minutes had passed between Bran's departure and Troy's order to halt and stand fast, and the ship itself had not only kept moving, but was also shifting and bobbing on the waves around the anchor chain. The whole horizon was just equally featureless darkness, and Troy's only real clue as to the ship's orientation was the direction of the wind. There were no landmarks, no stars, nothing visible in the sky behind the dense overcast. The rumbling stormclaps in the distance carried in every direction and only added to the disorientation. To make matters worse, a slow morning fog was building around the vessel, further obscuring anyone's guess as to which way they might go if, or when, they finally gave up and decided to eulogize their captain and weigh the anchor. Bran had better know what he's doing, Troy thought, because if he didn't, everyone on board might be cooked.

A number of impossible decisions weighed upon the navigator in those long, empty moments. How long could he keep the *Marvu* stationary before he had to concede the loss of his closest friend and move on? How would he explain these circumstances, let alone a decision to abandon Bran to the deep, to the crew? Two people had seen Bran go over with their own eyes. That left potentially sixty people on the ship who would have to learn of the event secondhand, and decide for themselves whether or not they believed it, and how they felt about it if they didn't believe it at all. Bran was neither impetuous nor impulsive, and this was a crew who knew very well that their captain would not just throw his life away to the fish on their first day at sea, on the most heralded voyage of their careers. Would that infernal bird ever return to the prow and guide the ship out of these waters, and would the Kalamaii be inclined to render a favorable wind? Troy had to consider the possibility that such a flagrant and unpredictable sign of instability from the ship's captain might persuade the deities to reconsider the *Marvu's* credibility and intentions with regard to the sacred Kalama temple and its vulnerable monks. Omnia might have been only a day's ride from wherever they were now, but if they charted the wrong course in this climate, they could sail for a thousand years and never see land again.

Troy reduced the matter to this basic formulation. Their survival now depended entirely on whether or not they were ever permitted to see the stars again. A well-motivated Kalamaii could keep the storms and clouds going indefinitely, which was somehow almost less terrifying than the prospect of just keeping it up for a very long time. The stars would guide them home, or the bird would guide them onward. Without one or the other, Troy was just the highest ranking soul among the damned. He was sure he could no more force the bird to comply than he could compel the wind to blow. Apparently, the only person aboard the ship who might compel that bird was the Kenjah presently burning brightly beneath it. Troy had a sinking feeling he would likely have better luck persuading the bird than the Kenjah, if the circumstances demanded persuasion. He shuddered and shoved the feeling aside. He was very tired, and now also completely helpless. It was not an ideal way to start a new command. Sixty three souls.

Come on, Bran.

One becomes a captain, Troy reflected, by being the very last person on the list of possible people who might do something stupid and get everyone else marooned and murdered. It was basically in the job description. It was not explicitly written into the commission that way, but it was certainly in there between the lines somewhere. The tension was building in his mind, but he was wearing it well enough, he hoped. He had to remind himself that he was not the only person onboard living through a potential existential crisis between faith and rationality. Time was passing, and each moment that ticked by was likely one less moment that his friend and captain had to live. And in this state of sensory deprivation, with no stars and no movement, time itself became an abstraction, and it was impossible to mark the increment of its passing.

Time.

Troy turned to Talthielle, who had been standing beside him quietly and contemplating these dilemmas from his own point of view. He looked deeply into Talthielle's eyes and held the vacant form of a question without sense or syntax, and he could see in Talthielle's grave expression that the clocksmith understood the question very clearly, and was fully awash with pleading reservations. The old tramp was injured and exhausted and confused, and possibly desperate. Talthielle winced a painful wince, and almost imperceptibly shook his head. *We have to wait. Give him a chance. If there's one thing she respects, it's got to be audacious courage.* This is what Talthielle wanted to say, but all Troy could see was one more dead-end. The navigator finally came face to face with the inevitably obvious conclusion. He had no control, and no agency, and would make no decision at all until something around him changed. *Bran, you've got all the time in the world. Good luck out there captain. I hope you know what you're doing, because I sure don't.* He nodded to Talthielle, and reluctantly deflated into resignation.

The *Marvu* stood fast, dead in the water.

(Radula Teuthida)

Bran shivered in the dark and damp as he came to. He was soaking wet and freezing, but he was not drowning, nor was he being masticated and dissolved into his elemental nutrients. All good signs, he supposed. The creature had rescued him. Perhaps not his first choice of venues for a parley, but his gambit had worked, or at least he hoped it worked, and that *she* wasn't just savoring his flavor for a little while. Bran absently wondered what he tasted like, and tried to think of something else. He was nearly frozen to the bone, but this... *space,* in which he found himself, was something just shy of comfortably warm. He could see nothing, and he struggled to breathe against the irregular gaseous composition of the air around him. But he could hear the slow and voluminous pulse of her twin hearts beating, and when his shuffling around indicated that consciousness had returned to him, he suddenly heard her voice booming in his mind, rather than in his ears. It was indescribable.

"Well now, curious sailor. What to make of you? I've seen plenty of your kind swimming away from me in my time. I'm not sure I've ever met one of you coming the other way. I'm very tempted to eat you on those grounds alone, just for the pleasure of trying something new!"

"Eat me then! And be done with it. You will not torment me, Kalamaii. If i was afraid of you, I would not have come."

"Whether or not you fear me, sailor, is of course, immaterial, don't you think?"

"Just as immaterial as whether or not you eat me."

"Do you want me to eat you?"

"I want someone to tell me just what in Dab is happening on my ship."

"Well that's easy. Your crewmen are topside and surveilling the sea for signs of your carcass. You'd know that if you hadn't *left* your ship, but then I suppose, they'd all be doing something else right now, wouldn't they? Like sailing to provision my people instead of wasting my time. Okay then, can I eat you now?"

"That's not what I mean and you know it."

"Then SAY what you mean, sailor. If you speak in riddles, I will eat you. I might eat you for a pun, so choose your words carefully."

Bran, in truth, preferred very much not to be eaten. As his eyes adjusted, be dimly became aware of the meaty glottal structure in the rear portion of the space he was thawing in. It was imperative to remain on this side of that structure, he decided. Perhaps if he lowered his voice a little, she might lower hers. When she spoke, he felt like his skull might implode from the pressure.

Choose your words, Bran.

"Among my riders, there are two Kenjah, one Viermah, and a character who claims to be *Epozia.* They say they are going to the temple to plead with you to return with them to sacrifice yourselves to Lavaris, the old man in the mountain, to persuade him to release the spirits of the dead into Omnia before its inhabitants burn everything to the ground trying to kill each other. Kalamaii, it is not my intention to speak to you in riddles, but surely you understand me when I say I can count at least twelve things in that little explanation that don't make any sense at all. As I am sure you know, we offer passage to anyone who will make themselves useful for a voyage. Most of my shipmates began their careers this way, and this has long been a general and mutually beneficial method of obtaining passage from one part of Omnia to another. It is a common practise. Only this time, my ship and its crew are tasked with the sacred honor of upholding the peace between our kind and yours by bringing your annual tribute. We have among us riders whose intentions may be contrary to your interests, and therefore may compromise our ability to fulfill our sacred obligations in some way which I can neither predict nor control.

"Someone told me today that I have no control. I have not come to you to redress the offense to my pride. I have come to you because my responsibility as captain of my ship simply cannot be contravened by strangers, or lunatics for that matter, especially when our intended errand is of such great importance. Everyone has a story, and everyone seems to have a role to play in it, but none of them seem to have all the same pieces of that story assembled the same way at the same time. According to our customs, which these inlanders seem to disregard, if my authority over my ship and its mission is nullified or incapacitated in some way, I must defer to an authority higher than my own. Kalamaii, you are the only authority in these waters to whom I would ever relinquish my command. So here I am, immobilized by two seemingly impossible contradictions. I guessed you would not eat me, and in point of fact, I would be thoroughly grateful if you did not eat me, because I and my ship are already in your service and in the service of your people. It is a great honor to us that we were chosen to bear tribute as our forebears have done.

"We would sooner throw these interlopers overboard than come all this way to offer you insult or injury. But I must consider it equally plausible that our doing so might be just as insulting or injurious to you and yours. If you follow my meaning, Kalamaii, then you can see that I have been presented with a circumstance which only your judgement can arbitrate. So, what say you?"

There was silence, or a close approximation of it between the rumbling drone of dueling heartbeats. Bran was not in the company of an insolent subordinate, and would not browbeat a response from the creature whose meaty glottal structure stood so readily by to settle a hostile dispute, so he waited patiently and tried to steady the beat of his own racing heart, and to take in as much of what little good air there was to be found. *Ursal* deliberated at her own pace, and at length, graciously responded in more conciliatory, and less skull crushing, tones.

"You flatter me, sailor. I might just keep you around if you keep it up. So you're here to defer to my judgment. You threw yourself into these frigid waters, swam against the tide and wind, screaming my name until your strength failed you, and offered me your own delicious skin, just to ask my opinion about these matters occurring aboard your own ship, which, as you say, is presently sailing in my service and the service of my people. I must admit, I can count at least ten things in that little explanation which I find enormously gratifying. Curious little creature. I can taste your courage and your fear, but I think I understand your position. Lesser men would have never dared to risk such certain death to treat with me in person. You are either an impetuous fool, or you possess the ethereal spirit of legends. I suppose it is a matter of perspective, which of these you are. No sensible captain would commission the *Marvu* to an impetuous fool, I think. It is a worthy ship, and your crew seems to be quite capable. And I admit, I rather prefer the version of this story in which I and my people are the beneficiaries of the heroic and honorable service of a captain who possesses the ethereal spirit of legends. I confess, it does make me want to eat you, all the more. But then, that would only confirm all the terrible little stories you tell your younglings about me to pacify them in their beds at night.

"Yes, captain Bran. I am well aware of the goings on aboard your ship. So Talthielle has assembled his quorum, or thinks he has anyway, and he is coming to see me. He wants to persuade me to give up my eyes to Lavaris so that Omnia can see itself as we Kalamaii see it. His Kenjah will give their luminous skin so that Omnia can feel. The birdling will surrender his golden feathers so that his countrymen will know divinity, and the last clocksmith will yield his precious time to increase the days of strangers. It all sounds very lovely, doesn't it?" *Ursal* sighed long and deep. It was a curious sound, more deeply felt than heard.

"But none of it will come to pass."

Bran's heart sank in his chest. He warily eyed the meaty glottal structure behind him, and that sense of mortal trepidation returned all at once, like an ominous flood of ill omen.

"My feeling has been that it would not, Kalamaii. I have had strange and terrible dreams of late. Perilous and unspeakable things. They are all trapped, and none of them know it, though I do suspect that some of them know more than they pretend. Truth is a strange thing, Kalamaii. Among inlanders, anyway. We sailors tend to regard such things differently, I suppose. These riders have all given themselves to a noble cause, which they do not know is doomed already, because while they have given over their lives to their cause, they still guard their precious secrets within themselves and from each other."

"Truth is the sea floor in deep water, captain. Everyone is sure it exists, but none among them will ever lay eyes upon it while they breathe. It is the place where they dispose of their fanciful theories and contentious dogmas. Talthielle has already failed, and he is only just now discovering that fact. He has not the life left within him to offer, even if he survived the arduous trek to treat with Lavaris. None of them know what is waiting for them at my temple. But you do, don't you captain? You've seen her, haven't you? The Magnificent One. You've dreamt of her? Of her incomprehensible beauty, and her awful sacrifices? None of them will be permitted to leave my island once they've arrived. Talthielle's reign has ended. Your Kenjah will not go to Lavaris, captain. Nor will the birdling, for that matter. Omnia's fate is beyond their reach. Its salvation is not theirs to grant. I am sorry, Bran. Your riders' noble errand is itself, errant, and has been so since the moment it began."

"But they *will arrive*, if that is your will, of course?" Bran felt some cautious tinge of encouragement creeping in from the cold. He had begun very casually but conscientiously tiptoeing away from the rear of the space, as if his chances of survival depended in any way upon proximity. Her voice had softened, but he supposed his flavor might not have. Bran really wanted to see his ship again. He did not want to see what was behind door number two, behind him, even the least little bit. "We will bring them to you, to dispose of as you will. I will tell them nothing, if discretion is what you require of me. And, um, I'm just going to say this one part out loud. I don't mean to be any more presumptuous than I've already been, and I am grateful for my rescue and for your confidence..."

"I'm not going to eat you, Bran."

"Please do not eat me. I really don't want to be eaten. I'm not begging, you understand... Just saying."

"If you don't stop prattling, I might eat you."

Bran was quiet. He breathed deeply, and all things considered, the air was really quite pleasant after all. *Ursal* seemed to be deliberating with herself again, and Bran had no further reason to intrude. He had inched his way across the space to the point farthest from the meaty glottal structure in her throat, and his heartbeat had gradually slowed until it was nearly beating in time with the twin hearts of the Kalamaii. He could see, dimly, the walls above him lined with dull teeth and groves of suckers and ganglia. Things that would amuse his houseguests for almost as long as they would haunt his nightmares. He touched nothing, and said nothing.

"Ok sailor. You have my gratitude for your faithful service, and my respect as well, might I add, for your unconventional valor, as it were. I won't eat you this time. But I might eat you later. I reserve the right, of course. For now, though, I suppose, it's time to get you back to your ship and get the *Marvu* back into the wind. Pleasant dreams sailor. We will meet again, I think. I'm rather looking forward to it." Bran was about to speak kindly in response, but the space shook violently and suddenly, and Bran tumbled over as concussive spasms tremored through the walls around him, and suddenly it felt as though he was aboard his ship as it was being tossed through the air. He felt movement all around him without, but could see nothing moving at all within. In a flash, his eyes searched for something he could grab onto, but found nothing in time. Once again, he was head over heels and rolling, scrambling for any hold he could find, until he found himself quite breathlessly holding onto the only structure that would support his weight without lacerating his skin. It was meaty, and glottal, and in it he could feel the quickeninging vibrations of thudding parallel pulses.

Bran held on for dear life.

***

Vaullus was the first to sense Brinka's imminent collapse. Konjo was the first to notice when it happened. Both of them had fallen into a dreamlike trance as they permitted their starlight to illuminate the night sky in the search for Bran. When Brinka's failing body reclaimed her mind, the link between the Kenjah was briefly disrupted. She stumbled and flickered, and might have fallen over the railing of the oh-four if Vaullus had not acted quickly and wrapped his talons around her shoulders, beating tornado winds from his broad wings to try to hold her upright long enough for her own instincts to take over. She let out a sharp yelp and fell to her knees, glowing pale like the quartz in Talthielle's staff. Vaullus landed beside her and instinctively tried to soften the blow of her head hitting the deck by cradling her in his feathers. He cooed at her and cawed loudly at the crew for aid, wordless, but in shrieks and tones no one present could fail to interpret. The bird was calling for help, and Konjo had already crossed the weatherdeck and was practically running up the ladderwell to reach her. Troy missed only a beat trying to take in what was happening, but he fell in step and was right behind Konjo when he appeared at Brinka's side. Konjo was the color of citrus and shaking when he saw the pleading look in the bird's eyes. Somehow, the bird knew better than he how serious the circumstances were, and Konjo was prepared to trust that visible urgency, though he did not yet know what to make of it.

As Konjo cradled his beloved in his arms, Vaullus laid a gentle wing across his shoulder and chortled softly in his ear. When Talthielle and Lua appeared on the oh-four, they were greeted by a new spectacle. Vaullus seemed to freeze for several breaths, as if the bird were about to experience a seizure of some kind, and then a look of blank confusion washed over its face as if it didn't know where it was or what was happening. When the spell passed, it seemed to reorient itself, and then it turned from the Kenjah to Troy and looked right into the navigator's eyes with a new sense of urgency and excitement. It jumped up and down and beat its wings at Troy in an obvious attempt to communicate some new message in a primitive and limited way.

Vaullus jumped up on the rails and spun around several times, facing the bow, then Troy, and around again, each time looking directly into Troy's eyes and beating his wings intensely. When it was sure it had Troy's attention, the bird leapt and glided gracefully back down to the forward railing where it had been stationed most of the day. It spun around again to see if Troy was watching, and then chose its mark on the black horizon and pointed. Then it turned around again and repeated the process a few more times, cawing more and more loudly. Troy understood the message, but had grave misgivings.

"No, stupid bird! I am not leaving without my captain!"

At this, the bird turned again to face him, and everyone on deck witnessed the rather comical and disturbing spectacle of an angry albatross soaring back to the oh-four and seeming to slap Troy hard across the face, which left the navigator dumbfounded and confused, and not a little indignant. Troy briefly wondered to himself how long they would last out here if he just throttled that bird with his own hands, but before he could even finish the thought, Vaullus had glided down again and resumed his post. Troy looked down at the Kenjah and back to the bird, and then he heard Lua speaking forcefully behind him. "Troy, he's telling you it's time to move."

"I know what he's telling me young lady, but my friend is still out there in that freezing water somewhere, and I'm not leaving without him." Troy spun on her furiously, but checked himself. Lua was opening her mouth to speak her mind when another voice boomed from the Kenjah, half-conscious on the deck between them, so loud and deep it even frightened Konjo. Brinka went crimson, and seemed to even startle herself as commands flowed from her lips.

"Aft crewmen, take in the anchor! Linemen, port and starboard, all sails to full. Pilot, fifteen degrees starboard and hold. All hands, prepare for high winds! Battle Stations! Lookouts, return to your duty stations. Rovers, seal all hatches below!" And for a painfully long breath, no one aboard moved. A hard surge of cold air whistled in from the stern as Troy looked down at Brinka in her state of mortal delirium. He was utterly baffled, and just stood there with his jaw hanging down, until Lua snapped him out of it.

"TROY! It's time to GO!"

Troy gasped and looked around in every direction, trying to process the scene, and then his wits returned. His voice thundered over the rails. "Carry the orders! Bring in the anchor! Full sail! Fifteen points starboard and hold. All hands: BATTLE STATIONS!" They heard Hinds and Garrison below shouting orders, and suddenly, the *Marvu* was buzzing like a hive. Troy flashed one last nervous and unconvinced look at Lua before he dashed below to help his shipmates. After he went down, Nanok appeared, behind Lua and Talthielle, who were now stooping around Brinka with expressions of grave concern. He reached for something appropriate to say, but he was just as confused as everyone else involved, if not moreso, and the best he could come up with was

"Hey, how come *she* gets to drive!?"

"Talthielle, what's happening to her?" Konjo's face was shrinking with tears and worry, and in his eyes there was earnest panic. Brinka had gone limp, and seemed nearly lifeless, though Konjo could feel her heart beating just as steadily as he had ever heard it. Her skin had gone pale again, like ash around a dead camp fire at dawn. But when Lua leaned in beside Talthielle and whispered Brinka's name, her eyes fluttered open, and she began speaking euphorically in something almost like a child's voice. "Lua! I've seen her! I've seen her Lua! She's beautiful! I can't believe it! I saw her just as plain as I see you now! Lua!"

Lua did not look at anyone else huddled around but Brinka, and only smiled her gentle smile.

"I know, my love. I know. And she has seen you as well. Don't be afraid, child. You're going to be okay, I promise. Everything is going to be okay. Just you rest now, and don't worry about a thing."

Brinka's eyes widened and glowed as though she'd just been given a new pet or a thousand flowers. She actually squealed with delight, pulling herself up around Konjo's shoulders and squeezing him like a pillow. "I saw her! I saw her!" To everyone but Lua, Brinka seemed hysterical.

"She's got a fever!" Talthielle shouted. "Let's get her down from here and into bed. She needs rest." He and Nanok began trying to help Konjo and his betrothed to their feet, when the forward watch poked his head through the ladderwell and shouted for Konjo.

"Kenjah! The captain requests your light, if you can spare it. Our eyes adjusted to your colors, and we are all starblind now in this darkness. We need you, Konjo!" Konjo was about to protest when Brinka put her hand on his and found his eyes. She was not scared or delirious, Konjo realized. When their hands touched, he felt her clarity as though he was sharing her dreams. She was shaken, but she was calm.

"Don't worry, Konjo. I'll be fine. Your shipmates need your starlight. Will you shine for me, my beloved? Help them find their way. When this is over, I'll be waiting for you. Go Konjo. Shine!"

Konjo kissed her hand, and then her face, and smiled. Konjo was the color of all of her stars.

Troy had to shield his eyes as he watched the Kenjah make his way to the prow, where he laid a gentle hand on the bird's wings. The *Marvu* soon found its wind, and was away, riding high on its keel in a pelting wind, cold and mercifully dry. He nodded to Lua and Talthielle, and the remainder of the conscripts as they climbed down the ladders to get below to the Kenjah's cabin, and he whispered his rudder commands to the pilot as he logged the movements of his winged compass needle. Soon, his own relief was politely but firmly shooing him away from the helm, insisting that the captain had a proper navigator, and that the captain was not required to drive the ship as well as command it. Troy reluctantly relented, and allowed himself to be relieved, quietly musing that the word somehow just did not really apply in situations like these.

He climbed down to the weather deck and took his post beside the forward deck officer, where he had been an hour ago. He thought of Bran out there in the deep darkness, numb and treading water on some aimless and doomed errand, compelled by lunacy beyond comprehension. At least driving the ship had given him some sense of control over the world around him, something he could feel responsible for. Now, standing beside Nabul, he just felt hopeless and helpless. After some long and contemplative moments passed in near silence, Talthielle and Nanok returned to the weatherdeck, explaining that Lua had *insisted*, as she does, that she and Brinka be left in peace and quiet. Talthielle had tried to protest, he assured them, but Lua would have none of it, so at last, he had conceded.

Troy couldn't help but laugh at this. "You'll get used to her, I suppose." And then, after a moment, he chuckled again, in spite of his nerves. "Good luck with that, librarian." Nanok laughed, and even Konjo snickered a little. Talthielle just looked very tired, and not a little defeated.

Moments later, the whole exchange was all but forgotten, and the *Marvu* felt as though it was no longer floating, but flying. The ship seemed to be gaining speed, even beyond the pressure in its sails, which almost seemed to be going slack, as if they were catching more forward wind and less aft. All hands quickly found tight grips on cold rails or thick ropes or whatever else was handy, and held their breath as the waterline seemed to be receding beneath the ballasts, which spilled their contents into the sea in four great fountains until they were empty, and then the keel itself was clearly visible to everyone brave enough to peer over the rails to see it. The *Marvu* was no longer a ship at sea. Konjo and Vaullus held onto the rails and to each other as they each felt their legs no longer so surely footed.

A loud scream pierced the night air as a clumsy sailor in the aft station lost his grip, and then his footing, and went tumbling over the rails into the drink, but there was no splash. A moment of collective fear and panic whipped through the hearts of the crew as many of them saw their man go over, but it was a difficult feeling to share with the overwhelming sensation of being lifted out of the water by some unseen force below. Troy was about to shout for Man Overboard, though he had no idea what anyone could do about it under these peculiar and alarming circumstances, but the words died on his lips when he saw something he just could not explain. The crewman, whom Troy had seen rolling over the starboard railing on the stern, fell out of view below, but then could be seen, and heard, moreover, shouting nonsense and falling *upwards* along the same path he had fallen the other way. This was a mindmelting and inexplicable feat which made Troy question his very sanity, until in the darkness his eyes made out the gargantuan shape of a long, coal black arm, which had wrapped itself around the terrified sailor, and was now gracefully plopping the man down on the stern, exactly where he had stood only a moment ago.

The man hit the deck scrambling for the nearest rail post, which he hugged with both hands and feet, chest heaving and eyes as wide as they could stretch, and the appendage which had saved his life vanished just as quickly as it had appeared. The sailors and riders stared at this unbelievable miracle with flat incredulity, and did not yet see the leviathan mass rising up out of the sea in front of the ship. Nabul, became aware of it first, and cried out for his captain. Troy, Konjo, Talthielle, and Nanok all turned around at once, and saw every stark detail. Troy whispered in disbelief, lines from the old invocation, *"Behold, her majesty of the deep, the Matriarch/ Behold, the goddess of the sea, High Priestess of the Temple, the Kalamaii./ Ursal has come, in all her wrath and splendor./ Death has come, to rend our ship to splinters./"*

And then there was a voice, unlike anything anyone aboard had ever heard. It was at once deep and wide, like thunder overhead, and also high and shrill, like the foghorns of a flotilla. No one wondered at its source.

Ursal was speaking:

"And woe to me, and unto thee, the mastheads all were toppled/ The sky above became the sea, and death beneath us cobbled/ we mouthed our prayers for peace and mercy/ and all our souls she swallowed."

Her eyes were alive with light, like a constellation of moons hanging low in the midnight horizon. As she opened her gaping maw, screams of terror grew in the bellies of the crewmen and rose to a symphony of shrieks and pleas and cries. Her face seemed to stretch into unnatural contortions, and the top half appeared to lift itself off of the bottom half, as if she might fit the whole ship in her gullet in one piece. Men clung desperately to their sanity, even as they clutched the rails for some illusion of safety. They would have clenched their eyes, but none could look away. Troy cursed himself, and that damned bird as well. He had been in command for barely more than a whole hour, and already, his whole crew was damned. He cried out the only word he could think of, at the top of his lungs, "Paaaaaarrrrrllleeeeeeeeyyyyyyyyyyyyyy!" But he couldn't even hear his own voice in the chaos.

Everyone watched, helpless and waiting, clinging to anything they could hold. Troy noticed that neither the Kenjah, nor the bird, even seemed moved at all, though they held on just as tightly. Troy saw the creature shove one of its long arms into its own mouth, and thought she might be prying it open wider to swallow the *Marvu* whole. And then he saw the greatest thing he would ever live to see in all of his days. All the voices aboard the *Marvu* fell silent, and awe overcame them, one and all. Emerging from the creature's awesome maw, at first only a speck of dust by comparison, and then growing larger and clearer as it grew closer, Troy saw

Bran, wild-eyed and grinning a toothy grin from ear to ear, flying upward from the thing's throat and floating down like a dove until his feet touched down beside Troy and Konjo and the bird, and the long black arm that held him uncoiled itself from around his chest and tousled his hair a little before retreating amongst its many gyrating peers.

"Hiya Troy! I would be very relieved, old friend, if you would consider standing relieved."

"Captain, you crazy old *swelu*! You just can't know how relieved I stand." Troy forgot himself for a breath and threw both hands around Bran's shoulders and shouted loudly, and his shouts were returned by a whole chorus of grateful and bewildered sailors. "Welcome back, you peanut-headed bastard! Don't you *EVER-*"

"Yeah, don't worry Troy. I promise you my feet are not leaving this ship for anything but dry land for the rest of my days. No worries there at all. I'm not doing that again! No way, brother. We can shake on it!"

The *Marvu* was returned to its keel, and their was a tremendous gurgling hiss of ballasts taking in water. The form of the great hulking leviathan towering over the prow lowered quietly lowered itself back into the sea. It moved ever so slowly as it did so, that the *Marvu* would not be sucked under with it as the waters rushed inwards from all sides to fill the void *Ursal* left behind. Everyone looked on in awe. The creature they had seen today, however large, had still been far away. From this vantage, the scene was that of a colossal mountain range sinking below the surface in a matter of moments, only a stone's throw away. Bran turned to Talthielle.

"A flair for the dramatic? Librarian, my friend, we've got to get you some better words."

Talthielle shrugged. "As you can see, captain, there are few words in our languages which even dare to come close to capturing her...*presence*. I am happy to see you are well, and I am sure your motives are entirely beyond me. I would love to hear this story. Not tonight, obviously, but soon!"

Bran nodded. "Someone told me today that I have no agency, librarian. One does not become captain of a Gunship like the *Marvu* by accepting such foolish premises. Yeah, Talthielle, I wholly agree. Definitely not tonight. I think I need a bath and a smoke and whatever sleep I can reclaim. Dawn comes early to the night owl." Bran turned to his crew, who were all awaiting some kind of explanation or resolution they all knew they would not receive tonight. "All hands! Resume normal stations. Day crew, to your bearthings. Get some rest men. Let us hope that tomorrow is less eventful. Thank you all for your efforts. Dismissed!" As the offshift crew began filing away from their lookout posts and toward their pillows, the captain put his hand on Troy's shoulders and felt the strain and exhaustion.

"Have I missed anything, old friend?"

"Could anyone be away from this ship for an hour and not miss anything, captain?"

Bran laughed aloud from the gut. His relief at not having been eaten was finally beginning to set in. He felt a new and profound sensation of gratitude for every little detail of his ship and crew that he hoped would never leave him. "Fair enough, Troy. Fair enough. I hope you'll tell me all about it, in the morning! Talthielle is correct. Not tonight. I think I'm done, and I think you are too. Get some sleep my boys. Talthielle, Nanok. Have I got a story for your books! Good night everyone." And with that parting salutation, Bran disappeared for the night. The navigator, the librarian, and the Viermah all graciously followed his lead.

The remainder of the evening belonged to Nabul and Stilver, and Vaullus, and the starless sea, and the darkness. The *Marvu* settled into its proper depth and found its wind, and began making its way out into the open waters beyond the midshelves. In a few days, it would stop to cast its nets and haul in its keep for their island visit. In a few more, the Kalama temple would come into view, and the ship would discharge its sacred function, enjoy a few days of rest and gratuity among their hosts, and then it would leave this strange world behind for the version of normality to which they were all properly accustomed.

That was the plan, anyway.

***

Konjo was the color of midnight and fading fast when he returned to his cabin. He found Brinka alone and waiting for him. She was glowing and euphoric, but he could see the weariness in her eyes. They both needed sleep as badly as they needed to be near each other, and tonight, they would finally have both. Konjo climbed into the ship's wool and wrapped his arms around his beloved. Their lips pressed against each other and their hearts beat in time. Brinka touched his face and gazed into his eyes. She would show him what she had seen when their shared dreams overtook them. The Kenjah were the color of soft choral in each other's embrace, and soon, sleep and dreams found them and carried them through the dawn. Away in the corner, the Pathfinder stone in the Enigma Blade flickered.

Three Kenjah sat in a circle around firelight. Two of them were young and vibrant and full of life. The third was ancient, whithered, and worn. Her papery skin was the color of wheatgrass. An intense light shone in her eyes as she spoke. Only the foreground could be discerned in the dancing firelight. Everything beyond was obscured by the balance of darkness in every direction. They sat in the dirt, wearing old robes and holding hands. Their eyes were closed. In their minds, they shared a vision of a tumultuous pond, beset on all sides by flames and smoke. This, she explained to them, was the future. If they did not extinguish the flames and settle the surface, they would all suffocate and drown. Their mission no longer belonged to them. Their fates had been indelibly altered by a force of will. The ancient one had dissipated her strength, and would now make one final play for the salvation of Omnia. She had contrived her own solution, and made it manifest, but at great cost. The younglings listened to her words attentively. They witnessed scenes of hostility and conflict and destruction in flashes and fragments. The suffering of the Kenjah, the indifference of the Viermah, the abdication of the Kalamaii, and the cruelty of men. They could not stop the war, or prevent its coming. But they could end it, and if they lived, they were the only ones who could do so. Troubling omens and foul winds portended a period of great darkness and strife. Omnia would convulse and conflagrate, and all of its children would rise against each other. Something must be done to repair their wounded hearts and still their fearful ways. Omnia's hatred could only be subdued by love, and the love between the Kenjah younglings was the strongest love to be found. A child of starlight would appear to lead the lores out of their darkness and into grace. A child of time, of sight, and of divinity. The child must live. It would learn the ways of the Kenjah, the Viermah, and the Kalamaii, and of the Epozia. And then it would return to Omnia, after learning the ways of the men on their ships at sea, and when it spoke, the lores would listen.

Brinka and Konjo were the color of goose down when they awoke to the ship's bells of reveille. They sat up, locked in each other's eyes, saying nothing. Their moment of revelation had come, and they understood their own footsteps for the first time since their miraculous reunion in the Titan. The world they knew had taken a somber turn, and they cared. Because the world they knew had given them each other once, and then had broken itself to give them each other again. The hostility and cynicism they had experienced in Flask was spreading with the four winds. It wasn't scarcity or claustrophobia. There was plenty of food in Omnia, and endless expanses of unsettled territory. It was a sickness of the mind.

The men, and the lores they hunted, were all set adrift in time and isolated from their collective past and shared futures. The garden that had been their birthright had been transformed into a wasteland of vanity and wont.* Their forebears had abandoned them, and fearful loneliness crept into their hearts. Fear of the unknown, fear of the other, and fear of suffering. They banded together around divergent languages and skindeep superficialities, and became atomized multitudes. Omnia had been for all, of all, and by all, but was now reduced to an empty prison of self.

Konjo touched her stomach with reverence, and smiled at her. Their own lives were changing. Their exclusive devotion had been to each other. Themselves against the world. Marla's bed had bequeathed them a stake in the future of that world in which they lived. Out of impossible love and a few lyptus berries, they had created life. The life of that child would bind their cause to the fate of Omnia. They stood to dress themselves and perform their morning rituals.

As they were finishing, a soft tap at the hatch to their cabin broke the silence. Brinka turned the dogs and opened it, revealing a forlorn sight. Nanok was standing with Lua and Bran, and behind them stood the trio of flag officers, all looking solemn and morose. Nanok's feathers had returned while he slept, but they fell lifeless and limp at his side, and the Kenjah saw tears in his swollen eyes.

"Talthielle has passed away in the night. Lua found him this morning, on his knees beside his bed and slumped over it, like he was praying. I am sorry Kenjah. We've lost him."

No one had words. The Kenjah went a sanguine scarlet as the news washed over them. Their clocksmith had met his end. His life force had flickered out like a candle, and was extinguished. Konjo reached to his face to wipe the first tear away, and then let the rest fall. Brinka wrapped herself in his arms and buried her eyes in his chest, weeping. Nanok stepped into the cabin and wrapped two full wings around them both. They all felt as though the air had been sucked out of the space. Their throats burned around thick knots, and the pain of loss enveloped them.

Bran stepped forward and spoke softly. "Shipmates, I offer my most sincere and heartfelt condolences for the loss of your friend. I confess, I had many doubts about him, but I have come to understand that he has given his life to bring you all here to me. With respect to his sacrifices, you have my oath, and the oaths of my men, that we will spend nothing short of our own lives to bring you where you are going, if that is what is required of us.

"My friends, no one spins a better sea story than we *swelus*, and none but us are better at dismissing the wild tales we hear as nothing but. But the things we have seen, the things *I* have seen, on only the first day of this voyage, have persuaded me that the story unfolding now is much greater than the sum of its parts. That we may play some role in it only adds to the honor of my crew and the glory of this ship. You are each hereby relieved of all duties.

By order of the captain, the *Marvu* is now and shall remain in your service until we can aid you no longer. We will provision the Kalama, and we will remain on station until you three can decide what comes next."

(The End of an Epoch)

The crew was gathered in ranks along the port and starboard railings, facing midships and standing at rest. All were dressed in the ceremonial ornamentation of their ancient custom. The sails had been taken in. The *Marvu* had cleared the midshelves in the night, and the waters were too deep to anchor. The ship bobbed in gentle winds, and Vaullus perched on the prow facing the weatherdeck, observing the scene of a grim funeral procession at sea. Nanok and Bran emerged from below deck at one end of a stretcher, with the Kenjah towing the rear. Talthielle, the *Epozia*, was neatly wrapped in seven layers of the ship's cleanest linens. The quartz in his staff lay over his heart. After some well reasoned debate between Lua and Brinka, Lua had prevailed upon Brinka to keep the clocksmith's stones, but Brinka argued rather forcefully for a compromise. Two blue stones were clenched in Talthielle's closed fists, his arms crossed over his chest in his wrappings. Nanok insisted on keeping the hairshirt the clocksmith had worn, but he paid for it with a feather from each of his wings, and these were affixed to the nomi leaf on the handle of the walking stick Marla had crafted.

The five of them marched slowly down the isle between opposing ranks of crewmen. The band on the stern played a melodic dirge. Troy and Lua waited for them on the bow, while Garrison and Hinds stood their traditional posts as forward and aft deck officers. The sky above was grey and low, and it draped the souls beneath it in a misty chill. Having nothing else but ship linens to wear, the Viermah and Kenjah wore Marla's robes and broaches. Nanok wore his helm, bezzled with the stone Talthielle had given him. His bow and a homemade quiver of arrows were slung at his back. Brinka noticed that the shape of the Enigma Blade on her hip was identical in its hilt and curvature to the ceremonial blade that Bran wore. Its Pathfinder stone glowed with her skin. His hung sharply by his side, and had a shine of its own so clear and bright it seemed to reflect the sun through the clouds. Konjo's blades hung across his shoulders in their sheaths. It is the *swelu's* oath that no soul at sea should ever go to meet death unarmed.

Vaullus watched as the procession halted before him. Three crewmen from each rank laid hands on the stretcher and relieved the attendants. They held it between their waists, arms and wrists locked. The old tramp wasn't very heavy. Bran turned to his attendants and saluted them, and then gave the command at arms. All the crewmen and officers drew sabers of their own from scabbards on their belts and held their blades high, edges facing the opposing rank. Their unburdened fists snapped to their sides and they lifted their eyes to the heavens above. Bran called for parade formation, and each of the crewmen held their swords to their chests and turned one quarter turn forward, and then lowered the tips of their blades to the deck.

Bran looked down at Talthielle's form and tried to comprehend its spirit. Their lives had overlapped by a single day, and no more, yet that one day was so immensely and utterly pregnant with significance that he could barely hold the whole thing in his mind. The King of Caught Fish. An ancient soul from a forgotten time trying to save a doomed world from its own cynical failures. The clocksmith who would barter his life to release the souls of Omnia's dead and bring peace again to troubled lands. His last words that anyone could remember had been something about *Ursal's* indescribable nature. Here, and gone. Lua had said that Talthielle never made it any further than this, but this was also the farthest he'd made it. Bran pretended to understand what that meant, and supposed he somehow basically got it anyway. Life was rewriting itself around him, and he was a blind spectator to revisions he could never be conscious of, before or after the fact.

Lua was not crying, but she wasn't far off. She held a book clutched in her arms, and was draped in an ornate woollen cloak of her own. Brinka noticed that the stone in her blade matched the stone in Lua's broach, forming a small translucent sun cradled in an inset the shape of a crescent moon, the symbol of the clerics in the Order of Tranquility. Vaullus looked upon Brinka with such tender affection, and then down at the fallen clocksmith with deep remorse. The crew was assembled at the ready, and the procession had reached its end. Bran would address the attendants and all assembled, and then he would yield to Talthielle's companions to speak their hastily prepared eulogies. Even as his lips began to move, Bran had no idea what he would say. What could he say?

"The last time I attended one of these unfortunate gatherings, it was to celebrate the life of my closest friend. Some of you aboard now served with me under Pike's command. He was a man who lived a remarkable life. He was honest, and kind, and fearless. He was, when he lived, a collector of stories. Our ship's library swells with evidence of his love of history and drama and poetry. He sought wisdom and guidance from every living soul, whether benevolent or maligned, whether real or fanciful. And he could make you laugh until you wet yourself. In all my days, if I ever live to be half the man he was, I'll have lived a charmed and fulfilling life. I miss him, and he is missed by everyone who had the chance pleasure to know him. He was a pioneer. A man born in charted seas who sought out the unseen stars beyond the horizon. He literally made the world a bigger place. And a better one, I think. And that's how I remember him.

"The soul whose body we so humbly commend to the deep, this day, was called Talthielle. He devoted his life to a singular cause, unto the very end. His cause was not the preservation of his own life, or even the lives of his friends. His cause was the salvation of strangers. He was a creature of Time and Memory. The integrity of his system of moral value was predicated on his understanding of the relationship between our past, present, and future. This, I think, is what he meant when he said he wanted to free the spirits of the Omnia's ancestors. In his mind, a peaceful and prosperous coexistence was the first casualty of our collective amnesia. We forgot the struggles and toils and aspirations of those who came before us, of those who labored to build the world we now take for granted. And in forgetting, we have forgotten ourselves. I don't know if that's how he would have said it, but I hope and pray that my words do his cause some justice. Let us not forget our shipmate, Talthielle.

"Who among us would make such a sacrifice? Who among us could muster such selfless dedication to a nobler cause? I don't ask to challenge your worthiness, my friends. I ask, because Talthielle reminds me that we all live with the capacity to do and be more than we are. Talthielle could see into the future because he appreciated the past and paid attention to the present. Without a careful consideration of all three parts, his gifts would have been meaningless. Do not forget the past, my friends. And do not fear the future. But most importantly, do not forsake the present. Live and die for the love of this world, and of everyone in it. Live and die as this one did. Our shipmate, Talthielle.

"Goodbye, *swelu*."

Bran lowered his eyes in a moment of silent reverence. Lua smiled and touched his hand. He wasn't sure how he did, really, but he knew she would approve in her supportive way. Nanok and the Kenjah had not actually determined which of them would go first prior to the moment at hand, and after a brief and intensely relatable moment of awkwardness, the Viermah straightened himself, and gazed upon the linen form laying in the stretcher. He knew precisely what he would say, and offered a little prayer for the wits to form the words in order.

"I hated him. I've hated him all my life. And I'd never even met him. I blamed him for the loss of my father, whom I never even got the chance to know. How could I have known he wore a hairshirt every day I've been alive, or that my father gave his life in service of the same crazy cause as this clocksmith laying here now. A new friend has given me a tome of my own father's thoughts and adventures. And I keep thinking..." Nanok's voice was heard to crack, ever so slightly, "that if I hadn't come here with this person who's been my very nemesis my whole life, I might never have seen this book, or gotten the chance to know my father as anything other than an unwitting victim of some cruel and malicious schemer. Talthielle, the *Epozia* clocksmith, whom I've hated so passionately for so long, was not only the one who gave me the chance to learn that my father was a hero, in his own right, but it stands reasoning that he was the one who gave my father the opportunity to become that hero I get to read about now. This same opportunity he has now offered to me.

"A few nights ago, I was roughly bound and hooded by my own kith and kin, whose motive for just handing me over to these peculiar strangers I still do not understand, and I was delivered very forcefully into their service. It is as if destiny itself has just thrust its arm through the ether and grabbed me by the throat and wrists. The Kenjah beside me were the clocksmith's conscripts, and at first I mistook them for prisoners, like myself. It took less than a day to realize that no such force could compel their starlight against their will. They have come with Talthielle, as I have, to do what is in their power to reconcile this world with itself. Their story is a part of mine, just as my father's story and my own are a part of theirs. We are all a part of your story, just the same. I think, if our friend had the chance to say one last thing, before his time came, he would have expressed gratitude to all of you here today, for your hospitality, for your decency, and for your courage. In his stead, may we extend our own gratitude, with warmth and feeling. Thank you for helping us."

Nanok put his hand on Talthielle's shoulder, and curled his wings beneath his cloak against the cold air. The Viermah do not say goodbye to their departed. But he held the words in his mind, and in his heart, nonetheless. *Goodbye, Talthielle.* The Kenjah put their hands on his arms and nodded their mutual approval. They looked at Bran and Lua, and at the crew, and then at their captor. Konjo and Brinka were the color of saphire when they spoke, and they spoke as one, in their magical and mesmerizing harmony. As they began, Vaullus hopped from his perch and landed on Brinka's shoulder, once again. This time, nothing odd happened at all. She just looked up at him with respect in her eyes. Konjo politely nudged the bird with his elbow, and Vaullus dutifully shifted over to her other shoulder, nodding his crest in assent and flapping his wings a little to hold his balance. When he was calm and stable, they spoke.

"Captain, shipmates, and friends. We Kenjah are unaccustomed to hospitality. We are a rather insular people. We rarely travel, and more rarely do we travel far. Our numbers have grown fewer and fewer as time has gone by, and when we travel anywhere, we are usually alone. We are greeted as strangers, often with hostility and paranoia, though none among us wish anyone harm. We are an honest people, and when we are given the chance to be, we are also gentle."

Troy, the navigator, was listening intently to the Kenjah's speech when the dim realization donned on him. The strangest feeling of *deja vu,* a sense that he had heard these familiar words somewhere already. He squinted beneath his bushy eyebrows and tried very hard not to reach for his beard, as he often did when he was confused or puzzled. He felt, for a moment, as though the skies were darkening ever so slightly, perhaps imperceptibly. He could swear he had lived through this very moment, though he knew that to be impossible. *The world we had known before we met...*

"...Talthielle was a cold and uninviting one, and for all our efforts..."

...we believed that all we had in the world...

"...was each other."

Vaullus cocked his head to the wind, sensing some subtle change in the pressure before anyone else. Troy noticed the bird, and the bird noticed Troy. Bran and Lua sensed some fidgety exchange occurring in repressed pantomime among his ship's guidance system, threatening to distract from the solemnity of the occasion. Bran would have no lapse in bearing--

And then Bran and Lua became aware of a change in the air as well.

"Omnia tore us away from each other. It was Talthielle who intervened and offered us an alternative fate. It is because of Talthielle that we are here today, together, with all of you."

You know, it's funny, but...

"...we aren't sure if Talthielle had anyone else left in the world but us before we came aboard. Anyone that would have celebrated his life with us today and mourned his passing."

We did meet one soul along the way, Troy was sure he felt the skies darkening around him. It was an unnerving feeling. Out of the corner of his eye, he thought he saw a hint of trepidation in his captain's countenance. Lua had turned her head just a little toward the forward seas, trying not to be rude as the Kenjah spoke, but also feeling drawn in some primordial way by some elusive presence.

"...whom Talthielle seemed to hold in high esteem. We are sure she will be sad to hear the news. But now, look what changes a few days can bring! Talthielle goes before us to Lavaris, with more friends nearby to send him off than we Kenjah have had in the whole of our lives." The Kenjah were not oblivious to the sudden shift in the attention spans of those around them, or to the odd sensation that something was happening, just out of reach of their own periphery.

Troy, Lua, and the crew could divert their attention no longer. Even the Kenjah cut off their clumsy speech and turned to face the growing swells off the bow and the darkening skies above. The six crewmen holding Talthielle's stretcher redoubled their grip and tried, unsuccessfully, to hold their bearing. After a few moments, the funeral oratory was lost on the winds, and all hands were bearing witness to their third unbelievable spectacle in a day's time. Troy broke the silence,

"Captain?" But he did not know what to say next. Bran, of course, had no reply.

Two long, onyx tentacles broke the water's surface, rising up over the prow railing in a twirling dance, at once intriguingly graceful and dreadfully terrifying. They crawled over the rails and touched the deck between Troy and Lua, who obligingly stood aside. The arms twisted and bent themselves and seemed to both bulge and contract at the same time, until they melded into the shape of a maiden. Gradually, her lines and details found definition, and everyone who could still breathe gasped out loud when they saw the figure of a woman appear where only two tentacles had been. What remained of them between herself and the sea below coiled into an imperceptibly thin tether which ran from the back of her neck, over the prow railing, and into the water below. Troy recalled his own dream in vivid detail, and half wondered if he was not dreaming the same dream again in this moment.* She was now standing straight, only inches away from him, and stretching her limbs in an absent kind of way, as if there were not sixty living souls transfixed by the sight. This was *Ursal*, the sea goddess of the Kalama, come to pay her respects to the dead.

The gripping silence was shipwide. When her transformation was complete, and she was comfortable in her own skin, she seemed to finally take notice of everyone else aboard, staring at her in disbelief. A wry smile in the corners of her eyes betrayed her amusement at the dumbfounded faces gawking at her terrestrial form. She looked around at each of them and studied their appearances, trying to recognize and place their identities with what she already knew of them. Bran, she had already encountered. Troy, she deduced from his forwardmost position in the funeral ceremony. She knew Lua by her broach and her cloak, the insignia of the Order of the Tranquility. This left only the Viermah and the Kenjah, and of course the fallen clocksmith on the carrier, wrapped in linens. *Ursal* tried out her limbs and lifted her hand to Vaullus, who flitted gleefully to the perch she offered. She stroked his feathers lovingly, and then looked around at everyone attending, all at once, to try to take in the memory of the scene.

Troy half expected to see the deckboards creaking and cracking beneath her weight, but decided this must have been a product of his own imagination as his mind tried to process the impossible scene in his dream. In form, she seemed as light and effete on her toes as the bird perched on her arm. She looked up at him and smiled, and he knew she could read his thoughts. Nanok was the first to break his own paralysis. He removed his cloak and offered it to her.

"I never thought I'd live to meet a goddess in the flesh." She paused for a breath to study the familiar lines in his face and the shimmering gold hue in his newly grown down, and then she stepped into the cloak and permitted him to wrap it around her naked flesh and fasten the broach at her neck. He kept his eyes respectably fixed upon her own as he did so, and his fingers were agile and delicate in their motions. He could not have looked away, or elsewhere, for that matter, if he had tried.

Ursal nodded her gratitude for his gentlemanly gesture and bearing, and whispered in his ear.

"I am not a god, Nanok. I'm just bigger than you." After a silent moment between them, she touched his face. "You look just like your father."

She offered her hand to Lua, as one greets an old friend, and Lua laughed and wrapped her arms around the Kalamaii. "Your highness, it is good to see you, though the circumstances are regrettable. You sure do know how to steal a show, my lady." *Ursal* returned Lua's embrace and kissed her cheek.

"It is wonderful to see you also, Priestess."

Ursal turned to Bran, who was visibly mistified, and the Kenjah, who were similarly entranced. She touched Bran's cheek, and then stunned him nearly out of his wits when she took his face in both hands and kissed him, long and deep. He might have protested, had not every muscle in his body turned to jelly in her arms. "You taste just fine, captain. I told you we'd meet again."

Bran stumbled and muttered and mumbled and tried to form words and failed. After some nonsense and helpless gibberish, he finally managed to squeak out the only coherent thought he could muster. "I, um, of course, I-- I stand...*relieved.*" When the words left his lips, he fell silent, and sagged a little. Relinquishing command of his own ship was no easy thing to do, even to the most majestic and powerful authority he would ever encounter. He tried to restrain his own foolish pride, and to some extent, he succeeded. She sensed his inner turmoil, and would not punish him for it or take offense.

"I relieve you, captain. Be assured, your worthy crew and sturdy vessel will come to no harm under my stewardship. You have my respect, and I will be honored to have such a capable mate at my side. The *Marvu* is yours, and I vow to return it to you in the same condition I received it."

At last, *Ursal* turned a tender eye to the humble Kenjah, now awestruck and reverent. She reached out to them and took each of them by hand.

"My friends, as I am sure you've guessed by now, I am *Ursal.* You have journeyed far to meet me, and we have much to discuss. Please accept my deepest and most sincere sympathies. Your companion was a dear friend of mine, and we have known each other for ages. My hearts mourn his passing. He has given his all to bring you here, and that is no small thing. He must have believed very strongly in you, and for that, I offer you my friendship in kind. Your path is long, and the way is hard, and there is still much that has not been revealed to you, though I suspect by now you know much more than you did when you set out on this journey. There is time, and we will talk. For now, if you will permit me, I should like to say a few words of my own for the last of the great servants of the seasons."

Ursal threw open her cloak behind her like a cape, and if she had any idea what an unnecessary distraction it was, she gave no indication. Some of the brighter members of the audience might have considered that in light of the frigid temperatures to which the creature addressing them was accustomed, the comfort offered by the woolen cloak in the warm air was likely less than ideal. Nanok had merely accommodated his own modesty. Whatever the word meant to her, it surely was not a superficial consideration. She had already transformed herself enough for their sake. Her coal black eyes and hair and her dark skin glistened in sunless skies. Her chest and shoulders were broad and full. Everything below was essentially amorphous, though her legs, many observed, were quite amazing interpretations of the real thing. They made her seem tall by proportion, but she stood just shy of Brinka's height. This was a conscious decision she had made with purpose. Indeed, throwing back her cloak had merely been intended to free her hands as she spoke. Her kind communicated in silent pantomime, in a rhythmic choreography of motions and gestures which have everything in common, aesthetically speaking, with dancing. She would move her hands as she spoke, though often in unusual and unintuitive ways that only made sense to her.

Among the many thoughts she collected from her captive audience, it was Nanok's which actually made her blush self-consciously, and briefly consider covering herself. Words Nanok would not have dared to speak out loud, and could not therefore be held against him.

If she's not a goddess, she'll certainly do until I meet one.

Ursal made a point of not looking at him as she giggled at his impropriety. There are no appropriate reasons to humiliate a fan... Bran stifled the urge to whisper into Troy's ear his suspicion that he almost preferred her the other way.

"*Marvu*, riders, shipmates. Each of you born beneath the brightest stars. Destiny has woven your paths together like so many threads of tomi, into a thick and unbreakable chord which no anchor could strain. In this moment, your lives are irrevocably entwined with my own. According to our ancient custom, I have commandeered your vessel. You are my crew, and I am your captain. You will tell your children and grandchildren of the time you sailed under the command of the Kalamaii, and they will think you senile old loons who've tipped their cups a little too often. This mate of ours, whom we commend to the deep today, he is the wind that pushed your sails to me. Talthielle was *Epozia*. He was the last of his kind, and therefore also the last of his Kin. His has, for many long seasons, been alone in the world. None of us here could imagine the world through his eyes, but he has spent much of his life trying to see the world through ours. What must he have seen?

"When my seasons were much fewer than they are now, your kind and my own were at war. We were petulant, greedy, territorial, and paranoid. Enough time passed for us to learn and grow and comprehend the error in our ways. Enough of you were willing to do and live as Talthielle has done, and lived to earn our respect and our cooperation. Though we were the monsters in your children's stories, enough of you contemplated the possibility that we might be more than that. Some of these courageous souls took a risk. They came to us unarmed, waving flags of surrender, and offered their lives in exchange for a lasting peace. They were willing to face the possibility of horrible death because they believed we might be made to reason. To listen. To deal fairly if only given the chance."

Ursal looked down at Talthielle and paused for a few breaths to collect her own thoughts. The words she had whispered to Nanok came into her mind. She turned her eyes to his and found him enraptured, but listening intently. There was a seriousness in his expression that she took to mean he understood the point she was making and respected it. He really did look just like his father. Nanok gave her a gentle nod of encouragement, and she continued.

"The sickness of the mind that troubles your inland kin is not new. It is perhaps Omnia's oldest geological structure. It is a flaw in the grand design. That which is different is uncomfortable, and either remains inaccessible and grows more uncomfortable by proportion of time and distance, or it invites curiosity and exploration until it is understood, and then it ceases to be different, and ceases to be uncomfortable. When you meet my people, you will doubtless find them very unusual and different. Some of you will be uncomfortable, and others will be curious. Don't you see? Everything that happens between you after proceeds from that simple distinction. Confusion and paralysis breeds fear. Confusion and courage renders the stuff of adventure and enlightenment. If you understand me, *Marvu*, my friends, my shipmates, may I beg you to put the fear and paralysis out of your mind, and be compelled by the courage of your curiosity. Do not see strangers and threats among my people, and they will never see strangers and threats among you. The past is the shared soil where all of our roots mingle and intertwine. This is what Talthielle understood about all of us. We may be lured into the cynical thought that we are all just stuck here together. The truth, my dear friend once told me, is that we all *got here together.* I can find no fault with his reasoning.

"He asks us to remember the past. To look our ancestors in the eyes once more and confront their contributions and mistakes and leaps of faith and fears and dreams and ideas. Behind Lavaris's gates, the dead abide in unity. None outrank another. None will outlast another. None will suffer while another prospers. None will be indentured, or bend another to their own will. They lived as they died, as children of Omnia. Talthielle walked among the first of Omnia's children, and died so that he would not walk among the last. Talthielle has brought us together."

Ursal leaned in and lifted her hands in what qualified as an effective display of wizardry.

"*Marvu*, my shipmates. I am not a god, I'm just bigger than you. I admit that I possess, as our friend says, *a flair for the dramatic*, but I am no tyrant. I have not come to bind you to any cause against your will. I ask you of you only what Talthielle tried so hard and got only so far just to ask of me. Will you commit yourselves, of your own free will, in good humor and good faith? As our Kenjah say, will you set your fists and your footsteps to our noble errand? *Marvu*, will you sail with us?"

It took a few breaths for the crew to be sure she stood on the question, but it took no time at all for their resounding affirmations to fill the misty sea air. Bran, for his part, was proud of his crew. Nanok and the Kenjah hooped and hollered with enthusiasm. *Ursal* was duly pleased at the response, and lowered her hands to quiet the rallying cries of her shipmates. When silence returned and they regained their bearing, she turned her eyes back to the clocksmith in his funeral garb. She tried to hold his spirit in her mind and recall the time they had spent together and the words they had shared. She would shed no tears from the eyes these creatures could see, but deep down below in the darkness where her material form existed *en masse,* the Kalamaii wept for her comrade. He had been as much of an elemental force to her as she must have seemed to the crew of the ship she now commanded.

There had been a time when the Dab was the seat upon which the *Epozia* observed the six axes of creation. Before the waters receded over the subsequent aeons and the children of Omnia took their first gasping breaths. There was only the still sea surrounding the peak of the great mountain those receding waters revealed. The *Epozia* looked out upon the rippling waves and saw their futures, like the shadows of images on the cavewall in firelight. This was the beginning of their power. The Kalamaii were born in those seas, and ruled much of the world until the waters began to fall away. Then came the Kenjah, the creatures of starlight who lived in the caves and canyons. Then the Viermah, who took to the skies from the lofty boughs of the great sinnana. They all communed as one, and breathed life into the creatures of dust who came and broke the land below and brought up food from the ground. The race of men, the fifth and final lore, and a truly troublesome and contentious lot, to be sure.

Lavaris would not require a representative among men. He would accept one, of course. But only four of the five lores were needed to constitute a quorum, the idea being that it would most likely be a belligerent fifth which demanded the urgent attention of the others. Some speculated that Lavaris himself was the Progenitor of all of Omnia's lores. Others posited that he was the first of the *Epozia* to cross over from the living to the dead. Lavaris himself has never spoken on the subject. *Ursal* supposed she might get the chance to ask him about it some day.

"Talthielle, servant of the seasons, King of Caught Fish. To your endless rest you go, and it is only your body we leave behind. In our hearts, your endless light remains. Your kin await you above, and mine await you below. May the sea keep you and bless you.

Goodbye, old friend. We'll take it from here.

She could hear nothing but her own pulse in the silence that gripped the souls aboard her ship as she bowed her head and stood aside. Vaullus had found his respectful distance on the railing beside her when her speech began (just before she threw her cloak back), and before the crewman could commence their final obligation, the bird hopped onto Talthielle's staff and lowered his brow to Talthielle's chest and caressed the clocksmith's head with both wings. Somewhere, far away, Brinka, the Queen of the Epochs, wiped tears from her eyes and whispered, "*Thank you for this, Talthielle. Thank you for brining them through the darkness together. I will never forget you, my sweetest friend.*" Brinka was the color of weathered linen, but the light of a thousand stars shone in her eyes.

Vaullus returned to *Ursal's* shoulder and hung his head in quiet reverence. The crew of the *Marvu* stood still and quiet at rest, and watched for their captain's signal. *Ursal* snapped to attention and placed her hand over her chest. Bran and Troy and the deck officers squared their shoulders and faced forward. The crew lifted their blades to the heavens above as the each opposing rank turned midship on their heels, then they brought their swords to their hearts. The crewmen carrying Talthielle took slow, careful steps in unison toward the prow. If Talthielle had been a criminal or a traitor, a very different kind of ceremony would have taken place at the stern, but it was considered bad luck to throw a good friend behind you.

Bran and Lua relieved the first two crewmen at the foot of the stretcher. *Ursal* and Nanok relieved the next two, and then the Kenjah relieved the last two. Troy awkwardly resisted the urge to protest when Vaullus kindly flitted over to his shoulders. He did look up at the bird in a quizzical and mildly put off kind of way, but he did not protest. The pallbearers each took turns looking around at each other, taking in their final moment together with a fallen companion. Nanok was openly crying, and was the last to look up from his captor's motionless form in ship linen white and meet the eyes of his friends. Konjo and Brinka were the color of gravestones on a cloudy day. Bran and Lua locked eyes and shared a moment of solidarity for their strange new friends and the even stranger circumstances which had befallen them, and then everyone turned to the Kalamaii.

Talthielle slid feet first into the sea with hardly a splash, and was gone forever.

The pallbearers observed a long and poignant moment of silence, and *Ursal* watched the shadow of the clocksmith's form drift down from the surface and pass in front of her on its way to the bottom. When he landed, she covered him in mounds of soft sand and drove his staff into the sea floor above his head as a marker. Above, she took Nanok's hand, and he took the Kenjahs', and so on, until all of the pallbearers were joined with bowed heads and closed eyes. She showed them what she really saw beneath. All manner of sea creatures swam to her from every direction, each carrying dazzling stones of every conceivable composition and size. Talthielle's friends looked on in wonder as these creatures carefully cooperated in a stunning choreography, placing the stones in odd, concentric rings around his body first, with the larger stones, and then filling in the spaces between and above those with smaller and smaller stones, until they had constructed a perfectly hemispherical altar over Talthielle's grave. Only his staff could be seen, protruding from the place where his body lay beneath the stones. As a finishing touch, *Ursal* lit his quartz and let it shine over the stones, which cast brilliant constellations of rippling light in all directions. Each of those present in the circle to witness the spectacle marveled at the grandeur of the gesture.

Above, they opened their eyes at last and saw in their hands only an empty stretcher where their friend had been. The hero had done his good works and gone on to the next place. The time came for the rest of them who lingered behind to do the good work of carrying his light with them, and to see to the business of finishing what he started. They handed off the stretcher to the crewmen, who made their last ritualistic show of marching the thing below decks and concluding the ceremony. *Ursal* broke the circle and shook the hands of her fellow bearers. After an appropriate number of breaths passed, so that the transition need not be abrupt, she found Bran's eyes and held them for a long time. She took a deep breath and mustered within herself a spirit of adventure, and smiled.

"What do you say, sailor? Wanna go catch some fish?"

Some of the strain and pressure and anxiety seemed to finally wash away from the lines in his furrowed brow, and something of a mischievous grin slowly crawled over his chin. His eyes twinkled a little as he snapped a somewhat exaggerated, but technically unreproachable salute. She lifted her hand to her heart in response, and he spun two quarter turns on his heels, almost gratefully assuming the duties of first mate.

"*Marvu!*" he shouted, "Prepare to sail!"

The crew promptly sheathed their swords and gave a hearty shout of approval, and complied.

(The Beginning of an Epoch)

A full moon rose in clear skies strewn with innumerable stars over the Kalama temple. Horns blasts sounded the imminent arrival of long awaited provisions when the Watchers spotted the *Marvu* on the horizon, legging its way towards the floating island's great makeshift harbor and riding daringly low on its keel. There was a flurry of excitement among the monks who had been eagerly anticipating the signal to begin their preparations. In kitchens across the island, stoves were lit and pots and pans were filled with the makings of endless delicacies. Nearly every home would contribute something to the evening's feast. The dishes would reflect their own unique personalities and individual tastes.

Entire divisions of monks were assigned to the docks and piers to greet their guests and to assist with the offloading of cargo. Others were already busy laying out long tables in the courtyards around the temple, which stood in the center of the floating island and could be seen rising over the homes and shops from any vantage point, anywhere along the coastlines in every direction.

The harbor itself was a little rounded cove on the leeward side of the island, and from above, the way Nanok would have seen it in his mind, the island resembled the shape of a fullish crescent moon standing on its points, which was also the shape printed on hundreds of ceremonial flags speckling the landscape. The dense and luscious foliage, which covered nearly every inch of the island in some form or other, had at one point all been imported transplants from the various regions of Omnia, but over time, every species of verdure in these ancient canopies* had adapted beyond recognition, resulting in a vibrant shroud of fascinating color, the effect of which on newcomers was a disorienting sensation of something between the familiar and the exotic. Visitors intuitively recognized shapes and forms they knew they had never laid eyes on in their lives. One observer famously described the feeling of witnessing exaggerated elements of one's own home in the throws of an utterly delightful fever dream. Another once commented that this was what their own world would like if any of them were good at living in it.

    The scale of beauty and bounty of their home was not lost upon the Kalama, but the perennial expressions of shock and awe on the part of visitors never failed to amuse the monks, and over time this phenomenon instilled such a sense of pride among them that they took ownership of their own aesthetic and the phenomenon became self-fulfilling and self-perpetuating. There were simply no better cultivators in all of Omnia. The stock of samples and seedlings which would return with the *Marvu* were the stuff of legend to inlanders, and only served to enhance the allure and intrigue of the many fables and stories and superstitions associated with the Kalama. This exceptional quality permeated every facet of Kalama life. Its people were taller, leaner, faster, and generally more adept and coordinated than their inland counterparts. Their voices were melodic, and their eyes were penetrating. Their wit was undeniable, but it was as often somewhat inaccessible to strangers whose modes and perceptions and idioms were alien to these enchanting scenes. They laughed from their guts, and they lived by inviolate moral codes which they cultivated with as much purposeful deliberation and creative flare as they expended on anything that grew from the ground.

Torches lit the island, and great fires burned in the lighthouse towers stationed at either of the crescent's points to aid the ship's navigators safely into the harbor at night. Smaller fires were sparked and stoked in the grills and pits around the long tables, and sea oil candles burned in the windows of every home, hut, and shop. But the brightest light to be seen that night came from the belltower of the temple. It burned with the brilliance of a dying star, and all the other lit flames seemed pale by comparison. And unlike all the other flames on the island, which danced and flickered and licked up at the cold sea winds, this light was motionless, and so nearly blinding against the dark skies that it cast everything beneath in even darker shadows, and the busy monks had to shield their eyes when walking inland from the shore. Though the *Marvu* was still more than a league out, Vaullus had already left the ship and returned to his master's side.

Ursal had also left the ship, and had slid quietly onto the island from the windward side, disguised as a child and donning garb hung from lines between two empty cottages on the beach. She took a circuitous path to the temple through hedges and bushes to avoid attention, and also to string her tether between footpaths and walkways where it could bury itself in the soft peat and evade discovery. She made her way up three stories and had barely turned the knob to enter the belltower when she was confronted by a robed figure waiting in the shadows. He was nearly hysterical and unable to contain himself, and stood on no ceremony.

"Is he coming? Did you see him?"

Ursal was not startled by the figure, and was not surprized at his unbridled enthusiasm. She laughed a polite and respectful laugh and took his hands in hers. "Yes, I've seen him. I suspect he'll be the first on off the ship, and he might not even wait until it enters the harbor."

"Does he... does he know I'm here?" *Ursal* could see a reservoir of mixed emotions in the figure's eyes, even in the dark shadows thrown by the blinding light. Impenetrable sadness and reticence mixed with unbridled joy and relief. He had waited along time for this night, and had played it out a thousand times in his mind, but still could not be certain how it should go. She could hear a jumble of questions turning over in his mind, each one followed by a corollary of self doubt and analysis of whether or not he should ask that question. *What does he look like? Is he strong? Is he happy? Is he okay? Does he... know?* Under the circumstances, she could not help but admire his restraint, however unrestrained he might have seemed. She knew there were more questions he was scared to ask, because he was unsure he could live with the answers. *Should I meet him? Will he be happy to see me? Or will he hate me when he realizes that I'm not...*

"He doesn't know, not yet anyway. They don't even know she is here, I don't think. They've been turning over their mission incessantly since they lost their friend. They don't know how it can be done without Talthielle, or if it can be done without him. The Kenjah are with child, and there can be no talk of sacrificing their unborn as a casualty of war, let alone as the cost of a lasting peace. Konjo and Nanok are adamant that, if any thing, the whole thing must be delayed by several years, at the very least, and then reconsidered at some latter date." *Ursal* knew that her companion was uninterested in these matters, and could only concentrate on the most significant moment of his own life, fast approaching. She held his hands to her cheek and kissed his fingers. "You will get to meet him. We could not let either of you come all this way for anything less. He is brave and strong and charming and funny, and beautiful, just like you my love. I can't say how he will respond when he learns you are here, but whatever happens, you must respect his feelings. They have all had a very strange and difficult journey, and it has taken its toll on all of them. You will be proud of him, no matter what. Of that I have no doubt. The Kenjah believe they have seen visions of what is to come, but they have seen only what she would permit them to see."

Ursal turned to Brinka, Queen of Epochs, holding her station and her starlight unwaveringly.

"So at long last, you have brought them all home? I know your conscript will be pleased."

The ancient Kenjah maiden was the color of sunlight. She held the rails in front of her with both hands, and did not even turn her head to speak. Nothing could take her eyes off of that ship, slowly paddling its way into the harbor. As it passed the lighthouses, the sound of music could be heard on the breeze. The ship's band had taken up a lively shanty on the prow, and no one would have failed to guess who it was about. *Ursal* could hear the words, even if her companions could not. She was intently aware of the reaches of her own vanity, but even she couldn't help but to cringe a little at the gushing prose of admiration and awe set to lutes and toms. She hoped that she had not deprived her tireless monks of their own due praise for the festivities which would follow by upstaging them all for whole weeks in advance. She was sure the musicians aboard the *Marvu* would have plenty more wonderful stories to write and sing about when their visit was concluded.

"I still can't believe you actually went aboard." There was a coldness in Brinka's voice that *Ursal* had trained herself to tolerate. She had hoped that it would begin to thaw when Brinka finally saw the ripening fruits of her allconsuming labors. The Kalamaii were unaccustomed to unchecked insolence. But what could she do?

"After all you've done to bring your Konjo through to the other side of this awful ordeal, you would not begrudge me my last opportunity to see my friend and to pay my final respects?"

Brinka leered at her out of the corner of her eye and stared off into the horizon. "You could have seen him when they threw his carcass off the ship."

The figure in the robes and shadows took a long breath and bit his tongue. *Ursal* would have none of it. "How, after all of this, do you still have the strength to hold against him all of his failures, when if not for his success, and his sacrifice, may i remind you, your bones would be rotting in a ditch outside of Flask, and Konjo's would be baking in the sun in the hillside above the Titan? You're only here because he believed in you. If not for him, none of this would have been possible. Brinka, that's got to count for something. You've got to let go!"

Brinka spun around on her, blazing pulses of lightning from sinew to sinew, with blue fire in her eyes. "He was a fool! None of this would have been necessary if not for him. And I must do no such thing! I owe him nothing." *Ursal* would not be so easily intimidated. She permitted herself to exchange the child's form for the woman's, and gave herself an extra inch on Brinka just for good measure.

Brinka's eyes burned with hatred and contempt and rage, but at her worst, she would not openly challenge the Kalamaii in her own home, and *Ursal* knew it plainly enough. The robed figure could never be so sure, and decided to risk some conciliatory interjection.

"Brinka?" was all he could come up with, but it did the trick. Brinka closed her eyes, and her starlight faded to empty nothingness. Brinka was the color of the shadow between the stars.

"I'm sorry. I know. I just..." and the ancient Kenjah had no more words. She covered her face and stifled a mute scream into her palms, and ran into the temple in silence to be alone.

The robed figure in the shadows stepped into the torchlight and put a gentle hand on the place on *Ursal's* neck, just above her tether, and massaged the base of her skull with deft fingers. *Ursal* bowed her head and sagged into his arms. He could feel the stress in her almost as intensely as she could.

"She's going to ruin a perfectly good party. You know that, right?"

Ursal took in all the cool sea air she could fit into her crafted lungs and sighed from the very core of her soul. "She'll come around. I hope."

Valishnok let his wings free of his robe and wrapped them around her tightly. "Me too."

"I can't believe he's gone. It just doesn't feel real. Or fair." She turned herself around in his embrace and buried her face in his chest, wrapping her arms around his hips. "I've got to go soon. I wish I could stay. I've missed you, my love." *Ursal* looked up into his golden eyes and searched for the comfort she always found there. "Be patient with him, please? You've had forever to wait for this moment. He won't even know it's coming. He's going to need time. He is very proud, and I don't wonder where he gets it." She laughed and smiled and nuzzled his chin with her brow, and buried her cheek in his chest again and held him tighter.

"I know, my love. I know." He kissed the top of her head and stroked her coal black locks. Reluctantly, at last she pulled away and gripped his hands in her own. "I'll see you soon. Wish me luck with him, and kiss me, and get out of here before you're seen." *Ursal* complied on all three points, and finally let him go. She made her way out of the temple and back out into the sea in the darkness of shadows, like a thief in her own land, and made herself whole again in the deep waters beneath the island. Her mind was full and her hearts were heavy. She thought of the Viermah and the Kenjah, and the priestess, and wished she could have a little reprieve, a little tranquility of her own.

Valishnok was little more than a whisp of shadow in the hollow of the belltower without Brinka's light. He watched the *Marvu* with sharp eyes as it slid gracefully into the docks and came to a halt alongside the longest pier. He watched the aft crewmen lowering the anchor, and the linemen already tossing out the moorings to the monks below. He searched the weatherdeck for signs of riders, but none had yet come above. The captain and his officers were standing on the prow talking with the liaisons and supervising the docking maneuver. The Bridge and crow's nest were empty, and energetic sailors bustled about to and fro, pulling down their sails for repairs and faking out the halyards.

The crew of the *Marvu* would have several more hours offloading their cargo, and the riders would all likely have volunteered for brigade duty. Valishnok would have never guessed that the second time he met his son in his entire life, he would be meeting a fully grown *swelu* disembarking an ancient Gunship. *Ursal* was right, none of it seemed real, let alone fair. In his mind, he understood Brinka's frustration with the whole entire world and everyone in it, but in his heart, he had to believe that reconciliation was possible. He was going to need every bit of possible he could find tonight.

Below him, the sounds and smells of a great feast coming together were intoxicating. The Kalama were beginning to straggle into the courtyards toting bags and crates full of food and drinks. A special place was prepared for the captain and his officers and riders and crew; a proper headcount had been requested as soon as the *Marvu* had pulled alongside the pier. The night air twinkled with the light of candles and torches, and a bonfire was already being lit in the center of the southern terrace, surrounded by stools and benches and carved stumps for revelers to sit on. Great plumes of smoke were rising into the starlit sky. The enthusiasm was palpable. But Valishnok could feel the knot in his stomach and the tension in his shoulders. Omnia was drifting towards war. Its heroes and saviors were on a Gunship moored to a floating island hidden by storm clouds, far enough away to be protected from the fallout and carnage. They believed they had come here following the noble aspirations of a messianic clocksmith to recruit a mythical sea goddess, on an errand of self sacrifice to reconnect the past with the present.

Valishnok knew that none of them would be permitted to leave this island until the child was born. And this was just one more thing his own son would hate him for. They would never see the *Marvu* or its captain again in their lifetimes. Talthielle was dead, and the Queen of Epochs lived. As for Lavaris, who could know what the old man in the mountain would say to a burned out Viermah, his Kalamaii bride, and their bitter, bereaved Kenjah mistress? Valishnok worried about Brinka. Her light did not fade, but there was a darkness in her spirit. She had finally got her way, but the number of chances she had given Omnia to deliver her Konjo and his bride had taken its toll. He sensed a jealousy in her. Would the old Brinka tolerate the young? Would she bear her own endless suffering just so an unbroken version of herself could live? Would she go through with this thing, now that all the pieces were finally finding their places in the incomprehensible puzzle she had devoted her life to? Would she forgive Talthielle, now that she had seen for herself just how complicated saving the world really was?

The offloading had begun. Valishnok watched the crewmen and monks pulling crates and barrels down the gangplank and sorting them out into long rows on the docks. Some of these were already being towed away to storehouses and shops. The *Marvu* rose a little on its keel with every load. He wondered about the provisions. What did Omnia have left that the Kalama needed? What could Omnia produce that was not wholly inferior to its Kalama counterpart? Was the whole ritual just an elaborate act of deference to the symbolism of peace? The inlanders paid the monks so that their shipping lanes would go unmolested by the creatures of the deep. The Kalama, in return, repaid the inlanders with tokens of their own independence and superiority, just as a reminder that their way of life was still evolving, while Omnia slowly collapsed beneath the weight of its own cynicism and apathy and delusional paranoia. The whole thing was just a war tax. The monks may live in devotion to the Kalamaii, but it was Omnia who truly served.

And now Omnia was sending its problems.

***

Brinka, Queen of Epochs, sat alone in her chambers, meditating on these same questions. Her wild eyes glitched and fluttered as she traced the competing ripples in her mind. She saw a multitude of threads weaving and unweaving a tapestry of causes and consequences, but she could not see any of them far enough to glimpse some kind of acceptable outcome. *Ursal* and Valishnok would commit to the arduous journey and the grim conclusion, and the three of them would submit themselves to Lavaris, but she could not see beyond the quorum. She could not hear Lavaris answer their call. She could not even see his face. She needed certainty, and could not find it. But what disturbed her more were the things she *could* see.

She saw the city of Call smouldering in ruins when the *Marvu* returned, and much of the Verdant burning behind it. The war had already begun, and Talthielle had been too late. Had he known? Surely, he had seen the same things Brinka saw now, and it certainly made an impression on her.* She saw Marla's body hanging prostrate between trees over the road through the marshes. She saw the ancient Silver Bridges broken by the Viermah so that the men could not could not trespass from the south. She saw the villagers in Waterside destroying the merchant rafts and slaughtering the sailors. All of this chaos because of Jorgan. Brinka had just traded one martyr for another. Talthielle would never have murdered Jorgan to save the Kenjah. But he would have never gotten both of them on the *Marvu* otherwise. Hard choices had to be made. Talthielle had not possessed the courage of his convictions.

Jorgan's death set off the same chain of events that Konjo's would have triggered. The townspeople were enraged when they found his cold, mangled corpse, and it took them no time at all to start pointing fingers. Only this time, everyone blamed someone different. It was the greedy merchants on their rafts. It was the malevolent old swamp witch. It was the mountain trash from the north, or the strange and troublesome branch dwellers in the great forest to the east. No one blamed Jorgan for being a hostile, contemptuous old misanthrope who hated everyone and everything with every beat of his black heart. The absence of any clear and definitive scapegoat just amplified their anger and hysteria until it reached a fever pitch, and their wrath just spilled over onto anyone and everyone unlucky enough to be nearby. And this was the motley world Talthielle had expected his conscripts to give their lives to save?

Brinka, Queen of Epochs, was beginning to have other ideas. She had set out on this path aiming for some pristine kind of science, but now found herself settling for heavily distorted art. Her loneliness and contempt had grown roots that ran beyond the lowest depths of her core, so deep that it seemed she had sprouted from them, rather than the other way around. Her mind and her feet and her fists wielded nearly absolute control over the world around her, but it was the grief that pulled the reigns now. She had witnessed the brutal and merciless death of her beloved in so many scenes and so many shades, as though the only possible end that Omnia had ever conceived for Konjo was torment and suffering.

Every time Brinka reset the day, some invisible hand intervened to thwart her design, and the same tragedy just happened over and over again, each time in a different way. She wondered if Talthielle had known the real truth of his craft, that the future does not want to be changed. The whole of existence was just one long, forceful, and elaborate attempt to create a single, interminable, insufferable moment called Now. It was a cold prison with insurmountable walls and iron bars and no windows. Brinka had waged her war against the Now and had nearly spent her strength beating her head against those unbreakable stones, swinging, clawing, thrashing in the blind darkness, just trying to conquer the intangible monster on the other side.

At last, the monster had conceded its precious designs and yielded her Konjo, oblivious and wholly enraptured by that naive, young, beautiful, and unbroken version of herself that knew nothing of the carnage her counterpart had witnessed, and less still of the carnage that Brinka, Queen of Epochs, would wreak upon Omnia for its treacherous belligerence. The time had come for governance. She heard *Ursal* whisper in Nanok's ears at Talthielle's funeral, *I'm not a god, I'm just bigger than you.* No, the Kalamaii was not a god. Omnia's wrathful god had yet to reveal herself. But the time was coming. Either Lavaris would release his dead, or Brinka, Queen of Epochs, would fill his kingdom to its very brim. Omnia would be reunified with its past, or it would simply join it.

These were the things Brinka thought about when she was angry. But she knew that any such tantrum would inevitably deprive Konjo and his betrothed of any kind of future whatsoever, and thus defeat the entire point of all of her efforts. The child must live. She could accept no other outcome. This was the measure of her success or failure. She would go to Lavaris with the Kalamaii and the old Viermah, and they would throw themselves at his feet and offer whatever he demanded, and the world they left behind would be fundamentally changed.

If this didn't work, then Omnia would learn the way of the yoke and the bridle, and suffer under the whip of its first and last Kenjah clocksmith. Omnia's living would labor under a vengeful and impatient governess who would not require a civilization of old dead to break them of their transgressions. Brinka tried to control her breathing and center herself. Her moment was approaching. The lifetimes of two *Epozia* had been spent in the space between two full moons. Tonight was one for celebration. The starlight of three Kenjah had been wrought from the shallow, sunlit graves of two. Their quest was complete, though they didn't know it yet. The Queen of Epochs would not permit her own godchild to return to Omnia in the grip of conflagration and chaos. It would remain here, among the Kalama, under the considerable protections of the Kalamaii, until it was old enough to rule, or rebel, or whatever else its heart might desire.

Try as she might, she could never make out its face on the distant ripples breaking upon the horizon of her perception. Was it he or she? Was it wise? Funny? Tenacious? She knew that it lived, but sensed from the fog that obscured her sight that her own days would reach their terminus before the child reached adolescence. No matter. She could see it, and it existed. What mattered was that her own decisions did not rip that vision away. That vision which had revealed itself for the first time in the restless waters of her mind only when the gurgling pleas and beating pulse of that malingering shopkeeper finally subsided beneath his own death rattle. When he died, the Kenjah survived. When he died, they lay in Marla's bed as honored guests rather than as hunted fugitives. When he died, the spirit of the child took its shape in her mind. The spirit of the child was the revelation. She had found the magical key that unlocked a sacred, hidden destiny, buried beneath the endless mediocrity of probable outcomes. The child that Jorgan and his friends had stolen from her, and from her Konjo. The child that had ultimately been rescued from those vicious beasts in Flask, by Talthielle.

She heard *Ursal's* stinging words in her mind, and in her heart, she knew the Kalamaii had spoken truth. But rage and grief are truths of their own, and they are jealous truths, at that. The roots of Brinka's rage had breached her own sea floor and kept growing, but the Kalamaii was right.

"How, after all of this, do you still have the strength to hold against him all of his failures, when if not for his success, and his sacrifice, may i remind you, your bones would be rotting in a ditch outside of Flask, and Konjo's would be baking in the sun in the hillside above the Titan? You're only here because he believed in you. If not for him, none of this would have been possible. Brinka, that's got to count for something. You've got to let go!"

If not for Talthielle... She loved him. She cried when his body broke the waves. She hated him. She cried when she broke his wrists and throat. The priestess had been right as well. Talthielle had deserved better. He might not have made it to Lavaris. But he made it to the *Marvu*. He got her that far. What if that really was his level best? What if he really had given his whole life just to get her out of Omnia, just to give her the power to choose her own ideal outcome, even if it was at the expense of his own? She could not dissociate the meddling schemer, the wryly grinning old tramp, from the serious and sincerely dedicated guardian angel. What would he have said if he had seen the trouble and chaos of the mess she had made without his tutelage? Would he have agreed that the child was worth it? Or did he die before she could ask him, just so he wouldn't have to answer?

She was tired of infinite rhetorical loops. She was also just tired. Talthielle was gone, and out there in the harbor, his conscripts were getting ready to take their first steps back onto dry land. She still did not know if she would meet them in the flesh. Her plan was to steal away with *Ursal* and Valishnok aboard the *Marvu* in the dark of night, while the Kenjah slept. She might never get the chance to see them again, but she could not contemplate any useful purpose for revealing herself. Like Valishnok, she wrestled with the conflict between selfish sentimentalism and the selfless sacrifice. How would they see her? Could she look them in the eyes? Could she bear the pain and guilt without breaking her resolve? Brinka, Queen of Epochs, was the color of smouldering embers. She was sore, inside and out. Her skin stretched over her brittle bones, and there were bags beneath her eyes. Her teeth were sharp and short from grinding them through the night when she permitted herself to rest. She was not frail, or weak, or feeble. But she had long outlived that enchanting vision of her youthful vitality. She had to remind herself, often, that this had all been for Konjo.

To require of him that he know how she suffered was just pure vanity. She loved him, and she would tear her own skin from bone to save him, just as he would have done for her, as he *had* done for her, over and over again on the road to Call. He had endured torture and torment, every single time, without hesitation or fear or failure. She would give herself for him, and for Talthielle, if that was what was required, if that was what would render Omnia habitable for the two of them, and for their children. Brinka did not care about Lavaris, or about Omnia's petty bloodfeuds, or the ingratitude which seemed to be written into the code the world operated upon. The Kenjah would have each other, and they would be happy, and they would never know, and perhaps they *should* never know, what had been sacrificed to wrench them both from their own grim fates.

The bells were sounding above. The offload was completed, and the monks would be gathering in droves to greet the crew and riders. Her moment had come, and she was stuck in a state of paralysis. So many life-or-death decisions had brought them all here, together, tonight. So much complexity, so many intersecting ripples and interwoven threads. She wanted to see him so badly. To touch his face, just one last time. To see her younger self, and lay her hand on the belly that carried the child the world had taken away from her. The child she would never even get to meet, let alone hold, and love, and teach, and protect. Brinka rose, and sat, and rose, and sat again. Brinka had tears in her eyes.

***

Konjo and Brinka met Lua and Nanok in the library for a cordial toast once the last of the ship's stores were on the ground. Lua poured a fifth for Uncle Talto and set it down on the table between them. The *swelu* custom for honoring a fallen comrade was to clink the unserved first, and then raise their drinks to clink them together before knocking them back. Each of them had too much to say to say anything at all, so they toasted their fallen friend in silence. In solemn moments, they had all learned to expect Nanok to finally be the one to break the silence, but Nanok seemed preoccupied and withdrawn. The Kenjah were mildly concerned, and tried to nudge the sullen Viermah into the proper spirit. He did not resent their efforts, and did not want to drag down the mood, so he insisted he was okay, mumbling something about a disagreeable breakfast and his gratitude that the ship was finally sitting still on its keel. Lua knew he had finished the Book of Valishnok. He had tried to return it, but she insisted that he keep it. The book was all that the poor birdling had left in the world to connect himself to the family that had gone before him. When she saw the tear in his grateful eye, she knew the *Marvu's* library would survive an empty spot on its shelves.

All were robed; none were armed. The Kenjah had decided to forego the ship's linens. They craved the light of the sun and moon and stars on their bare skin. Nanok had grown rather fond of the trousers and decided to stay in them. Lua, for her part, carried a small satchel, neatly stuffed with everything in the world she still cared about. Of the four of them, she was the only one who knew she would not be leaving the island when the *Marvu* pulled its moorings and unfurled its sails. She had pried it out of Bran, plying him with several extra rounds one night, shortly after they took in their bulging nets, and nagging him until he gave up the truth of his encounter with *Ursal*.

"It's a shame. That we should have made it this far without him." Brinka was restless. Something nagged at the corners of her mind. A nameless feeling of anxiety and dread. Of having missed something critical. Konjo felt it too, and could sense that what levity she could muster was dry and forced. Nanok was despondent, and Lua was distracted. The four of them made lousy company for anyone but themselves, but their shared sense of antipathy for their fast approaching moments of truth and consequence somehow gave them the comfort of solidarity, and made them fellows in the storm. It made them shipmates. "He had so much to teach me, and has instead only left me with as much to learn. I owe him my life. And I don't know how to repay him. I would honor him if I could."

Konjo took her free hand with his own in concurrence. "My life was taken from me, ripped away was everything I ever loved. Talthielle gave her back to me, and I will remain unto the end of my days in his debt. I lost all sense of purpose, and was prepared to lose all that which remained in its shadow. But his light shown upon my path, and his light has guided me to purpose. Konjo and Brinka will remain in his service until our own starlight is spent." Tears glistened in the Kenjahs' lavender eyes. "Whatever it is, we will see it done." Brinka squeezed Konjo's hand, approving, and drew him nearer. "We only wish we knew what was required of us, now that he is gone."

Nanok was watching Lua watching the Kenjah. Lua felt scrutinized in the moment, and could likely speculate why, but could not bend her tongue to the truth. She nodded along in solemnity and sipped from her goblet, saying nothing. Her sympathies were not airs. She mourned the plight of the clocksmith's worthy conscripts, who were now unmoored and set adrift without his guidance. She met his eyes coldly, not daring him, but begging him to hold his own thoughts long enough for the last bells to sound. She sensed he understood, but Nanok valued his own freedom, *differently.*

"Did he have to die, priestess?"

The Kenjah sensed the tension between their friends, and tried to comprehend its meaning. They turned to Lua with the imploring expressions of the lost and desperate who seek the impossible, and just in time to see her constrain a flash of impatient fury. Lua took a deep breath through her nose and finished her drink. "I cannot change the past, Nanok. And I have no wish to relive it. Do you understand?"

"Did he have to die?" Nanok had found his mark in her eyes and resolved to hold it fast.

"Damn you! Nanok! I beg you to let me off of this ship. I know you understand me."

"You're free to go, priestess. No one is holding you here." Nanok was trying to tell her something. He did understand. He understood perfectly. A wave of dim revelation softened Lua's features. Her mind cried out for noise, for chaos, for anything that could distract her from the vague glimpses his demeanor portended. She had to turn away. She had to sing. To cry. To laugh. She could not let her mind rest on the truth. She grabbed him by his wings and kissed him deeply, and filled her mind with love for her friends. She grabbed the decanter between them and downed what remained of it, and took each of the Kenjah's hands in her own and clasped them together.

"This is the way Kenjah. It is the only way. Trust your friend. He is here for a reason, I think."

With these cryptic words, Lua turned to Nanok with mournful eyes, as though she might never see him again. To him, she said only this. "Be careful Nanok. And good luck." Then she turned on her heels and rushed out of the library. The Kenjah were baffled, and looked to Nanok for an explanation. For the first time since his journey began, Nanok believed he understood why he had been chosen. He looked over his Kenjah companions in silence and tried to gather his racing thoughts. He had expected some other kind of response from Lua. Some kind of real answer. But it was not until she answered him that he could see the whole puzzle in his mind. *I beg you to let me off of this ship.* Suddenly, all the pieces fell into place. She could not save them. She was powerless to help them. She was a conscript, herself. Trapped here aboard the *Marvu* and cursed to witness these events over and over and over again, into perpetuity, until her captor was satisfied. Chills ran down Nanok's spine as he realized how closely his clumsy tongue had brought them all to being sent back to the quarterdeck beneath a new moon. She wanted him to try. But she could know nothing of his thoughts, or risk spoiling all the progress they had made, only to see it wiped away in a streak of light and a horrible sound, and be the only one alive who knew how far they had come.

That's why she gave him the book. Her captor could not know what it contained.

"Nanok! Don't just stand there you mute! Something is happening! What do you know? Speak, by Dab! Or we'll wring it out of you! What did you mean by that? When you asked her if Talthielle had to die? Where has she gone? Nanok, say something!" Brinka was holding him by the shoulders and nearly shaking him, as if her answers might fall out of his feathers like mites. Nanok's eyes were sad. He reached up, slowly and gently, and took her hands into his own in silence. He pushed her backwards, ever so softly, just enough to make her step back on her own. He put her hands into Konjo's and whispered.

"This is the way, Brinka. This was always the way."

A staccato bell rang furiously over the ship, signalling man overboard.

The Kenjah heard the bells and tried to make sense of them, looking around in confusion. Nanok did not take his eyes off of Brinka. "We're out of time, Brinka. You have to go back."

Brinka and Konjo were the color of dense fog. "What do you mean we have to go back? Go back where, Nanok? What is happening?" Her voice was as perplexed as it was urgent.

Nanok spoke softly. "You have to go back to the Titan, Brinka. You have to save Talthielle. Something is wrong here. There isn't time to explain it, but I think if we get off of this ship, we don't leave this island. We lose control over the future, and you may lose your powers. You have to take Konjo back to the Titan, where you met Talthielle. You have to tell him she's gone mad. He is the only one who can help you stop her."

"Nanok, stop who? Who has gone mad? What are you saying?"

The bells stopped, and then beat wildly again. They heard shouting on the deck above, and the shuffling of boots. They could not make out the words, but the commotion was evident. Someone had gone over the side, and crewmen were diving into the harbor. Nanok suddenly became very forceful and intense. He grabbed each Kenjah by the shoulder and shouted at them.

"You can save Talthielle, Brinka. Your other half is out there, right now, probably already bending time just to get here fast enough to stop you. She's gone mad, Brinka. All the hurt, all the loss, the grief, the trauma, the failure. It has corrupted her mind."

Brinka's eyes narrowed, and Konjo gripped her hands as they shared the thought. "Nanok, who has gone overboard up there? Why did Lua run away like that. Nanok?"

Nanok bowed his head, trying not to think about it. It didn't matter anyway. None of this mattered now.

"Nanok, I don't know *how* to go back! What has happened to Lua!"

"Yes you do, Brinka. Remember! Remember when your beloved embraced you again, for the first time. Remember when your soul was returned to your body. Remember yourself there, in his arms, just as you are now. Remember Brinka!"

There was commotion in the ladderwells, and more frantic shouting. Something was happening in the passageway outside. Nanok was nearly beside himself now.

"You can do this Brinka! You have to go back. Find Talthielle, and tell him everything you remember. And then find Marla. I will try to meet you on the road there. Remember Kenjah, you won't be there alone. She's coming! I'm going to try to buy you some time! Focus, Brinka! You can do this! You are the Queen of Epochs. You have powers you can't even comprehend. Listen to me! You have to take the Pathfinder with you, the sword that Marla gave you. Go and pull the book I pulled. You'll drop down below when the sparring chamber falls. Get back to your berthing and get that sword! Nothing else there matters, do you understand! When you have it, hold on tight to each other and just see where you want to go. See the Titan, Brinka! Remember it!" Nanok released their hands and clapped them both on the shoulders, hard. "Go Kenjah! And good luck!" Nanok left them stunned and speechless as he turned and rushed out of the library, just as Lua had done.

Breaths passed, and the Kenjah tried to gather their scattered wits and make sense of Nanok's wild ravings. They heard more shouting outside, closer now, and the clatter of things slamming into bulkheads and things breaking. They heard Nanok give a war cry, and it startled them into action. Konjo held Brinka's hand and they dove into the partitions, trying to remember the exact book Talthielle had instructed the Viermah to locate, that last fateful night he had been alive. Brinka found it first, and they looked at each other for some sign that this was the right thing to do. The shouting was right outside the library hatch now, and they could hear screaming over the turning of dogs.

Konjo put his forehead to Brinka's and they pulled the book together. They heard the hatch swing open just as they felt the floor seem to disappear beneath them. There was a loud crash above and the sound of greased pulleys squeaking beside, and suddenly they were one deck below. They heard the commotion above, and a scream, followed by a gurgling sound and a dull thud on the overhead. Konjo pulled Brinka to her feet, and they were running now, through a hidden passage that led out into one of the main corridors. They recognized the markings on the bulkhead and understood where they were, and they ran back down the passageway to their cabin in the midship.

Konjo twisted the dogs and slung the hatch wide as he dragged a befuddled Brinka into the space and closed the hatch tightly behind him. She was coming to her senses on the way, as a matter of necessity, and within seconds she was diving under their luggage for the Enigma Blade. She stood and fastened it to her hip while Konjo barred the door with anything and everything he could throw in front of it. The commotion had already followed them down, and they could hear heavy footsteps and a grueling wail outside, and drawing near.

Brinka took a deep breath, and took her Konjo in her arms. The Kenjah were the color of starlight now, and burning brightly. The stone in Brinka's sword was already awake and alive, glowing like sunshine on still waters. Konjo enfolded his beloved and held her as tightly as her bones would allow. "Remember, Brinka. As if either of us could ever forget."

"I love you, Konjo. I sure hope this works."

"I love you too, Brinka. I believe in you. Let's go."

(It Doesn't Have To End)

Far beneath the surface of the mild waves that lapped against the artificial shores of the Kalama island, *Ursal* listened to Talthielle's mournful conscripts clanking their glasses in honor of their fallen. Even from this distance, she could feel the somber tension in the air between them as they each strained to feign their best reveling spirits. She recalled something from one of her last conversations with the old wandering clocksmith, when her own seasons were fewer. They had been drinking on a desolate rock which jutted up from shallow shelves south of the port city of Cradle, where the first morning sunrays crawled out of the sea and began their daily trek across Omnia. The rock was not visible from the shore. Only sea creatures and seasoned *swelus* knew of its solitary existence. It was said that this stone cast the first and last shadow in the whole world, each morning and night, and the attentive could mark Omnia's seasons by the angle of that shadow. For those who could reach it, the stone promised the greatest view of either a sunrise at sea, or a sunset over Omnia, ever to be found in existence. It was a place for lovers and thinkers and adventurers.

Its shape had been carved in part by the sea itself, and by generations of whittlers and masons who each felt individual compulsions to ply their trade on the rock. It was wide and tall and round, and graffitied all over with the chiseled engravings of its visitors' names and aliases, and tidy little beatitudes between the faceless strangers who formed a kind of anonymous and ad hoc temporal collective around the ancient volcanic guyot. She had asked him how he was feeling. He said that he felt like he was in a footrace against himself, and yet had only himself to whom to hand off the baton in the race. She said she supposed the imagery made sense to him, but would sound like nonsense to anyone else in the world. Now, listening to the riders on the *Marvu,* she thought she finally understood.

Ursal could hear the sadness and frustration in Lua's voice as she ran from the library.

She remembered Talthielle, harried and tired and not a little inebriated on that rock, watching the sun come up over the sea. She put her arm around him, and emptied her mind. She bid all the waves in eyeshot in every direction to be still and calm. Soon, the two of them seemed to be sitting amidst a vast expanse of polished glass. The sun's rays, reflected, shone even brighter than the sun itself, and as the sun rose over the morning, the stone seemed to be enveloped in perfect light. Talthielle gazed out over the unassailable beauty of time and space at its most restful peace, and *Ursal* handed him a little blue stone she found on the ground beside where they sat. Like everything else in this place, it was worn smooth by ages of wind and rain and the passing seasons.

Talthielle turned it over in his hands and studied its mysteries, and thought of the future.

"Where will you go, Talthielle?"

He shrugged and sighed and leaned back on his elbow, putting the rising sun behind *Ursal's* chosen form. She heard him muse to himself that the vision was a rare and subtle improvement upon the grand design. "To my grave, I suppose. It's not my first choice, mind you. But I can't see any way around it. And I can't see anything beyond it. I wish I could just stay here. I suppose if I did, Omnia's problems would eventually learn to swim, and would come searching for me."

"Throw it, Talhielle."

"I don't want to."

"Why not?"

"Because everything I see here is perfect, just the way it is." Talthielle turned the stone over in his hands and rubbed it with his fingers and thumbs. "What could I possibly add to perfection?"

"Where will you go?"

"I think I'll follow the sun inland, to Riel, and then up towards Flask. I don't know where I'll end up after that. My visions tell me that I'll find what I'm looking for there."

"And what are you looking for?"

Talthielle sat himself upright over crossed legs and let his hands fall into his lap.

"The future."

Ursal looked down at the stone in his hands, and then out to the gleaming horizon ahead.

"Throw it."

Talthielle closed his eyes and bowed his head and thought of peace, and then he flung the stone out into the sea, spinning his finger along the rounded edge sideways, so that the smooth face caught the sun on one side and the water on the other. It skipped long, and skipped again high, and then glanced over the surface a few more times before disappearing forever, from his point of view. He could not have seen her catch it, but had he known she kept it, he would have approved. A constellation of little ripples appeared everywhere the stone touched the still water, forming a trail of overlapping concentric rings of dancing light, of dreams and shadows, breaking in any direction only against themselves and against the lonely rock, where two souls sat in reverent observance.

Ursal heard the splash when Lua went over the *Marvu's* rails. And then she heard the bells, and the shouting. She thought of Talthielle, running against the wind, always on his own heels, leading and following his own shadow against the tides. His whole view of reality had been defined by the continuity of causality, by the tireless nature of change over time. They had lived their lives as elementals. She could enchant the sailor and the fisherman, or she could terrorize them. But he could teach them how to become better versions of themselves. He was not merely a servant of these seasons. He was Omnia's last best hope for a second chance. Possibility was the language of his virtue. He would not break still waters to break the peace. The waters he broke were already tumultuous, and he broke them only to guide the waves, and to spare the riders. Omnia's problems couldn't swim.

Lua could swim, but she didn't. She tore a blade across her throat as she leapt, and dropped it. Beneath the surface, *Ursal* caught them both, and kept them. She sent tethering tendrils up the sides of the temple and revealed herself to Valishnok, startling him even at his most resigned. She wrapped her hands around his face and held his sad, but courageous eyes. She kissed him, and he kissed her, and then he nodded, and closed his eyes. He would not get to meet Nanok. None of them would be permitted to leave the island. It was over, and it was now for some other version of themselves to live and breathe and learn and choose. There's only one way to beat a clocksmith.

"My love," he whispered. She snapped his neck, and held him in her arms as he crumbled.

Ursal wept, and waited for the flash of light, and for infinite nothing, and beyond.

"Good luck, Kenjah."

***

The clocksmith, having offered his ante, quietly awaited as Konjo deliberated. It did not matter how much time had passed. The clocksmith had all the time in the world. That was the point. It mattered, Konjo supposed, in the sense that the longer Konjo sat there, stone faced and stupid and staring deeply into this old man's striking eyes, the more likely it became that the other patrons, themselves one and all never fully unaware of the Kenjah, no matter how hard they pretended, might begin to speculate in their own vulgar ways. Damn them all, of course, but circumstances now seemed to preclude the need for drawing attention, be it the right kind or the wrong. Konjo conceded that this had been the nature of his first round, in grand fashion, drawing attention to himself. One less round remained, and from this moment forward, what he did or said or did not say or do, mattered. That was the nature of the bargain. That, with the prospect of redeeming the life of his own beloved Brinka.

"You have my attention, and you may have much more than that, I begin to see and will try to accept. But as you have spoken, so shall you set your feet and fists. I will listen, and I will consent to help, whatever to and whither you may incline. But as you have me, you will now assent that I have you as well, and just the same. When this arrangement concludes, I swear on the color of stars, old man, the fates of yourself and my beloved shall be entwined. If she be shade and you be false, then shade too shall you be . You will fill no more of a cloak than she, and to this and nothing more must you agree." Konjo was the color of blood in battle, and stood and offered his hand.

The old clocksmith, of course, understood the Kenjah's colors and comprehended the Kenjah's meaning. He raised himself up to meet Konjo's eye and grasp the length of his outstretched arm, both hands, with sleeves retracted, skin to skin. "Konjo, my boy, I would have it no other way. We are agreed." A proper contract thus enjoined, and many explanations demanding, Konjo released the old tramp's hand and began to form the first of many inquiries in a row, as the process might naturally be expected to proceed, but before the words could reach his own tongue, as soon as the clocksmith's hand was free, both of the old man's hands shot to Konjo's brow and the world around him went momentarily dark, but just as it happened, it unhappened just the same and the old man's hands went, neutral, to his hips, just a few woolen sleeves beneath an even more pronounced twinkle in those old blues than before.

Konjo, prepared to protest and not a little embarrassed by the futility of his own reflexes, tried to compose himself in that instant, if for no other reason than to refuse to be made to overplay his hand once more, but there was something in the way the light around him changed (Kenjah are sensitive to these things, by now reader, you must surely see), and he spun around in a moment's panic to find his Brinka's beautiful, haunting shade dissipated. A million waves slammed against the shores of his mind and heart at once, from all directions, and he was overwhelmed. Too many questions crashed into each other in the lane between his mind and mouth for any of them to manifest. Konjo was shaken and alarmed and confused. *Brinka was gone!*

Konjo whirled around to the old clocksmith once again, prepared to do much more than protest, but once again, before his hands could raise themselves or his lips could purse, the old clocksmith put a gentle arm on Konjo's shoulder and gently cocked his head towards the Titan's doors, where what Konjo now witnessed, following the nod as one cannot help but doing, even when a good brawl is brewing (and sometimes especially), what Konjo witnessed at the trail end of the old man's glance broke him, broke him as nothing else, conceivable or otherwise, ever could. Konjo swam in color and nearly collapsed, but for the gentle grip of the old man's hand. Impossible. Impossible. Impossi...

"Konjo." Her perfect voice. Her fragile frame. Her knowing eyes. She was the color of life.

"Brinka?"

As Konjo's hand raised to meet with hers, Talthielle felt the dim flutter of candles and torches protesting a gust of soft wind rippling through the Titan, and thought it peculiar for a moment, but passed it off to the intrusion of inclement weather brewing behind the heavy doors as they closed.

He watched them collapse into each other's arms, and had expected nothing less. The Kenjah were the color of azure seas, just before sunset. He heard a peel of thunder outside the tavern; a real storm was fast approaching from somewhere over the eastern swamps. At length, the Kenjah pulled themselves apart and drank each other in with loving eyes, and whispered something unintelligible to each other before turning to Talthielle. His time was now.

"I am Talthielle. I tire of questions easily, and I can tell both of you will burst at the seams if your questions go unanswered. For these things, there is time, I assure you, but the time is not-"

"Clocksmith! Before this night is out, you'll have plenty of questions of your own. Right now we need you to skip the monologue, pay the man for another round, and prepare to put this place behind you with all haste. We've got to get to Waterside and persuade Jorgan to get out of it by sunup. Then we've got to find Nanok on the road to meet Marla, and get ourselves to the *Marvu* before the Order of Tranquility does. We will meet the Kalamaii about a half day's ride from Call, if we're lucky. And Talthielle, you should know now that there is another clocksmith in play. It's a long story, and we're happy to explain on the way, but we have to go now. I mean, we've got to have a round between us first, obviously, but then we definitely have to go. Do you understand?"

The wry smile had gone out of him, and he most emphatically did not understand.

Konjo leaned forward and clapped him hard on the shoulder.

"Whaddaya say, old buddy, old pal? *What have you got to lose?"*

(Rest in Peace, Brent Hinds: 1974-2025)

The End.

Look for the sequel to this book,

Brinka

coming in the fall of 2026

Also by this Author

<u>Cigarettes for Breakfast</u>

Sam Solvierro is a brilliant author and a broken man, conscripted by a messianic devil to bear witness to the end times.

As society's institutions crumble, humanity surrenders its freedom to its machines in exchange for protection from its own destructive excesses. Sam is shown bits and pieces of the lives of a few influential people whose interconnected paths lead them towards a common but uncertain future, dragging the fate of the species behind them in tow.

This story transcends time, space, heaven, hell, dreams, and reality. As Sam begins to discover that they are all one and the same, his own life begins to change

Scan the code to purchase this book!

Look for the following titles in the future.

The Principles of Rational Eschatology: A Thoughtful Analysis of the Five Destinies of Man

Corn, Coins, Cash, Checks, Credit, and Crypto: A History of the Evolution of Currency

The Way of Wisdom is the Word: A Remembrance of William F. Buckley, Jr.

Coffee at Midnight: The Sequel I Swore I Would Never Write.

Suspected Militant: Dehumanization and Drone Warfare.

Snakes, Roaches, and Mosquitoes: My Life in the Buckle of the Bible Belt.

Steven Harkness is a father, a writer, a veteran, and an honors graduate with a Bachelor's in History and a Master's in the Arts. He lives in Louisiana with his teenage son and two dogs. Steven is a painter by trade, and owns his own business. He spends his days rescuing and restoring old homes in his community, and spends his nights streaming, longboarding, and playing the bass. Steven was homeless several times as a child, as well as a ward of the state, and lived in three different crackhouses before he was old enough to vote. He has read and written voraciously since adolescence, but has carefully avoided the publishing racket until now, due to the ubiquitous decline of literature in American culture. His mission is to replace mythological concepts of rapture and judgment with the Principles of Rational Eschatology in the collective consciousness. This philosophy centers around the belief that the human species must contend with the inevitability of extinction, and that the prospect of avoiding such a fate may unify the human race behind a common cause which theological worldviews have traditionally failed to acknowledge.

He is prejudiced against robots, hippies, tweakers, and libertarians, and will likely die anonymous and poor.

Find out more about this author at

www.stevenbharkness.com